CRISIS AT PROXIMA

BAEN BOOKS by TRAVIS S. TAYLOR & LES JOHNSON

ORION'S ARM

Saving Proxima • *Crisis at Proxima*

SPACE EXCURSIONS

Back to the Moon • *On to the Asteroid*

BAEN BOOKS by TRAVIS S. TAYLOR

Ballistic

THE TAU CETI AGENDA SERIES

One Day on Mars • *The Tau Ceti Agenda* • *One Good Soldier*
Trail of Evil • *Kill Before Dying* • *Bringers of Hell*

WARP SPEED SERIES

Warp Speed • *The Quantum Connection*

WITH JODY LYNN NYE

Moon Beam • *Moon Tracks*

WITH JOHN RINGO

Into the Looking Glass • *Vorpal Blade*
Manxome Foe • *Claws That Catch*

Von Neumann's War

WITH MICHAEL Z. WILLIAMSON, TIMOTHY ZAHN, KACEY EZELL, JOSH HAYES

Battle Luna

BAEN BOOKS NONFICTION BY TRAVIS S. TAYLOR

A New American Space Plan • *The Science Behind The Secret*
Alien Invasion: How to Defend Earth (with Bob Boan)

BAEN BOOKS by LES JOHNSON

Mission to Methone • *The Spacetime War*

WITH BEN BOVA

Rescue Mode

ANTHOLOGIES

Going Interstellar (edited with Jack McDevitt)
Stellaris: People of the Stars (edited with Robert E. Hampson)

CRISIS AT PROXIMA

TRAVIS S. TAYLOR
LES JOHNSON

Crisis at Proxima

This is a work of fiction. All the characters and events portrayed in this book are fictional, and any resemblance to real people or incidents is purely coincidental.

A Baen Books Original

Baen Publishing Enterprises
P.O. Box 1403
Riverdale, NY 10471
www.baen.com

ISBN: 978-1-9821-9375-1

Cover art by Dave Seeley
Models used for cover art by John Douglass

First printing, November 2024

Distributed by Simon & Schuster
1230 Avenue of the Americas
New York, NY 10020

Library of Congress Cataloging-in-Publication Data

Names: Taylor, Travis S., author. | Johnson, Les (Charles Les) author.
Title: Crisis at proxima / Travis S. Taylor, Les Johnson.
Description: Riverdale, NY : Baen Publishing Enterprises, 2024. | Series: Orion's Arm ; 2
Classification: LCC PS3620.A98 C75 2024 (print) | LCC PS3620.A98 (ebook) | DDC 813/.6—dc23/eng/20240621
LC record available at https://lccn.loc.gov/2024026767
LC ebook record available at https://lccn.loc.gov/2024026768

Printed in the United States of America

10 9 8 7 6 5 4 3 2 1

Dedicated to the late
Richard "Uncle Timmy" Bolgeo

Smart people with good intentions and
high moral standards can solve any problem.

PART 1

LIVING ON AN ALIEN WORLD

CHAPTER 1

February 15, 2101 (Earth calendar)

"How's the newest addition to the family?" Lorraine ("Rain" to her friends) Gilster asked as she greeted Roy Burbank on the doorstep of the modest, two-story stone house that he and his wife, Chloe, had finished renovating and occupying barely a month before their son, Jeremiah, had been born. Fintidierian houses looked a lot like their counterparts back on Earth; they were both designed for, and occupied by, humans. Human anatomy drives many design decisions and since Fintidierian humans (many called them "Fintis"), and Terrans were the same, so were their housing needs. Nonetheless, Rain continued to be surprised at how similar this strain of humanity was to its distant cousins back on Earth. They'd been separated for tens of thousands of years, but in all that time, they hadn't diverged all that much. Roy had the look of a tired, but proud, father on his face. Of course, this was another common trait between the two strains of humanity, and since both Roy and Rain were of the same strain—they had voyaged to Proxima Centauri b from Earth together less than a year ago—the cross-cultural similarities of one's parenthood had not been more than a passing thought.

"He's healthy. Especially his lungs. That boy can cry. Makes his older sister want to run out of the house screaming herself," Roy said, a big grin breaking out as he spoke. "It's good to see you, Rain. Is Mak with you?" he asked, looking past Rain and out into the yard. She and the *Samaritan*'s chief medical doctor,

Dr. Maksim Kopylova, had met aboard ship on the journey from Earth to Proxima Centauri b and married less than a year after arrival. The pair had the approval of everyone who knew them from aboard the ship, not that that mattered to either of them. They were definitely a good match.

"I hope you're not disappointed, but he had to stay at work this afternoon. A lot of kids are coming down with the sniffles and, well, the locals still prefer to have their precious little darlings seen by the more technologically advanced Terran medical doctor rather than one of their own. I can understand that for serious illnesses, but for the sniffles? *Come on.* The local doc is a lot more experienced diagnosing the various flavors of the common cold circulating here than an Earth doctor."

"As we, of all people, should know very well after what we all went through this last year. I'm beginning to think we should rename this world The Planet of the Sick Head. I think we all had one big symbiotic intelligent sinus infection most of the year," Roy said jokingly while instinctively rubbing the side of his nose as he spoke.

Rain could relate. She and Mak had had many conversations on the topic. The early Proxima b atmospheric analysis the crew of the *Samaritan* had performed found no major pathogens, but it had surely missed the vicious varieties of the common cold that were circulating. Cold viruses that none of the Terrans' immune systems had ever before encountered. And encounter them they all did, one cold after the other, at first causing Mak to wonder what he'd missed in the initial survey. Only after realizing that no one was dying from the infections did he calm down and stop second-guessing his initial sampling and analysis. Cold viruses on Earth mutate constantly, infecting and reinfecting people on a regular basis. Here, the Terrans were perfect petri dishes for every variety of virus in circulation among the locals. Fortunately, in the last few months, the number of people catching colds had dropped dramatically as their immune systems adapted. Mankind could now travel between the stars—but had yet to cure the damned common cold.

"Agreed. Fortunately, I'm starting to feel more and more like my old self, and *you* don't sound congested at all," she remarked.

"No, I'm fine. Samari is still sniffly, but I think that's more because she's eight years old and would be catching everything that comes along here or back on Earth."

Rain hesitated, knowing that she was intruding on Roy's time off. His son, Jeremiah, was only a few weeks old, and Roy had been on leave helping to take care of his wife, daughter, and newborn son on some well-deserved leave. Earth-trained engineers like him were in huge demand on Proxima b as the locals tried to learn every Earth-modern engineering trick and tool they could. Technologically, the locals were nearly a century behind their Earthly visitors, but they were quickly catching up.

"Rain, I can tell by the way you are fidgeting that you aren't here on a purely social call," Roy observed, his grin turning into more of a slight smile. "I would invite you in, but Chloe, Jeremiah, and Samari are all napping and the last thing I want to do is wake them up."

"Listen, if this is an inconvenient time, I can come back," Rain responded, starting to back away toward the porch stairs.

"Not at all. But we'll have to talk out here. Take a seat," Roy said, motioning to one of the three rocking chairs adorning the small porch. The chairs were made from a local tree, similar to the oak family back on Earth, and were stained with a clear stain that highlighted the tones of the wood. Thanks to the red dwarf star around which Proxima b orbited, to see the tones in a way they were used to seeing, the settlers from Earth had to use full *Earth* spectrum lights. The dim reddish light from the star around that b orbited, Proxima Centauri, made everything look a little dingy and some colors that the Earth human eye was used to seeing simply weren't visible except using the lights the crew brought from Earth. Green, for example, looked mostly black when viewed outside on a clear sunny day. Amazingly, most of the local plants, which were genetically similar to those found on Earth, had adapted the photosynthesis cycle to work across a broader spectrum to allow for the fact that Proxima Centauri emitted almost no green light. There was heated debate among the Earth geneticists as to whether these adaptations occurred naturally or were genetically engineered. The latter, of course, opened up a whole host of questions that would have to be addressed.

They sat and Rain took a deep breath.

"I've been racking my brain about that radio signal for the better part of an Earth year and I'm no closer now to deciphering it than I was when I first detected it last spring. Without a decryption key, we'll never be able to know what it says." Rain was referring to the strong, directional radio signal she had detected shortly after their arrival on Proxima b. A signal that originated in a region of the sky exactly where the ancient hieroglyphics they had found on the Fintidierians' forbidden continent, Misropos, indicated was the origination or home place of what the Terrans called the Atlanteans. The Atlanteans were apparently a strain of alien visitors, maybe also human, who had ruled Proxima b some fifty thousand years ago, enslaving the local population, before they mysteriously died out. Discovering this had almost resulted in the death of the entire crew of the *Samaritan*, sent to help the people of Proxima b. But the continent where the ruins were found was a forbidden location under Fintidierian law, something the people of Earth did not know at the time, and they nearly started the first interstellar war by simply going there. The locals thought that whatever killed these ancient people might be a contagion, so they required that everyone who visited there be quarantined for a time upon their return. This also gave time for the diplomats to smooth things over as best they could. Officer relations were now better, but still a bit strained.

"I'm a hardware guy, not a coder. I would not know a decryption key if it punched me in the face," Roy declared.

"Yeah, I know. That's kind of why I'm here. We may not be able to find out what they are saying in the signal, but we can figure out who's sending it. Or, at least, *from where* they are sending it. That's why I need your help," Rain said. She could feel her own pulse rate increasing. She knew what they had to do, and she needed an ally to convince one of the two ships' captains to go along with her idea. Roy was the key. Everybody respected and liked him. After all he'd been through on his "accidental" trip to Proxima b, he had made a lot of friends. A lot.

"I don't understand," Roy responded. "What can I do?"

"Okay, look. You haven't had so much advanced math that you've forgotten high school trigonometry, have you?" Rain asked with just the hint of a smile. She hoped he hadn't forgotten, but you never knew...

"I never showed you this?" Roy rolled up his sleeve and pointed to a small tattoo on his right shoulder.

Rain looked closer at it. The tattoo was a red sine-wave pattern with a black line underneath it. Underneath the black line was a blue cosine wave. She studied it briefly and clearly was confused.

"A sine over a cosine?" she asked.

"Yes. That way, I always will have a tan!" Roy laughed triumphantly at the trigonometry joke. He could tell it didn't take Rain more than a microsecond to understand that tangent equals sine divided by cosine, and she groaned.

"I assume you got that before you were married."

"I did. And I was quite drunk."

"I bet you were. But it appears you do recall high school trig."

"I think I can hold my own with Pythagoras," Roy retorted, smiling back.

"Great!" Rain directed the conversation back on topic. "When we see a star in the sky, we can tell in what direction it lies, but our radio simply doesn't have the resolution to tell us from which particular star along our line of sight the signal comes from. There are dozens, if not hundreds, in that one small slice of the sky where the signal originates. The signal is somewhat directional, that's why no one on Earth ever picked it up. Now, if we were on Earth and the signal had been directed toward us there, then we might have been able to figure it out in the time we've had since we first detected it last spring. This is where trigonometry comes in. On Earth, to locate a deep space radiation source, one emitting light, radio, or whatever, and find its distance, astronomers would plot its relative location in the sky at some time of the year, let's pick the spring equinox and then again in half a year, at the fall equinox. In six months, the Earth has gone half an orbit around the Sun and the source's location in the sky has moved, relative to where it was in the spring, by ninety-three million miles times two. By similar triangles and knowing the angle subtended by the star compared to them in the spring and the fall, we can identify sources and calculate their distances out to thirty-two hundred light-years or so. But that's with Earth orbiting optical telescopes. When we look through the atmosphere, the light gets distorted and smeared out. From the Earth's surface, using the best ground-based telescopes, we're limited to three hundred and twenty light-years, give or take. We have the same problem here, only worse. We're looking at longer wavelength radio waves, which makes it harder still to do from the ground."

"I see where you are going," Roy said. "What you want to do is pinpoint the star from which the Atlantean signal originates.

Given that this screwy planet's year is only eleven days long, shouldn't you already have done that? We're on the other side of the star having our equinox every five and a half days."

"That's exactly the problem. We're only zero-point-zero-five AU from the star. Five percent of an astronomical unit. That's not much. Only four-point-six million miles. Multiply by two and you get over nine million miles. Compared to one hundred eighty-six million back home. The base of the triangles we can make here are simply too small for the trigonometry to tell us much of anything. The strength of the signal hardly varies at all over that distance. We need to increase the size of our triangles' bases. We need to take the measurements in space," Rain explained. She stopped and looked expectantly at Roy.

"That should be easy enough. Just take the *Samaritan* or the *Emissary* out far enough to get a better measurement," Roy suggested, shrugged his shoulders, and made a palms-up gesture.

"Exactly. And when I asked Captain Crosby, he said we couldn't risk leaving orbit until we'd worked out some sort of formal treaty with the planetary government about trade policies. I don't understand what that has to do with taking the ship out of orbit, not the system, for a few weeks to take some measurements. I couldn't convince him. But I'm hoping you can. He trusts you. And you know as well as I do that this is important."

"Rain, let's assume you get what you need, and you figure out where the signal is coming from. It won't help us decode it. What's the point, other than intellectual curiosity?" Roy asked.

"I think it *is* close. It would have to be for the Atlanteans to have come here and kept some sort of communication with home. This isn't some sort of tachyon beam, this is radio. It's limited to the speed of light, which means it probably isn't twenty-five thousand light-years away or what would be the point in keeping up some sort of communication? Sure, for us to talk to Earth takes over four years each way with an actual two-sentence conversation taking nearly nine years. It must be something similar for the Atlanteans or what would be the point?"

"And if they are that close, you want to go there," Roy noted. It was clearly a statement, not a question.

"You bet your ass I do," she declared. "And I'm sure there will be many others from both ships that agree. We have enough people here to keep working on the fertility problem, or whatever it is, while the rest of us go on to see what we can find out about whoever is behind this whole thing."

"What 'whole thing' would that be?" Roy asked.

"How it happens to be that this planet and Earth both have biospheres compatible with Earth-based life and Earth life, with the same DNA. We are no closer to understanding that than we were when we left Earth. If anything, the mystery has gotten deeper."

"Rain, if I agree to help you, then we need to get one thing perfectly clear: I'm *not* going. Anywhere. I didn't want to come here to begin with and for over four years I thought I would never see my wife again, let alone even meet my daughter. And now I've got a son. I have no intention of going anywhere near either of those ships when they leave orbit, to the outer parts of the Proxima system to take your measurements, and certainly not on another yearslong trip to another star. The only place that might tempt me is a trip back to Earth and only then if my family were coming too. Nothing is going to separate me from them again," Roy asserted in a tone that was unmistakably resolute.

"Yes." Rain smiled. "I realize that, and I would never ask. I need you as an advocate."

"Well, what you suggest sounds reasonable, so don't be offended at my next request," he said.

"Okay," she replied, her curiosity hard to contain. "Shoot."

"I'm an engineer. Early in my career, one of my more intimidating bosses had a poster behind his desk quoting W. Edwards Deming, the man largely responsible for Japan's economic recovery after World War Two. It said, 'In God we trust; all others bring data.' I'll need to see your calculations and make sure that they're right before I put my neck out."

"I suspected as much." Rain's smile broadened and she replied, "I wouldn't have it any other way. I'll send over everything later today."

A small cry, followed by a much louder one, came from one of the upstairs windows.

"It sounds like Jeremiah is awake. I'd better tend to him. Thanks for coming by," Roy said as he began to make his way toward the door and back into the house.

"You do that. And tell Chloe that I said hello."

✧ ✧ ✧

"Staff meetings. We fly four and a half light-years to explore a new world, forsaking our extended families, friends, and everything else we knew and loved about home and here we are, gathering for yet another damned staff meeting. Who'd have bloody thought?" asked Neil Polkingham, one of the few Brits on either of the two ships and a key member of the biology and fertility team that was still puzzling over the Fintidierians' fertility crisis. The crisis that prompted the *Samaritan* and then the *Emissary* to leave Earth and travel to Proxima Centauri b.

"Neil, I've been to many staff meetings in my life and most of them are complete wastes of time. But I must admit that Nkrumah does a decent job with them. He usually has an agenda and almost always finds ways to end on time," observed Dr. Chris Sentell. Sentell, a forty-five-year-old biologist, was recruited for the mission to Proxima based on his work at a genetics research firm in Atlanta, where he focused on finding breakthroughs to cure inherited genetic diseases. In addition to his professional commitments, he had a passion for fishing, often spending weekends on Earth by the riverside, enjoying the tranquility and thrill of the sport. Sentell's speech carried a distinct Southern accent, reflecting his roots and upbringing in the American South.

"I consider them parts of the job. If they get long and off track, well, that's when I stop paying attention and get myself prepared to return to the lab," added Dr. Rich Gilliam. Gilliam, like Sentell, was a biologist and before joining the mission served as the chair of the biology department at UCLA. Renowned for his exceptional contributions to the field of biology, he had earned several international prizes that recognized his outstanding achievements.

Gilliam and Sentell had arrived aboard the *Emissary* not long after the *Samaritan* had made orbit. They spoke as they made their way down the hall toward the conference room.

Polkingham and the combined biology teams, with what support the locals could provide (extremely limited support, given the knowledge and technology gap between the Terrans and the Fintidierian humans), had been working for months trying to isolate the source of the problem. So far, they'd had no luck. Over the last century, there had been fewer and fewer Fintidierian females born, causing a demographic catastrophe that, unless reversed, meant their extinction in just a few decades. The project lead,

Dr. Kieran Nkrumah, chaired the biweekly meetings that brought all the research teams together to discuss their recent results, plans, and problems and viable solutions to the latter. As much as he hated to be pulled from his work, Polkingham grudgingly admitted they were necessary. But that didn't prevent him from complaining. He rather enjoyed the role of curmudgeon.

The building they were using for the research was the most modern and well-equipped biology lab the Fintidierian city of Gwonura, a municipality of three hundred thousand people near where the Terrans had made planetfall and set up their base camp. Like most Fintidierian buildings, it looked like something you would see in an old 2D movie set in the USA circa 1945 to 1950, with lots of concrete, austere windows, high ceilings, and exterior pillars.

The local equivalent of the community college had been quickly modified to accommodate the specifications provided by the Earth team and, much as Polkingham was loathe to admit—at least publicly—they had done a respectable job. They had much of what was needed in terms of infrastructure, including a sterile room with laminar flow, multiple autoclaves, a plentiful supply of dry ice and liquid nitrogen, and some functional—though rather large, loud, and clunky—centrifuges. From the *Samaritan* and the *Emissary*, they'd brought down the more sophisticated equipment like their microarray scanners, microplate readers, some UV-Vis spectrophotometers, among other things. They brought to the surface their rapid gene sequencers but not their gene splicers. Those remained aboard ship where only the properly trained Terran crew could use them. Advanced gene editing was not something they wanted the locals to learn too much about yet.

Polkingham and his colleagues entered the auditorium-style lecture hall and took their seats near the center right, as was customary. Most everyone else was already in the room, including Nkrumah, who was pacing back and forth in front, seemingly lost in thought. The lights were set to the Earth normal spectrum, as was now the custom when Earthborn and native Fintidierians were intermingled. To the biologists' amazement, once the Fintidierians were exposed to the full Earth spectrum, they were able to fully see every color those from Earth saw: red, orange, yellow, green, blue, indigo, and violet—ROYGBIV. The local humans had the genes to see more colors than should have been possible had they originated on Proxima b. They were so excited that they actually requested to have Earth normal lighting whenever possible.

Polkingham noticed that the native Fintidierian biologists were slowly getting more intermingled with the Terrans and not just keeping to themselves. When they first arrived, getting the groups to not self-segregate was a huge challenge. Then, the ice began to break. At first the Fintidierians seemed to gravitate toward the Asian members of the Terran group, which made some sense. People, at their core, tended to be tribal. And since the Fintidierians were descended from Terrans who were presumably brought to Proxima b from Asia, they naturally found affinity first among those that looked most similar to themselves. Never mind that their genetic ancestors parted ways fifty thousand or so years ago, they were "cousins." Then the other barriers began to break down both in the biology lab and among the native population. Now they were well on their way to seeing each other as fellow humans, regardless of the planet and ethnic group from which they originated. There were even a few Terran-Fintidierian couples now.

Nkrumah moved to the lectern and loudly cleared his throat, getting everyone's attention, and waved to them to be seated. The many conversations died down to whispers, then silence. Nkrumah was not a physically imposing figure, quite the opposite. He was rather short, far shorter than the average Terran, closer in overall physical build to the Fintidierans, who also tended to be somewhat smaller in stature than their Terran counterparts. His voice was not one that would instantly garner attention in a crowded room, yet when he spoke, people paid attention. What he lacked in physical stature he made up for many times in his intellectual stature. Many considered him brilliant. And he had walked away from one of the most prestigious universities on Earth to join the expedition to Proxima b. His work curing inherited conditions and diseases *in utero* had won him a Nobel Prize nomination and the thanks of millions of people around the world who had their children born without many of the diseases previously passed from generation to generation, including cystic fibrosis, hemophilia, muscular dystrophy, and sickle cell anemia, to name a few. That was why he was here. If the female fertility problem—or the male fertility problem, whichever the case might be—could be corrected *in utero*, then he could figure out how to do it.

The meeting began with a series of status reports from each of the research subteams, the latest birth statistics from each of the planet's provinces that showed the male/female conception and birth rates were not getting any better, and finally, the two bits of data that Polkingham had been personally waiting to hear. The first came from Nkrumah himself, in his heavily accented English.

"First, the good news. As you may recall, we have successfully established five fertility clinics, one in each province, where we are performing *in vitro* implantation of Terran female embryos into Fintidierian women who volunteer for the treatment. The local doctors are fast learners and their success rates are now nearly as high as those back on Earth. Between the two ships, we brought nearly fifty thousand female embryos, and our goal is to get as many of these gestating as quickly as possible. We've been tracking the pregnancies of the women who have undergone the implantation, and their pregnancies are proceeding as one would expect of a normal pregnancy, without any higher incidence of rejection, miscarriage, or other prenatal adverse issues. This is excellent news."

There was a bit of applause, but mostly polite silence. It was good news, but all in the room knew that fifty thousand female births were not enough to solve the immediate problem. Not even close. As the native female population aged, the number of unattached males exploded, with all the negative social consequences that one might expect. The Fintidierians were experiencing increasing crime, truancy, markedly fewer choosing to continue their education beyond the minimum (one of the reasons it was so easy for the biologists to take over the community college facilities), suicide, and an overall sense of despair. They desperately needed to figure out what was causing the problem and fix it. Soon. Or this culture would likely soon descend into chaos and anarchy before it ultimately died out.

Nkrumah cleared his throat again, in what those assembled knew was his custom when he wanted them to be quiet and pay attention. It worked.

"Now, for the bad news. Since our arrival nearly a year ago, there has been increasing fraternization between the Terran crews and the local population, as would be expected. To date, there are thirty-seven pregnancies: twelve are women from the *Samaritan* and *Emissary*, the rest are Fintidierian. All the pregnancies are thankfully proceeding normally, with no detectable problems in either group from the... genetic mixing."

The last comment drew some guffaws from the audience, proving that even biologists and fertility experts had base reactions to sexual innuendo. They were still human, after all.

"Unfortunately, all but one of the natural matings resulted in male fetuses. One of the Fintidierian women, who for now asks to remain anonymous, is pregnant with a daughter," announced Nkrumah.

The audience this time did not react with applause, but with not-so-quiet murmuring. The news, to Polkingham and everyone else, was distressing to say the least. Nkrumah motioned for people to quiet down and continued.

"And now for the most interesting and useful bit of data. If there is a silver lining, then this is it. The woman in question, the one carrying the female fetus, is a Fintidierian. The father was a Terran who had remained aboard the *Emissary* almost the entire time since our arrival, only coming to the surface a few days before he, um, had an encounter with the woman in question. Now, it is difficult to tell for certain with only one data point, but this strongly suggests that there is something in the local environment causing the population imbalance. Something that this crew member may not have been exposed to for long enough to affect him and his sperm. This also suggests that whatever the environmental factor is, it may only affect the men. Men, after all, determine the sex of the child."

Nkrumah then began walking the audience through the multitudinous data collected on each and every pregnant couple, noting results from blood tests, genetic sequencing, health histories, etcetera. The question-and-answer session lasted nearly two hours before the meeting was adjourned.

Polkingham listened to every word, took copious notes on his datapad and in his mental checklist, trying to not miss anything relevant to the avenues of pursuit that he and his team were considering next. He was in his element, and he loved it. He really wished it were more of an academic debate and not something as time critical as saving this world and its culture.

CHAPTER 2

Charles Jesus was a man used to dealing with obstinate politicians. He would be the first to admit that he, too, could be quite obstinate when the situation called for it. But he really didn't like dealing with people pulling the same trick on him, especially since he knew all the signs that this woman was stalling and not negotiating from some real, unalterable position. The question was why? Jesus, unlike his more famous and godlier namesake, was no saint. He was quite sure that the woman with whom he was negotiating, Secretary General Balfine Arctinier, the one who had successfully managed to exasperate him, was also not a saint. No one who can rise to be the chief executive of a government, especially a planetary government, can have done so without making compromises and getting dirty. It was, unfortunately, the nature of high-stakes politics and, in the history of humanity on Earth, it was rare for someone with scruples to reach the pinnacle of leadership. The only possible exception he could think of was the twentieth-century US president Dwight Eisenhower, and he wasn't so sure about good old Ike. There had to have been a skeleton in his closet somewhere.

Arctinier was close to wrapping up her latest diatribe, and to Jesus it sounded like a bunch of gibberish. Of course, since she was speaking in her native tongue, which Jesus had only learned on the trip from Earth, he could only understand everything she said when he was intentionally concentrating. He had done fairly well with that early in their meeting today, but he was getting fatigued with her repetitiveness and that had caused him to tune out and miss most of what she had just said. He suspected she was droning on and on in her native tongue for that exact purpose. He would have to wing his response.

"Madame Secretary General, I understand your military does not yet trust us. And I deeply regret that we had to make that trip to Misropos without your express permission, but it was essential for us to gain confidence so that we could trust *you*. And, if we are being honest, I think we both came out of that experience with trust issues. For what you consider very valid reasons, you were keeping an important part of your history hidden from us. And when we suspected there was something there that you did not want us to know, we acknowledged that we undertook a mission there in violation of our agreement to remain in one location. But please know that what we learned has given us important historical context that will, hopefully, aid us in finding the cause of the Gender Plague and perhaps its cure. I want us to move beyond that event from a year ago and look at the situation today and where we need to be tomorrow," Jesus noted, careful to not repeat word for word what he had used in his last appeal to her, paraphrasing enough so that it would be (hopefully) heard as a new argument.

"Ambassador Jesus. It is not that simple. Yes, your people have been model visitors since our rather rough start, but it is simply too soon for us to feel comfortable with one of your ships scouting and surveying all the other planets in our system. Despite the fact that we don't yet have spacecraft as capable as yours, these are our planets and any Atlantean artifacts that might be upon them are part of our heritage and belong to us. We realize you really don't need our permission to do this, and we have no way to stop you, but I hope that our strong objections are enough to keep you from ignoring our wishes," Arctinier said.

Jesus fixed his gaze upon this head of state with whom he was sparring—not really yet negotiating since that would take both parties being willing to give and take—and briefly wondered what her ancestors had looked like when they separated from their Earthly cousins' genetic tree branch those millennia ago, and how and why they had been brought to Proxima Centauri b. Cause and effect had always fascinated him and this was no different. He didn't dare pause too long, and when he sensed that enough time had passed to make it appear he was deep in thought, which he was—just not about the topic they were discussing—he responded.

"We will gladly take a delegation of your choosing with us as we begin the exploration, and I commit to make them full partners in viewing, assessing, and deciding what to do with or about any Atlantean artifacts they might happen to find." Jesus was going out on a bit of limb here. When he left Earth, he was given some pretty firm limits as to how much technological insight he could give the Fintidierians, and having them on one of the ships was specifically discussed as a no-no. Fortunately, the ones who set the rules were over twenty trillion miles away and might not even know he broke the rule for another four years—if he decided to tell them.

The offer caught Arctinier by surprise and she did not do a particularly good job of hiding it. Jesus smiled to himself but managed to have his outward appearance remain stoic.

"Mr. Ambassador, that is an intriguing offer. I will have to discuss that with my staff," she countered, rising from her chair.

From experience, Jesus knew that meant the meeting was over and he was dismissed. He gave the customary local bow—which was thankfully not much different from what was customary in Japan, a country to which he had traveled many times as part of many delegations—thanked her for the meeting, and backed his way out of the room.

Now Jesus would have to explain to Mike Rialto, the *Samaritan*'s chief of security, that he'd invited the Fintidierian military aboard one of his ships. Rialto was just going to *love* that.

They would be like kids in the candy store. But if they were to find any Atlantean artifacts in the system, then it would have been worth it. Things last longer in the vacuum of space where they are not subject to the extreme weathering of a planetary biosphere. In vacuum, they were likely to be in fairly good shape, or at least in better shape than what they'd found in Misropos. The Atlanteans had come to Proxima Centauri b, and Earth, from the look of it, when Earth's humans were running around battling woolly mammoths in the latter part of the Pleistocene, during what was commonly called the Ice Age. If the Atlanteans, whoever they were, were that advanced fifty thousand years ago, then who knew what they might have left around the Proximan star system. He was determined to find out. Just one more kid in the candy store.

Jesus did not get back to his office until well after noon. On the way back, he stopped off at his favorite Fintidierian restaurant, which had a name that translated roughly to "the slab of beef with as few vegetables as possible," for a sampling of what its name advertised. The local grass-fed beef was to die for, and he enjoyed every bite, undisturbed by politics, news, or anything even remotely concerning all the issues he had to juggle as the ambassador. Unlike many others he knew, Jesus had no problem "turning off" his job to enjoy some downtime, especially if it involved steak and wine. Unfortunately, the local wines, unlike their beef, fell short of his standards.

When he arrived at his planetside office, located in a renovated elementary school not far from the city's central park, he was no longer worried about the security implications of the offer he'd just made to the secretary general; that would now be Mike's worry, not his. He paused to say hello to his Fintidierian aide, Sam Smith, an up-and-coming civil servant in the Fintidierian diplomatic corps. Of course, Sam Smith was not his real name—who could have that as a real name? Smith's real name was Sgurom Smyo, and, like many of the Fintidierians who worked with the Terrans, he'd adopted a more Terran-sounding one. It seemed that gave him some stature with his friends, who all wanted to work with the exotic visitors from the stars. Earth names were quite the fad. Smith informed him that his next meeting would be in thirty minutes with Roy Burbank and Rain Gilster. They had not provided a topic.

Jesus spent the time pacing in his office, using his net-connected contact lenses to scroll through and answer or ignore the many messages that were awaiting him after being out for most of the morning. He made a practice of turning off the contact lenses and aural implant network interfaces during important meetings. Not because he didn't want to have instant access to all the information that might be relevant and available from the vast data library they brought with them from Earth, but because he did not want to risk someone hacking the system and eavesdropping. Granted, on this technologically backward planet, such hacking was not likely, but "not likely" did not mean "impossible." Jesus believed information security was far more important than ease of network access.

Jesus heard a knock on the door and instinctively looked at the time. His thirty minutes had gone quickly. He walked to the door and opened it, seeing Sam and his two visitors standing in the outer office.

"Come in. I'm just catching my breath after another wonderful morning's discussion with Secretary Arctinier," Jesus announced, knowing full well that his guests would be put at ease by his apparent lapse of formality in front of his aide. Jesus had no doubt that Sam reported most everything he heard while working with the Terran ambassador. Making such casual statements publicly would, hopefully, lull the Fintidierians into underestimating him when it was time for him to be underestimated. It was simply another move on the diplomacy chessboard.

Roy and Rain came into the office and Sam dutifully closed the door after them as he returned to his desk.

"How may I help two of my favorite people?" Jesus asked.

"Ambassador, as you know," Rain began, "my team and I have been working for months trying to decipher and learn more about the radio messages being beamed here by someone, perhaps the Atlanteans. We've done all we can do from the ground and to make any sort of progress, and we need to take either the *Samaritan* or the *Emissary* to the outer solar system so we can get a better baseline and learn from where the message originates. I've worked out the details with the communications engineers on both ships and either one can be easily modified to get the data we need."

"Well, I—" Jesus started.

"Before you object, I want you to know that I asked Roy to double-check all my calculations and confirm that the radios on either ship should be capable of picking up the signal and determining its strength relative to what we pick up here. By triangulating and measuring the relative signal strength, and unless the source is much farther away than we think, then we should be able to pinpoint from which star system the message originates up to a distance of a little over a hundred light-years. Personally, I think the source is close. If it were that far away, then what would be the point? Roy?" she asked, speaking rapidly.

"Rain, things have changed and I—" Jesus interjected, trying to not be rude. This time, Roy cut him off.

"Ambassador—Charles, I want to let you know that I looked

over Rain's calculations and agree with her assessment. By taking these measurements, we can determine where the signals originate once and for all. It may not seem as urgent or important as solving the Fintidierian fertility problem, but I can't help but believe there may be a connection to what happened to the Atlanteans thousands of years ago. I found no mistakes in her calculations or conclusions" Roy said.

"That's good to know, Roy. I've been talking with the secretary general and—"

"I know she's got some reason she doesn't want us to leave orbit, but you have to convince her that doing so might help resolve this crisis. This is important," Rain added, finally pausing for a breath.

Jesus raised both his hands and made a T-shape with them.

"Time out! Time out!" he exclaimed.

"Wha—" Rain started to say, but could tell by the look on Jesus's face that he had the floor and she should be quiet.

"I agree with you. And I think the secretary general might allow us to make it happen. My meeting with her this morning was on a related topic and I made her an offer she is not likely to refuse, in exchange for her blessing to take the ships and do some exploring of the other planets in the system. While they are away, they can take all the measurements you need," Jesus said, smiling and leaning back in his chair.

"Both ships? If they go to opposite sides of the system, then we will get an even better baseline! That's wonderful news. When can they depart?" Rain asked.

"Oh, Secretary General Arctinier has not yet given her approval, but I expect it any moment now. Once we have that, I expect the ships will be able to depart within a few weeks. We might need to do some training of a few locals to join the crews, but that can be expedited. To save time, I recommend you go ahead and start working the details of what you need with the comms people on both ships," Jesus responded.

"Thank you, Mr. Ambassador. Thank you!" Rain said, rising from her seat to shake his hand.

"Thank you, sir." added Roy.

"My pleasure," Jesus replied, chuckling to himself. *If only all my decisions were so well received.*

✧ ✧ ✧

"Are we sure the Terrans aren't listening?" asked the secretary general as she looked around the room at her three top advisors. Arctinier decided to keep her inner circle small on all matters relating to the Terrans. After all, they were aliens on her world and from what she could tell from Earth's history, courtesy of the Terrans themselves, they were far from the united planetary government that she represented. Their history was filled with even more wars, more spying, and more covert operations than even her own world's sordid past. As much as she liked Ambassador Jesus and the rest of the Terrans she'd met, it was difficult to put their callous trespass on Misropos in the past and not have it influence her current thinking regarding trust. She had to wonder if Jesus was his real name. From what she could discern about the Christian religion's savior of the same name, his "turn the other cheek" and "love your neighbors" admonitions were just the characteristics one would want to have in the forefront of a potential opponent's mind as a way to put them at ease. If the Jesus she met with this morning was like the historical Jesus, then he should be trusted implicitly. *Ha! Not a chance.*

"As best we can tell, the room is secure," Lortay Vistra, her secretary of internal security, replied. The Fintidierians had no equivalent to a secretary of war or defense secretary since they had not been at war with anyone for quite a while. Sure, there were always discontents who made trouble, but they were far short in capability to warrant any sort of defense forces. No, the national police under his authority were more than enough. Perhaps. With the Terrans' arrival, the verdict was still out.

"For all we know, they could have one of their miniature drones in here listening to every word we say and we would never know it. From what we learned in some of their fiction and media stories, they seem to have the capability to build flying microphones the size of houseflies," the chief of staff added.

"Raolo, they very well might. But no matter how good their technology is, they cannot be everywhere. And I am sure their flying insects have batteries with some sort of lifetime storage and usage limit. We will have to keep moving our meeting locations around and hope we don't develop any discernable habits that will make our choices predictable. After all, we didn't decide where to meet today until barely an hour ago," Arctinier replied. The object of her rebuke, Raolo Vinsavan, was unfazed. That's why she liked him. He expressed his opinions and did not really care if they were accepted or rejected. But he was determined to be heard and had been right far more often in his advice than wrong.

"We are as secure here as we can be anywhere. If we let our paranoia get ahead of us, then we'll quit talking altogether and that would be disastrous," Vistra said.

"I agree. We need to get on with it. As you know, the Terrans have been wanting to use their ships to explore our star system and, at your request, I've been steadfastly refusing. Well, today they finally offered what we were hoping they would offer—places among the crew for some of our people to accompany them in their search for artifacts left by the Wrackvulta—or, as the Terrans refer to them, the Atlanteans," stated Arctinier, leaning back in her chair to watch for the reactions from her staff.

"I must say, you played that well," Vistra said as he, too, leaned back in his chair and took a deep breath. "With their technological superiority and their callous disregard of our quarantine protocols last spring, I was sure they were going to ignore us and do as they please. It appears you were right to take a hard line. They might actually be sincere in what they've been telling us."

"Be careful to not generalize their response under this particular circumstance. We have many, many reasons to be wary of them," Vinsavan replied.

"Whatever their reasons, they caved and now the ball is in our court. I told Ambassador Jesus I would respond to his offer expeditiously. Unless there is objection, I will accept the offer this afternoon," she declared.

No one objected.

"In that case, I would like Lortay to provide a list of candidates to join them in their expeditions in two days. I need ten people for each ship, and I want most of them to be above reproach with expertise relevant to finding and understanding any artifacts that might be out there. We have to take the search seriously and not just as an opportunity to gather intelligence on their technologies and capabilities. If we send them a list of military people and politicians, they will reject it outright. Raolo is correct in one thing: they can probably access our communications and systems more than we can imagine. If we claim someone is an experienced anthropologist, then this person damn well better have the pedigree one would expect. But I do want some, one or two on each team, to have as their top priority gathering the intelligence we need."

"Madame Secretary General, I have another item that we have discussed before, and it is becoming more and more urgent. Before the Terrans arrived, the fertility crisis was driving us to a complete breakdown in the social order. People were not showing up to their jobs, depression and suicide rates were climbing steadily, especially among young men, and the stock market tanked—taking most peoples' savings with it. The prospects for future profits are zero if there is no one here to buy anything. We were facing anarchy. The arrival of the Terrans seemed to put a pause to all that. With their advanced technology, there was general optimism that the fertility problem might soon go away. Well, it has been nearly a year and that has not happened yet. And we are starting to see the optimism bump-reverse itself. Unless there is a breakthrough soon, then I fear the societal depression will return," Vistra said.

"I had an update from the surgeon general on the progress of the joint medical team this morning. The good news is that the Terrans are implanting the first of thousands of female fetuses in women volunteers and, so far, they seem to be 'taking.' Granted, that's not nearly enough, but I think we should have a deliberate publicity campaign to highlight this minor success. It might help prolong the optimism and delay the inevitable chaos," Arctinier commented. "Also, I want you to implement a more vigorous effort to find top young students in science, technologies, and mathematics who can be apprenticed to Terran scientists. I have spoken to Ambassador Jesus on this issue and this is not a request from us to them. I made the point that this is a requirement."

"Ma'am, many of the citizens are somewhat reticent to work with the Terrans, while others are quite eager to do so. They are afraid of them," Harma Oo'ortava explained. The old woman had a look on her face that suggested she might be fearful of the Terrans herself.

"Harma, as secretary of commerce for our people, figure it out," Arctinier ordered. "We have lists of our best. Now find some of them willing to apprentice to the Terrans. Not a request, Harma. A requirement."

"Yes, ma'am."

"And the bad news, Secretary General?" Vinsavan inquired.

"The bad news?" Arctinier looked puzzled.

"Yes, ma'am, you told us the good news about the fertility efforts," Vinsavan said. "What's the bad news?"

"Ah, yes. I see. The bad news is that, of the natural conceptions involving Terrans, there is only one that is female."

"Shit," uttered Vistra.

"There goes the genetic diversity argument," Vinsavan said.

"I'm afraid so," Arctinier agreed. "It seems our saviors are as susceptible to whatever is causing the problem as we are."

"Shit, shit, shit," repeated Vistra.

Arctinier could not agree more. She felt like the entire planet was in a bucket of it.

CHAPTER 3

For Mike Rialto, the *Samaritan*'s chief of security, it was a nightmare come true. Ten Fintidierians, none of whom he had any chance to vet, or even meet before today, were now wandering around his ship, mostly unsupervised, getting into who knows what. Rialto knew that Captain Crosby didn't like the situation any more than he did, but their hands were tied. Ambassador Jesus had made an agreement with the Fintidierians that these scientists now on board the *Emissary* could accompany the *Samaritan* as it spent the next two months scouting the Proxima Centauri system for artifacts left behind by the Atlanteans. As usual, political decisions were made without consulting those who had to implement them and, well, it all rolled downhill from there. He and his security detail would have to do the best they could to contain any risk to the ship.

This likely meant that each of the ten scientists—and he seriously doubted they were all scientists—would have a crew member as a "shadow" for the duration, like it or not. Rialto would much rather have them each be intentionally supervised by a crew member, but that was ruled out by the captain and Ambassador Jesus. He was not necessarily worried about deliberate sabotage, since the Fintidierians had likely sent only people they trusted to not create an interstellar incident. However, if he were in their shoes and had the chance to observe alien technology nearly a century ahead of his own, among the various scientists would be a few intelligence gathering experts. In other words, spies. Even the non-spies would be soaking up as much as they possibly could during their time aboard ship. His shadows would mostly try to keep their assigned Fintidierian in sight and intervene only if they did something that looked dangerous or suspicious. The Fintidierians were not stupid and would soon figure out they were being watched.

To top it all off, none of his visitors had been trained for life on a spaceship and nearly all of them had required the vomit bags within an hour of coming aboard. Until they got underway, and the Samara Drive kicked in to provide some acceleration, they would be in microgravity, essentially "no gravity," with all its usual side effects. He could not be too hard on them for getting sick—nearly everyone did when they first experienced prolonged microgravity. *At least being nauseous will likely keep them from making any mischief for a few days.*

Rialto was pulling himself down the corridor using the handholds that were installed along the top of each shipboard corridor. They were put there for just this purpose, to expedite moving down the ship's long central corridor and those that fanned out from it. Plus, it was fun. They were spaced more than ten feet apart and enabled crew members to have a controlled "dive" from one end to the other by pushing off the wall and flying down the corridor to the next handhold. Some of the crew amused themselves by dividing into teams and flying from one side to the other, each group starting from a different end, timing their torpedolike flights to crisscross each other like some sort of synchronized swimming event. Of course, there were those who were less coordinated, and they tended to plow right into another member of the crew, causing some bruising, but, thankfully, no broken bones yet. Ah, the joys of long-duration spaceflight...

"Chief Rialto, please come to the bridge." The chief heard the summons via his cochlear implant. He reached up and tapped his collar to activate his microphone, exactly like the characters in the old twentieth-century sci-fi shows he watched with his grandfather as a child, and replied, "Copy. On my way."

He wasn't far and the trip to the bridge took only a few minutes, seven at most.

The bridge was a flurry of activity as the crew prepared to make way for the first time since they had arrived at Proxima b. The bustle of activity had a positive energy to it, and Rialto liked it. It felt good to be going back into space, even if they wouldn't really leave the neighborhood.

"Mike, there you are! Come on over, we need to chat." The speaker was Rialto's ground-pounder counterpart, Commander Mike Rogers. Rogers. A SEAL, Rogers was one of a few active military who had come along with the *Samaritan* to Proxima b. He was there in case the locals had turned out to be unfriendly. Rialto was never sure how fewer than a dozen Navy SEALS could hold off an army of Fintidierians, but he didn't doubt they could, at least for a while, and he was glad they were there. There was something reassuring about the militarily trained and fit can-do men and women in his team. They exuded security, confidence, and serious damned trouble—for anyone who crossed them. He was floating next to Captain Crosby and Dr. Enrico Vulpetti, the man responsible for getting the *Samaritan* funded and, by virtue of his connections, who got himself invited along for the ride. Of course, the fact that Vulpetti was a brilliant PhD aerospace engineer might also have boosted his qualifications. That, and the fact that he was both extremely helpful and a nice guy.

"Two Mikes. What a concept," Vulpetti said with a smile. "Maybe you guys should open a sandwich shop or something."

"Ha! Not like we've never heard that before," replied Rogers. Rialto nodded and smiled.

"While Dr. Vulpetti and I go over the list of suggested destinations provided by the Fintidierians, I want you two to work together on security plans for aboard ship, which Chief Rialto will be responsible for implementing, and for any landings and site visits, which Commander Rogers will run. The chief and I have discussed at length what to do with our guests aboard ship and I want our SEALs to help out where they can. But let's be clear: if anything arises, I want the chief's people to be the first to intervene. We don't want to escalate beyond neighborhood policing unless we absolutely need to do so. That said, the safety and security of this ship and its crew are my top priority. Anything that jeopardizes either of those cannot be tolerated, and it's up to you, both of you, to make sure nothing happens," Captain Crosby ordered.

"Yes, sir. My team is good with that," Rogers noted, nodding toward Rialto. "Mike, shall we go to your office to discuss?"

"Absolutely." When Rialto first met Rogers and his team, he

was wary of their real orders and intentions and whether or not their two teams would end up in conflict during the long trip. All his fears were unfounded, and both men ended up being fairly close friends. He was looking forward to strategizing with Rogers about how to keep their Fintidierian friends out of trouble aboard ship. He was also wondering what Rogers had in mind for security if they found any sign of the Atlanteans within the system. If the Atlanteans were as advanced as the records indicated they were, who knew what dangers they might encounter.

Crosby watched his two security leads swimming away through the air down the corridor, eagerly engaging each other, no doubt already brainstorming possible scenarios and everything that could go wrong. That was exactly what he wanted them to do. He then turned his attention to Vulpetti, who was also watching the two Mikes depart.

"Do you think we'll have any trouble?" Vulpetti asked as he was turning his head back toward Crosby.

"I have no idea. I hope not, but I cannot bet on hope," Crosby replied.

"I understand. I'm just glad we have them." He paused, then continued. "You asked me to pull together some destinations for us to investigate after we get the radio measurements for Dr. Gilster, and I have some ideas. I met last night with the lead Fintidierian scientist, Mr. Bob—he's an archaeologist who specializes in all things Atlantean—and we drew up a list of potential destinations."

"Whoa. Wait a minute. 'Mr. Bob'? That doesn't sound like a Fintidierian name," interrupted Crosby.

"It's not. His real name has so many consonants in it that Earth humans can't pronounce it without insulting him and his entire family. He finally gave up and asked somebody, one of ours, what name he should pick, and the smart-ass suggested 'Mr. Bob.' So, it stuck," Vulpetti explained.

"Another question. How is it that they have an expert on Atlantean archaeology? I thought Misropos was off-limits and visiting it was tantamount to a death sentence." Considering that the Fintidierian secretary general had nearly firebombed a Terran ground team out of existence for merely visiting Misropos, he was sincerely curious. Even the secretary general seemed surprised when she learned of the ruins there that pointed toward the existence of the ancient Atlantean visitors to her world. *Is she that good of a liar?*

"Well, I asked the same thing and all I got was a smile and a cryptic answer that went something like this: 'There are forbidden subjects and then there are *forbidden* subjects. For some, me included, forbidden just makes a subject more enticing.'"

"Remind me to ask Rialto to have his best people shadow Mr. Bob while he is on my ship. I've told them there are definitely some *forbidden* areas on the *Samaritan*. Please continue." Crosby's curiosity was now in overdrive. Learning about the Atlanteans, and what capabilities and technologies they might have or have had, was becoming something of a hobby for Crosby. He had pored over the photographic records taken in Misropos, chatted with everyone who was there, and spent more than a few sleepless late-night hours wondering what else the universe had in store for them to uncover during this trip. He felt a little bit like Captain Robert FitzRoy, with the *Samaritan* being the modern version of the HMS *Beagle*.

"Since we're going out to five astronomical units for the radio measurements, we should have our infrared telescopes on wide-angle scan and our radiation sensors set to maximum sensitivity once we're two AU from the star. Chances are that any technological artifacts in deep space had some sort of nuclear power source, fission or fusion, and once they are activated and used, they take a long time to cool off—in terms of waste heat and radioactive decay products, which can cause the heat. Depending upon the amount of initial radioactive material, it could still be shedding alpha particles for tens of thousands of years. Granted, we would need to be fairly close to detect anything and, given the volume of space around a star, the chance of accidentally stumbling across something is very small. But it isn't zero and sometimes dumb luck pays off."

"What about the other planets?" asked Crosby.

"Since we and *Emissary* will be going out a hundred eighty degrees apart, we'll be passing closer to Proxima Centauri c, which would be best to visit on the way back in since its only at one-point-five AU from the star. Given the size and dimness of Proxima, c is likely to be in worse shape than Mars—which is about the same distance from the Sun. There are eight dwarf planets about the size of Ceres between c and the system's Kuiper

Belt. I've consulted with navigation, and they've plotted a trajectory that should allow the *Samaritan* to easily visit three of them on the way back to c and b. *Emissary* can hit four, leaving only one that we can't easily reach," said Vulpetti.

"Only planets, then? You didn't need to consult with Mr. Bob for that," Crosby observed.

Vulpetti smiled. "I saved the most interesting for last. Mr. Bob said that his study of the ancient records and pictographs suggests that the most likely location to find something interesting is on c's innermost moon, c Prime. The planet has three moons, all ranging in size between Phobos and Deimos—in other words, pretty small. He showed me a pictograph that in the background seemed to depict the Proxima Centauri star system and there was a big starburst right next to c and two other moons. In the foreground were a bunch of Atlanteans walking out from what looked like a tall, skinny pyramid. I think it is some sort of lander and the artist is conveying that those getting out of it are from the star around Proxima c."

"I'm looking forward to meeting Mr. Bob. Why don't you and he join me for dinner tonight in my cabin?" Crosby asked.

"I'll ask him. And have you decided on a departure time?" asked Vulpetti.

"Tomorrow morning."

"That soon? Wow. That's great news. I haven't been this excited since we left Earth," declared Vulpetti, once again grinning.

"So, you've been to Misropos?" asked Crosby, between chews. Since they were still in microgravity and not the useful and mild one-fifth gravity that they would experience once the *Samaritan* activated its Samara Drive and began accelerating the ship to its first destination, they were eating ZG rations. ZG standing for "zero gravity." The food wasn't bad, it was just unappealingly packaged in plastic squeeze tubes. The evening meal was fried chicken, mashed potatoes, and green beans—mush style. Mealtime in zero gravity was not the sexiest part of deep space travel.

"Twice. The first time was when I was a student at the university and beginning my research. We all knew something of Misropos, the part about it being contaminated and off-limits, but none of us believed it—at least, we wouldn't admit that we believed it. The foolishness of youth. We had heard rumors of ancient ruins there, of buried treasures, lost secrets of the ancients, and more. From what I have read, you have similar legends."

"We do, and based on what we found here, we are rethinking a number of them," said Vulpetti.

"My friends and I knew there had to be something there. Many legends have as their basis some sort of factual event or person. We were convinced that the stories we had heard as children and adults had some basis in fact, and, as archaeologists, we decided that it would be up to us to find them and bring their secrets to the world. So, we rented a boat, bought enough provisions for our own miniature archaeological expedition, and set out for Misropos. Given all we had heard about the forbidden nature of the continent, we expected to see a large military presence blockading the route. In case we were stopped, we had a plausible cover story rehearsed and ready to provide. To avoid being stopped, we had several alternate routes planned to our final destination—which, I might add, was not far from the ruins you investigated," Mr. Bob said.

"But how? We found the ruins using hyperspectral imaging from space. They were mostly hidden in the forest," Vulpetti inquired through a partial mouthful of foodstuff. He swallowed, nodded, then squeezed a bit of mashed potato into his mouth. "Go on. Please."

"In the university library there were ancient books, mostly mythologies, describing the heroic deeds of long-forgotten heroes and their pantheon of gods. Tales of love, conquest, and great heroism—usually resulting in them winning the hand of a princess or some such. Most people considered them pure fantasy. But we found a pattern in the stories. A consistent set of underlying locations and events that seemed common to most, if not all, the great stories. Some of the books had maps describing where the events took place and nearly all of them touched certain regions of forbidden Misropos. We simply stopped reading the stories as literature and began reading them as embellished history texts and it became clear to us that there was something on Misropos that we needed to find and understand. And it all pointed to the region of Atlantean ruins."

"What did you find?" asked Crosby.

"Not what you found, that's for sure," said Mr. Bob, smiling. "But we found enough to convince us we were on to something. We found evidence of prehistoric habitation, the remains of buildings that should not have survived in the harsh conditions of Misropos, and evidence that these buildings were far more sophisticated in construction than even our modern buildings. For example, there was a cave around which were some still-standing square rock blocks, obviously artificially constructed. In the cave, we found evidence of past habitation such as pottery shards, arrow heads, that sort of thing. And then we found some long metal bars embedded within the rock walls to a depth of at least six feet. The bars were not steel, though they were certainly every bit as strong. It took us more than two days to chip away the surrounding rock to get one loose so we could bring it back to the lab with us. We asked a friend, a chemistry student, to help us identify the metal, and he did. It was titanium."

"I bet that was a surprise," Crosby added.

"An understatement. The titanium rod was of a purity that our industry was only then beginning to have an idea of how to make. And, based on the artifacts we found surrounding and built upon it, the rod had clearly been in that cave for many thousands of years. It changed our lives forever and was the catalyst for us pursuing as much information as we could concerning Misropos and the ancient civilization that once lived there."

"I have to ask. It's our understanding that going to Misropos is punishable by death. And yet, here you are," Crosby said.

"My friends and I were very careful to not let anyone know where we had been or what we found. Our chemistry friend was extremely curious, but after a fashion he stopped pestering us about it and moved on with his own career. We all eventually graduated and began our own academic careers as archaeologists, officially studying more traditional historical artifacts and cultures. But in our spare time, we gathered and continued our foray into understanding the ruins and lost civilization on Misropos. A couple of years later we took another trip there and found more artifacts, though none as compelling as the titanium rod. On the return trip, we nearly got caught by a military patrol and after we arrived home, we heard on the news about some smugglers caught off the coast of Misropos who were summarily shot for violating the quarantine. At that point, we were a bit older and less bold in our risk-taking. We decided to not make any more trips."

"How did you continue your work?" asked Crosby.

"You would be surprised what is on display or in the vaults of our world's museums that point to the ancient civilizations on Misropos. An anomalous tool here; an inexplicable hieroglyph there. Once you look at old things with a new filter, you can sometimes find more than meets the eye," observed Mr. Bob.

"Mr. Bob and his colleagues have been sharing their findings with our team and I think they will be of immense help in understanding any artifacts we might find out here on the trip. We're still putting together the pieces, and having locals with firsthand experience in the history and mythology of their world instead of just us outsiders making guesses has been a tremendous help," Vulpetti said.

"In that case, we need to make a toast," Crosby announced, reaching into a side drawer built into the table and removing three small squeeze tubes, each containing a red liquid. "What do you think of Earth wine?"

"I've not yet tried it," Mr. Bob said, reaching out to take one of the tubes.

"You are in for a treat. We don't have much of our supply left, but this is a special occasion," Crosby remarked as he gave the remaining tube to Vulpetti and opened his own. Crosby watched Mr. Bob's expression as he took his first suck.

Mr. Bob grimaced but managed a smile. "No offense, but I think I prefer Fintidierian wine," he uttered as he carefully pushed the tube of wine back onto the sticky mat before them. It was clear he would not be taking a second sip.

CHAPTER 4

Rain was ecstatic. She and the *Samaritan*'s communications team had been monitoring the as-yet undecipherable radio signal as they progressed away from Proxima b and toward the outer regions of the star system and, until now, the signal strength had been fairly constant. At approximately four AU, there was a small but noticeable drop-off in signal strength and what looked like the beginnings of a small sidelobe. By five AU they were solidly out of the main beam and even passing out of the weak first sidelobe they had detected. From the data so far, there might not be any more to detect. Sidelobes were an annoying reality of directional radio systems and even the advanced civilization broadcasting the mysterious signal had not been able to completely escape the fundamentals of radio transmissions and suppress all of them. Still, with a signal as strong as the one they had been monitoring, having only one detectable sidelobe was an achievement.

As soon as the signal strength went to zero, Rain had her triangulation data. With luck, she might not even need the data from the *Emissary* to complete the analysis and determine its source. And luck was with her. A few seconds after running the algorithm with the new trigonometric data, she had her answer: Luyten's Star.

Via her contact lens, Rain pulled up the stellar database and began reading about Luyten's Star. Like Proxima Centauri, Luyten's Star was a red dwarf—which made sense. When Earth humans began searching for potentially habitable exoplanets, they looked around stars like the Sun—a yellow dwarf main-sequence star. Might the Atlanteans not look for a habitable planet around another red dwarf like their own? Of course, she had no idea if the beings sending the radio signal were the same ones as the Atlanteans who had visited Proxima b millennia ago, but it was the team's working hypothesis. Observations from Earth indicated that Luyten's Star had five planets, one of which, Luyten b, was in its habitable zone. Luyten b was less than three times more massive than Earth, which made Rain cringe at the thought of trying to walk on its surface with all that extra gravity pulling on her already-out-of-shape self. Like Proxima b, Luyten b orbited much closer to its star than Earth at only nearly one tenth of an AU, which meant that it completed an orbit, its year, once every eighteen days. Given the luminosity of the star and the planet's distance from it, the surface temperatures ought to be nearly identical to those on Earth. And it was only twelve light-years from Earth; approximately sixteen light-years from Proxima b. Farther than she'd like, but within reach. *And, if all pans out, reach it we will.*

She was so excited that she nearly ran from the room to inform Captain Crosby. *Calm down*, she thought. The positional data would be coming in soon from the *Emissary,* which was now reaching about the same distance from Proxima Centauri as the *Samaritan* but on the other side of the star. Once she had their data, she could run it through the algorithm to confirm the analysis and make sure there were no unexpected errors. She could not imagine what those errors might be, but as an experienced radio astronomer, she knew that "crap" sometimes interfered with otherwise good data. She would wait until she had another set of data before she made any sort of announcement.

Rain did not have to wait long. Shortly after noon the next day, the *Emissary* passed out of the main signal and through the first sidelobe, giving her all the corroborating data she needed. The signal originated at Luyten's Star, most likely from Luyten b. Now she could tell the captain and send the good news back to Proxima b.

"Captain, we're in orbit around c Prime," announced the ship's navigator, Lt. Ricardo "Rick" Alexander. Alexander was the unsung hero of the *Samaritan*'s flight from Earth to Proxima

Centauri, working with the demoralized Roy Burbank to make sure the ship arrived safely in orbit around Proxima b. One of his "other duties as assigned" at the time was to make sure Burbank remained engaged in his work so that he would not have too much time to brood over being separated from his family across multiple light-years. In the process, Alexander and Burbank had become close. Alexander's efforts were subtle but appreciated by Captain Crosby.

"Give the science team the go-ahead to begin their mapping," Crosby said. He knew the mapping shouldn't take long, given that c Prime, Proxima Centauri c's smallest moon, was only approximately 150 square miles in area—roughly half the size of New York City. The ship was equipped with multiple optical, infrared, and ultraviolet telescopes with high-resolution imagers that could discern features to well less than a few centimeters. In addition to the telescopes, the ship was using its radar to map the moon's contours and synthetic aperture radar to penetrate several feet below the surface, allowing features such as caves to be found and charted. On their way back from collecting Dr. Gilster's radio data, they'd stopped and gathered similar data from c's other two moons and two of the system's dwarf planets located at two- and three-point-five AU, respectively. They, and the other two moons orbiting Proxima Centauri c, had been devoid of anything artificial they could detect, though the data they accumulated got both the *Samaritan* and Finti scientists excited. Scientists apparently liked seeing things for the first time, even if they looked like rocks to untrained eyes—like Crosby's.

"We've got something." The voice was that of Enrico Vulpetti coming from the far side of the bridge where the visible-light mapping data was being rendered on a display. Crosby could hear the excitement in his voice. Before he could ask anything, Vulpetti and Mr. Bob began talking to each other rapid-fire, and Crosby did not want to interrupt them—yet.

After a few minutes with no indication that they were going to bring their captain into the discussion anytime soon, Crosby decided to interject himself into their dialog. "Would one of you gentlemen care to enlighten the captain as to what you've found?"

"A cluster of pyramids, slightly north of the moon's equator! Three of them, each with a base about three thousand square feet. They are clearly artificial," remarked Vulpetti.

"Why does it always have to be pyramids?" asked Crosby. For centuries, some people attributed the construction of the great pyramids of Giza to aliens. Now they had found real pyramids that could only have been fabricated by aliens, or aliens who otherwise looked human, if they were built by the Atlanteans.

Crosby pushed off the deck toward the scientists and the display upon which they were now showing what they'd found. Now that the ship was no longer accelerating to reach the moon, his body told him they were again in zero gee. Except they weren't. C Prime was so small that in order to quickly map its surface, they were circling it but in a powered trajectory, not a simple gravitationally bound orbit. This meant that there were subtle, small accelerations occurring all the time that were barely perceptible to humans, and those minor accelerations caused him to misjudge his own personal trajectory so that he nearly missed the handhold he was targeting and came very close to bowling over Vulpetti. Vulpetti was so engrossed in his data that he didn't seem to notice.

"What? Oh, of course. Ha! I understand. And I have no idea why it has to be pyramids," said Vulpetti without looking up. "Here are the high-res images from our first pass. The shadows are rather long due to the sun angle, but on our next pass we'll cross at a slightly different angle which should allow the computer to subtract them out and give us a clean image."

Sure enough, on the screen Crosby saw three pyramids on the small moon's surface, plain as day. Their bases were not individuated and separate. Instead, they overlapped, with the resulting pyramidal shape being somewhat truncated on the bottom as one structure's side wall emerged from the lower portion of another's wall. It sure looked like one structure with three triangular apex roofs. Most interestingly, they looked pristine. Almost new. But out here on an airless world, and one with little gravity, there was no atmospheric weathering, and, from a long-term degradation point of view, there was no way any disturbed surface regolith would remain close to the moon's surface to slowly sandblast the structure. Regular micrometeoroid impacts, common to all planets and moons, would simply launch any ejected dust on an escape trajectory away from the moon instead of creating much of a spray that would travel any significant distance, as might happen on the Earth's moon. It could be a hundred years old, a thousand, or tens of thousands. Based on what they found back on Proxima b, it was most likely the latter. These pyramids were ancient.

"And there's more," announced Vulpetti, as he brought up a new set of images that overlayed the previous one with what appeared to be a soil-depth profile from the SAR. Under each pyramid, connecting them, were a serics of tunnels. "They are connected underground and one of the tunnels seems to extend farther into the ground than our radar can penetrate. At this resolution, they appear to be intact."

They stared in silence at the images as more data poured in, giving a clearer and clearer picture of the ruins.

An area in the rightmost pyramid slowly turned a semitransparent red.

"Well, well, well," said Vulpetti. "More and more curious by the moment. The infrared sensor is picking up some heat from down there. It isn't much, but it's enough above background to be significant."

"A power plant?" asked Crosby.

"If this is as old as we think it is, then I doubt it could be either a fission or fusion power source. I can't imagine something like that still being operational after thousands of years. We don't see any solar panels and c Prime isn't showing any sign of geothermal activity. I would put it in the category of 'something we will have to find out.' When can we go?" Vulpetti asked.

The airlock next to where the planetary shuttles were docked to the *Samaritan* was larger than most. It was, after all, located next to the shuttle dock for a reason—to allow the crew to don their spacesuits before boarding the much more cramped shuttle. Nonetheless, it was designed to be an airlock and could be fully functional with or without atmosphere. Its white walls appeared more stark than most due to the intense "natural light" spotlights that illuminated every cubic square inch of the walls, floors, and ceilings.

"I hate these damn suits." Joni Walker fidgeted at the arms as if she could adjust the space suit to a more comfortable fit, but the one-size-fits-all system was what it was. She continued to moan about it as she and her two fellow SEALs wriggled their way into the pressure suits that would keep them alive on the airless c Prime. "Once we got to Proxima and found that the air was breathable, I never thought we'd have to deal with these damned things again." Retired Space Force Chief Warrant Officer 5 Joni Walker had volunteered for the opportunity to take the one-way trip to Proxima Centauri as soon as it had opened up. When they met while in training for the mission, Rogers was immediately impressed with her diverse capabilities, which included spacecraft construction and repair, power and nuclear technologies, space and exo-terrestrial construction, and piloting. Today she was their pilot, taking them to the archaeological site on the moon's surface.

"Stow the shit, Walker. That's why we kept training," Rogers said, also struggling to fit into his suit system.

"Kiss your mother with that mouth do you, Commander?" The chief warrant officer 5 shot the navy officer a bit of a scowl. CW5s typically only took shit, and orders, from officers with a lot more metal on their uniforms. "Besides, looks like you could use some custom-fitting to your own LCVCG," she added to emphasize her expertise and why *she* was there. As was typical of the military, equipment names, including uniforms, were often unpronounceable except for the contractors who made them—including their Liquid-Cooled Ventilation and Compression Garment (everyone just called them long johns)—but she wanted all to know that she paid attention to detail, and this was one way to do that.

"Right," Rogers grunted. He continued to struggle into the suit.

The LCVCG microfiber garment was much easier to wear and offered more mobility than early twenty-first-century spacesuits, but it was still no fun. They had to be careful to not dislodge the Excreted Fluids and Solids Compression Under Garment, or EFaSCUG, carefully positioned underneath. SEAL 3, Jozef Horváth, saw Rogers also struggling and tried, unsuccessfully, to contain his guffaw. CW5 Walker grinned and nodded.

"Like I said, these damned things are a pain in the ass." Walker laughed.

With the garment now fully on, all Rogers had to do to get it to feel "right" was wiggle, squirm, and bounce around a few times while puffing out his chest and flexing his shoulders until the garment fell into place. Finally, it conformed to his shape. Next to put on was the backpack with the oxygen tanks and the sealing of a few small connectors between it and his suit. Last was his helmet. Now, he was ready. A few minutes later, so was the rest of his team. The third SEAL, Horváth, was a quiet and very capable guy whom Rogers had also grown to know and appreciate during their time together. Like everyone else on the ship, Horváth was a volunteer. He was a first-generation American whose parents had immigrated to the US from Slovakia after the great economic reset of 2066. Before they departed Earth, Jozef's parents invited the entire *Samaritan* SEAL team to their home in Long Island for a huge blowout of a meal with plenty of vodka. In Mike's book, Jozef was good people.

He and the SEALs would be accompanying Drs. Vulpetti and Shavers, Mr. Bob, and Walker to the surface. It was Carrie Shavers's first time in the suits since their emergency drills onboard the *Samaritan* during the journey from Earth, but, interestingly enough, she was the first to get completely suited up. As the *Samaritan*'s only astrogeologist and planetary astronomer, she'd naturally said yes to the opportunity to join the two-month solar system exploration. She also didn't hesitate to agree to joining the team going to the surface. From what Rogers could tell, she was in scientist nirvana at the thought of exploring yet another new world. All *he* wanted was for the EVA to be over, with everyone back in the ship safe and sound.

Rogers, now fully suited up and ready to go except for dropping the visor in his helmet, began to inspect his gear—again. Headlamp—check. Utility belt with almost every tool known to man—check. Sidearm loaded with plenty of extra ammo—check. Finally, he checked his primary weapon, a modified SIG Sauer carbine. In theory, any weapon that used a bullet should work fine in the vacuum of space. In theory. Reality was a lot different from theory and when lives were at stake, Rogers and any trained professional would want a weapon that worked in practice as well as theory. Bullets carry their own oxidizing agent, so there was no need for atmospheric oxygen to ignite the propellant. But without the atmosphere, the wide temperature variations in space were a problem. Direct sunlight might make the gun hot enough for the ammunition to explode spontaneously, which would not be a good thing. A gun kept in the shade might eventually become so cold that the primer in the firing cap might not work at all. The wild temperature swings and the vacuum of space also caused most lubricants to bead up and seize parts together. To solve these problems, the SEALs' weapons had built-in thermometers, heaters, and microcooling units to keep them in their optimal temperature range. They used a special lubricant that had been designed just for that purpose by the Space Force Research and Development office back on Earth decades prior. Their spare rounds were kept in clips and magazines that were similarly temperature controlled. He'd opted against having anyone on the team bring anything heavier—like grenade launchers. This was an archaeological expedition to a site theoretically abandoned thousands of years ago. It was unlikely they would be battling space monsters—he hoped.

Rogers looked around and saw that the rest of his team were performing similar last-minute inspections of their gear, as were the two scientists, who had quite different gear, and Mr. Bob. To no one's surprise, Mr. Bob took the longest to get suited up and needed a great deal of help from the support staff. The sum total of Mr. Bob's time to train in the suit had been during their journey from Proxima b, not enough for him to become proficient. Additionally, he'd yet to attempt it in microgravity. Hopefully, it was enough to keep him from doing anything stupid. A few minutes later, everyone was ready.

"Alright, people. Let's get aboard the shuttle and get this show on the road," Rogers ordered as he motioned for the group to join him in boarding one of the *Samaritan*'s four drop shuttles. Designed for taking up to twenty people from the *Samaritan* to a planetary surface, one with or without an atmosphere, each shuttle was its own mini spaceship equipped with nearly everything one would need for a monthlong trip in space except for a Samara Drive. The photon drive that had brought the *Samaritan* and the *Emissary* to Proxima b required way too much power to operate than the designers had wanted to install in a ship meant for near-space orbital and orbital-to-surface hops, so its propulsion was much simpler—and limited in range. It was good enough for what it was designed for and that was all they needed. A military transport it was not.

Thirty minutes later, Walker undocked the shuttle, eased it away from the *Samaritan*, and began her descent toward the moon below them. "Relax and enjoy the short ride. We'll rendezvous and dock with the moon's surface in less than forty minutes," she said.

Rogers kept his eyes glued to the windows and displays that

showed the view 360 degrees around the shuttle. He was now "on duty" and that meant he wanted full situational awareness.

As promised, and unlike the ride from the *Samaritan* to the surface of Proxima b, there was no turbulence. After all, the moon was too small to have an atmosphere and they were simply moving through the vacuum of space—where there was nothing to cause bumpiness.

Thirty-nine minutes later, there was a small puff of dust as the shuttle set down on the gray surface of c Prime. No one spoke as Walker powered down the shuttle systems, leaving only the reassuring thrum of the ventilation fans as ambient noise.

"Ladies and gentlemen, welcome to c Prime," she announced as she rose from the pilot's chair. "In a few minutes we'll enter the air lock, cycle out the air, and open the hatch to begin our walk over to the Atlantean artifact. I don't know if you noticed, but from my perspective as a pilot, our landing here was more like a docking maneuver. This rock doesn't have much mass and, as such, the gravity is very weak. It's enough for the shuttle to remain in place and for you to walk—but barely. If you walk too fast, say over three miles per hour, you might find yourself launched into a ballistic trajectory up and away from the rest of us and I really don't want to have to do my own acrobatic routine to come and fetch you. Does anybody want to tie off to someone else while we walk over?"

There were no takers.

"Alright then, visors down and follow me," she said as she moved to the back of the shuttle and the airlock. The rest of the team followed, with Rogers bringing up the rear.

It took less than fifteen minutes to get through the airlock and out onto the surface. It was all Rogers could do to keep himself walking forward without taking little jumps like he saw the early Apollo astronauts do when they first arrived on the lunar surface. Here, it would be even easier, and Rogers could easily see himself taking a flying leap and reaching escape velocity. *Not today.*

The surface of the moon looked a lot like Earth's moon. It was gray, covered with craters, and regolith into which their boots made shallow boot prints. It was also like the lunar regolith in that after only a few steps, the gray dust began to adhere to their suits, making them look like they needed a good cleaning. Looking up from the surface, however, and the similarity with the Moon became more striking. The horizon of this much smaller body was far closer and stood out in starker contract given the lack of atmosphere and the blackness of space just beyond.

Walking across the dead surface, routinely scoured by the intense ultraviolet light emitted by Proxima Centauri, made Rogers more sentimental toward both the verdant Earth and his new home, Proxima b. With the exception of the clearly artificial structures ahead of them, this world was truly dead, devoid of life, and would almost certainly remain that way forever.

Ten minutes later, they were standing in front of what looked like a door to the leftmost pyramid. While the clearly artificial structures were large, towering above the humans by at least as much as a three-story building, they were far smaller than the pyramids of Egypt. The door was only a little larger than those to which they were accustomed. The door was metallic, but the pyramid appeared to be made of the same material as the moon's surface. Rogers knew that many of the structures back on Earth's moon were made from lunar regolith that had been superheated, sintered, by microwaves, fusing the densely packed dust into an impermeable solid that could be shaped as needed during the heating process. Whoever built these had apparently done something very similar.

Mr. Bob, Vulpetti, and Shavers were taking pictures and examining it from every angle. While they did so, Rogers had Walker and Horváth check out the other structures, which were clustered close by.

"Commander Rogers, I think we've figured out how to open the door," Shavers informed them.

"Great. Let's try it after my team gets back from recon," Rogers replied.

A few minutes later, Walker and Horváth returned.

"The middle one doesn't have any openings. This one and the one on the right have the same type of door," Horváth briefed them, motioning toward the door in front of them as he spoke. "Nothing else to report. Just cold-looking alien walls."

"Dr. Vulpetti, you may proceed," Rogers said, bringing his carbine from being slung over his shoulder to the ready. The other two SEALs did the same.

"If I'm right, and if there is any power left in the system, then all I should have to do is place my hand on the pad right here," Vulpetti observed as he placed his glove on a hand-sized pad slightly below what appeared to be a control panel with various buttons and even a small dark screen.

Nothing happened.

"Well, damn," Shavers sighed.

The trio of scientists stood staring at the door and the likely control panel to its right as if it were a rattlesnake ready to strike.

"Did you push on it?" asked Shavers.

"Push on it? Well, no. I placed my hand on it. It looks like a hand reader that I've seen in company offices back on Earth," Vulpetti explained.

"If there's no power, a hand reader won't work. Give it a push," she suggested.

Vulpetti again placed his hand on the reader, leaned slightly forward, and pushed.

The pad moved inward two inches and the right-side edge of the door slid sideways, making an opening of nearly six inches, stirring up a bit of dust from around the edges as it did so.

Reacting like he'd just stuck his hand in a pit of snakes, Vulpetti removed his hand from the panel and stepped quickly back too energetically. Shavers quickly reacted and tugged him downward by the left wrist.

Rogers's training kicked in. He quickly stepped forward and brought his weapon to the ready.

"I'll be damned," Walker remarked, panning her light through the opening.

Rogers turned on his headlamp and peered around the door into the newly made opening. "There's a small room and another door on the far side. It looks like an airlock," he said.

Rogers put his hand on the plate, now indented in the wall, and pushed. Hard. Nothing happened.

"Well, let's try it the old-fashioned way. Horváth, Walker, give me a hand," Rogers ordered, making a space for the other SEALs to reach over and around him. Together, they were able to slide the door open enough for a person to squeeze through, though it would be tight.

"I'll go first," Rogers said, waving off Shavers, who had begun moving for the door.

"Because I'm a woman?" she asked.

"No, because I'm a SEAL . . . with a gun," he commented as he turned himself not-quite sideways and went through the opening into the dark room beyond. His headlamp illuminated the small room, which was only slightly larger than the airlock on their shuttle. It was completely empty, made of what looked like metal or plastic, and was featureless except for two identical control panels—one next to the door he used to enter and another beside a door on the opposite wall. If he didn't know better, he would assume he was in an airlock at some human outpost in the solar system instead of in one created by aliens on a moon in another star system. The control panels in the room did not have the pressure plate below them; instead, there was an old-fashioned lever like those in every Earth-made spaceship.

"I guess the Atlanteans were as cautious as we are. It looks like these doors are designed to be openable even if the power goes out. Walker, you are with me. We'll cycle through the airlock and into the structure first. Horváth, you stay with the scientists and come on through when I radio you that it's okay," Rogers said.

Fortunately, the inside mechanism made closing the outer door much easier than opening it, and opening the interior door was just as easy. When they opened the inner door, they continued to be greeted by darkness. To Rogers's surprise, there was no detectable atmosphere in the building. In the God-only-knows-how-long that the structure had been abandoned, someone had either vented any interior atmosphere to space or it had slowly leaked away. Rogers bet on the latter. All it would take over a decent span of time was for only a few meteorite strikes to put enough holes in the walls to allow any air within to escape.

Seeing no immediate threats, Rogers summoned the rest of the team through the airlock and into the building.

The room in which they found themselves was unremarkable. Along the walls were what appeared to be display screens and one additional door on the far side of the room. In the center of the room were several desk-height pieces of built-in furniture that Rogers assumed were control panels—apparently powered down and dead, of course.

They spread out around the room and began taking videos of everything they saw, transmitting the data immediately out to the shuttle, which then relayed it in near-real time to the *Samaritan*. They also began touching the desk surfaces, the walls, anything and everything, hoping their presence might activate some system. They had, after all, detected residual heat coming from the structures, which could indicate low-level power still flowing somewhere to *something*.

Nothing happened.

"Alright, let's keep moving," Rogers said as he moved toward the door that presumably led to the middle pyramid. It, too, was lever activated and relatively easy to open.

Rogers peered into the darkness of the next room, only it wasn't completely dark. It took a moment for his eyes to adjust, but within the room along the two side walls he saw multiple dimly glowing boxes, each slightly over six feet in length and three feet in depth. As he peered around the room, he saw that not all the boxes were glowing, some were dark. Sixteen in all, with five glowing faint green and one a dim orange.

"They look like coffins," Mr. Bob observed. It was one of the few times he'd spoken since they entered the pyramid complex.

"Or the cryobeds we use on the *Samaritan*," Shavers added.

Rogers walked slowly into the room, followed by the rest of the team. Seeing no immediate threats, he approached one of the coffins with the green glow while the rest of his team spread out to examine others. As he neared it, he knew their suspicions were correct. Each box had a semitransparent cover. Through the green glow and heavily frosted cover, though he could not make out many details, it was clear to Rogers that within the box was a human body.

"You're right. There's someone in this one," Rogers observed.

"This one too," said Shavers. She was standing next to another of the green glowing boxes.

"These too," added Horváth.

"And in the orange one," Walker said.

"I can't tell if the body is intact or not. The glass is too fogged up to see much. It sure looks like someone in cryosleep," Shavers said.

"It will be a miracle if any of them are still alive," Vulpetti said. "If our assumptions are correct, then they may have been here for over thirty thousand years. Unbelievable."

"Don't touch anything," Rogers admonished.

As he spoke, Mr. Bob's gloved hand touched the frosted window covering one of the green glowing cryobeds. Upon hearing Rogers, he pulled his hand back.

At first, nothing happened. Then Rogers noticed that the room was not as dark as it was previously. The walls themselves were beginning to emit a dull, reddish-colored light that was soon bright enough to eliminate the need for those assembled to use their headlamps.

"Alright everyone, circle up, civilians in the middle. SEALs, you know the drill," Rogers ordered.

The scientists and Mr. Bob moved toward the center of the room with the SEALs taking up position around them, guns at the ready. The lights brightened and then stabilized at a level that reminded Rogers of a summer evening right before sunset. Bright enough to see, but with a hint of dimness.

"Really, is this necessary?" asked Vulpetti.

As he spoke the lighted boxes, cryobeds, whatever they were began to glow more brightly and upon each of them, in areas previously dark and unremarkable, various lights began to glow, some flashing, some varying in brightness.

"I take that back," Vulpetti muttered nervously in a hushed tone.

"Oh my God, they're being awakened," Shavers announced. "We've got to do something!"

Rogers knew she was correct. Though it was extremely unlikely that any of the bodies in the cryobeds were still living, the last thing they wanted to do was accidentally awaken a bunch of sleeping Atlanteans only to have them immediately die from being exposed to hard vacuum and extreme cold. If the power system had been operating for thousands of years to keep them alive, then he owed them more of chance to live than that.

"Everyone, I don't believe we are in immediate danger, but they are. Fan out. See if you can understand enough of what's going on to stop it from happening. If they are waking up, then we need to get them some ambient atmosphere and heat or they're not going to last more than a few seconds," Rogers said.

To the scientists' credit, they moved forward quickly. Rogers let them focus on the individual cryobeds while he decided to close the door to the room so that any atmosphere this building might decide to provide would not immediately leak away.

He immediately checked his suit's external environmental monitoring system and detected no sign of change. If some sort of environmental control system knew the room was uninhabitable, then it was unable or unwilling to do anything about it. Of course, if it was as old as they thought, then that would not be a surprise. Getting anything to last that long and still be functional would be quite a coup against the second law of thermodynamics. Nonetheless, when he reached the door, he closed it.

He quickly and methodically scanned the walls, searching for any sort of control system that was still functional that he could try. Of course, without knowing anything concerning the Atlanteans—their language, their culture, anything—even if he found a control panel, he would not know what to do with it. There had to be something he could do.

"Commander, the shuttle has the Biohazard Containment Tent. It's big enough to cover two, maybe three of the cryobeds!" Shavers exclaimed. "We brought them to use when we first landed on Proxima b in case we detected pathogens in their atmosphere."

Rogers immediately reversed himself and began opening the door he had just closed. "Horváth, you and Dr. Shavers get over to the shuttle as fast as you can and come back with that tent," he said.

"But it isn't vacuum rated," added Shavers as she approached the door. "Not sure it will work."

"That's why Horváth is going with you to bring back some spare oxygen tanks along with all the portable MLI he can carry. It'll be leaky, but it might be good enough until the *Samaritan* can get us something better. Now, go!" Rogers shouted as the door was finally open.

"Are you getting all this, *Samaritan*?" Rogers asked, changing his aural implant from broadcast-only mode to now allow two-way communication. Broadcast mode was usually preferred for any remote operations team to avoid the inevitable chatter from third-party observers who might distract those in harm's way from being fully situationally aware in their potentially hostile local environment. Those on the ship could have overridden this mode to allow direct contact via the implant, but they had not done so in this case, allowing Rogers maximum freedom to control the situation.

"Copy that, Commander. We're prepping the other shuttle for immediate launch with a medical team and a vacuum-rated rescue inflatable. The soonest it can be loaded and on the ground is approximately forty minutes," replied Captain Crosby.

As Rogers was speaking, he noticed that the top of one of the green glowing cryobeds had opened, releasing a miniature snow shower of ice crystals upward into a graceful ballistic trajectory elongated by the low gravity of the moon. Walker, the closest of the group to that particular cryobed, rushed over to investigate and then stopped.

"This is bad. The poor bastard never had a chance," said Walker as she stood transfixed, staring into the now-open cryobed.

Rogers activated his corneal implant and accessed Walker's video feed, immediately regretting doing so. Inside the cryobed was a naked human male with coal-black hair and a muscular frame. His body was grotesquely distorted, ballooned outward to twice the size of a normal, healthy male, and his skin was shriveled and cracked. His face bore the expression of a person in a great deal of pain.

"Alright people, that's one. It appears he was alive when the cryobed opened. If there's no obvious way to stop the awakening process, then let's try brute force to keep at least a couple of the beds sealed until we get the tent. Let's pick two beds close together, a green one and the orange one. Two of us on each one. Put every muscle you've got into keeping those lids secure and closed until the tent gets here and in place," Rogers said.

As he spoke, another of the green-lit cryobeds opened, emitting the now not-so-pretty spray of ice crystals. Rogers and Mr. Bob moved toward the orange-lit bed while Vulpetti and Walker moved to the adjacent green one.

Rogers tried to make out more detail beneath the frosted window and could not. He just knew that whoever was under that lid deserved a chance to live.

Shavers and Horváth exited the airlock and were back on the moon's surface heading toward their shuttle. Taking full advantage of the low gravity, both were taking long, loping strides that carried them three to four feet above the surface before being pulled back down to the moon while trying not to launch themselves into orbit. It reminded Shavers of the flying dreams she had when she was a child. In those dreams, she discovered that she could jump into the air and, with a great deal of concentration, remain there, suspended a few feet above the ground, for longer than should have been possible for a normal person. It made her feel special, like she and she alone had the gift of flight. In these dreams, she would run and then leap for the sheer joy of being suspended in midair for a few extra seconds while her peers all immediately returned to the ground. But those were childhood dreams that she had long forgotten. It took the reality of leaping on an alien moon to remind her of them. It was exhilarating.

"Hey, watch out!" Horváth shouted, bringing her back to reality. She was so caught up in the moment that her last leap had been a bit too forceful and had carried her just a little too far, too fast and now she wasn't coming down as fast as she should. In fact, she was barely coming down at all. From what she could tell, she was going to overshoot the shuttle completely. She panicked as she attempted to force herself down to the surface, without success, and went into a tumble. Without any reaction force, there was nothing she could do to alter her now-ballistic trajectory across the moon's surface. She began to hyperventilate as she tumbled onward.

"Shavers! Listen to me. You've got to straighten out your body to reduce your spin rate and orient yourself. You're coming back down, but you'll reach the ground a good thirty yards on the other side of the shuttle. You've got to prepare yourself for hitting the surface. If you come in headfirst you will need to go into a roll to avoid hurting yourself. And I can't nursemaid you and carry the tent and oxygen bottles back to the pyramid by myself," Horváth told her as he loped along, trying to catch up with her without launching himself into a similar trajectory.

At first, Shavers did not process what Horváth was saying. All she could think about was how fast the world was spinning and how she was now going into orbit around the moon—perhaps never to come back down. Slowly, as the panic attack subsided, she mentally replayed what she'd heard and attempted to straighten her body. It helped slow down her spin, but it did not eliminate it. She could now also see that she was not going into orbit, but rather coming down a long way from the shuttle. As her body continued to rotate, taking her head downward, she fought hard to keep the panic from returning and concentrated on slowing down her breathing.

"I hear you," Shavers remarked. "I'm okay. I can do this." She only half believed what she was saying. But she was going to try. *Feet first—run with it to slow down. Headfirst—go into a roll.* She repeated this to herself over and over as she dropped closer and closer to the surface. *Feet first—run with . . . Hmph.* The thought abruptly ended as she landed on her feet with her upper torso leaning slightly forward. She came to a stop and stood there, taking deep breaths.

"Shavers! Are you okay?"

"I'm okay," she said, looking back toward the shuttle she had just flown over. "I'll be right there. We have some Atlanteans to save." With that she began to lope back toward the shuttle—taking much smaller steps.

So far it was working—mostly. The three Earth humans and the Fintidierian were successfully keeping the lids on their two cryobeds closed as whatever mechanisms within them were trying to open them. Unfortunately, one by one, the other unattended cryobeds repeated the same cycle of opening and death as the first two and there was nothing they could do but watch. For these time travelers across tens of thousands of years, death came quickly. Unfortunately, though they were mostly successful at keeping the lids closed on the cryobeds, Rogers could see an occasional puff of atmosphere and ice crystals leak out along the seams. Unless something changed soon, instead of a quick decompression death, the occupants would die from hypoxia.

Rogers peered through the still-frosted covering between him and the now-awakened Atlantean within the cryobed with wonder and empathy. At first, the newly awakened occupant just lay there, assessing his surroundings. Then he tried to push open the lid. When it didn't move, he frantically moved his hands left and right, presumably looking for some sort of manual release mechanism. When that didn't work, he began to panic and alternatingly started pushing hard against the covering and beating his fist against it. Rogers could only think of those horror stories he heard as a youth about people thought dead being buried alive with their fate only discovered when people exhumed the coffins and saw scratch marks in their inner lids. He also wondered if the trapped Atlantean realized he was being kept in the cryobed by two people sitting atop it. The poor guy must be terrified. *I wonder if he can feel the cold.*

Rogers glanced at his partner, Mr. Bob, and gave him a smile that he hoped was visible through his helmet's visor. "Mr. Bob, hang in there. You are doing great. Without your help, this guy would be dead."

"I'm not sure he shouldn't be dead, Commander Rogers," Mr. Bob replied. "He might have whatever disease wiped out his kind and so many of mine. Plus, if the records are to be believed, he was one of the actual monsters who enslaved my people."

Rogers knew that Mr. Bob was responding to a lifetime of conditioned belief that anything associated with the continent of Misropos, the newly discovered Atlanteans first and foremost, was dangerous and must be avoided at all costs. This cultural belief had almost resulted in the firebombing of the *Samaritan* crew when they investigated the ruins there shortly after their arrival on Proxima b last year. Truth be told, though he knew the risk was low, he would be happier to have the medical experts from the *Samaritan* dealing with the problem of the Atlanteans instead of him and his team.

"I realize this is difficult for you, but this man might have the key to stopping the fertility crisis. Keeping him alive might actually save your people," he replied.

"Commander, we're coming through the airlock. We'll be there with the tent and air tanks within a couple of minutes," said Horváth.

"We've got a couple of awakened Atlanteans who I suspect will be mighty grateful," Rogers said.

Two minutes later, Shavers and Horváth ran into the room carrying the biohazard tent, multiple-layer insulation blankets, and two oxygen tanks. It did not take long to set up the tent and begin filling it with oxygen. Rogers's environmental sensor showed the atmospheric pressure in the tent that now covered both cryobeds slowly rise to barely under eighteen kilopascals and level off. The tanks were still pumping air in but the leakage rate from the tent kept it from rising any higher.

"We can't open the cryobeds. The pressure in the tent is still only half that on top of Mount Everest, less than one sixth of sea level. That's not enough to keep them alive if we get them out, but hopefully enough to keep them going long enough in their cryobeds until the real pressurized tent arrives, hopefully with a couple of spare space suits," Rogers said.

"Uh, Commander, I think we have a problem. The Atlantean in our cryobed has stopped moving and gone limp," announced Walker.

"Shit," Rogers uttered.

"What do we do?" asked Walker.

"Stay put. Opening the lid will only make things worse. Maybe the med team will be able to do something once they get here," Rogers said. Then, speaking into his implant, he added, "What's the status of the next shuttle?"

"It's on the way and should be landing near yours within two minutes. Drs. Kopylova and Thomaskutty are with the team and ready to do what they can," replied Captain Crosby.

"Thanks, Cap'n. That's great news." Rogers was feeling optimistic for the first time since the cryobeds began activating.

"Commander, you and your team are to remain in the rescue inflatable with the doctors to provide their security. Let me be clear: If you perceive any threat to you or any member of the team, you are to use whatever force necessary to remove that threat. Am I clear?"

"Yes, sir. I understand," Rogers said, looking to his team to affirm that they heard also. All heads nodded.

The next fifteen minutes felt like an eternity. When the secondary crew entered the room carrying the rescue inflatable, more oxygen tanks, and a large radiant heater and power supply, Rogers allowed himself a sigh of relief.

"Aren't you guys a sight for sore eyes," Rogers declared.

"Good to see you too, Commander," Mak responded. "Let's see if we can keep our new friends here alive, shall we?"

"I'm afraid one of the two might be in serious trouble. The other one, the one I'm sitting on, looks pretty agitated—but healthy," Rogers noted.

"Let's hope they are as human as our Fintidierian friends. I know how to treat humans suffering from hypoxia and recovering from cryostasis, but if they're truly aliens, then I'm not sure how much help we will be," Mak said.

CHAPTER 5

Cold. Dark. Is that light? Why is it so cold? Why can't I move?

Merciful sleep.

What? Where am I? It's so cold. Are my hands tied? Why are my hands tied? The light is too bright. Why am I here? Where is here?

Calm down. Rest. Think.

Voices. I hear voices. I don't understand them. They aren't speaking the dialect. Where am I? Am I a captive? How long has it been? Don't let them know I am awake.

More sleep.

"I will not allow *it* to set foot on the planet. Period. The discussion is over."

Charles Jesus was once again descending into frustration at the obstinance of his Fintidierian counterpart, Secretary General Arctinier. They had been discussing the matter of finding a living Atlantean and what to do with her—*it*, according to Arctinier. Once the cryobed was opened, the naked body of the occupant made it very clear that what they had thought was a "he" when peering through the frosted lid was actually a she. Of the sixteen cryobeds the crew of the *Samaritan* found on c Prime's innermost moon, only one, the one that had been in the bed emitting an orange glow, appeared to be still alive. Unfortunately, the other living one died before the medical team from the *Samaritan* could get their life-saving equipment in place. The survivor, who, after examination, was determined to be fully human with what appeared to be Native American ancestry, was now safely in the *Samaritan*'s infirmary under strict quarantine protocol. She had not awakened after passing out, presumably due to the low atmospheric pressure to which she was subjected while awaiting rescue. But she was very much alive, with her brain waves indicating she was in a very deep sleep—and dreaming.

In addition to her apparent Native American ancestry, the detailed examination provided by Mak and his team uncovered that her body was heavily augmented in much the same way that was projected to shortly be the norm on Earth. There were implants in her eyes, at various points in her brain, within her skeletal structure, and alongside several of her internal organs. Mak and his team were completely unable to determine the purpose of the augmentations. Theories ranged from they were needed to keep her alive on Proxima b to suggestions she was modified to be a weapon. It was because of the latter possibility that Captain Crosby had her physically restrained and under continuous guard by two from Rialto's security team.

The ship was back in a low orbit around Proxima b and, according to Mak, it was only a matter of time before their guest became conscious. So far, the medical facilities aboard the *Samaritan*, which were extremely well equipped given the nature of their mission, had failed to detect any sort of pathogens on or in the sleeping Atlantean. For this reason, Crosby proposed, and Jesus agreed, that the Atlantean should be brought planetside and placed in a secure facility there until they could communicate with her and determine her intentions. Arctinier most emphatically did not agree.

It had been nearly two months since the alien base had been found and the team led by Drs. Shavers and Vulpetti made their astounding discovery. The news spread rapidly and soon thereafter there emerged two opposing political camps, both vying to have their views guide any next steps. The first group, which the Earth humans supported, called for immediate autopsies of the dead Atlanteans to find out more about them and, hopefully, gain insight into the still-worsening fertility plague. Maybe there was a biological connection between the ancient Atlanteans and the plague that could be uncovered using the Earth's vastly superior biological science capabilities. This was the side that Jesus hoped would hold sway. The other, which he now knew had the support of Secretary General Arctinier, was that the dead Atlanteans—and the living one—were simply too risky to even study and must simply be destroyed. In the case of the living one, executed.

"Secretary General Arctinier, we came here to help find the cause, and hopefully a cure, for your fertility crisis. Studying these people may result in the breakthrough we need to accomplish that goal. With regard to a biological examination of the dead Atlanteans, we are already well underway, and I consider making that decision to have been fully within my prevue. I will agree to not allow their bodies to be brought to the surface and that all of my crew be thoroughly checked and rechecked to make sure that no pathogens are transferred from our ancient friends to you or the rest of my crew," Jesus said.

"Given your *obvious* superiority, I must reluctantly acquiesce on that point," she muttered.

Her mentioning the Terrans' superiority, in Jesus's opinion, was borderline insulting. In one short year, she'd gone from being thankful to have more technologically advanced help to resenting it. *Not a good trend.* Jesus made a mental note to bring up this growing resentment in the next all-hands meeting to see if others were experiencing anything similar in their interactions with the locals.

"But on the other, I will not give. The alien must never be allowed to come here. The risk is too great," she said.

Jesus sat impassively, try to not show a reaction of any sort. Internally, he was steaming.

I'm alive! How long has it been? Where am I? And of what family are these voices that I cannot understand? Where are the rest of the rest of my *family?*

Rakwar Frawka, Guardian of the Leader, slowly opened her eyes—but only slightly. She did not want her captors—and captors they were (why else would they have her restrained?)—to know she was awake. The bright lights were at first unbearable. Intellectually, she knew she had been asleep and in darkness for a long time, making her eyes overly sensitive to even normal light levels, but the brightness and inner fear of being blinded almost overrode her intellect. Almost. She closed her eyes and instead activated her augmentations.

She could now hear not only the conversation taking place

between the two people in the room with her, but also those in the next room and, from what she could tell, passersby in the corridor. The hum of the electronics all around her made her realize she was either the captive of some unknown race, definitely not The People, or she had been in cryosleep for a long, long time. When she left the colony world, the primitives were far from having a technological culture themselves.

Her radiation scan turned up the usual visible and radio frequency emissions, but also the telltale low-level gamma-ray and neutron signatures of a fusion power system. There was also the background radiation emissions characteristic of Proxima Centauri, the star around which she had spent most of her adult life in service to The People.

She then performed a self-diagnostic and was surprised to learn that none of her body augmentations had been disabled. Were her captors truly ignorant of what that meant? That these restraints would do no more to hold her than were they not even present? She was at first surprised that she was not hungry, then she realized that the tubes connected to her body must have been providing nourishment while she recovered from cryosleep. There were no traces of any foreign substances in her bloodstream, so it was clear that they had not yet tried to interrogate or torture her.

She had to get free, make contact with The People, and warn them that some primitives, likely very dangerous primitives, were nearby and had defiled one or more of their facilities at Proxima Centauri. In the years since The People had been expanding their domain from star to star, they had never encountered others with a level of technology even close to their own. The threat was obvious. She had to warn them.

Calmly calling upon years of training, she took a deep breath and triggered the rapid release of epinephrine into her bloodstream, increasing her pulse rate and blood pressure and her lung's oxygen processing capabilities, and then activated the cascade of hormonal responses to flood her system with cortisol, allowing her enhanced musculature to respond at its full capability. Barely two seconds later, she was off the table and began neutralizing the threats in the room with her.

"Mak, she's got to wake up eventually. There's no good physiological reason for her to still be unconscious. She's not in a coma, her brain activity suggests she's sleeping. Based on her brain activity, we thought she might be waking up a few hours ago, but it was only transient. Since then, only a few blips, the most recent being just a few minutes ago. She might be waking up and then going back to sleep, cycling between the two," Dr. Sindi Thomaskutty said, one of the many medical specialists who had come to Proxima b with Mak and the rest of the *Samaritan*'s medical team.

Mak and Thomaskutty had been poring over the physiological data they'd collected from their Atlantean patient since she arrived in the ship's infirmary. As it became clear that she was one hundred percent human and not some alien where the services of a veterinarian might be more useful than a physician, their task became easier. As they had learned from gene sequencing that the Fintidierians were of human ancestry, with ancestors likely from somewhere in East Asia fifty thousand years ago, so too was their Atlantean, but with ancestry that suggested she, or they, came from Earth much more recently, perhaps only ten thousand years ago, likely from somewhere in the Americas.

And then there were the curious physical changes resulting from her many surgical implants. The embedded electronics in multiple regions of her brain, ears, eyes, hands, legs, and feet. The latter with connections to her brain running there in parallel with her spine and spinal cord. What appeared to be tiny servomotors were implanted at many of her joints, suggesting they were there to augment her physical strength and, perhaps, response times. Curiously, unlike what had been happening on Earth with the advent of the genetic engineering revolution, there was no indication in her genome that she was similarly modified. Of course, the technology the Atlanteans used to perform genetic engineering might be so much more advanced than Earth's that the *Samaritan*'s equipment simply could not discern that it had been done. The augmentations were a wild card that Mak didn't like. He was not exactly the paranoid sort, but it was beginning to look like their guest had some capabilities beyond the typical human and that could be a problem.

"The tox screens are still clear?" asked Mak, referring to the many toxicological tests they had performed to determine if their Atlantean guest carried any pathogens or contaminants that could endanger the crew of the *Samaritan* or the people of Proxima b. After seeing the ruins on Misropos and accepting the theory that some sort of disease or condition caused the Atlanteans to die off in the planet's ancient history they'd become a bit paranoid. Understandably so.

"Completely clear. Based on the data, she can come out of the isolation tent anytime. She is as healthy, or healthier, than you or me," replied Thomaskutty.

Bang! Snap!

Mak glanced toward the isolation tent containing the Atlantean, the source of the noise, and had his growing fears confirmed as he saw her rise from the table, snapping the arm and leg restraints like they were not even there and tear through the side of the isolation tent like the proverbial knife through butter. He started to shout and alert the two security guards outside the door but he never had the chance as the naked Amazon lunged through the air like an acrobat in complete control of her body in microgravity. As she closed the distance at the last moment she rolled over and kicked him in the upper chest, just below his windpipe, knocking him across the room, incapacitated. Thomaskutty was not so lucky, the single kick that began with Mak sliced sideways and caught the shorter doctor on the side of her neck, causing it to make a sickening snapping sound as she crumpled and drifted into a lifeless spin from the momentum of the kick.

Mak took in a deep breath and immediately regretted it. He undoubtedly had multiple broken ribs and perhaps a collapsed lung. He hurt and could taste blood. The pain was excruciating, and he struggled to remain conscious long enough to see what their "visitor" was now up to.

The Atlantean made a beeline for the computer interface and after studying it momentarily, she steadied herself into place with her left hand and gave it a fast and vicious punch with her right that loosened it enough for her to pull the cover completely off. After sorting through the various wires and fibers in the console, she apparently found what she was looking for and pulled a small bundle of fiber-optic cables from within and grasped it firmly in her right hand. As she did so, she tilted her head upward and froze.

Guardian of the Leader took little pleasure in incapacitating her captors, knowing that the ones she attacked were not likely among those in charge and were simple healers. She had no personal quarrel with them, but as part of whatever group had found her and were now holding her against her will, they were expendable and a threat that had to be neutralized. It felt good to be moving and the thrill of executing a killing blow, even against untrained opponents, invigorated her.

Quickly assessing the technological level of her captors, she knew where she had to go to achieve her most urgent goal. She found it relatively easy to remove the viewscreen and access the electronics and optronics below. Using the sensors embedded in her fingers, she quickly tapped into the data flowing through the wires and fiber optics running through the console. Most were routing simple, unencrypted information concerning the health and status of various ship systems and those in the medical bay in which she found herself. As she allowed her consciousness to tap into the data flow and visualize it, the relative rate at which time passed around her physical body seemed to slow to a mere trickle. Looking around the data flowing through their systems all around her, she had to resist the urge to follow every thread, especially those that ran into the ship's core data storage hub in which she was sure she could find out more about the humans that surrounded her, their history, and their motivations. There might be time for that later. For now, she was looking for something much more specific. *There.* She found it. Now all she had to do was make a few tweaks to its command-and-control algorithms and then her immediate mission would be accomplished. *Finally!* All was now ready. Guardian of the Leader briefly paused before executing the software sequence she had just crafted. In the time it took for her body to draw another breath, she thought about what she had discovered while scanning their systems. The spacecraft in which she found herself had originated in another star system and was not crewed by descendants of those she knew from Proxima b. Fusion power. Photon propulsion. While primitive compared to her own technological level, these humans were not as far behind as she had hoped. They might actually be a significant threat to The People.

She quickly modified her previous work and this time unhesitatingly commanded the algorithm to execute.

Captain Crosby and Dr. Cindy Mastrano, *Samaritan*'s chief engineer—known as the "CHENG"—were on the bridge discussing the options the scientists and engineers aboard ship had come up with for potentially accessing the computer systems they'd found on the moon below. That is, if the builders even used what

Earth humans considered to be "computers." Who knew what technologies they possessed, and whether or not they were even accessible and understandable to another technological culture trying to access them.

"There is clearly a still-functioning power source on the moon, or all the cryobeds would have failed long before now," Mastrano noted. As was her habit when she was deep in thought, she paused and ran her hands through her long black hair, now interspersed with gray.

"Do we know what caused all the others to fail?" asked Crosby.

"Not all of them, no. But a few of the ones that failed had been holed by micrometeorites, likely the same ones that pierced the exterior walls and allowed the atmosphere to escape. Though the likelihood of having some piece of interplanetary rubble traveling at twenty to thirty kilometers per second hitting you at any given time is extremely low, the probability of being hit over a long enough period of time is rather large. And if they've been here as long as we think, thousands of years, then the probability of at least one hitting a cryobed is not small. We're still looking at the other beds, those not holed, to see if we can figure out a cause. But we won't likely know unless we can tap into their computers and understand what we find," the CHENG replied.

"It may be that we have to leave that for the next team that comes out. The ambassador would like for us and the *Emissary* to return to Proxima b to get together all the specialists we may need from each ship for the return effort. *Emissary* is already on its way back," Crosby said.

Without warning, the lights on the bridge went dark, triggering the emergency lights. Crosby and Mastrano were startled only momentarily before allowing their training to take over. Mastrano moved away from Crosby, pushing off to glide across the room and into the chair at her duty station. Crosby buckled his seatbelt and activated the status boards on his personal console. Only those tied into the emergency network were active.

"CHENG, get me the ship's status as soon as possible. We need to find out what's going on. I don't hear any alarms or see any obvious damage or threat," Crosby said as he scanned the few systems that he could access.

"Nothing yet, Captain," Mastrano added as she busied herself at her own console.

Crosby hoped she had access to more of the ship's systems than he had at the moment. From a ship point of view, the bridge crew was both dead and blind—not a situation that he wanted to remain in for long.

The ship lurched and Crosby felt the momentary tug of his inertia trying to keep him from moving from whatever motion and orientation the ship had been in to whatever ones it was now moving toward.

"CHENG?" Crosby asked impatiently.

"It felt like the ADCS thrusters fired to reorient us, sir. But I can't see the status board to confirm," she replied, reporting on the Attitude Determination and Control System.

"Do what you can," Crosby said and then slammed his fist onto the arm of his command chair opposite to the one from which his console originated. "Dammit, the intercom system isn't working either. I can't access it via my console or my implant." Then he remembered that he should be able to access specific individuals via his ear implant.

"Mike, this is Captain Crosby. I don't know what's happening but I would bet it has something to do with our guests. Check in with the guards you have in the infirmary and make sure everything there is under control," Crosby said.

"I'm one step ahead of you, sir. I contacted the team and they're going in now," replied Rialto.

Crosby gave a sigh of relief. His crew was the best and he should have known that Rialto and his team would be one step ahead of him. Now he had to do his part and regain control of the ship while they figured out what happened.

Guardian of the Leader knew she had only moments after executing the software command before her captors would send someone to check on her. She also knew that whoever might come would likely not be healers and therefore more of a threat. Though she would like to have remained immersed in their network for longer to learn more about these mysterious humans, there was no time. She let go of the optical cable bundle and moved toward the door, placing her feet against a bulkhead and balling herself into a ready crouch like a coiled rattlesnake ready to strike as she did so.

Right on schedule, the door opened and two men carrying what she could only assume was some sort of weapon entered the room. Taking advantage of what remained of her element of surprise, she launched herself toward the first man to enter, knocking him sideways as she grasped the side of his weapon to make sure the tip was not aimed at her and raised her knee to strike him in the groin. The two of them rolled and struggled for the weapon and were pulled slightly toward the aft wall due to another firing of the attitude control thrusters. They continued to struggle across the room and into the wall until she finally managed an elbow into his solar plexus, stunning him momentarily. As he crumpled inward from the blow, his finger reflexively squeezed the trigger on the weapon and fired a burst of projectiles into the nearby wall. Using her remaining forward momentum, taking into account the recoil she experienced from her impact with the now-incapacitated man, she swung the weapon around toward the second man entering the room and grasped what she had observed was the weapon's trigger, discharging another short burst of projectiles into him.

The second man had been raising his weapon to fire but never had a chance. The projectiles struck him in the torso, releasing a spray of blood that filled the air. She then pulled the weapon from the first man's now slack grasp and used its butt to strike him in the head.

The immediate threat was now behind her, but she knew she was not out of danger. It would not be long before her escape was discovered. She had only minutes to reach one of the ship's shuttles she had learned of when tapping into their computer system. If she could get there quickly and get off the ship, then she might be able to find a way to either hide until she came up with a plan to reach any others of her kind who might still be alive in-system or to kill herself cleanly so that no amount of interrogation or torture could get her to betray The People.

In her head, she visualized the layout of the ship and found the quickest route to the shuttle she would use for her escape. In the dim lighting of the hallway, she activated her optical enhancements, which gave her the visual equivalent of the audio enhancement she had been using since awakening. No one could possibly sneak up on her now. She set out for the shuttle, determined to make her escape.

"Sir, someone interrupted the command-and-control circuits with a pretty damn ingenious block. I should be able to remove it momentarily now that I've found it. Stand by," the CHENG announced.

"Very good. But will you be able to know if there are any other surprises in there? If someone can modify the C and C, then they could do damn-near anything," replied Crosby.

"Answering that will take some time. Once we have full system access, I can start running diagnostics. To be safe, as soon as the system is restored, I'll put the fusion reactor on standby and put a block on it so no one can give it a command except you or me," Mastrano said without looking up. Her hands flew across the console in front of her.

Crosby started to reply when his implant signaled that he had an incoming call from Rialto.

"Captain, I can't raise the guards in the infirmary. I've alerted all my staff and asked Mike Rogers to get his SEALs ready to help. I'm nearing the infirmary now. The door is open and . . . oh, my God. The Atlantean appears to have gotten loose. We've got casualties here. I'm alerting the team. A security detail is already on its way to the bridge," announced Rialto, not bothering to sign off from his communication with Captain Crosby.

"CHENG, I'm deaf and blind here. We've got a killer Atlantean loose on the ship and I need my eyes and ears," Crosby said. He knew Mastrano was working as fast as she could, but Crosby had to alert her to the news he'd just heard—as if it would give her incentive beyond what she had already . . .

Crosby looked up as the reassuring face of Mike Rogers entered the bridge and closed the hatch behind him.

"Captain, my team is under Mike's command until we find and neutralize the Atlantean. I volunteered to come up here to secure the bridge personally. We can't discount the probability that she might choose to come up here to seize control of the ship," Rogers said in his best "I'm a SEAL and no one should ever forget it" tone. On that point, Crosby was never going to forget. Having one of the two Mikes securing the bridge was as reassuring as it could get.

"Thanks, Mike. There are no circumstances under which we relinquish control over this ship. None," Crosby declared, pausing only momentarily to make eye contact with him. Rogers's slight head nod confirmed that his message was received. If the situation were to go that far south, Rogers knew what he might have to do to keep the ship out of alien hands—anything he deemed necessary. Even if that meant self-destruction.

Guardian of the Leader encountered two unarmed crew members on her way to the shuttle and incapacitated both with blows that were meant to be nonlethal. Unfortunately, her long time in the cryobed had dulled her reflexes and at least one most likely died. She could tell from the crunching sound she heard when her hand struck the man's windpipe. Any remorse she felt was more for herself and her lack of fine control than sympathy for the victim. He was a casualty in the eternal war between those who can be enslaved and those who are strong enough to enslave them. Being alone here, she knew that should she be captured, she would fall into the first category—her superior knowledge and technology could be far outmatched by sheer numbers. This was a lesson she had painfully learned in her last few days on Proxima b.

There! Immediately ahead was the shuttle and no one was around guarding it. She knew that was not likely to last. Now that those who controlled the ship knew she was loose, they would undoubtedly surmise that escape with one of the shuttles might be her plan.

Her final leap allowed her to grasp the handhold outside the open shuttle hatch and to swing her torso through the hatch and into the shuttle in one fluid motion. She briefly noted the presence of multiple security cameras in the room to which the shuttle was docked but paid them no heed. By the time they figured out how to remove the blocks she had placed on their systems, she would be long gone and their cameras would only show an empty room and a missing shuttle. She closed the door behind her and settled herself into the pilot seat, activating the shuttle's controls as she did so. Being independently powered, the shuttle had not been affected by the meddling she'd done to the ship's central computer network.

She glanced at the controls and decided she would have better control by tapping into the computer system directly—so she smashed her fist through the panel to access the wiring bundle underneath, quickly finding the one she was looking for.

Bang!

Momentarily distracted from the task at hand, she looked back toward the hatch and saw an armed man on the other side banging on the outside of the hatch. She noted that he, too, was armed with a projectile weapon but that did not concern her. There was no way any of the weapon's projectiles could pierce the shuttle's hatch. But she did not know what other weapons he might have at his disposal. He might have something that could damage the shuttle and prevent her escape. She assessed her options and decided that fleeing offered her the best chance of success. As much as she might relish fighting and killing the man, she dared not take the time nor run the risk of him having something more lethal at his disposal. She turned back to what she was doing before the man distracted her.

Success! The shuttle's systems came to life as her awareness permeated the small ship's cameras, sensors, and operating systems. The shuttle became her body; the cameras her eyes; the magnetometers and particle sensors her tactile and olfactory input; finally, the now-fully-powered propulsion system her legs and she was ready to run free.

Slowly, she separated from the *Samaritan* and began to run.

To Crosby, the seconds seemed like minutes, the minutes like hours. As he received status reports from around the ship in his earpiece, the more frustrated he became. The Atlantean left a trail of bodies from the infirmary through the central ship corridor, as she made her way... where? That was not yet clear. The security teams were rapidly searching, but none had yet encountered her. All the while, he waited as his CHENG and her team tried to regain control of the ship.

In less than a second, the lighting went from dim with a red tint to full spectrum bright, accompanied by the reassuring hum of various electronic systems coming to life all around the bridge.

"We're back in business! The block has been removed," Mastrano announced with a note of triumph in her voice.

"Good work. Now I want complete situational awareness. Where is she and how do we stop her?" Crosby asked.

"Captain, this is Rialto. One of my men reports that she's taken Shuttle Two. He arrived at the docking hatch just as the shuttle detached and began moving away. He confirms that the Atlantean is in the shuttle."

"Captain, Shuttle Two has undocked and is moving rapidly away from aft," confirmed Mastrano.

Crosby took in all the information and tried to focus his thoughts. *The Atlantean has to be stopped. Who knows where she's going and what she might be fleeing toward. Is there some sort of warship hidden out there that she might reach?*

"CHENG, what is the status of the Samara Drive?" asked Crosby. The Samara Drive was the propulsion system that had opened the stars to human exploration and settlement and enabled the rescue mission to Proxima Centauri. Powered by the ship's fusion reactor, the Samara Drive emitted an extremely intense beam of UV light that functioned as reaction mass to accelerate the *Samaritan* (and the *Emissary*) at up to one gee for extended periods of time, allowing the ships to reach a significant fraction of the speed of light. It was the ultimate space propulsion system. It was also potentially deadly, as a rogue freighter had fatally discovered back at Earth shortly before their departure. A second in the photon exhaust would fry any spacecraft and severely damage most natural objects.

"Power up the drive and put us on a trajectory opposite to the shuttle's path. I want our exhaust rammed right down her throat," Crosby ordered.

"Uh, sir, we've never done that sort of thing before. We usually use the navigation system to go places, not fry things in our wake," Mastrano responded, but she rapidly executed the commands required to do as she had been instructed.

"It's time to do something new, then," Crosby said.

"The drive will be active in sixty-seven seconds," she noted.

"Sound the acceleration alert. I want everyone buckled up when we start moving," Crosby said. Two seconds later, the terse repetitive beeps of the acceleration alarm could be heard throughout the ship. The crew was trained to react quickly to the alarm, with their most recent exercise having everyone bucked up with one minute of its sounding. But that time didn't include securing injured crew. The *Samaritan* was not a warship, but a ship of exploration. Worrying about crew injured by internal combat had not been part of any of their simulations. He hoped the crew could react in time because the Atlantean had to be stopped and this was the only way he could figure out how to make that happen.

"Fifteen seconds," announced the CHENG as Crosby felt the ADCS thrusters reorient the ship thirty degrees, presumably to keep the thrusters pointed toward the fleeing shuttle.

✧ ✧ ✧

It felt good to run through space, even with a ship as primitive as the one she'd commandeered. The distance between her and the *Samaritan* was growing, and she was starting to feel confident that she could escape. From her brief time in the bigger ship's computers, she had determined that it was not a ship of war and that it had no external weapons. Once she was undocked, there was simply nothing they could do to stop her.

Her new external eyes noticed that the *Samaritan* was shifting its orientation. They had apparently regained control of it and removed her block. *What are they up to?*

She watched as the ship's long axis kept alignment with her departure vector, matching it exactly but poised to move in the exact opposite direction. Were they going to run away from her? Did they think she had some sort of weapon with her that she could use against them?

She accessed her memories of the ship's systems, running through them one by one as rapidly as she could, trying to see if there was something she missed. They were clearly in control and acting to keep her in a constant relative position for a reason and she had to figure out why.

On the bridge of the *Samaritan*, Mastrano was counting down. "The drive will be active in three . . . two . . . one . . ."

The drive! It was a photon drive. Guardian of the Leader suddenly realized that if they brought it online with her in its exhaust path, then . . .

The ultraviolet light emitted by the Samara Drive was invisible to the human eye, so there was no "death ray" to see as the drive sent the intense beam of light outward to propel the ship on its programmed course. Crosby knew the drive was active when his command console told him it was, when he felt the acceleration of the ship, and when he saw the escaping shuttle disintegrate before his eyes.

"Cease acceleration," Crosby said.

The ship lurched as the drive stopped and zero gravity returned.

"We got her, sir," Mastrano remarked.

"So, I see," Crosby responded, rubbing his eyes. Only then did he realize his heartbeat was elevated, his palms sweaty, and that he desperately needed to throw up. He had never before killed someone, and he felt desperately ill. "Yes . . . at what cost?"

"CHENG, you have the bridge. I need to go to the head," Crosby said as he unbuckled from his chair and propelled himself toward the hatch and the bathroom beyond it. He wasn't sure he could get there before the contents of his stomach demanded an immediate exit, but he would try.

He made it to the head with moments to spare. Fortunately, bathrooms on spacecraft were designed to accommodate people with space sickness, since most people become nauseous and throw up when they are first without gravity. Because of this all-too-common problem, a vacuum receptacle was easily accessible to Crosby as he entered the room. As he used it, he figured out that he might be the first person to use one due to vomiting after killing someone.

It took him a few minutes to control the nausea to the point where he was no longer debilitated, and he returned to the bridge.

"Are you okay?" Rogers asked as Crosby passed. Crosby knew that Rogers had probably killed many in his tenure as a soldier and could probably readily guess why Crosby had his sudden exit. He wondered how someone could get used to doing such a thing. Used to it to the point of signing up in the military to kill people for a living. Crosby made a mental note to talk to the suddenly more imposing Mike Rogers, after they got the situation better in hand. Most likely over drinks. A lot of drinks.

Crosby regained his seat and scanned the situation board.

"CHENG, how's my ship?" Crosby asked.

"We haven't found any additional blocks, but I've found an anomaly that occurred while we were locked out that you should be aware of," Mastrano said, looking up from the status board and toward Crosby. "She redlined the power input to the ship's directional transmitter and sent a message that kept repeating until we regained control of the ship."

"A message? Where was it sent? And what did it say?" asked Crosby.

"We have no way of knowing the contents of the message. Once we regained control, it was deleted from the buffer and the transmitter shut down. When I said she 'redlined the power,' I meant it. She almost burned out the transmitter circuits with all the power she put into the signal. As to where it went, you'll have to ask Dr. Gilster."

"Ask Rain? Why? Oh. Are you sure?" Crosby asked.

"Positive. She sent the message to the same coordinates we came out here to better refine—to the star system that's been broadcasting toward Proxima b. Luyten-b," Mastrano answered.

"And you're sure she left no surprises in the system for us to discover later?" he asked.

"Not totally sure, but fairly confident. I won't know for sure until I complete some additional diagnostics, but the system looks clean."

"Very good, keep me informed."

"Captain, this is Mike. I've got an update on the casualties." Rialto was still broadcasting directly into Crosby's ear implant.

"Mike, I'm sure Commander Rogers would be interested in hearing what you have to say. I'm putting you on the speaker," Crosby declared as he routed the call from his ear to the normal intraship comm system.

"We've got two injured who are now in the infirmary. Dr. Kopylova has multiple broken ribs and a collapsed lung. Dr. Nkrumah said he should be fine but he's going to hurt like hell for at least a week. The other is Bob Roca. He's got a broken nose and came damn close to having a broken neck. He's resting now but keeps insisting to the doctor that he needs to get back to his station to help Mastrano keep the ship running," Rogers said.

"That sounds like Bob," Mastrano added, smiling.

"Who are the dead?" asked Crosby.

"Dr. Thomaskutty and one of the Fintidierian scientists. I don't know his real name, but our people had been calling him Dr. Xanadu. Both had their necks snapped."

"Thomaskutty? My God, I had breakfast with her this morning," Mastrano uttered.

"That's not going to go over well with our hosts," Crosby said.

"Captain, it's my fault this happened. I underestimated the threat and should never have left the Atlantean in the room without both guards being in there also," said Rialto.

"Mike, you and your team are among Earth's best. This is not the time for recriminations. We need to learn our lesson and move forward. Right now, we need to make sure the ship is secure and reassure the crew that the danger is past. I'll be leaning on you and Rogers to have your people be seen patrolling the ship twenty-four-seven until we get back to Proxima b," Crosby ordered.

"Yes, sir. Thank you, sir," replied Rialto.

"Mike, I'll meet you in the aft conference room to work out the patrol schedules in ten minutes. That work for you?" Rogers asked.

"That'll work. See you there."

After the connection was broken, Crosby leaned toward Rogers. "I will give the scientists on the planet notice that we will be departing for Proxima b in two days. That should be enough time for us to make sure our guest did not leave any surprises for us in the computer system or anywhere else on the ship. And if what happened is anyone's fault, it's mine. Make sure Mike understands that. He's a good man and he doesn't need to beat himself up."

"Will do, sir."

"Well, if you aren't the prettiest sight a man can hope to have when he wakes up," croaked Mak as his eyes opened and adjusted to the light. Holding his hand and leaning over him, wearing a big smile, Rain looked back at him. His voice was strained and as he drew a breath after speaking, a sharp pain shot across his chest. He winced.

"Shhh. I don't want you to associate complimenting me with being in pain," Rain replied, squeezing his hand.

"Jesus, don't make me laugh. It hurts too badly." Mak took a shallow breath and tried his best to not wince. He only partially succeeded. "Did they catch her?"

Rain frowned and kept squeezing his hand as she answered, "Yes, but only by killing her. She got off the ship, going God knows where, and the captain used the ship's drive to destroy her shuttle."

"How is Sindi?" asked Mak.

"Sorry." Rain's frown deepened. "She didn't make it."

This time Mak's pain was more than physical. He and Sindi Thomaskutty were not merely colleagues, but close friends. It was her that he had confided in when he needed advice on how to interact with Rain and not make a complete fool of himself. He couldn't bring himself to say anything in response. He suddenly felt very, very tired.

"You rest," Rain said. "I'll be right here and there's not a force on this ship that will get me to move."

Mak attempted a smile, squeezed her hand as best he could, and closed his eyes. Less than two minutes later, he was asleep.

CHAPTER 6

"Two days? How can we possibly finish what we have to do in only two days?" Dr. Carrie Shavers asked, unable to contain her exasperation. Since they landed and discovered all the artifacts in the pyramids, she had been working at 125 percent of normal speed and efficiency. And she knew they were getting close to uncovering something, she did not know exactly what, that would rival the discovery of the sleeping Atlanteans—hopefully something a bit less deadly. She was in that state of mind that some would call "flow." When she reached it, it was like time stood still and all that mattered was the unfolding of the task at hand. It was euphoric.

Late yesterday, and it only seemed like moments ago, they had been able to power up some of the systems in the room outside the cryobeds. On the workbenches they had discovered were embedded video screens, not unlike the ones that were now ubiquitous back at Earth. Throughout the solar system, people had grown accustomed to the flexible graphene displays that now covered nearly everything used in a normal day, allowing instant access to information and some very interesting camouflage or video simulations. They were becoming even more popular recreationally as virtual reality simulation rooms. And the Atlanteans appeared to have used them extensively.

The problem was that when the screen powered up, incomprehensible patterns were displayed and no one on the team had the slightest idea of what they meant. Were they welcome screens written in Atlantean? Error messages from a malfunctioning computer system? Or simply visually appealing artwork evoking an Atlantean aesthetic? The team quickly confirmed they were touch sensitive and it was all they could do to keep the Fintidierians from simply touching them to see what happens. Though, to be fair, as time was now in short supply, the "see what happens" approach might have been the way to go.

They had just finished lunch and had a good four or five more hours of work left in them before they would return to the shuttle and bed down for the night. Shavers intended to make the time count, especially now that the atmosphere they'd pumped into the room was, finally, warm, and somewhat comfortable. Whatever materials were used in the construction of the pyramids acted as a tremendous heat sink, absorbing almost all of the heat they pumped into the room for the first day or so before the ambient air temperature began to noticeably rise. The warm air had allowed them to remove their spacesuits, making the job of figuring out how what things worked in the pyramid much more tolerable.

"If that's all the time they are going to give us, then I think we need to do like Mr. Bob has been urging. We need to touch the various symbols and see what happens," Shavers mentioned to no one in particular.

"Now wait a minute, Doc. All we did was walk into the cryobed chamber and the Atlanteans started thawing and then one of them went berserk on the ship, maybe damaging it and, by the way, killing two people along the way. How do you know that you won't be turning on the self-destruct mechanism or the 'sterilize the room' command?" Chief Warrant Officer 5 Joni Walker protested.

"She may have a point," Dr. Vulpetti added. "Mr. Bob said he recognizes some of the symbols on the screens. They are similar to some of the runes in Misropos."

"And?" Walker asked with a shoulder shrug. "The last time we talked, you guys still don't know what any of those runes mean there either."

"Well, that may be strictly true, but working with Mr. Bob, we have some theories," Vulpetti replied. "Mr. Bob, tell her what we've been discussing."

The usually silent Mr. Bob looked uncomfortable being asked to speak. Shavers knew it was because he was not a native English speaker and that he was afraid he would embarrass himself in front of the Earth scientists that he thought were a lot smarter than he. Of course, Shavers knew better than to equate intelligence with knowledge. There were many people with lots of knowledge who just happened to be clueless as to how that knowledge should be applied to solve problems in the real world. She had certainly dated enough of them.

"When I was studying the symbols from Misropos, there was one that appeared in many places. In English, Dr. Vulpetti told me you would describe it as a target symbol with three wavy lines underneath it. Here, this is a picture your team took of it when you were in Misropos."

"We did some searching, and it is nearly identical to some ancient runes from back on Earth, this one related to ancient India. It refers to one of the chakras. Translated literally, it means 'wheel,' and refers to energy points in the body. They are thought to be spinning disks of energy that correspond to bundles of nerves and areas of our energy in our bodies that affect our emotional and physical well-being," Vulpetti interjected.

"It's an 'on' switch," Shavers remarked.

"It's an 'on' switch," confirmed Vulpetti, smiling.

"Okay, let's assume you are correct. What then?" Walker asked, still looking skeptical.

"Then we... wing it," Vulpetti said.

"I agree. We've got nothing to lose," Shavers added, feeling the comfortable excitement building in her chest. It was a high and she loved it.

"Nothing to lose? What if it doesn't mean 'on,' but rather 'initiate self-destruct sequence'?" Walker added again.

"Well, then you will at least have died a meaningful death. What can be more meaningful than exploring millennia-old ruins in the hopes of saving a planet full of people?" Vulpetti asked, smiling.

Walker looked pained, obviously torn as to the best approach forward, and truly didn't agree with the others.

"Alright, you win, I guess," Walker declared. "'Fortune favors the bold,' as they say."

Shavers walked over to the screen on the middle console that glowed a pale blue color with the chakra symbol prominently in the middle. Without so much as a pause, she pressed her palm against it.

The symbol disappeared from the screen, turning it completely black. A few seconds later, the screen came back to life and then every screen in the room lit up. Each had a display of symbols that all appeared to be in different combinations. A cursory glance told Shavers that some were common, some more common than others, but each screen appeared to have unique symbols or common symbols in a unique order. There was also a faint odor of ozone in the air, likely caused by electrical circuits getting warm for the first time in millennia.

"Could we build systems to be active this long?" Shavers asked.

"I doubt it," Vulpetti replied. "A few hundred years, probably. But thousands? No way."

"Okay. I'm still in favor of pushing ahead, but I think it might be a good idea to send what's on each screen up to the *Samaritan* for the computer to run some pattern-recognition algorithms—and to see if any of these symbols are in a database somewhere," Shavers said. She was eager to press forward, but she couldn't bring herself to completely ignore Walker's cautionary tone.

"Who knows? Maybe some of the symbols will be in a database somewhere like the chakra," added Vulpetti. "Mr. Bob, walk around and see if you recognize any other symbols."

On cue, Mr. Bob began walking slowly across the room, pausing to stare at each screen as he went. As he did so, both Shavers and Vulpetti set up the multiple minicameras they'd brought with them and started the data relays up to the ship.

"Dr. Shavers. Please come look at this," Mr. Bob motioned to them. His voice was soft, but she could hear a tinge of excitement in it.

Shavers walked to where he was standing and looked at the screen to which he was now pointing.

"Does that symbol mean the same thing to you as it does to us?" he asked.

"I know I've seen it, but I can't place it. It looks like it might be a star," she said. "*Samaritan*, are you getting this?"

"We sure are, Carrie. Running it through the computer now." Shavers recognized the voice but could not place the name of the female crew member who responded. She was terrible at names, even after being so close to the crew of the *Samaritan* for so many years; matching faces and voices with names was still a challenge.

"Got it! It's the Star of Ishtar, or sometimes called the Star of Venus. Ishtar was the Mesopotamian goddess of war and love. Babylon had a similar deity that was often associated with the symbol, the goddess Inanna. For both cultures, she was the goddess of love, sex, fertility—and war."

"On Earth, Venus is the closest planet to Earth, yes?" Mr. Bob asked.

"Some of the time, yes. What does the symbol mean to you?" Shavers asked in response.

"It means the planets and stars. It is our symbol for all things astronomical," Mr. Bob replied.

"Press it," Vulpetti admonished. "I have a hunch."

Shavers looked at the assembled team and saw approving faces and nods, even from Walker. Without further hesitation, she reached out her palm and touched the symbol on the screen.

In the air, immediately above the console, appeared a three-dimensional starfield with Shavers standing at its center. She could still see the room and her team, but they looked hazy and indistinct as she peered through the thousands of stars that now floated around her. She looked up, down, and around and saw the distribution of stars in each direction was different, as would be expected. But what was her perspective? Where in the universe was the center at which the display had placed her?

"Are you seeing this?" she asked.

"Yes. It appears my hunch was correct. You're in the middle

of what looks like a 3D star map. As we look through it, you appear to be a little fuzzy. Are you okay?" Vulpetti asked.

"I'm fine and, for the record, you are fuzzy too. I'm trying to get my bearings and figure out where I am," she said as she raised her hand and moved it through the projection. As she did so, the orientation adjusted, following the motions of her hand like swiping across a touchscreen that changed the perspective in a two-dimensional map. Earth's astronomers used similar three-dimensional star maps, so the experience was somewhat familiar.

"I'm going to need some help from the *Samaritan*'s computer to figure this out," she noted as she lifted one of the minicameras to eye level and scanned the view she was seeing, from the inside out, and in as many directions as she could.

"We're on it," said the unknown female crew member.

"That's good because I can't tell what's what. It's embarrassing. In the space dramas, I'd suddenly say, 'a-ha!' and start manipulating everything as if it were second nature. But I'm overloaded and just can't," Shavers replied. It was embarrassing. Like in graduate school, it was taking her more time than she would have liked to learn a new concept.

"We've got it! Without moving your arms around, turn to face Mr. Bob," her *Samaritan* contact said. "There. At the center where you are is Proxima Centauri, as you might expect. That yellow star just in front of you is Sol. If you look to your left side just a little, you'll see Alpha Centauri as a brighter yellow star. The distances between stars don't appear to be at scale, but you might have noticed that you can stretch out or contract the distances by moving your hands as you did a moment ago."

Shavers turned her head as directed and was a bit startled by the appearance of a bright yellow dot not more than a few inches from her face. She raised her hand and pushed it away toward the bright star and, sure enough, it moved outward from her. She could control not only her viewing orientation, but the relative distances between the stars in the simulation. It was then that she noticed the dim dots of light that were even closer to her head than Alpha Centauri. She peered at one of them and then cupped her hands to encircle it. She slowly pulled her hands apart and the small dot grew to a size comparable to a grapefruit. As she looked at it, she realized it was the planet Proxima b. She could now see details of its surface, including the landmasses and various bodies of water. She reached out to touch it and was then able to change its orientation relative to her eyes, making it spin as she did so.

Next, she reached out toward Sol, pulled it toward her, and then expanded the view. As she moved her hands outward and drew the solar system closer to her, she saw the familiar Saturn and Jupiter, followed by diminutive Mars and, finally, Earth. When she caught sight of home, her heart skipped a beat. The blue oceans and wispy white clouds evoked an emotional reaction that she allowed herself to indulge in for a few seconds before she pulled herself back to the task at hand. *Something's not quite right.*

She saw the familiar continents of North and South America, Eurasia, and Australia. But then she realized what had caught her eye only moments ago. *There!* In the South Atlantic, due west of Capetown, there was a large island with which she wasn't familiar. She knew there were islands in the South Atlantic, but this one was far larger than any she remembered—nearly the size of the United Kingdom.

She manipulated her hands to zoom in as close as possible and found that she was not able to do more than the equivalent of a high Earth orbital view. That said, its presence was unmistakable. She carefully examined other continental features and found that all looked like she remembered, giving no clue as to when the image was taken. Knowing a bit of Earth's geologic history, that meant the photo could be as young as a few thousand years or as old as tens of thousands—or even more. She made sure her camera feed was sending everything to the ship and decided to move on.

Next, she zoomed back out to an interstellar view and reoriented herself, locating Luyten's Star. *Let's see what's hiding there*, she thought as she moved her hands to draw herself closer to the red dwarf that seemed so popular to the Atlanteans on Proxima b. As she did so, she cupped it to allow a view of any planets there, but before she could zoom in, the entire three-dimensional projection vanished—as did the power to every display screen in the room.

"What? Did you do anything to cause that to happen?" Shavers asked, looking at the faces of her colleagues, who appeared to have been as surprised by the power loss as she was.

"No. But we'd better figure out what happened so we can try

to get the systems powered up again. The day is almost over and that just leaves us tomorrow before we have depart. Who knows when we'll get back," Vulpetti said.

Shavers agreed, but she was a bit distracted processing what she saw of Earth and the large island that featured so prominently when the images were taken, but which didn't exist now. All she could think of was the lost kingdom of Atlantis and the myths surrounding it. She would write up her observations when she got back to the ship and then compose a message to Earth for someone to investigate the site. Of course, by the time anyone on Earth got the message, over four years would have passed. By the time they did any investigating and sent a message back, more than a decade. Who knew where she and her shipmates might be in a decade?

CHAPTER 7

The *Samaritan* and the *Emissary* had been back at Proxima b for just over two weeks when the news of their discoveries on c Prime broke, including both the real, live (and deadly) Atlantean and the radio message she'd sent to Luyten's Star. The news was not well received among the general public. In fact, for the government and overall social order, it was an unmitigated disaster.

Fear. Though most of the population had been ignorant of the details revealed from the forbidden continent of Misropos until they were recently made public, their culture was full of myths, fairy tales, and angst related to their prehistorical enslavement by the Atlanteans. To the anthropologists from Earth, looking at Fintidierian culture with the knowledge that mass enslavement of their population had occurred in a largely forgotten history gave them an entirely new perspective to interpret what they observed.

Children's stories describing in gory detail how misbehaving youngsters would be punished by gremlins and evil creatures that lived for no other purpose than torturing miscreants were now seen as the product of oral traditions handing down the all-too-real experiences of their ancestors when they did not satisfy their Atlantean masters. Similar to *Grimm's Fairy Tales*, which, when read from an adult perspective, *were* quite grim, to *Struwwelpeter*, old German folk stories were the closest things to which the anthropologists could compare Fintidierian stories. In *Struwwelpeter*, a boy sucks his thumb and has it cut off. The Fintidierian counterpart has a boy who refuses to do his household chores and gets his toes removed; his teenage brother is castrated. Gruesome stories all. Most had to do with children who did not meet their parents' expectations suffering dismemberment, torture, or death. It was easy to see how these transitioned from an oral history of enslavement—which would have been passed on to future generations by telling stories, primarily to young people who had not personally experienced the horror—to becoming cautionary stories intended for children.

Adult literature, radio, and television drama also had elements that were undoubtedly derived from stories handed down across time. The Fintidierian version of Shakespeare did not write about such things as love, power, and conflict. Rather, she wrote of the consequences of disobedience to authority, the dangers of innovation and critical thinking, and the fear of the outsider. When looking with this new awareness, the Terrans could see the influence of the long-dead and departed Atlanteans everywhere they looked.

The latest news appeared to have uncovered deep-seated fears among the population.

And the situation was quickly moving from the cultural and historical to the current and political. At first, there was condemnation of the Terrans violating Misropos and endangering the Fintidierian population. When it was clear that there was no disease risk on Misropos, and the Atlantean history became well known, the public began to get xenophobic. Outside of the medical and governmental districts, where Terrans were once enthusiastically greeted, they were now merely tolerated. That initial outrage soon cooled and the public's view of the Terrans plateaued. Then came the news from c Prime.

TERRANS MUST STOP MEDDLING IN FINTIDIERIAN POLICY AND LAW! was a popular headline in the newspapers. EARTHERS VIOLATE FINTIDIERIAN SOVEREIGNTY and EARTHERS WILL BRING DESTRUCTION TO THE PLANET were others. Each contained lengthy editorials describing how the discoveries should be carefully managed by the Fintidierian government with the Terrans participating only as observers. Some were even beginning to question the motive of those who came from Earth. SAVIORS? OR ENSLAVERS? was the most disturbing headline. Shortly after it appeared, Roy and Chloe Burbank's home had rocks thrown through their windows, prompting the local authorities to post around-the-clock guards at their house. They were not alone. In just one week, there were over a hundred acts of violence or credible threats made against the newcomers.

When news of the Atlantean's escape and radio message to Luyten's Star was made known, the mass protests began. Around government buildings all over the world, crowds gathered and asked their leaders what they were going to do to protect them should the Atlantean enslavers return. Would those from Earth protect them? Would they run away? Or worse yet, would the Terrans join the Atlanteans in oppressing the Fintidierian people? And was the fertility crisis just a convenient excuse for welcoming their Earthly saviors who might actually just be there as puppets for the Atlanteans—as an interplanetary Fifth Column?

It was with this as backdrop that the Fintidierian government called for an emergency meeting with Ambassador Jesus.

"And why, exactly, do I need the SEALs to accompany me to the meeting?" Jesus asked. He and his advisors had just completed their own emergency status meeting, going over the rapidly worsening situation and the steps they would need to take to preserve their primary mission, that of helping the Fintidierian people, while at the same time protecting their people from the Fintidierians.

"For the same reason we're bringing many of our people back into the compound, at least temporarily," Mike Rogers replied. "The threats are increasing and all it will take is a few hotheads to ignite a riot, or, worse yet, a massacre. We may still have a technological edge when it comes to protecting our people, but there are too few of us for that to be able to keep us safe. There are a couple hundred of us and a billion Fintidierians. Allowing you out of the compound to cross public streets and into the governmental sector for the meeting provides too easy an opportunity for those hotheads to make their first move. Are you sure Secretary General Arctinier won't come here?" Rogers was usually a silent member of Jesus's cabinet meetings, but Jesus was not surprised he spoke up in this meeting. Since the Misropos fiasco, there had been virtually no need for him to bring up any security matters. Things had changed.

"Given that we are the visitors on their planet and that we are trying desperately hard to not be perceived as a threat, asking her to come to us would be a public relations disaster and only embolden the opposition. It would look like she was coming to us because we are somehow her superiors. No, I need to go to her," Jesus stated in reply.

"I'd like to accompany you, along with at least three of my team," Rogers offered.

"I'm planning to meet with the secretary general alone. If I agree to a security detail, it certainly won't be four heavily armed SEALs. We aren't at war with these people and the display of force, or potential use of force, will send the wrong message," Jesus said.

"Mr. Ambassador, I must disagree with you," Captain Crosby countered. Jesus respected Crosby's judgment on most matters, particularly in matters of security. He had juggled the roles and responsibilities of his shipboard security detail versus the role of the SEALs with clarity and forethought. So far, they had seen eye to eye on the precautions taken planetside with regard to protecting their people.

"Captain, you'll have to explain," Jesus said.

"It isn't organized violence we're concerned with here, at least not yet. It's the opportunistic hothead that we need to deter. There isn't much better a deterrent than seeing fully suited, armed-for-bear soldiers. Otherwise, you will be needlessly exposing yourself to danger that, if the worst happened, would make the situation here much, much worse."

"Especially for me," Jesus noted. He wanted to disagree, but he could not. His instincts told him to decline the military escort, but his brain said that would be foolish. Instead, he decided to compromise.

"Very well. Mike, you and one additional SEAL can accompany me in the transport we will take to the meeting. Others of your team can be in one of the shuttles overhead keeping an eye on things, preferably out of sight way overhead and only making their presence known in the event of an emergency," Jesus said.

"I can live with that," Rogers agreed, leaning back in his chair.

"I can have the shuttle in place with an hour's notice," Crosby added.

"Well, then. We have a plan. I'll respond to the secretary general and let her know we accept her meeting invitation. Is there another item of business?" asked Jesus.

"Yes, sir. There is," Crosby said. "And you will likely want to bring it up in your meeting with Secretary General Arctinier."

"Go on."

"Captain Jacobs and I met with Dr. Gilster to review the results of her analysis of the radio signal's source and to discuss the unknown message the Atlantean sent there. We agreed that he should take the *Emissary* and depart immediately for Luyten's Star."

The room was silent. Even Jesus was at a loss for words, a situation that no one close to him would ever believe possible.

"That would take years, correct?"

"About eighteen years absolute, yes. Not so many for the crew," replied Crosby.

Jesus looked across the table at Captain Jacobs, who nodded in affirmation.

"Why?" Jesus asked.

"Because we need to know what's there," Jacobs asserted. "It sure looks like the Atlanteans are a threat not only to this planet, but also to Earth. We've got two ships and both are not needed here. Your work on Proxima b requires the medical teams, not the ships and their crews. It won't be too much longer before those aboard the *Samaritan* start wondering why they are remaining aboard and not intermarrying with the locals and establishing new lives planetside. They signed up for a one-way trip and the latter part of that plan has not yet materialized. My crew is a different story. They are mostly active-duty members of the Space Force and did not necessarily sign up for a one-way trip, though as members of the military, they know any trip might end up being so. Many are starting to wonder what their next assignment will be. Many, perhaps most, think that they will take the *Emissary* and return to Earth. And we would, if circumstances had been different. So, from a personal point of view, if we are going to make this trip, then we need to get going. There is no time to ask Earth for permission. With the time lag, we'd have to wait at least nine years to get our answer.

"That explains why we need to go soon, but not the urgency of going as soon as possible," he continued. "It is our opinion that we need to depart immediately so that we don't allow too much time to pass between the arrival of whatever message our Atlantean friend sent and our arrival. We may need to diffuse what is likely to be a complicated situation, rife with potential misunderstanding. And that requires expediency."

"And you are telling me, not asking?" Jesus retorted. Though he phrased it as a question, it was a statement of fact. He had jurisdiction on all matters relating to the Fintidierians and some say in Captain Crosby's actions since his was a diplomatic, not military, ship. Captain Jacobs, however, had complete and independent control of his ship and crew. Where and when he decided to go was his responsibility to decide.

As expected, Jacob's affirmative response to Jesus's non-question was to simply remain silent.

"And I am the one who has to inform Secretary General Arctinier that her visitors are sending a ship to call on the people who once enslaved them. I'm sure she will simply love that," Jesus said.

"I really don't see any alternative," Jacobs countered. "As an officer of the Space Force I am sworn to protect the United States of America and, in this case, all of Earth, from all enemies—foreign and domestic. The Atlanteans are as foreign as one can get. Before we depart, I plan to send a complete status report of the situation and my plans to Earth so they can begin preparing for what might be a future confrontation with the Atlanteans. Hell, they might decide to send some newer ship to join us there. I doubt the timing can be worked out to have us arrive at the same time, or even close. But that will be up to them to decide. My course of action is clear."

Jesus had to agree. If the Atlantean had awakened and been cooperative, then it might be a different story. But she wasn't. And they have no idea of the contents of her radio message. There did seem to be a compelling case for the *Emissary* to make the trip. He just did not yet know how he would deal with the diplomatic fallout.

"Alan, I know you have a dedicated and fiercely loyal crew. But as you just said, they didn't necessarily sign up for a one-way trip. With the travel times we're discussing here, for all practical purposes, that's what it is going to be. With the time it took for the *Emissary* to get to Proxima b, plus the time spent here, adding another eighteen years to Luyten's Star and then, optimistically, a decade or so to get home, their tour of duty will end up being as much as thirty years or more. Any family or friends they left on Earth will have long forgotten them when . . . if . . . they finally return home," Jesus noted.

"As you said, my crew is dedicated. They swore the same oath to the Constitution that I did, and I expect they meant it. They will also understand the importance of our mission. It would not be an exaggeration to say that the survival of the human race might well depend upon the actions we take. I can count on them. Besides, the relative time aboard ship will be much less than thirty years," Jacobs added.

"May I ask about Dr. Gilster's plans?" Jesus asked.

"She and Mak want to join the *Emissary*. In fact, I think we would have to use Commander Rogers's team to keep them, mostly her, from doing so," Crosby said, rejoining the conversation. "Which brings to mind another pressing question: Will any of Rogers's team be joining the crew of the *Emissary*?"

"That's a damn good question!" Rogers exclaimed. "My team signed the same oath Captain Crosby mentioned, but like the civilians aboard the *Samaritan*, they signed up for a trip here, not a series of interstellar deployments. I'll have to meet with them and see what they think before I make a decision. I believe you'll need some protection when you arrive, but I sure as hell don't want to order any of them to go."

"Well, no offense to Commander Rogers, but the *Emissary* did come with its own contingent of Space Force spec ops personnel," Captain Jacobs asserted.

"None taken, General." Rogers nodded, using Jacobs's official rank and not his ship title.

"How soon do you plan to depart?" asked Jesus.

"Next week," Crosby said.

Fintidierian Secretary General Balfine Arctinier sat in her office, alone, having just dismissed her closest aides to give her time to mentally prepare for the meeting with Ambassador Jesus. The more she considered the symbolic nature of his name, given that he was the political leader of the Terrans sent to Proxima to "save" them from extinction, the more she wondered if it was his real name, one he assumed to intimidate them, or The One True God's idea of a joke. With the seriousness of every crisis now faced by her people, if it were a joke, then it was not a very funny one.

The fertility crisis was not any closer to resolution and the people's hope that was aroused by the Terrans' arrival was definitely beginning to fade. Her political opponents, primarily

Senator Garpur and his acolytes, were using the events in space to destabilize their society, stoking fears and encouraging the riots, all in the name of weakening her ahead of next year's election. There was outrage when the people learned more of the nature of the ruins on Misropos and that their leaders knew about them and yet continued to keep it secret, promulgating the "contagion" lie regarding why the small continent was kept off-limits. A lie that spanned millennia.

She did not believe the Terrans were conspiring with the mythical Atlanteans, which the general public now knew were not so mythical, yet she couldn't help but wonder about the timing of the events that had recently transpired. The Terrans just happened to find Atlantean ruins and a live, murderous Atlantean as they were trying to figure out the exact source of the mysterious radio signal from space—which, coincidentally, was the destination of the radio message the rogue Atlantean transmitted before her death. Coincidence after coincidence, after coincidence.

It was too much for the population and almost too much for her. She was going to suggest the Terrans temporarily return to the compound they'd lived in after their arrival and while under quarantine. She could protect them there. Many had moved out of the compound to live among her people; some had actually married Fintidierians and "gone local." For the former it would be inconvenient; for the latter, difficult on the Fintidierians involved. But it was for their own safety, and she hoped Ambassador Jesus would accept that.

The door to her office opened with her assistant announcing that the ambassador had arrived.

"Send him in," she said as she rose from her chair, then walked around her desk to greet Jesus as he entered.

"Thank you for coming to meet with me on such short notice, Mr. Ambassador," Arctinier remarked, offering her hand in the type of handshake she knew the Terrans preferred and to which they were accustomed. She tried to smile.

"It is my pleasure, Madam Secretary General," Jesus replied, taking her offered hand and grasping it. His grip was not too tight and not too soft. She returned it in kind.

They sat in the two chairs on the area rug in the center of her office. She found it much easier to negotiate and reach agreement with a peer this way. Remaining behind her desk for meetings was something she only did with subordinates or those she was trying to intimidate. She knew intimidating Jesus would absolutely not work, so she did not even bother trying.

"Mr. Ambassador, I am sure you are aware that the threats and acts of violence against you and your people have increased dramatically since their return from the outer solar system," she said.

"We are. And I am concerned," Jesus responded. "Not only regarding the safety of my people, but also about the success of our mission."

"I'm glad we are in agreement. I hope you will also agree that we need to take some measures to keep both safe, even if they are somewhat... unpalatable."

"That depends. What do you have in mind?" asked Jesus.

"I would like to move all your people and their families back into the compound until this all cools down. Even better would be if some or all of your people returned to their ships. This would, of course, be a temporary measure," she added.

"Temporary? How temporary?" Jesus asked.

"Just until the threat against them subsides—a few months, perhaps," she said. Of course, they both knew that such measures could quickly become permanent. It would all depend upon the fickleness of the public—and the actions of the opposition.

"I share your concern for the safety of our people, but I don't believe retreating into an armed compound and separating ourselves is the best way to win over hearts and minds. Please don't forget that the crew of the *Samaritan* are here to stay. They gave up their lives on Earth to live among your people and help solve the crisis you now face. Placing them in the compound for any length of time, especially after living for nearly a year of intermingling, would be akin to placing them in jail for a crime they did not commit."

Damn. He was not going to make this easy. Though she firmly believed he and the Terrans were peaceful, she could not forget that as long as their ships orbited the planet, they could do whatever they damn well pleased. Since their arrival, she had learned a great deal of their history and technical capabilities, even though they had skillfully left out information from their encyclopedic data dump beamed from Earth over the years. Most notably, she'd learned about the whole Cold War thing and the tens of thousands of atomic bombs that ostensibly kept it "cold." From what her cadre of aerospace engineers told her, their visitors could also simply drop projectiles from orbit, with their kinetic energy upon impact having effects similar to those of atomic weapons but without the radiation. No, she could not force them into their compound. Jesus had the upper hand here, ill intent or not.

"I see. We both know that I cannot force you into the compound and, I assure you, I would not do so even if I believed I could. Other than the increased police presence near where your people live and work that we've already put in place, there is not much more that I can do. We must work together to ratchet down the threat of violence. It would help if we were able to announce significant progress in the search for a cure. Do you have any notable updates?" Arctinier was briefed daily on the joint team's progress in searching for a cure, but she also knew that there might be work going on that her team was not part of. It did not hurt to ask.

"Unfortunately, I don't have any news on the biology team's work. I will let you know as soon I hear anything," Jesus offered with a frown and a shrug.

"I would like for you to look at this." Arctinier handed him a folder. Jesus opened it and started reading.

"What's this? Graggyon Oo'ortava?" he muttered through the pronunciation of the name. "Physics student at Gwonura Institute for Learning..."

"The first volunteer apprentice," Arctinier said with a raised eyebrow.

"Apprentice?" Jesus repeated rhetorically. "Okay, a physics student. He could sit in with Dr. Burbank or maybe Rain's team..."

"No!" Arctinier exclaimed—a bit too harshly, perhaps. "I'm, ur, sorry. But, please no. I want him on the fertility crisis team. This young man is smart and talented. He will learn anything and everything he can and not be in the way."

"Why the fertility crisis team?"

"We have to show a combined, ur, team effort," Arctinier insisted.

"Oo'ortava? Related to Secretary Harma Oo'ortava by any chance?" Jesus asked.

"Ambassador, I must explain," Arctinier added shyly. "We queried thousands of potentials. We have a few who agreed to meet, but none are willing to immediately start work. Harma's nephew was one of the potentials. He's a good kid. I asked her to pressure him to say yes. We must, Charles, *must* start showing some solidarity. Please, help me here. Put this young man as an apprentice to your fertility crisis team."

"I see," Jesus agreed. "Sometimes, who you know turns out to not be a blessing, huh?"

"A blessing?" Arctinier took a moment but then smiled. "Haha! Yes. But, I think this is the opportunity of a lifetime for any young scientists from our people, even if they do not realize it yet."

"We have a saying back on Earth, Madam Secretary General," Jesus said. "'Fortune favors the bold.' If this lad is bold enough to take the position, I will get him there. And hopefully, his fortune will favor us all."

"Indeed." Arctinier leaned back in her chair and exhaled as if she were happy to have gotten that conversation off her shoulders. "Was there more?"

"Well, yes. I do have another item to make you aware of. I would have requested a private meeting to discuss it if you had not already done so," Jesus said.

"Go on."

"Given that we are now certain that the radio broadcast Dr. Gilster and her team detected originates at Luyten's Star and that this was also the intended destination of the message broadcast by the Atlantean when she commandeered the communications system on the *Samaritan*, we are dispatching the *Emissary* there immediately. This should alleviate some of the safety concerns you raised earlier. Just over half of our people will be departing on the *Emissary* within the next several days."

Do these people realize how difficult they are making my job? This news caught Arctinier flat-footed, and her mind began spiraling into speculation of how the people would respond to this bit of news. Outwardly, the only way she was able to remain calm was by relying on her years of training as a professional politician. Inwardly, well, that was a different story.

"I am glad you informed me first. I will need some time to figure out how, in turn, to inform the public without further inflaming them. That will make my deployment of additional police protection all the more important," she said.

"And we certainly appreciate that, Madam Secretary General. I realize you are not happy with this development, but I believe the impact will be minimal. Given the distances involved, the *Emissary* will not reach Luyten's Star for another eighteen years—plenty of time for our team to have found a cure and for things here to calm down."

Arctinier knew that in eighteen years, either she would be in retirement sipping mixed drinks at cocktail parties as a large cohort of children, male and female, were graduating from schools all across the planet, or she would most likely be dead from the chaos that would inevitably be part of the collapse of the civilization if no cure were found. She could not imagine anything in between.

"Well, then, let's plan on success and see how we can get the people to share our optimistic views," she said, painting her most convincing, though totally artificial, smile on her face as she extended her hand to formally end their meeting.

"I am all for optimism," Jesus returned as he grasped her hand and rose from his seat. "For what it's worth, I mean that. I am convinced that if a cure can be found, then our combined team will find it. As for the *Emissary*, I simply cannot predict what they will find at the end of their journey. For that reason, I choose to be optimistic there as well."

CHAPTER 8

Aboard the *Emissary*, Five Weeks Later

When Alan Jacobs was asked to take command of the *Emissary* on its mission to Proxima b, he readily agreed. It was the only time in his military career that he was asked if he wanted a particular job instead of simply being ordered to take it. He had been laser-focused on taking the next ship to the stars since he'd learned about the capabilities of the Samara Drive and visited the *Samaritan* before it left the Sol system in search of the saboteur who tried to get that ship lost in space. He got his wish. He had cut his teeth flying the old nuclear thermal rockets that were limited to speed far less than the speed of light, and now he commanded one that came close to nature's ultimate speed limit, that of light itself. Times had certainly changed. Being widowed and having seniority, with over twenty years in the Space Force, he had topped out as a full-bird colonel. There wasn't much left to his career; he didn't believe himself to be brigadier general promotable. Or at least he hadn't until the offer to go on the *Emissary* as the ship's captain. Jacobs had jumped at the opportunity. Of course, had his wife not died in a tragic ski accident five years previously to him taking the deep space missions to the outer Sol planets, his answer might have been quite different. But that was a different life. He was here. Now. He had been promoted to a one-star. He was captain of a starship. He was now on his way to whatever might await them at Luyten b.

They couldn't travel as fast as the radio message sent to Luyten b by the renegade Atlantean, but they wouldn't be too far behind it when they arrived. Relativistic time made things complicated, but for the crew of the ship who would be traveling at close to the speed of light and have their clocks slowed, it was complicated in a good way. The time they spent traveling would be a good deal less than that which would pass on Earth and Proxima b.

Drs. Gilster and Vulpetti had been over their calculations many times and members of an independent team confirmed them. Luyten b was both the source of the message beamed toward Proxima b and the destination of the message sent by the murderous Atlantean. Now they were on their way to find out what was there.

Operating the Samara Drive in the Proxima b system was much less complicated than back at Sol. *Emissary* and *Samaritan* were the only two ships in interplanetary space and therefore the risk of the Samara Drive's UV exhaust roasting an errant ship was zero. They only had to make sure that the beam didn't have line of sight with Proxima b until they were sufficiently far away for the beam's divergence to make it harmless.

They were now accelerating at one-half gee and enjoying not having to deal with zero or microgravity, which was, as far as Jacobs was concerned, the one and only drawback of spaceflight. He'd never quite gotten over experiencing nausea every time they were in free fall, despite spending over twenty years in space. It was only by his force of self-control that it did not become an impediment to his career. He simply willed himself to not get sick and that sort of worked. Enough to prevent him from vomiting, but not enough to keep him from being miserable every time the acceleration went to zero.

That said, he could grasp what happened to his body in zero gravity conditions. Cardiovascular deconditioning, fluid redistribution, and all the physiological changes he and most people were easy to understand. There were correlations in their everyday lives that people could draw upon to make sense of it. It was the relativity that he still had trouble with. Both ships had experienced its effects on the journey from Earth to Proxima Centauri, the *Emissary* more so than the *Samaritan* due to its faster speed. Improvements in the Samara Drive over the brief time between each ship's launch had made a dramatic difference in the travel time from the points of view of both the crew and those folks back at home.

That voyage made the trip he and his crew were now embarking upon seem easy, almost trivial. Given the time they would need to accelerate to more than ninety-eight percent of light speed, those at Proxima b, and Earth—if they even knew the trip was happening—would require just over eighteen years to cover that approximately sixteen light-year distance between here and Luyten's Star. From his perspective, and that of the rest of the *Emissary*'s crew, however, the trip would take a mere five or so years. There would be nearly a year of acceleration to 0.98c. Then there would be three years of cruising at max speed. And that would be followed by a year of deceleration for system arrival. Finding where to enter and what planets to approach might take several more months. Most of that time they would spend in the cryobeds. Commensurate with the improvement of the Samara Drive had also come improvements in cryobed technology that now allowed the aging process to slow while they were asleep. Instead of sleeping away six years of life, their bodies would only age approximately one year for every ten they spent in the cryobed. Taken together, the human race was now a truly interstellar species and Jacobs couldn't help but wonder what additional advances had occurred after they left Earth. Would they arrive at Luyten's Star and find another Earth ship already there?

His crew was now a mix of those from both the *Emissary* and the *Samaritan*, with a few Fintidierians thrown in for good measure. Of the latter, Jacobs really enjoyed the company of Mr. Bob. He had learned more of Fintidierian history and culture in their mealtime conversations than from the official Proximan Encyclopedia his people had shared with those from Earth, who were now known as "Terrans" or "Earthers" by most Fintidierians. The latter term was catching on among the Terrans as well. It was far simpler to say than "Earth humans" and conveyed a retro feel to all involved that was somehow fun.

Mr. Bob had talked him through his life and explained how he and his cohorts reacted to the fertility crisis as well as the news that Terrans existed—and were coming to visit. Apparently, and unbeknownst to those traveling from Earth to Proxima b, the culture there was on the verge of mass suicide. Literally. The government had plans to mass-distribute cyanide pills to any who wanted to die and avoid the coming societal collapse, and the misery and despair that would accompany it. Surveys indicated that more than eighty percent of the planet's population was considering that option up until the radio messages from Earth were made public. That's when hope reemerged and the plans for euthanization were scrapped. Unfortunately, given that Terran medicine had not yet found the cause or the cure of the fertility crisis, the doomsday sentiment among some was again gaining traction. Jacobs suspected the whole thing would be resolved, one way or the other, by the time they awakened at the end of their journey.

Some of the passengers were entering the cryobeds directly while most of the crew was still awake and making sure the ship was performing as it should. The ship's computers were considered reliable enough to not require Jacobs and his crew to awaken more than once during the journey, to "check on things." Even knowing that complex systems sometimes fail, Jacobs was not that concerned. He knew his ship and believed to the core of his being that it would not let them down during the long trip. If it did, well, he would probably not wake up and would never know.

"Captain Jacobs, we've got an estimate on how long it will take to reconfigure the reconnaissance probes. CHENG says they'll need another two days, tops," Lieutenant Marcus Keaton, the *Emissary*'s newly minted weapons officer, explained.

Though the crew of the *Emissary* was mostly members of the Space Force, it was essentially still a ship of peaceful exploration, not a warship. Built generally along the same design specifications as the *Samaritan*, but with an improved Samara Drive, it was never envisioned that the ship would need to carry any sort of armament. Apparently, none of the utopian scientists and engineers back in the Sol system recalled any of the science fiction movies from humanity's past and had left their home system completely unprepared for what dangers might actually be out in the depths of space. Jacobs saw as extremely ironic that a ship run by the United States Space Force for the most part had very little in the way of weapons built in. That was, of course, not including the Samara Drive itself, and the five nuclear devices stowed away in the ship for safekeeping that only he, the CHENG, and his XO (executive officer) knew about.

The ship did have an armory, but that was to equip the USSF Spec Ops security and landing teams as well as the SEALs for use on any planetside excursions. While adding some sort of weapons system to the ship was discussed, briefly, before departure from Earth, it was determined that adding such systems to the nearly completed ship would cause its launch to slip nearly two years. Given the urgency of sending additional medical personnel to Proxima b, and that the Proximans appeared to be far behind Earth in terms of technology, the political leadership decided to not wait and send the ship out as is. At the time Jacobs hadn't disagreed with the decision simply because at that time there was never any thought of going to other, potentially hostile worlds. He was now regretting that decision and working to see if there was anything they could do to give the ship some teeth. The Atlantean they had encountered was anything but friendly and certainly their technological peer or, worst case, their superior.

It was Lieutenant Marcus Keaton's idea to modify the ship's reconnaissance probes to be kinetic energy weapons. Each probe was a smaller version of the unmanned *Interstellarerforscher* robotic scout ship that had led the *Samaritan* to Proxima Centauri after that ship's Pulsar Interstellar Navigation System, or PINS, had failed and nearly left them adrift between the stars. Originally designed to do the same thing as the *Interstellarerforscher*—carry scientific instruments to survey a region of space and report back to the Emissary what was found—each probe massed nearly two hundred kilograms and carried its own scientific instruments, a microfusion power plant, and a small, but very capable Samara Drive to propel it at nearly the speed of light on its journey. It was the combination of speed and mass that inspired Keaton to suggest it as a weapon. Capable of accelerating at twenty gees to more than ninety-five percent the speed of light, each probe could have the explosive force equivalent of more than one million Hiroshima bombs. That was more than enough energy to destroy a spaceship, likely enough to obliterate a small moon. There was one drawback: to reach 0.95c, it would have to accelerate for over sixteen days. In a combat situation, they might need to use them in situations with flight times considerably less than that, perhaps as short as seconds or minutes. Even then, a two-hundred-kilogram chunk hitting something after accelerating only ten seconds would reach a speed of four kilometers per second and pack quite a punch—more than enough to cripple the *Emissary* or *Samaritan*. He would certainly not want to be on the receiving end.

The other drawback was the combination of time and distance. With the right sensors, such a missile would be easily detectable and, with enough lead time, anything in its flight path would be able to maneuver out of the way. Given that they weren't designed as missiles, the onboard navigation system was not capable of such rapid retargeting. This was where teamwork came into play. Once they began working on modifying the probes to become missiles and were discussing the issues, one of the engineers suggested rigging the fusion drive to overheat and explode before impact so that instead of a ship having to dodge one fast, but very predictable missile, it would be subject to a barrage of rapidly moving debris, turning the interstellar rifle into a shotgun. While the explosion would not be the result of a nuclear process, just simple rapid, unmitigated heat buildup, it would be enough to disperse the debris across a large angle and dramatically increase the likelihood of hitting something—under the right circumstances.

And then there was the Samara Drive itself. As they had so successfully demonstrated when the shuttle carried the fugitive Atlantean, the ultraviolet exhaust of the ship's propulsion system could be quite a devastating weapon. Of course, that, too, had its limitations. It was the ship's propulsion system and, as such, was limited in how it could be targeted. To engage a target fore, the ship would have to rapidly rotate on its axis to bring the aft pointing in the correct direction. And, as it was being used as a weapon, it would be pushing the *Emissary* away from the engagement in a direction opposite to it.

Adding their measures together, the *Emissary* was not going to be completely helpless in a fight. Just mostly helpless. Jacobs sincerely hoped that none of these plans would ever have to be implemented, but as a Space Force captain, it was his job to be prepared. And he was very good at his job.

Jacobs activated his comm link and set it to be an all-hands message through the ship's speaker system. "This is Captain Jacobs. As you know, we are headed for the Luyten b star system to find out more about the source of the radio signals beamed at Proxima b, and to find out who the awakened Atlantean was so eager to contact before her death. Though this is not a ship of war, we are doing everything we can to assure that we are not helpless when we arrive at our destination. I would like to commend the creativity of the crew in coming up with the stingers we hope we never have to use.

"Some are already in the cryobeds for the duration of the trip and the rest of us will soon follow suit. While we're asleep, the ship's sensors will be scanning what's ahead, monitoring the radio signal from Luyten b for any significant changes, and listening for news from both Proxima b and Earth. If there are any significant changes, the ship will awaken me and select members of the crew to decide a course of action. If nothing changes, then we, like everyone else, will remain in cryo. The plan is to begin awakening the crew when we are three weeks out from the system's heliopause, which should give us plenty of time to get the lay of the land before we enter the planetary system. The ship will have been decelerating for quite some time, bringing us to nearly a standstill relative to Luyten's Star."

He took a dry breath.

"We don't know what we will find there, but I do know this crew is among the best that humanity has to offer with regard to the task ahead of us. At the risk of sounding overly dramatic, clichéd, and sentimental, we are truly going where no human has gone before. Let's do it well."

Four days later, Jacobs was in the cryobed as Mak made the final checks before activating the system that would put him under for the remainder of the trip. The system would not activate until Mak had placed himself in the adjacent bed—satisfying one of the many flight rules created by the psych teams back on Earth, that there was never a time when only one human was awake on the ship. It was one of the rare times when Jacobs waxed philosophical. Few in cryosleep reported dreaming and the bed's sensors bore that out. When in cryosleep, fewer than one in a thousand people experienced any sort of REM sleep whatsoever. And in those few, it was, at its most frequent, sporadic, and short in duration—perhaps once or twice in a year. It was the closest thing to death that Jacobs could imagine.

"Mak, do you believe in God?" Jacobs asked.

"Hmm? God? Well, yes, in fact I do. I was raised as an Eastern Orthodox Christian. My parents were very strong believers and they did their best to bring me and my two sisters up in the faith. Of course, like many people, I drifted from it during college and medical school, not giving it much thought until my mama died in a commuter train crash. I and my sisters were crushed, but though my *otets* missed her dearly, he seemed at peace with her passing. At first that made me angry, and I confronted him over it. It was then that I finally understood what it meant to be a believer. I wanted what he had. And now I have it," Mak said, a faint smile appearing on his face.

Jacobs turned his head upward and replied, "Well, I must admit, I'm not in the same camp as you, but I do believe there is something more than this experience we call life. Being out here, experiencing the enormity of it all, and encountering others like us just seems... improbable. That doesn't mean that I believe there is some mystical force that for some reason made itself known to an obscure tribe of primitives on an otherwise insignificant rock in the outer reaches of the galaxy. Far from it. No, if there is a god, or a purpose, then it must be larger than we humans. Then again, maybe it is all just a fluke of nature. Maybe we, the Proximans, and the Atlanteans are merely products of physical processes that precipitated out of the Big Bang. For some reason, I just don't like that answer. Should I be worried that I'm thinking about these things?"

"Captain Jacobs, I would be worried if you didn't. Only a fool doesn't look at the majesty of the world... worlds... universe around them and have such thoughts. And you, sir, are not a fool. Now rest easy as I activate our cryobeds. We shall soon be awakened and among the first of the crew worshipping the porcelain gods as we recover from cryosleep. A side effect of this process that I must admit I would like to avoid," Mak replied.

"To sleep and vomit." Jacobs, like Mak, smiled, and said finally, "Let's do this thing."

Thirty seconds later, and for another several years, Jacobs and Mak experienced nothingness firsthand.

CHAPTER 9

On Proxima b

"Wow. Vacuum tubes. I'm glad I brushed up on these babies before we agreed to help with this project. From the strong ozone smell, I imagine it gets pretty hot in here when these are operating," Burbank said, formerly of the *Samaritan* and now a freelance consultant helping Fintidierian companies upgrade their infrastructure using his knowledge of twenty-first-century Earth technologies. Roy was with his Fintidierian colleagues in a large room filled with glass tubes and wires. It was the regional power company's computer center that was responsible for keeping the lights on for just over a million Fintidierians in a city just a few hundred miles from where the Terrans had settled and now called home. He had to constantly remind himself that making comments about the primitive nature of their technologies, of which they were immensely proud, made him sound like an arrogant jerk. He did not want to be a jerk. He wanted to be helpful.

Roy had agreed to consult on the project, which would keep him from home for at least a week, perhaps longer. To Roy's surprise, his wife, Chloe, had readily agreed. "You need the time away," she'd urged. He was surprised because that would mean he would be unable to help with their two young children. Since their arrival, he had mostly been a homebody, taking care of the kids while his wife collaborated with the medical team to seek the cure for the fertility crisis. At first, it was a lot of fun. Spending time at home had allowed him to really get to know his daughter, who he had missed being with for the first few years of her life as she was traveling on the *Emissary* to join him at Proxima b. Unsurprisingly, it had taken her some time to warm up to this new person in her life, this "daddy," but once she did, they became nearly inseparable. Lately, though, he had grown restless. He was an engineer and he wanted to get back in the game. There was only so much he could fix and improve at home.

When the opportunity to consult with the utility company came up, he went for it. And Chloe was incredibly supportive. She knew he needed mental engagement and prodded him into accepting the offer. So, here he was. The utility was not asking to design or fix anything specific, merely look over their new, not-yet-online computer center and its interface with the local power grid and provide recommendations as to how it might be made more reliable or increase its performance. As he looked at the room with its thousands of vacuum tubes, miles of wires, and complex water-cooling system, he could not help but think about how all this computing power could be performed by the handheld he had in his right pocket. *It could have been performed by my father's cell phone*, he thought.

Roy had hoped to get to know his Fintidierian colleagues during the trip, but both men had been quite standoffish. At first, Roy thought it was the usual Terran/Fintidierian cultural divide coupled with the language barrier. And that could still be the root of the problem, though Roy didn't think it explained their reticence. His Fintidierian was now passable and their proficiency in English equally so. In their conversations so far, though brief and largely transactional, there had not seemed to be a communications barrier. Then he thought it might be the age barrier. Though he was still in his forties, a comparatively youthful age back on Earth, both Zakri and Hoproman were in their midtwenties. From what he could tell, he was roughly the same age as both men's fathers. But that didn't explain it either. In Roy's life experience, engineering was the language that crossed every cultural, social, racial, and political barrier. You could have two engineers from different countries, religions, ethnicities, or racial background and have them work together, joyfully, once they started talking about circuits, amperage, inductance, and induced *emf*. The language of engineering, the lure of the technical that appealed to those who chose to work in that field, superseded almost all other cultural programming and allowed people of radically different backgrounds to work together and break down barriers. But not with Zakri and Hoproman. When Roy had tried to engage them, they assiduously avoided him. And that was downright odd.

As Roy moved from the door and into the room to look more closely, he realized something. He smelled ozone in the air. Not just ozone, but that mix of ozone and dankness that only came from being in a room filled with hot electrical equipment that had been operating for years. It was normally a comforting smell, one of equipment working to perform its design goal and succeeding. But not in this case. He shouldn't have smelled anything in this room except perhaps a slight odor that comes from a vacuum tube's first use when the accumulated dust is burned off as it heats up. This was supposed to be the new control room. He was there to inspect it before it came online and had time to generate the level of residual ozone that Roy was now smelling.

"Guys, are you sure we are in the right place? I think this might be one that's been in use. I'm here to see the *new* control room," Roy said as he turned away from the glass-and-metal-filled room and back toward his Fintidierian colleagues who had been coming in behind him. Instead, he saw the massive metal door closing and heard it latch, leaving him alone.

"What's going on?" Roy shouted as he moved back toward the door. The door, designed to contain a major electrical fire, was closed and locked. He knew immediately that there was no way he would be able to open it from the inside. *Is this some sort of juvenile prank? What the hell is going on?*

Standing there long enough to take stock of his situation, Roy turned around to examine the room in more detail to see if there might be another way out. Figuring out why they locked him in would have to wait until after he found an exit route.

He found himself in a man-made cavern, at least fifty feet long and thirty feet wide with a ceiling that towered twenty feet overhead. Everywhere he looked were vacuum tubes of assorted sizes and shapes, capacitors, and other antique electronics that he had only studied in history books before coming up to speed on modern Fintidierian technology. As he looked at the tubes more closely, he realized they were different from what was in the design manuals he had been studying. They were larger. More primitive (if that were possible!). Less efficient. And the wiring was just too hefty to match the power needs of the newer designs he had expected to encounter. He now understood why the room smelled old and used. It had been. This must have been the old control room that was decommissioned.

Zakri and Hopromanbrought him here to trap him. But why? He knew the tensions between some Fintidierian factions and the Terrans were rising and that was why the government had provided additional security in areas where Terrans were living and working. If they had wanted to hurt him, or kill him, they could have done so long before now. The car ride to the power plant would have been ideal. They had driven on mostly empty country roads for quite some time, and they could have pulled over, killed him, and dumped his body any number of places and no one would have been the wiser. Why bring him out here? Was he being kidnapped? He and Chloe had no more money than anyone else, so if it were a kidnapping, then the motive had to be something other than money. He decided not to waste any more time thinking about motive and to remain focused on gaining his freedom. *I can figure out why later.*

He looked around the room and, for the moment, tried to ignore the siren call of the electrical equipment that filled it. There were windows, but they were nearly twenty feet overhead, near the roof, and each was covered with what looked like thick wire mesh. He didn't see any ladders or tables that he could use to get to them without disassembling and moving a significant amount of hardware. Making it all the more difficult were the massive fans that filled each one. With all the heat generated in the room, air maintaining air flow was especially important. They would also be in the way should he attempt to exit through one of the overhead windows.

Concrete block walls. Concrete floors. And lots of pipes, all designed to carry cold water from the local river, snaking throughout the room and connected to the heat sinks designed into each bench of vacuum tubes. He walked over to the closest pipe, which measured nearly two feet in diameter, and listened. Silence. Whatever water used to flow through the system was not there now. He studied the room's piping and saw that none were any larger. Two feet was simply not enough for him to get through even if he could get one of them open.

He paused. *That's it. No obvious way out. I'm stuck.*

Okay. Think. If this were Earth, I could just get on the net and call for help. Chloe has the family's emergency radio, so that won't work. And no one will miss me for a week.

What could they possibly want?

Chloe Burbank was in a good mood. She was not happy because Roy was away, she was happy that he was away to do something he loved. She admired his commitment to his family and very much appreciated him taking on the role of primary caregiver after the birth of their second child, but she knew that he would never be satisfied with that role alone. He needed to work. He was an engineer and, well, engineers needed to engineer things. She planned to continue working in the med lab while he was gone and was fortunate that next door were two very responsible Fintidierian teenagers, both boys, who were very good with children and eagerly accepted the opportunity to watch the kids while she was away at work. They'd babysat before when she and Roy had been on dates and the kids loved them.

When she entered the lab, she noticed that the normal guards were there as were at least three additional local police officers. She knew the reason for the extra security and was thankful for it. She was also thankful for the police officers who kept watch on her house. If the kids or their teenage minders had an accident, help was only seconds away. It was reassuring, though she wished it weren't necessary.

"Good morning," she said as she entered the building and greeted the receptionist.

"Good morning, Dr. Burbank," the male receptionist replied with a smile. For a Fintidierian, his English was surprisingly good. When she was concentrating on it, she tried to speak with the locals in their language instead of assuming they would use hers. In this case, stopping to reply would have taken too much time and effort, so she just smiled in return and nodded.

Chloe wished she could remember the receptionist's name but could not. He was fairly new, having started working at the job only a couple of weeks ago and was nice enough, but she'd not had the opportunity to chat with him—and that's what it would take for her to be able to commit his name to memory. *Another item on my to-do list.* He was also kind of cute, not that she was trying to notice.

She decided to take the stairs to the third-floor laboratory today. Exercise was not one of her scheduled time priorities, especially with Roy gone, so she thought she should take whatever fitness opportunity presented itself. She passed the elevators as the doors closed and noticed that two of her Fintidierian colleagues were inside, along with two men she did not recognize. She smiled as she passed them. She reached the stairway and decided she would bound up two steps at a time—just because.

When she arrived at the lab, her two colleagues, Drs. Guzma and Werma, and their three students were already there along with the two men from the elevator and three others she did not recognize.

"Good morning," Chloe said, this time speaking Fintidierian. It was then that she noticed that no one was working, they were instead just standing on the far side of the room watching her come in. "What's wrong?" she asked. And then she noticed the guns. Each of the men she did not recognize was armed and had their pistols drawn, pointing them at both her and the rest of her team.

The door behind her closed. She glanced over her shoulder and saw a woman, also armed, locking it.

"Good morning to you, Dr. Burbank." One of the men stepped forward as he spoke (in Fintidierian). "Please join your colleagues and do not make any noise, please. On your way, please place your backpack on the table to your right."

Chloe walked slowly toward the gathered scientists and carefully, and very slowly, removed her backpack. As she did so, she slipped her hand into the right side pocket on the backpack, quickly feeling each of the contents until she found her emergency radio and held the power button long enough, she hoped, to turn it on. She pressed the transmit button as she moved toward the table where everyone's belongings were in a pile.

"May I ask why you are threatening us with guns? Are we being taken hostage?" she asked, hoping that whoever was crewing the communications room at the compound was listening and would not be too quick to reply and catch their captors' attention. She stopped at the table and held on to her backpack, and the transmit button, pausing as if waiting for their answer before she would place it on the table.

"Best to be quiet for now, Dr. Burbank. Just place the bag on the table and step over there," repeated the man who she now presumed to be their leader. He was definitely the oldest in the group, by a long shot. With his gray beard and mostly gray hair, she guessed that he was in his midfifties, trim, and did not seem at all nervous. The others were definitely younger, by a decade or two, and none of them spoke.

She carefully placed the bag on the table and released the transmit button. *Please don't call back*, she silently prayed. *Just send help.*

As soon as she reached her colleagues, the man in charge told them to sit.

They sat.

What followed was some rapid-fire dialog among their captors, all spoken in Fintidierian, only half of which she was able to understand. If they had spoken more slowly, she might have understood more. What she picked up indicated that their being taken hostage was part of a broader activity and that their demands were now being made known to the government. All she could think of now was the safety of her children.

The two guards at the Burbank home began their shift chatting on the sidewalk just in front of the house. Both were experienced police officers, and neither was overly inclined to discuss the politics of the Terrans and what had recently been stirring up trouble in and around their activities. They were there to do their jobs and keep the peace. Besides, they'd gotten to know the Burbanks, particularly their oldest daughter who brought them cookies just every day.

The senior of the two, Officer Pak, noticed a man walking his dog coming down the street toward them and quickly assessed that he was not likely to be a threat. But when he saw two other men coming from the opposite direction with a pace that would have them all converge together at one time right where the two officers were standing, the hairs on the back of his neck began to rise. Officer Mnu didn't appear to notice anything and kept talking about how he and his fishing buddies had found a great spot to cast and drink beer over the weekend. Pak estimated that they had twenty seconds to determine if there was a threat... or not.

"We've got company," announced Pak, interrupting Mnu's description of the cold beers they'd imbibed during the weekend.

Pak nodded toward the coming two men and then the dogwalker. He slowly dropped his right hand, unsnapped his gun holster, and rested it there.

Mnu began walking toward the two men. "Good morning," he said as he stepped toward them. Neither man replied as they kept walking. Mnu raised his left hand, palm outstretched in the universal "stop" gesture and added, "May we help you?"

The bullet caught Mnu in the chest. Fired from a perch on top of a house across the street, the sound of the gunshot arrived only a second after the bullet. Mnu collapsed.

Pak saw his fellow patrol officer get hit and fall to the ground at the same time that he saw the two men reach behind their backs and pull out handguns. The man walking the dog just stopped and stared—Pak quickly determined that dog man was not part of the attack that was unfolding and hoped he would get out of his state of shock and run away, and to call for help. Pak's perception of time began to slow down as his reflexes allowed him to draw his gun and take aim at one of the two approaching men just as they had theirs fully drawn and pointed at him. He fired at the one on the left and then quickly shifted his position to the right, toward their patrol car, to avoid being a still target for the second man. Two additional shots rang out. The first came from the second man just as his friend fell from Pak's round impacting him in the chest. Fortunately for Pak, it was a bad shot—the round hit a tree ten feet behind him. The second hit the ground just inches from where Pak had been standing before he shifted his position. It came from the sniper across the street who had already taken out Mnu. Pak knew he had to get some cover quickly or he would have only a few more seconds of life. He dropped behind the patrol car to shield himself from whoever was firing from across the street. Unfortunately, this gave the second, walking gunman a clear line of sight for taking another shot.

The approaching gunman and Officer Pak fired at roughly the same time, and both were hit. Pak felt an agonizing pain in his upper left shoulder as he saw his target fall. He groaned and only through sheer force of will was he able to keep his focus on the tactical situation and not his now useless left arm and the blood flowing from it. Another round from across the street hit the roof of his patrol car just a few inches above where he was crouched.

Dog man was now gone, and a large car was approaching

rapidly from the same direction as the walkers. Pak suspected the car held more of the attackers and there wasn't a thing he could do about it. If he broke cover to run into the house and defend the kids, the man across the street would have an easy shot. If he sat still, the approaching car would be able to discharge its occupants and quickly take care of him. He opened the car door and, still crouching, reached in to grab the radio. Another shot rang out, this time shattering the car window just above his head—but missing him and the radio.

He just finished the distress call when the approaching car careened to a stop and three men jumped out, each armed and running toward Pak. He was able to take out one of the three before two bullets struck him.

Inside the house, the two teenagers, nicknamed "Bill" and "Ted" by Chloe, had just moments before been playing with the Burbank children when they heard the initial gunshots and saw Officer Pak take down the second gunman as they reached the window to see what was going on. Samari arrived just after them and peered through the lower part of the window as she stood between them.

"What's going on?" Samari asked, looking up at Bill.

"Let's get away from the window, it's dangerous," Bill said as he reached down and scooped up Jeremiah from the floor where he was crawling toward them. Though his heart was racing, Bill was not scared—just excited. He and his family had experienced the riots and civil unrest that were gripping their world before the Terrans arrived and had begun practicing survival drills for emergency situations, including those that involved armed gangs who intended them harm. They were the Fintidierian equivalent of "preppers." Bill and Ted were no stranger to guns, and they knew that unless they fled immediately to someplace safe, they would either be taken hostage or killed. Bill didn't hesitate.

"I've got Jeremiah, you take Samari. We'll go out the back door and get to the house where we can hole up with Mom in the safe room until the police get here," he said.

Ted took Samari's hand, bent over toward her, and softly said, "We need to get out of here now. I know it's scary, but we need you to be a big girl and not cry. You need to do exactly as we say, okay?"

Samari looked up at him with wide eyes and nodded her head. It was clear that she was valiantly trying to hold back tears, and her fear, and only barely succeeding.

The boys led the Burbank children to the back door and briefly stopped to see if it was safe to go out the door. If more people with guns were coming in from the back, their only other chance was to get out through the windows in the side bedroom. Bill cracked open the door and quickly surveyed the yard behind the house and had his hopes dashed. Another gunman was coming toward the door from the right and saw Bill just as Bill saw him. They briefly locked eyes and then Bill moved to close the door and lock it. He knew that would not stop the gunman, but it would at least slow him down.

"Another one is coming, and he's armed," Bill announced.

Samari, who had been heroically holding herself together until now, began crying.

Sensing the anxiety, Jeremiah joined in—wailing.

"Let's get to the master bedroom. There is a window there we might be able to get out of," Bill said.

Boom! The sound of a shotgun blast from just outside the back door jolted them to move. Bill was sure it was the sound of the gun being fired at the door to break the lock and allow the gunman to enter. It took him a few seconds to realize that the door was not damaged, which meant that the gunshot was for some other purpose.

They weren't going to wait around and see what happened. They had to get away and the master bedroom was their only option. They were just about out of the room when they heard someone rattle the back door.

"Cabri? Drui? It's Mom. Open the door and come with me. It's safe now." It was their mom.

Stopping mid-stride, Cabri (Bill) and Drui (Ted) returned to the kitchen. Cabri opened the door and was relieved to see their mother standing there—with her shotgun.

"Come, quickly," she urged as she motioned for the foursome to follow her. Their mother was a tall, thin, black-haired woman who walked with vigor and carried the shotgun as if it were an extension of her hand and arm. They'd been target shooting with her and knew she was a good shot but that didn't stop them from being surprised when they saw the bloodied body of the gunman lying on the ground just a few feet to the side of the door as they came out.

"He was so focused on you and getting in the house that he

didn't see or hear me come up behind him," she said to them and then leaned toward the still-crying Samari. "Honey, don't look at the bad man. Look at me and keep holding Cabri's hand. We're going to take you and your brother to someplace safe."

Drui, still carrying Jeremiah, Cabri, and Samri followed the boys' mother out the back door and toward her house two houses down on the right. They walked quickly, but not so quickly that Samari would trip and fall, which would have slowed them down.

After what seemed like an eternity, they reached the back of the house and quickly entered it.

After closing and locking the door, their mother said, "I heard the shots and knew something was wrong. Let's get in the safe room and then you can tell me all about it." She led them through the kitchen.

"Where are we going?" Samari asked through a sniffle.

"Just keep quiet for now and follow," the woman replied as she turned and led them down the stairs into the basement. As they entered, she closed a heavy steel door behind them.

The room was small, but well equipped. There were four cots, shelves filled with canned food and water bottles, and a wall that had firearms of varying types hanging from it: another full-size shotgun and two with pistol grips; multiple handguns; two hunting rifles; and an assortment of knives. Drui took both children to one of the cots and engaged them, trying to get them to stop crying. Of the two, Drui was definitely the more empathetic and most able to sooth children of all ages.

Cabri walked over to the gun rack, without hesitation took down one of the pistol-grip shotguns, and made sure it was loaded. His mother nodded approvingly as he walked to join her at the door to listen and wait.

"Mr. Ambassador, we have a problem." Captain Crosby was speaking on the secure, encrypted radio link to Ambassador Jesus from aboard the *Samaritan*. "Chloe Burbank used her satphone to let us overhear what sounds like a hostage situation at the bioresearch facility. From what we can tell, there are multiple bad guys with guns, and they've taken her entire research group hostage. So far, there's been no alert from the local police."

Jesus had answered Crosby's emergency call as soon as it came in. Fortunately, he was not in any meeting and was just at his desk planning the day and taking care of the mountain of bureaucratic paperwork the Fintidierians seemed to love. He had studied how bad real "paperwork" had been in precomputer societies, now he was living it. There was a mountain of papers on his desk awaiting him to read, skim, or ignore. All of that would have to wait.

"Has she been injured?" asked Jesus.

"Not that we can tell. We recorded the conversation, and it sounds like she was able to activate the phone for only a few seconds before they forced her to put it down. The phone is still active, and we know exactly where it is. Unless they've separated her from it, she's in the research lab."

Damn! Rogers and his SEALs are on the Emissary *bound for Luyten's Star, leaving only Mike Rialto and his team. They're capable, but they're not SEALs.* Jesus was running through the options available, and he did not like them. The local police were good, but they would not have the technical capabilities of the Terran team, even a ship's security team like that led by Rialto.

"Captain Crosby, how quickly can Rialto and his team be at the facility to effect a rescue?" Jesus asked.

"I've already alerted them, and Rialto thinks they can be onsite within forty minutes. Fortunately, they are planetside in the compound doing some training. He's to get back with me with options when they are en route to the lab. I know that you'll want to alert Secretary General Arctinier and coordinate with the local police. It's times like these that I don't envy you and your job. Up here, I would just tell Rialto to come up with a plan and execute it. Down there, I know things are going to be a lot more complicated."

"That depends," Jesus said. "It depends upon how fast their captors make their intentions known to the locals or how quickly they are discovered. I have a lot more confidence in your team than I do in the local police. Given the political situation here, I wonder how many police might be sympathetic to the political opposition."

"You don't plan to alert Secretary General Arctinier?"

"Not yet. Get your people there as quickly and quietly as possible and let them do their job. I trust your judgment. I don't need to sign off on whatever plan they come up with, but I do need to know what's going on so I can knowledgeably deal with the fallout," Jesus responded. *The last thing I'm going to do is meddle in the planning of a life-or-death hostage rescue effort, something I know nothing of. Plus, it gives me some small measure of deniability.*

"We will keep you informed," Crosby said as he cut the connection.

Jesus rose from his chair and walked to the window overlooking the building's beautiful courtyard. Every day he looked out the window and vowed he would take time to go out and enjoy the trees and flowers so carefully tended there, and every day he would somehow never find the time. *When this crisis is over, I'm going put a walk in the courtyard on my schedule every day.* He hoped he would actually follow through but knew that he probably would not. He sighed and began coming up with ideas of how to approach Madam Secretary General.

Thirty-five minutes later, Rialto and the three members of his security detail arrived at the research lab. From their vantage point across the street, all appeared to be quite normal. Whatever was going on inside had not yet made itself known to those outside or the serene scene of pedestrians walking this way and that would have been replaced with police cars and a sense of crisis. Surprise was still in their favor and, for that, Rialto was pleased.

Rialto had complete confidence in the capabilities of his team. First, there was his deputy, Christin Walker. She was a former police officer and the daughter of an astronomy professor who, because of her apparent lack of math skills, was unable to follow in her father's academic footsteps. She had always wanted to study space but could not, so she had jumped at the chance to volunteer for the trip to Proxima Centauri those many years ago as part of the security detail. She was quite good at her job and was a real people person. If there was going to be any sort of negotiation, she would be the one doing all the talking. Next there was Jayden Abioye. Abioye was the son of African immigrants to America and had a drive to excel and be the best that amazed and inspired all who came to know him. When they left Earth, he was the one about whom Rialto knew the least. But at every step of the way, from the Gaines crisis on their way out to the incident at Misropos, he'd proven himself to be more than capable. He had earned Rialto's trust and confidence. And then there was Keith Ruiz. Ruiz was quiet, capable, and what Rialto could only describe as "solid." When assigned a task, Ruiz completed it—on time and to the exact specifications required. It was a good team.

They readied themselves outside the lab complex and behind the corner of a building across and just down the street to avoid being too obvious. There was no sign that anyone had noticed them or paid them any heed.

"We don't know how many hostage takers are there and we can't really do much until we know the tactical situation. Ruiz, is the drone ready to fly?" Rialto asked.

"Powered up and ready to go." Ruiz nodded to him over the controller. He was holding a small quadcopter in the palm of his left hand and held up the controller with his right to emphasize the point. No larger than his thumbnail, the quadcopter could remain in the air for up to seven hours on a single charge thanks to its graphene capacitive battery, carried optics and onboard signal processing to give it ultra-high definition visuals and audio, and was covered in a thin layer of liquid crystals that automatically changed color to allow the craft to blend into whatever background it encountered. It was virtually undetectable unless you knew what to look for and where to look.

"Okay, let's see what we are dealing with. You reviewed the building's plans. If they are still in the main lab where the sat phone is pinging, then you should have an unobstructed view from outside the south window. Let's get her airborne," Rialto ordered.

Ruiz nodded and tossed the tiny drone into the air. Its rotors activated and immediately took it skyward. Ruiz had donned the control visor that allowed him to see what the drone was seeing as well as a heads-up display of all the tiny flyer's systems. He forced the control transmitter on and snapped it to a molle strip in his vest. Once the control icons appeared in the virtual view, he stood stock-still and moved his hands in the air to direct the tiny craft to its intended target. Rialto and the team quickly lost sight of the drone, leaving its flight totally up to Ruiz. They didn't have to wait long.

"I'm there and have a visual," Ruiz said. "I'm sending it to your datapads." Each of Rialto's team looked at their unfolded data pads, each as thin as a sheet of paper and showing what the tiny camera on the drone was seeing in high definition.

Despite them all seeing the same thing, Rialto always liked to discuss the tactical situation verbally to make sure he wasn't missing something. "I can see six people with guns and six scientists, including Dr. Burbank. They've barricaded the door and moved the furniture around to provide some cover in case someone makes a frontal attack. One of the terrorists is watching the window, but he doesn't seem to see the drone—a good thing. No one seems to be injured."

"What about elsewhere in the building?" asked Walker.

"That's my next stop," Ruiz uttered monotonically, not taking his focus from the controls. The view on the tiny screen changed as the quadcopter flew toward the top of the building.

"Air vents," he said, anticipating the next question. "Once I'm in the ventilation system, I can see into every room from the air vents. There's a huge opening on the roof with a fan. Getting past the blades will be a piece of cake."

The team watched, almost mesmerized, as the tiny ship raced into the ductwork, not so much a pausing before it zipped past the relatively slow-moving fan blades and into the wide aluminum duct that then branched out to the many rooms within the building. Ruiz, who had studied the structure's plans on the trip over, knew exactly where he was going. First, he would check the hallway outside the barricaded laboratory to make sure no one was out there keeping watch. Done. The hallway was empty.

His next stop was the lobby. It took another few minutes for the copter to reach the bottom of the building. It exited a vent on the back left of the atrium and hovered near the ceiling as the camera panned across the room, taking in the situation. There were two men sitting at a table, each with a larger backpack by their side on the floor. Ruiz flew closer and zoomed in on their open backpacks and saw the unmistakable butt of what looked like one of the automatic or semiautomatic battle rifles they had seen in use by the Fintidierian military. Each carried a detachable box magazine containing twenty rounds. They were clearly part of the opposition.

Next, the copter flew toward the receptionist desk and saw that the young and smiling (why was he smiling?) receptionist had a similar weapon just under his desk within easy reach. No one else was in the lobby.

The copter then flew down the hallway, past the elevators and to the stairwell. No one was visible.

"We need to act before the locals get wind of what's going on," Rialto said. "We have authority from the captain to move and that's what I intend to do. Here's the plan..."

Chloe was trying to understand what the Fintidierians were saying but caught only every other word. To find out what was being said, she tried to engage Dr. Werma, who was sitting just next to her. But as soon as she tried, one of the armed men turned his gun toward her and told her to be quiet.

Nothing much happened in the room. They were obviously waiting for something. That something was a call on the radio that the man she assumed was their leader answered as soon as the radio clicked to get his attention. She couldn't hear what was said by the person on the other side of the conversation, but the leader didn't appear to be pleased. In fact, his demeanor went rapidly from annoyed to angry. Then she heard words that she did understand, and they caused her heart to sink. "Find the children at all costs. Find them quickly."

The children? Her *children?* She started to rise and was pushed harshly back to the ground by the man who had previously silenced her. "If you do anything to my children, so help me God, I will kill you," she threatened, her worry becoming anger.

"If you do as we say, you and your children will be fine," said the man. "Now, if you try that again, I won't be nearly as polite. Sit down, don't move, and be quiet."

From what Chloe could tell, which wasn't a whole lot, it sounded like someone was trying to find her children and they had not yet done so. She knew the police were at the house protecting them and that gave her some measure of relief, but not much. Something to do with her children was going down and she did not like that.

Her thoughts were racing, trying to figure out what, if anything, she could do. And then she realized she was suddenly very tired. At almost the same moment the thought entered her mind, she saw only blackness.

Unseen by anyone in the room, a quadcopter hovering just inside the room's air vent had just released a burst of knockout gas, sufficient to put everyone in the room into a deep sleep. The gas, which had been brought from Earth by Rialto's team as a nonlethal way to deal with any sort of possible crew problems while in space, did the job for which it was designed with ease. Everyone in the room, good guys and bad, would not wake up for at least two hours.

At the same time the gas was being released upstairs, Rialto walked into the building's lobby and toward the front desk. The lobby was too small to use sleeping gas. Armed only with a pistol concealed under his light jacket and a knife in its sheath near his ankle, Rialto tried to look nonchalant as he approached the receptionist. He could sense the eyes of the two armed men at the table following him as he walked across the room.

Rialto was obviously a Terran, given his very European look among a Fintidierian population of common Asian descent and that undoubtedly put the people in the room on high alert. Using his best Fintidierian, he declared, "I'm here to see Dr. Burbank." That was the action phrase and as he said it, he reached toward the small of his back to draw his handgun. Before anyone in the room could react, the sound of breaking glass was the only clue that two ten-millimeter rounds, each traveling at over three thousand feet per second, impacted the men at the table, splattering their brains across three feet of carpet.

The "receptionist" reacted quickly but was, as anticipated, momentarily distracted by the shattering glass, allowing Rialto to bring his gun up just a little bit faster. Rialto put a round in the man's chest, knocking him backward and onto the ground. Rialto quickly rounded the desk and kicked the rifle far out of the man's reach. The receptionist was not dead, but he might be shortly if he didn't get medical attention. Rialto leaned over and searched him, making sure he had no additional concealed weapons. He didn't.

The doors opened and the rest of Rialto's team entered. Ruiz moved to make sure the two men were as dead as they looked while Walker and Abioye joined him at the desk.

"Ruiz, you watch our friend here and let Captain Crosby know we're in the building and on our way up to retrieve Dr. Burbank. Let him know that I would prefer the locals not arrive until we've got her back safely at the compound," Rialto said.

When the three members of the *Samaritan*'s security detail arrived upstairs, the sleeping gas had fully dissipated, leaving everyone in the room in a deep sleep. One by one, Rialto's team searched, disarmed, and bound the gunmen so they could no longer pose a threat to anyone—even if they awakened earlier from the gas then they should. They then carried the sleeping medical team to the elevator for transport to the ground floor.

Once there, Rialto and Walker carried Dr. Burbank out the door and to the van that had carried the team to the laboratory.

"I'll get her back to the compound. Captain Crosby alerted Ambassador Jesus that we were successful and he's now alerting the police. You and the team wait here to debrief them once they arrive. I suggest you stand outside and try to look harmless. We don't want the locals to think you are on the wrong team," Rialto told his men.

"Sure thing, Mike. Just take care of the good doctor and let us know if anything else is going down. I don't have a good feeling about this," Walker said.

"I'm on it," Abioye replied.

Lesson number one: Don't kidnap and lock an engineer in a room filled with electrical equipment and expect him or her to complacently accept their fate. While the hardware in the room was old and long unused, that didn't mean it was necessarily broken and not functional. Roy was easily able to pry open several of the casings to find vacuum tubes, Earth 1950s-era capacitors of various sizes, diodes, rectifiers, transformers, and as much copper wire as an engineer might use in a lifetime.

At first Roy thought about using the wires to trip his captors as they entered the room, but that alone wouldn't likely get him out of his predicament. There were at least two of them and even if they were both momentarily distracted by tripping, they were armed and one of them would likely recover before he could disarm or disable the other. Transformers, with all their embedded copper wire, were very heavy and he was sure he could either knock out or even kill a person with a surprise strike to the head using one—but, again, there were at least two of them. Physical force was definitely not Plan A. Besides, they were both younger and likely much stronger than he. No, he would have to use his advantages—his brain and his experience.

As he surveyed the gold mine—more appropriately the copper and silver mine—that he had laid out on the tables in front of him, an idea began to germinate. To make it work, he needed to see if any of the electrical leads or outlets in the room still had power. He grabbed some old, hardened, and flaky electrical insulation from inside one of the casings that had housed the now dismantled circuits as well as some copper wire and then began looking for a source of power. After examining every wall, every light fixture, and every conduit he could find, there were none still hot. No juice.

But he did find batteries—lots and lots of good, old-fashioned lead/acid batteries, God bless them. Most were dead. Others maybe not completely, judging by the faint sparks he was able to get when touching some of them. He grinned. Now all he needed was a little water. He followed one of the many pipes in the room until he found what he was looking for—an access point that he might just be able to open. What do you get when you mix water, batteries, capacitors, rectifiers, and some diodes with an engineer? The bastards who locked him in the room would soon find out...

After a little over an hour, Roy was not anywhere near finished with what he planned when he heard the door being opened. His heart raced as he quickly abandoned the equipment piled on the workbench and made his way as far from it as possible when the door finally opened and Hoproman peered in.

"I have food and water for you," Hoproman said as he sat a plate with a sandwich and a cup of water on the floor just inside the door.

Roy tried to look inconspicuous and resigned to his fate, hoping that the equipment he had moved would not be noticed. To keep Hoproman's attention on him and not the room, he replied, "You know that I will eventually be missed. My wife knows where we were going and will inform the authorities."

Hoproman said nothing as he simply stared at Burbank and then closed the door.

Roy walked toward the door and picked up the food.

"I might as well eat. It'll help me think," he muttered to himself as he took his first bite of what was a completely stale sandwich.

Then he got back to work.

Roy was pleased with what he had been able to kludge. In addition to the surprise that awaited his captors upon their return, he'd fashioned a weapon, what he now affectionately called "Thor's Hammer," out of a short piece of steel pipe and a medium-size electrical transformer attached to the end with multiple windings of copper wire. For good measure he had also secured the base plates of a few cathode ray tubes with their one-inch-long pins facing outward from the hammer. *Better to make them bleed.* He had no qualms about seriously injuring his captors—after all, they were the ones who pointed guns at him.

Now, all he had to do was wait.

He didn't have to wait long. Shortly after he got himself into position, he heard the door being opened and then saw Zakri stick his head into the room. Roy was hidden from view, but not behind the door as they might expect. He wanted to be far enough away to not get caught in his own trap yet not so far as to not be able to take advantage of whatever injured or stunned shape the men might be in after he sprung it. He was hiding under a table ten feet behind the door. They would almost certainly not be able to see him until they were all the way into the room.

Zakri looked back and forth, trying unsuccessfully to pick out Roy from among all the junk in the room. He briefly looked over his shoulder and asked Hoproman to join him in searching for Burbank. They were not speaking softly, and Roy was easily able to follow what they were saying.

Moments later, both of his Fintidierian captors walked into the room as they slammed the door wide open with a loud *clang.*

"Mr. Burbank, hiding is of no use. We don't have to make this difficult. If you come out now and follow our instructions without us having to come find you, and perhaps hurt you, then things will go much more smoothly for you and your family," said Hoproman in his best English.

Hearing that his family was somehow involved in whatever was going on just inflamed Roy and strengthened his resolve. *Don't you dare bring my family into this . . .* Roy remained crouched, motionless, with his hands on the wire that he would soon use to close the circuit on his primitive, but hopefully operative, step-up converter that he'd hastily assembled. If it worked, it would take the little remaining voltage remaining in the sixteen batteries he'd connected and step it up to a level that should give each man a quite painful jolt. He wasn't sure how much current he'd get, or what would be needed to actually injure the men, but he might incapacitate them long enough to swing into action, as it were, with Thor's Hammer.

The seconds seemed like minutes as Zakri and Hopromian slowly moved into the room. Roy became concerned when they abruptly changed direction and began walking the wrong way. If they went any way other than the path he envisioned, then his plan would simply not work. He had to do something to get them back on track, so he ever-so-slightly scuffed his shoe. *That* got their attention, putting them back on the correct path.

Hopromian noticed the puddle first, but not before both men were standing in the water that Roy had diverted from one of the cooling pipes, where it had pooled and become stale, to where it was needed. As he looked down to see what he'd stepped in, Roy closed the circuit.

Visually, there wasn't much to see except for the reactions of the Fintidierians. When the circuit closed, the little remaining power in each of the mostly depleted batteries flowed through a circuit Roy had devised that used capacitors, rectifiers, and a transformer to step up the voltage as high as he could manage. Both men stood suddenly as straight as boards and dropped their guns as their bodies spasmed from the electrical shock. There may not have been much to see, but the sound and smell created by the electrical discharge was one any good electrician, or engineer, would recognize as a significant one. As the shock subsided, both men crumpled to the floor.

Roy opened the circuit out of habit before he rushed forward. He needn't have bothered since the batteries were now fully discharged and not a risk to him or anyone else. Thor's Hammer, however, was quite a different story.

Roy could not bring himself to bludgeon the slowly recovering men in the head as they struggled to sit up and began searching for their weapons, but he had no qualms about hitting other body parts. Both men had their hands turned to bloody pulp in a matter of seconds. For good measure, Roy didn't wait to assess the damage he'd done to their hands before he similarly smashed their kneecaps, leaving both men writhing on the floor.

Roy scooped up both weapons and sprinted out the door. Though he was an engineer's engineer, and had no formal military training, he was no stranger to guns and had gone shooting many times before and after their trip to Proxima Centauri. He slung one rifle over his shoulder and held the other at the ready should he encounter anyone else at the site in his bid for freedom.

When he exited the building, he saw no one else. It didn't take long for him to retrace his steps to the vehicle that had brought him and his two captors to the site. Before he slid into the driver's seat, he used the butt of the rifle to smash the cover over the ignition system in the car so he could reach the wires and start it without having to worry about using what the Fintidierians used for keys. They didn't really look like the dongles that had been the norm on Earth for so long. The keys actually looked like cylinders with grooves and notches cut in them.

Roy pulled the wires free and found the one that would throw a spark against the chassis of the column. Then he took turns touching the hot wire to others until he heard the starter motor kick over. Once he found that one, he pulled it aside. He'd need that one. But first he had to figure out which wire needed to stay hot for the car's electrical system to stay on. He touched wires to the hot one until the dash lit up. He was quite sure he had it figured out, but there was only one way to find out.

"Come on, baby. Start for me," he muttered a bit between frantically and impatiently. "Come on."

He held the two electrical system wires together between his thumb and forefinger and twisted them until the electrical system on the car stayed on. Then he grabbed the ignition wire and touched it to them. The starter motor whirred. He tapped the gas lightly.

"Hot damn!" he shouted. "I'm out of here." He slipped the car into gear, and he was on the road back toward town—and his family.

As he drove, he replayed Hopromen's comments concerning his family over and over in his head, making him both angry and anxious to get back. *What the Hell is going on?*

"I don't know, sweetheart." Roy lifted Samari's hair and hugged his daughter to him tightly. "People who are desperate and feel like they have no salvation or are hopeless and helpless do very drastic and bad things sometimes."

"It's okay now, baby." Chloe smiled and pulled Jeremiah to her tighter. "Mommy and Daddy are here. And we're going to stay here at the compound until all this blows over. Here, you can run and play outside with nothing to worry about."

"That right, Daddy?" Samari asked.

"That's right, Samari. We're safe here."

"Can we do anything to help these people?" Samari asked.

"I'm sure we can." Roy patted her head. "I'm sure."

He looked at Chloe, who still appeared a bit hungover from the knockout gas. He gave her a confident sideways nod of the head and tried to smile. He figured her confidence in solving the fertility problem for the Fintidierians was a bit shaken too. He knew his was.

Roy, Chloe, and their children were all holding each other as they looked out the large living room window of the small quarters they had originally lived in when they had first arrived at Proxima. It was smaller than where they had been living for the past year, but it was safe. They were safe.

"I'll take the kids upstairs and let them sleep in our bed with us, if that's okay. I think I'll go ahead and crash now too. I'm bushed," said Chloe.

"I'll be up shortly. Mike Rialto is on his way over with some news he seems eager to share. I'll come up after he leaves," said Roy.

"Should I stay down here to see him?" she asked.

"Chloe, you look like you could use at least two full days of sleep. Go on upstairs. I call fill you in tomorrow," he offered.

She leaned over to kiss him on the cheek and whispered, "Good night."

Roy smiled and replied, "I won't be too long."

Ten minutes after Roy heard the last of the nighttime routine noises from upstairs, he saw Mike Rialto coming up the stairs to the front door. Roy hurried to greet him, afraid Rialto might ring the doorbell or make some other noise to wake up his now-sleeping family.

"Mike, its good to see you. Come on in," said Roy, motioning him inside. "Would you like some water?"

"No, thanks," said Rialto as he came in the room and sat in a chair near the window.

Roy sat back down in his chair, directly across from the security chief.

"What's the news?" asked Roy.

"We found where the kidnappers lived and searched their houses. In one of their houses, we hit pay dirt and found their manifesto," Rialto replied. "Before I fill you in, I need to get Captain Crosby on the line. He wants to be part of the discussion."

Rialto took out his radio and put it on the table. "Connect to Captain Crosby," he said, speaking toward the radio.

"I'm here." Crosby's voice came from the radio almost immediately. "Thanks for tying me in."

"Sam, it's good to hear your voice," said Roy as he leaned back in his chair. *Maybe I am getting tired after all*, he thought.

"I was going to tell Roy about the manifesto," interjected Rialto.

"Don't let me stop you," Crosby replied.

"Alright. We found what looks like a letter that was going to be delivered to the media after they had you and your family hidden in a safe house outside of town. We sent a team there also, but it was empty. It was well stocked with food and supplies, but no one was there," Rialto said.

"Because they were alerted somehow? Or because all the people were busy trying to kidnap us?" asked Roy.

"We think it was the latter, but we're not sure," Rialto responded.

"What did the letter say?" asked Roy.

"That they were holding you hostage and would kill members of your family one at a time, starting with you, by the way, unless we agreed to immediately leave the planet, return to our ships, and go back to Earth. They weren't going to release anyone in your family until *Emissary* was outside of the star system and *Samaritan* was ready to go," stated Rialto.

"These people were extreme xenophobes. They thought we were responsible for the fertility problem and used it as an excuse to come here and colonize or annex the planet," chimed in Crosby.

"Did they seriously expect us to do that?" asked Roy. "Most of the people here signed up for a one-way trip. I didn't, and six months or so ago, I might have considered going back, but not now. This is our new home. We came here to help them!"

"This is a new home for all of us," said Crosby. "We left our lives on Earth behind and most everyone is at peace with that. If we did agree to leave, then by the time we arrived back home, any life we might want to resume there would have been interrupted by decades. And given the unknown nature of the fertility problem, Earth would never let us leave our ships and return to the surface for fear of contamination."

"Is that all? Did you find out more about their organization? Most importantly, are there any more of them out there?" asked Roy.

"Unfortunately, its likely, very likely, that they were not acting alone. We've got some leads. We'll keep you posted," said Rialto.

Rialto stood and picked up the radio. "Roy, that's all we've got tonight. You look beat. We'll leave you alone so you can join your family and get some rest."

"Listen to Mike and get some rest. Tomorrow is another day," urged Captain Crosby as he signed off.

Roy walked Rialto to the door and shook his hand. "Thank you again for all you did to save my family today."

"I just did my job," he replied as he opened the door and exited.

"Good night," Roy said as Rialto walked down the path toward the sidewalk.

We're safe for now, Roy thought. *Well, safer than we were, anyway.*

This particular plot had been foiled, but what would follow it? If the Terrans didn't find an answer to the fertility problem soon...

CHAPTER 10

Proxima b

"Dr. Chris, you have to bounce it on the bottom more slowly or you'll scare them away." Graggyon Oo'ortava demonstrated the way to work the fishing rig again. Sentell watched carefully as the much younger man, who on Earth would be the typical age of an undergraduate student, demonstrated the finer parts of catching the Fintidierian orange-striped skiezel. As far as Sentell was concerned, they looked like a cross between a large-mouth bass and a sun perch. According to Grag, they tasted just as good as any fish anywhere when fried. Sentell couldn't wait to find out how they compared to their Terran counterparts.

Sentell tried not to be too overly excited over the simple fact that he might be the first Earther to fish on another planet. That thought rolled over in his mind, amusing and distracting him from the pure relaxation and essence of being on a lake with a fishing rig in his hands. But the vibrations of the line grasped gently between his thumb and forefinger were reassuring and kept his attention on the task at hand—catching fish.

"Got it, Grag. Low and slow." He focused a bit and worked the tip of his rod up to over a meter and then let it slowly settle back down. "My grandpa used to actually call this 'bumpin' the bottom' fishing. We would catch a fish about like this, called a bass, by dragging a plastic worm on the bottom."

"Yes, there you have it." Grag nodded. "Plastic worm? Hmmm, that might work here. We might have to see if we can make such a thing and give it a try."

"I'll see if I can print us a few of them." Sentell leaned back slowly in the seat of the three-person-sized boat. It wasn't much different from the bass boat he had back on Earth. Well, if you didn't consider that the boat he had back on Earth was made of a carbon composite material, damned near unsinkable, had sonar, depth gauges, fish finders, cushy seats and compartments, a beer cooler, and an electric motor that would propel the boat to a hundred and thirty kilometers per hour while this boat was made of wood, had Finti plastic seats, no instruments, and the motor was a smelly fossil-fuel-burning outboard contraption like Sentell had only ever seen in old fishing videos and movies. But fishin' was fishin' on any planet.

The water was a strange violet in the near dark lighting of the evening sun. There was almost no breeze and the boat gently rocked with the very small waves of the large lake. It was almost as priceless a feeling as he recalled fishing in Guntersville Lake back home. That was the best bass fishing on Earth. When he had told Grag of this, the kid couldn't stop talking about Gwonura Reservoir and how great the skiezel fishing was there. So, finally, just to get away from the crazy turmoil of the world for a few hours, Sentell had taken the young man up on his offer of a fishing trip to the lake.

"This is the life," Sentell said.

"The 'life'?" Grag was saying to himself and Sentell could tell the Fintidierian was trying to translate that in his head and wasn't quite getting it. He mouthed it again, "... the life..."

Chris couldn't help but laugh out loud as he watched Grag mouthing the words in deep contemplation. Even though Grag spoke perfect English, slang, euphemisms, metaphors, and similes were mostly still lost on him.

"Sorry, Grag. It means in my language that if I only had to do what I wanted to do, then this would be it. All I would do with my life is to sit here and relax and—HEY! A big one!" The canelike rod in his hands bent straight down. Sentell reacted quickly to set the hook.

"Hold your rod down or he'll throw the hook!" Grag warned as the skiezel jumped from the water. "Jerk and reel!"

"I've got him! Small-mouth do this back home!" Sentell did just as he had hundreds, maybe thousands of times on Earth, fighting the large fish as it cleared the water, shaking its head back and forth, trying to sling the lure from its mouth. The odd illumination from Proxima accentuated the orange stripes on the fish to the point that it appeared to glow like a fluorescent dye. It was beautiful. Sentell fought with the fish and did his best to keep the line taut. "It's a big one! Get the dip net!"

Grag was already kneeling over the side of the boat with the net as Sentell brought the fish to the edge near the aft end. The rod bent into almost a complete U-shaped curve and he had to struggle to keep the tip out of the water. The net slipped under the fish and then he lifted his pole as Grag lifted the net.

"We got it! It's female." Grag lifted the net quickly into the boat and grabbed the fish by the lower lip.

"I bet that thing is twenty-two skeens!" Grag sounded excited.

"I'm guessing five kilos. Can't convert to your system in my head."

"She's full of eggs," Grag exclaimed excitedly. "Female for sure. The males aren't as pretty. Wait until you taste the deep-fried fish eggs!"

"We'll eat well tonight," Sentell said as he looked at the female fish. The belly was engorged and bloated. The fish population was not having any problems with female fertility. The lifecycle of these fish was only a couple of years.

"If only we could learn from them." Grag looked sad for a moment. His excitement waning slightly to a more somber tone.

"How d'ya mean, Grag?"

"Why do all the animals thrive, yet we do not?" he asked.

"Well, probably because . . ." Sentell paused and looked at the fish and then back at the young man. Then he noted several birds circling overhead. He thought of the number of catlike animals and doglike animals that he had seen loose in the city. He also thought of the cattlelike farm animals he'd seen. Then he realized that they had not really looked into that as much as they should have.

"That's a damned good question, Grag. The animal kingdom seems to have no reproduction problems here, that is, except the humans." Sentell held up the livewell box lid as Grag plopped the fish into it. The fish banked against the lid and then splashed into the water. It briefly splashed about with the others already in there and then settled down. "A lot of fish to clean and it is getting late, don't you think?"

"Yes. I agree." Grag nodded. "We should head back before sundown and start cleaning them."

"What d'ya say we just hang out and eat the fish and have a few beers. I don't want to go back to the compound tonight," Sentell said. "All the guards and stuff are depressing."

"Great. We can stay at my family's place. You will be safe there tonight."

"Well, Grag, the sex of a zygote, as I explained to you at the lab, is the fertilized egg that forms after sperm fertilizes an egg, is actually chosen by the chromosomes in the sperm cell. The men carry the sex gene," Sentell mumbled around a mouthful of the skiezel. "For whatever reason it's the sperm-and-egg combination that seems to be where the problem is . . . maybe. Can't be sure. Polkingham thinks it is something else."

"Again, I was a physics student until you arrived. I am still learning the anatomy and biology. Perhaps my physics will be helpful along the way," Grag noted and then held up an empty bottle. "Another?"

"Damn right," Sentell agreed. The Fintidierian beer reminded him of the very bitter pale ales back on Earth. He could only guess that most of the beers were so strong to keep them preserved over longer periods of time. The Fintidierians were only now to the point in their culture and technological advancement that refrigerators with freezers were making it into every home. The Earth historical analog would put them at approximately 1950s-era technology. People were still likely preserving things through canning, smoking, salt, and sugar. The strong beers and wines didn't spoil as quickly. Hence, the beer was strong and bitter. In fact, he did recall that that was the very reason for the India Pale Ales back on Earth. They had been made extremely hoppy and strong to remain preserved on the long trips from India to Europe.

He watched as the young Fintidierian sat the bottle aside by the firepit. Grag looked over into the black cauldron and appeared to be nodding to himself. He reached into the boiling grease with the long screen ladle and scooped out the remaining of the filets frying there. The popping and sizzling sounds heightened as he stirred them up and withdrew them from the pot. He dumped them out on the tray with the others and then sprinkled them heavily with the spice shaker.

"What spice is that?" Sentell asked. "It's very good."

"Yes. It is my great-grandmother's mixture of sodium and potassium chloride, and a local spice plant . . . um . . . like your peppers," Grag explained as he continued to sprinkle the fish heavily.

"Last of the fish eggs, if you would like?" Grag offered the tray of fresh fried and spiced fish, pointing out the final large fried fish egg sack. Sentell noted how it looked exactly like the ones he'd fried back home. Animal life continued to be an amazement to him around every turn and new exposure or discovery.

"Think I will." Sentell grabbed the eggs and a couple of the pieces of fish for his plate and sat back down while Grag slid on pan holders, lifted the pot from the firepit, and sat it on the ground a few meters away. He stoked the fire and added a couple of logs, throwing bright orange embers upward against the night sky. Sentell watched them rise gently and then flow with the evening breeze. Grag then pulled a couple of bottles from the ice bucket and handed him one.

"I need to teach you how to make hushpuppies," Sentell offered around a mouthful of the fish.

"Hushpuppies?" Grag asked. "Quiet canine animals? Sounds gross! You eat dogs on Earth?"

"Of course not!" Sentell almost shouted, but then thought for a moment. "Well, some cultures used to, but it wasn't widespread where I'm from. In fact, it was against the law where I am from."

"Then . . . hushpuppies?"

"Haha! No animals at all in them. Let me tell you all about hushpuppies . . ."

Several bites and beer swallows later, their conversation returned to biology.

"Let me ask you, Dr. Chris," Grag said. No matter how many times Sentell had told him to drop the doctor part, he still insisted. He continued as he held out another large brown bottle in Chris's general direction. "I was wondering if . . . em . . . nope . . . can, yes, the word is can. Can the sex of a baby be determined through any technological methods? I mean, you came from the stars. Certainly, you can choose the sex of a baby on your world?"

"Hmm . . . yes is the correct answer." Sentell took the bottle and twisted the top off. The differences in little things interested him. The caps twisted in the same direction. Righty tighty. Lefty loosey. But they were not the type of single-twist caps on beer bottles like back on Earth. They were lids more like those of plastic soda or water bottles that took many turns to remove. He sat the top in the container Grag had nearby to collect them for reuse and reflected on the subtlety briefly. Then he took a long swig from the bitter ale. He liked it more and more with each swallow.

"So, back on Earth, every now and then we do that. People used to do it more, but it never really caught on accept in a few countries where women weren't considered to be as prized as men. I know it sounds dumb, but it happened at times. That went away a good seventy years ago, though. So, only in a few cases do people still do it. I guess they don't like the surprises or something. I don't know. Never had kids."

"But you can do it?"

"Have kids?" Sentell smiled, shrugged. "Sure. I guess I could, maybe. You know, with the right woman and all."

"You are joking with me, yes?"

"Yes, Grag. I was pulling your..." Sentell paused, not wanting to get into another explanation of expressions of the Earth languages. "...um, yes. I was joking."

"Funny." Grag didn't sound as if he truly thought it had been funny. "So, can you?"

"Of course. Sometimes a family might have a genetic proclivity for some gender-specific disease, and they will pick the other rather than gamble on the child getting the disease. One of the most common methods for determining the sex of a zygote is through what is known as preimplantation genetic diagnosis, or PGD for short. This process is typically used for medical reasons like I was saying. We can identify if a zygote carries a genetic disorder that is carried on the X or Y chromosome—in other words, sex-linked—or to help couples who are at risk of passing on a genetic disorder to their children."

"Interesting. How does it work?"

"PGD involves removing one or two cells from an embryo while it is developing. Then we analyze the chromosomes to determine the sex of it. But this is after the fact, and it won't cause the sex of the baby but will only measure it. It is done in vitro, you see. Once a zygote matching the right sex is generated, then the mother is implanted with the fertilized egg."

"This is what you have tried already, right?"

"Yes, we have done this but the zygotes we have all are male from you guys. The female zygotes we brought from Earth do implant nicely, though. For whatever reason, we can't create new ones here," Sentell explained.

"Yes, but can you choose the sex before fertilization?"

"I'm getting there." Sentell laughed and took another drink of his beer. "Just be patient."

"Sorry, Dr. Chris. I will be patient." The kid seemed hurt or nervous that Sentell was angry with him. Sentell laughed inwardly again at the communication differences. But he didn't want to get into some long-winded apology conversation either.

"Hey, no worries. We have other methods for determining the sex after the fact, like chorionic villus sampling—CVS for short. We also have noninvasive prenatal testing, which is a blood test that can be done as early as ten weeks in. Believe it or not, the mother carries fetal DNA in her blood stream at levels that are detectable."

"I believe you," Grag said seriously. Sentell tried not to laugh at the misunderstood expression as he found it to be continually amusing and an enjoyable interaction. He also thought it could be the beer.

"But to actually, truly determine—or more to the point, what we need here is to shape the sex of the zygote, well, that takes more work. The oldest method we have is to literally sort through the sperm before the zygote is made and separate them based on their X and Y chromosomes. At that point, the sorted sperm is used to fertilize the egg. We do this for in vitro fertilization—IVF—or artificial insemination. People have done it for nonmedical reasons, like I mentioned before, or because they want a boy and a girl or something. Don't know the motivations really. They vary. But it is done sometimes."

"I wish we could do it here."

"Well, back on Earth it would raise ethical concerns. For example, some people argue that using PGD or sperm sorting to select the sex of a child for non-medical reasons is some form of discrimination or some such nonsense. I don't know, maybe they think it is playing God or something. All that sounds like made-up turmoil to me—like news outlets only telling bad news instead of the good. I dunno. What it could do, though, is lead to a skewed gender ratio in a population. You know, actually, that is *exactly* what is happening here you see. So that is an example of this gone wrong. We need to figure out what went wrong."

"Yes, we do."

"Some people believe that using these methods to prevent the transmission of a genetic disorder is a form of 'genetic engineering' that raises ethical concerns too. But me, Hell, again I don't know. I think in the individual cases it's peoples' own damned business. I mean, if a couple wants enough boys for a baseball team or girls for fast-pitch softball team, whatever, that's their business. But here, well, here the problem is much bigger, and I don't know what to think."

"But, if I understand you correctly, we can choose the sex technologically to be male or female based on choice of the parents."

"Well, back on Earth we could."

"What if, Dr. Chris, that is what *is* happening here *on purpose*, or to some design?" Grag looked more serious than Sentell had ever seen him. "We now know our religion and mythologies are based on actual aliens from another world coming here and doing whatever it was they did."

"I see where you're going with this, Grag."

"Well, if you can select the sperm, couldn't the ancient ones who left have done something? Left something behind?" Grag asked.

"That is one working speculation. Not sure how to really test it as a hypothesis, though." Sentell sat his plate aside and stretched. He was full and couldn't eat another bite. The beer, on the other hand, was a different story. He was enjoying letting go and forgetting about all the craziness and friction between the locals and the Terrans. And the conversation with Grag was interesting and mentally stimulating, even with his brain dulled from the ethanol. But sometimes it was when the brain was relaxed and the stress removed that the breakthroughs happened. After all, Newton was relaxing in his family's apple orchard when he discovered his Universal Law of Gravitation.

"Hmmm, interesting, but really not sure how to test that idea," Sentell muttered again before leaning back in the chair and letting the tension flee from his body. He let out a long exhale through his pursed lips, making a motorboat sound—the old-school fossil-fuel kind.

"Not sure? How so? Just look for whatever you would do to cause the problem." Grag leaned back in his chair, sort of copying

Chris's movements. Then he stretched his feet closer to the fire to warm them. He tilted his head back and looked up at the stars. "You came from out there. Be the ancient ones. You think of how you would do this atrocity on an entire planet with your technology and knowledge. Then, learn how to undo it."

"Okay, I'll bite." Sentell looked up at the stars too. He had no idea which one was Sol or if you could even see it from where they were at that time of night. He was a research physician and biologist not an astronomer.

"There." Grag pointed. "That one is your star."

"Thanks. I see it." Sentell had no idea where the kid was pointing. He activated the star chart app in his contact lenses and let the embedded artificial intelligence find the star for him.

"Very different from our star."

"In more ways than one," Sentell agreed. "But similar in some of the best ways. Like fish and beer, for example."

Sentell nodded to the fish and then held up his bottle in the way he had taught Grag to do.

"Cheers my friend. Thanks for the great day." Sentell tapped his bottle to Grag.

"Cheers, Dr. Chris. You are very welcome."

CHAPTER 11

"Please explain again, Dr. Polkingham. How does this sperm sorting work?" Fintidierian scientist Filipineaus Cromntinier looked over his shoulder as he brought the sample into focus on the monitor.

"Well, Filip, this is called flow cytometry. We are using lasers and fluorescent dyes to sort the sperm," Polkingham replied.

"Lasers? Yes, the intense beams of light from atoms you have?"

"Well, yes, I guess that is one way to think of it, but we have lasers that are generated from various types of interactions, but they are typically due to the excitation of electron populations inverted from ground-energy population." Polkingham didn't want to get into explaining lasers. He was a biologist not a physicist. "We first have to treat the sperm with a fluorescent dye that binds to a specific protein on the sperm cell's membrane. The sperm are then passed through a flow cytometer, this thing here, which uses a laser to excite the electrons in the fluorescent dye, which then in response deexcite by releasing a light signal. The light signal is then used to sort the sperm into two populations: those that carry the X chromosome and those that carry the Y chromosome."

"And this works?" Filip asked.

"You can watch the live action here on the monitor. In this bin will be the X chromosome sperm and here the Y." Polkingham pointed to the monitor.

"Then what?"

"Aha! That is the right question." Polkingham smiled and turned to Sentell and the young Fintidierian physicist who had been assigned to him. "Once we have the sperm separated, I'll show you. Chris, have you spun up the microbots yet?"

"The computer is handshaking with them now," Sentell said over his shoulder while interfacing with the computer system across the lab. The Fintidierian scientist mouthed the words "computer is handshaking" quietly to himself, attempting to understand.

"Handshaking?" Filip asked.

"Ah, that is a word we use to say that the computer, our controller box, is connecting to the robots. Just like when people meet, they handshake."

"I see."

"Right here, Grag, that is the microbot I was describing," Sentell said as he turned back to his work.

"Why have you not done this experiment until now, Dr. Polkingham?" Filip asked.

"Well, to be honest, we didn't think of it. We've been looking for sicknesses and treatments to the overall cause rather than thinking about simply engineering the births. While we did try washing the sperm early on and using the washed mostly female sperm, it never worked. We just didn't consider brute forcing it. Dr. Sentell recently had the idea."

"Nope!" Sentell exclaimed loudly from across the lab. "Young Grag here thought of it."

"I did not, Dr. Chris. I simply asked you if it could be done," Grag said sheepishly.

"Do you have the sperm yet, Neil?"

"Yes. Done." Polkingham removed the sample from the separating device and carefully walked it to Chris's station. "Here are several thousand female chromosome sperm."

Sentell took the sample and carefully sat it in the open panel and locked it down into place. He then slid the panel closed and locked the door mechanism with a *snap* as it went into place. Once he toggled a few icons on the computer monitor, a view of swimming sperm was on the larger monitor above their heads.

"Okay, now for the egg." Polkingham nodded at Candis Twickingham, a PhD biomechanics engineer who also worked as a technician in the biolab. She was working with the miniature cryobed apparatus used to maintain the eggs that had been collected.

"The eggs have reached the appropriate temperature, Chris," she announced.

"So then, they're ready to go?" Sentell asked, not looking up from his station.

"Here. These are from sample X-138340. Fintidierian female approximately twenty-two years past puberty. The egg is viable," Dr. Twickingham said as she inserted the egg container into the microbot machine. The egg appeared almost instantly on the monitor overhead in a split section of the screen.

"Okay, now, Grag, I'll use the tweezers here . . ." Sentell explained as he worked icons on the computer. "I'll pick up the egg and plop it down in the sperm."

"This is what we have seen many times, Filip." Polkingham pointed at the screen. "At first the sperm look normal and indeed are strong swimmers. But then, the sperm seem completely uninterested in the egg once it is placed in the environment with them. We can't explain this. As soon as the egg hits the environment, the female sperm just stop swimming."

"How can that be?"

"We have no idea, yet." Sentell grunted. "But we can nudge them along."

"How so?" Filip asked.

"Microbots." Grag smiled. "From the stars."

"Well, I guess you could say that, bud." Sentell focused on his work and then suddenly a flood of small spring-shaped objects slightly smaller in length but larger in diameter than the sperm appeared on the screen. Even to the untrained scientist the image was clear. The screen showed a mix of nonmoving sperm, an egg, and a plethora of spinning springs.

"What are they?" Filip pointed.

"These are very tiny machines. Now watch as Chris controls them," Polkingham explained.

"It's like driving a remote-control drone," Sentell observed as he took the controller with both hands. He carefully used the left-thumb joystick to place crosshairs over one of the springs. The spring was suddenly highlighted on the monitor and then Sentell had control of it. "I can steer this bot anywhere I want it to go."

Sentell demonstrated a figure-eight pattern all the while describing how he was controlling the spring through magnetic fields. Then he slowly guided the spring in behind one of the docile sperm. The spring then engulfed the tail of the sperm.

"Got it," Sentell said as he guided the spring shaped bot up until only the head of the sperm was sticking out in front and the tail was protruding from the rear. "Now I have captured this sperm and I can drive it right into the egg."

The bot turned the sperm back toward the egg and Sentell steered it right into the surface. Once the bot forced the sperm through the outer membrane of the egg the magic of life suddenly began. And just like that for the first time in decades a female zygote from fully Fintidierian parents was formed.

"Voilà! We have conception," Sentell announced.

"From the stars!" Grag added.

"From the stars." Sentell smiled. "And we have all these other female sperm. Let's catalogue this zygote so it goes back to the right family and then let's impregnate another one!"

"You've done it, then?" Filip asked Polkingham.

"Well, we've gotten this far. Now we have to implant the zygote and hope the pregnancy holds," Polkingham replied. "But, while we haven't discovered the cause, we have discovered a work-around . . . perhaps."

"And this will work for any family?" Filip had tears forming at the corner of his eyes as he looked at the younger Fintidierian, Grag, who was grinning from ear to ear with joy and excitement.

"If I may," Sentell interjected. "We will fertilize several with each family set of gametes and implant up to quadruplets based on the female's health. There could be a very large boost in the female population soon."

"Dr. Cromntinier, they have saved us." Grag continued to cry tears of joy. "This could stop the riots and change our world! These people from the stars, sir, have saved us."

"Grag, buddy, it was your idea," Sentell noted. "My grandpa used to always say if you couldn't figure something out, take the day off and go fishin'. Thank you for that."

"No, Dr. Chris. Thank you!" Grag exclaimed. "And we can go fishing anytime you desire."

"Come with me, young man. It is time you meet Secretary

General Arctinier and tell her of this yourself!" Filip grabbed Grag's hand and shook it in the Fintidierian style vigorously. "My heaven, thank you, doctors!"

Filip took time to shake each of the scientists' and technicians' hands between wiping tears as they streamed down his weathered cheeks. He asked to watch the process a few more times before grabbing Grag by the arm and dragging him to the exit.

"Come, my boy. We've lots to tell the world."

CHAPTER 12

Proxima b

The cool air inside the monitoring station was a welcome respite from the heat outside. While the Proximan weather was typically mild this time of year, the local political heat was almost unbearable. For some time, the locals had gotten more and more worked up over the Terrans' presence there, and since the *Emissary* had left, many of the better-known faces like Rain and Max were gone with it. The climate was tumultuous at best.

The station, a sleek structure of some version of local concrete, metal girders, steel panels, and glass, was nestled in the midst of the alien landscape of Proxima Centauri b on the highest peak of the area the Fintidierians had set aside for the visitors from Earth. Roy Burbank adjusted his glasses and sat in front of the array of screens, the glow illuminating his determined face. Rain's instructions had been clear. She had found the original signal from Proxima back on Earth, a task that had changed the course of human history. Roy respected her brilliance and intuition, and he diligently tracked the Luyten signal now, waiting for any changes or additional information. He also kept watch on the *Emissary.* He made certain that there was a weekly upload of information beamed across space to the ship that was now nearly two thirds of a light-year away.

Roy Burbank missed seeing the superbright spacecraft passing overhead on occasion. Where there had been two, the *Samaritan* and the *Emissary*, now there was only the *Samaritan,* and it was often doing deeper solar system missions and not in any low Finti orbit. He missed some of the team who had gone on the eighteen-year one-way trip to Luyten's Star. A few he didn't really know, but he missed Rain and Max the most. They were his friends. They had been the couple that he and Chloe could invite over for dinner or cards or to shoot the breeze and hang out. But Rain and Max had been gone now for almost a year. Roy had sort of come to the conclusion that he'd never see them again. But then again, he'd once thought that about his wife and daughter, and that ended up working out pretty well. But that outcome had been completely out of his hands. Perhaps, he pondered, so was everything else. Things would work out. They would have to. He put it out of his mind. If it were meant to be that he'd see his friends again, then he'd see them and that was that. Or it was at least how he decided to compartmentalize the subject. He kept it in the same regard as all of the other craziness that was going on around the planet. Somehow, it would work itself out.

Work had even been more of a thing he had to do rather than a thing he *wanted* to do. For the first couple of months, he'd gone in day after day to maintain the dish array and the communications equipment linking them to the *Samaritan*. And he managed an uplink in the direction of the *Emissary* with daily bursts of news and data. He also maintained the communications link between Proxima b and Earth (or Sol 3 as some of the Fintidierians called it). But over time, his enthusiasm waned and now he forced himself to check everything at least once a week. Roy had plenty of other things on his to-do list as he was one of the most senior and competent hands-on engineers planetside. There was always something in need of being repaired, updated, tweaked, and the like.

He looked up from the tablet he was currently working with and out the window at the large ten-meter-diameter dish as it turned toward the Sol system. There had been something in the signal that he'd been seeing for months that didn't make any sense. Sure, the data stream from Earth was there, but there was something else: an increase in the noise floor sometimes, and then sometimes a decrease in the signal strength occurred, as if something were blocking the signal.

His fingers danced over the keyboard virtually projected in

front of him by his contact lenses, pulling up the daily data logs. The hum of the high-performance threaded multiprocessor computers whirring behind him in the large rack was comforting; the steady tone from the cooling fans had always worked better than sedatives for his nerves. This was his element. It was where he was at home—building, doing, engineering. He jumped slightly as he heard a soft background noise in the stillness of the station, like one of the local versions of a cat scurrying across the floor. Those damned things were everywhere and so far, he had yet been able to get close enough to pet one. The Radio Astronomy and Communications Ground Station was calm, and everything was running in order, well, accept for maybe that damned cat. He'd have to make sure they hadn't found a way into the place through a vent or loose panel or something.

But today, something was different. More than just the increase in the noise floor across the radio spectrum and more than a loss of signal, there was something else. As he scanned the spectrum, the large dish locked on to the signals from Earth, and the artificial intelligence and machine-learning algorithms homed in on the known signals and sources and began logging and demodulating them. But there was something unusual in the spectrum that was now well above the noise-floor background and was clearly a new source. Roy's eyes focused on the anomaly as he watched the waterfall of the RF, microwave, and terahertz spectrum pass by. A new signal, its source from the direction of Earth . . . but not. It was not at any frequency it should be if it were coming from Earth. Roy's heart raced.

"This can't be right," he whispered, recalibrating the instruments and running a diagnostic. The signal persisted, clear and strong. "Three-hundred-seventy four-point-seven gigahertz? What the hell?"

The modulated wave patterns and frequency suggested advanced technology for sure, but who used 374.7 gigahertz? Roy was certain that it was not a stray signal or a reflection, but something purposeful. He analyzed the data further and then had a thought.

"Uh, Nigel, you see this signal here?" he asked his AI as he highlighted the signal in the spectrum analyzer waterfall.

"Certainly, Roy. What would you like to know?" Nigel replied.

"If this were the *Samaritan* at top speed traveling toward us, what would the frequency be at the transmitter?" Roy rubbed his chin, realizing he hadn't shaved in a couple of days. Chloe usually reminded him of such things, or maybe she had and he was too distracted with all the repair jobs to pay attention.

"Assuming the *Samaritan* was traveling at approximately zero-point-nine-seven-c, the pre-blue-shifted frequency would be forty-six-point-three gigahertz. And it would be using a Binary Phase Shift Keying—BPSK—modulation scheme."

"Hmm. Okay then, demodulate it," Roy suggested. "Assume around that forty-six gigahertz to be the base frequency."

"I'm sorry, Roy, that didn't work," Nigel responded.

Roy thought it over in more detail. BPSK was a digital modulation technique that had been used in communication systems for more than a century and was the workhorse of long-range space communications. It represents binary data (0s and 1s) by shifting the phase of a carrier signal (RF, microwave, terahertz, optical, etc.). In BPSK, a phase shift of 180 degrees or π radians was typically used to encode one binary state, while no phase shift represented the other state.

The problem was that any transmitter moving relative to the receiver would have a so-called Doppler shift, which wasn't really a *shift* because Doppler has to do with sound. The red or blue shift in electromagnetic signals worked the same but that incorrect term continued to be used.

"We don't have the right transmitter frequency, Nigel," Roy said.

"Ah, yes of course, if the Doppler shift due to the high velocity is not properly accounted for, then it can result in a carrier frequency offset at the receiver," Nigel agreed. Roy sometimes got annoyed at how the AI would overexplain things to him. "Without the correct Doppler shift correction, the demodulation of a BPSK signal at interstellar spacecraft velocities may become impossible, and the received signal will prove impossible to be accurately demodulated."

"Haha! No kidding," Roy scoffed. "We need the transmitter frequency."

"Yes, I could start running all the base frequencies at once and demodulate the signal with each Doppler shift filter," Nigel suggested.

"Uh, hold on . . ." Roy bit at his lower lip, thinking about that course of action. "How long would that take, Nigel?"

"Uncertain. But there could be a very large range of frequencies from single-digit gigahertz up to a terahertz, with likely accuracy needed down to two decimal points," Nigel explained.

"That's like, uh, a million possible choices?"

"Correct, Roy."

"Okay, hold on. Let's try something else." Roy held up his hand as if telling someone to stop. After realizing nobody was there to see his hand gesture, he briefly laughed inwardly at himself. "Open me a channel to the *Samaritan*. Who's the CHENG now that Mastrano left on the *Emissary*?"

"That would be Bob Roca, Roy."

"Okay, get him on the line."

"Hold one minute, Roy," Nigel said.

Roy sat impatiently for a couple of moments, looking at the signal in the spectrum analyzer, whose screen literally looked like a waterfall. A blue background rolled from top to the bottom. The horizontal axis from left to right was low-frequency RF to terahertz. On the right half of the screen were two bright white lines (white being maximum measured signal strength) zigging and zagging back and forth, creating two irregular randomly moving tracks as they fell down the screen.

"Roca here." An audio channel opened almost startling Roy.

"CHENG, this is Roy Burbank down at the ground station," Roy said.

"What can I do you for, Roy? Haven't heard from you in a bit."

"Yeah, it's been a minute. Hey, man, listen, I'm detecting a radio signal coming from Earth that is blue shifted all the way up to three-seventy-four-point-seven gigahertz. I think it's a ship."

"No shit?" Roca questioned. Roy wasn't sure from his tone if he didn't believe him or was more surprised at there being possibly another ship.

"No shit," Roy retorted. "It looks like it's BPSK modulated, but we don't know the base frequency. I could have the AI run it, but it would take days. I was thinking of a quicker route."

"I'm listening."

"Well, I was thinking, if they have a Samara Drive, then you could point the optical telescope on the *Samaritan* at it and measure the optical spectrum up there. We know the Samara Drive physics. The ultraviolet light beam has a specific wavelength. You get me the color measured here and I can calculate how much it is blue shifted and therefore how fast the ship is going."

"Ah! I see. Then you can reverse calculate from the speed of the ship, the measured three-seventy-four-point-seven gigahertz signal, and apply special relativistic corrections to determine what frequency the ship is using," Roca replied. "Got it. Okay, shoot me the coordinates."

"Uh, just point the thing at Sol," Roy suggested, trying *not* to sound condescending.

"Oh, yeah, duh," Roca laughed. "I'll shoot you the spectrum in minute. Anything else?"

"Naw, that'll do it," Roy said.

"Alrighty, then. *Samaritan* out." The channel closed.

"Nigel, as soon as the spectrum gets here, run those numbers for me, okay?"

"Copy that, Roy."

Several minutes passed and then Roy's inbox dinged at him. He looked and could see it was the information from the *Samaritan.* Roca had come through. Roy opened the file making a tossing motion with his hand. The file opened virtually in front of him.

"Nigel?"

"Yes, I am working it."

"Good, let me watch."

"Sure, it is on your VR field of view now."

Roy watched as the AI expanded the multispectral image that had been taken, looking in the direction of the Sol system. The image turned into a spectral graph with the horizontal axis being wavelength short to long left to right. Then another graph appeared that looked like a single big peak with smaller sidelobes near it, looking like a sombrero centered right at 221.1 nanometers. That was the known ultraviolet spectrum of the Samara Drive measured with zero relative velocity between the ship and the sensor.

"As you can see here, Roy," Nigel interjected. "The stationary Samara Drive spectrum is centered at two-twenty-one-point nanometers. And here in the spectrum from the *Samaritan* looking back at Earth, we see known spectra from Sol and the other planets in the system. Filtering that out, we see here a spectrum centered at four-point-nine-five nanometers that looks exactly like a Samara Drive spectrum."

"Boom!" Roy slapped his hands on the tabletop so hard that the one old-school keyboard there bounced upward. "There you go, using special relativity the speed of the spacecraft must be..."

"Zero point nine nine nine times the speed of light!" Nigel exclaimed.

"Holy shit, that thing is fast!"

"Yes, it is, faster than the *Samaritan* for sure," Roca said.

"So, now we know the speed. What frequency are they broadcasting?" Roy pulled the 374.7 gigahertz signal back up on his screen.

"The base frequency is eight-point-three-eight gigahertz. Applying it to the BPSK demodulation correction now," Nigel said, and an audio signal started playing over the speakers of Roy's tablet.

". . . left Sol system approximately eighteen months ago and should arrive in the Proxima system in four Earth years. This is the interstellar ship Pioneer. *We are a privately funded effort to aid in the relief to the people and civilization of Proxima b. Our crew complement consists of one hundred and eighty women between the ages of eighteen and forty-six, twenty-two men, and various livestock samples. We are bringing modern scientific and engineering equipment and the latest research information on the genetics issues of the Fintidierian people. Our ship implements an updated Samara Drive pushing us faster than ever before. We accelerated from Mars and then left the Sol system approximately . . ."*

"Nigel, what was the date stamp on that message?" Roy asked. If they were receiving this message that was sent eighteen months after departure and they were now receiving that signal at Proxima, then they were getting close. In fact, they were probably already decelerating.

"It would appear that the signal was sent Proxima relative forty-one months ago," Nigel replied.

"Estimated arrival?"

"Six months to a year."

"Unbelievable." Captain Sam Crosby furrowed his brow as he leaned back in the command chair of the *Samaritan*. "Well, this is certainly unexpected. A private ship? Full of women volunteers and experts? That's quite the twist, isn't it? And they plan on doing what exactly?"

"You're telling me, Captain!" Roy Burbank nodded as he adjusted the shades of the ground station conference room. The evening Proximan sunlight was casting strange glares across the screen. "The *Samaritan* and *Emissary* missions were supposed to be the initial contact with the Fintidierians. Now we have another player in the mix, and they're bringing a whole lot of unknowns with them . . . and new female blood."

"Yes, but new blood under no particular command structure here." Jesus tapped his fingers nervously on the Fintidierian ash-like wooden table. "It's a delicate situation, no doubt. We need to consider the implications carefully. Who is the legal authority over them?"

"We've got to think of the best way to approach this," Cosby replied. "If they were merchant space farers then they'd be under my jurisdiction. Private citizens, well, I guess that becomes a diplomatic issue for the Fintidierians."

"Oh, they're gonna love that!" Roy muttered.

"Agreed," Jesus added. "But you are right, Captain. This is an immigration issue for the Fintidierians. We can offer some form of assistance, security, diplomacy, maybe, but this is a situation of migrants showing up on the Fintidierian border with no visas or passports."

"Well, we do have an uncomfortable decision to make here, gentlemen," Crosby started. "Do we keep it under wraps for now? I mean, we're not even sure what the Fintidierians' reaction will be."

"That's the crux of it, Captain. We've come a long way, and the Fintidierians have been more cooperative than we could have hoped," Roy said. "Right up until things went to hell and they kidnapped me and became violent toward us. Things are calmer now, but..."

"We don't want to jeopardize the progress we've made," Jesus agreed and then leaned forward toward the screen Captain Crosby was displayed on. "On the other hand, we can't keep something like this secret forever. The Fintidierians are likely to find out sooner or later. Secrets always have a way of leaking in my experience. And you say we have six months to a year until they are in the system?"

"That's right," Roy agreed.

"True, true, but right now only a few in my crew and you two know of it." Crosby made a gesture with his left hand as if to include the crew of his ship. "We should inform the Fintidierian leadership, but we need to do it carefully. We can't afford any misunderstandings or panic. And we can take our time as to when we do it. We don't have to rush and do it this week, even. We can take a month or more to think this through. We should take the time to think this through carefully. I mean, what if the Fintidierians want us to intercept them and turn them away? What then?"

"Fortunately, the Fintidierians don't use gigahertz signals yet. They're still down in the hundreds of megahertz. They are a long way from software-defined radios." Roy exhaled slowly. "They aren't likely to detect the signal. But what about any Earth transmissions directly to them? Are there amateurs broadcasting about the *Pioneer*?"

"Good point." Jesus shook his head negatively in frustration. "We'd better tell them before they find out and realize we were keeping it from them. Oh man, what a mess this is."

"Very well, we tell them. We tell them sometime soon, perhaps in the next couple of weeks." Crosby grunted. "Damnit. I'd rather have time to think these things through in more detail."

"What of the *Pioneer*?" Roy asked.

"What about it?" Jesus shrugged.

"I mean, uh, do I communicate with them?" Roy held both hands palms up. "I mean, they won't get the signal for months to a year, but when do we start communicating with them?"

"Oh, that." Crosby nodded in understanding. "No rush. I guess, let's wait until Ambassador Jesus there has a chance to write up a protocol for interacting with the Fintidierian immigration officials and then we send it."

"Ah, good idea, Captain. You could have been a politician." Jesus laughed.

"Careful, Ambassador, some would take that as fighting words," Crosby said with a smile. "I wouldn't wish your job on a yeoman."

PART 2

THE MYSTERY DEEPENS

CHAPTER 13

Proxima b

The biolab was buzzing with anticipation. It had been nearly a year since the success of using microbots to facilitate conception of a female zygote, and, in fact, several newborn Fintidierian girls had been delivered. All of them healthy, with ten fingers and ten toes—perfect little female humans. But the team faced another hurdle. While they had successfully managed to force the female sperm into the egg, they were no closer to understanding *why* the female sperm were non-motile than they had been when they arrived in the system years prior.

Dr. Polkingham brushed a red curl off his forehead using his fingers like a comb, his face etched with concentration. He intently observed the viewscreen in front of him showing the contents of a petri dish under a microscope. On the screen was a sample of the non-motile female sperm just sitting there. Oh, they could use the micromachines and push it along with magnetic fields to intercept an egg, and they had dedicated a completely new lab room for that ongoing and continuous process. The plan was to generate an assembly line of new female zygotes to be implanted into Fintidierian mothers-to-be.

The research lab had been repurposed. Now that they had discovered the main symptom, the driving goal was to uncover why that was happening.

A lot of time had passed since the groundbreaking fertilization experiment. An experiment that Dr. Sentell and Grag had conceived after a day of fishing. Polkingham was amused by that. He thought of so many great "eureka" moments throughout history where a discovery was made during the most amusing of activities. There had been the actual "eureka" moment with Archimedes. There was Newton and his apple. One of his favorites was Alexander Graham Bell's invention of the telephone. And, of course, the strange scenario around the discovery of the Samara Drive was more than amusing.

Polkingham hoped to have a moment like that someday. Maybe it would be today? He inwardly chuckled and reminded himself that those scientists made their discoveries after months, years, and decades of study and hard work. While he had worked his entire life in the field of bioengineering and genetics, he had only been on Fintidier a short while. It was beginning to seem like a lifetime.

The laboratory was alive with activity and anticipation. The viewscreens covered every wall with magnified images of sperm in various states. There were computer code and pull-down menus covering parts of several screens and atop that were the virtual screens the Terrans could access with their smart contact lenses and artificial intelligence assistants. Polkingham noticed that Grag and Professor Cromntinier, one of Fintidier's eminent scholars, stood together, trying to keep up with the flurry of movement and terminology being thrown around by the scientists from the stars. He also noticed their intrigued, yet slightly overwhelmed, expressions as he was distracted from his screen. It was then that he spotted Sentell approaching them from behind.

"Glad you two could join us for this," Sentell said as he slapped Grag on the back. "Who knows, maybe we'll figure something out today."

"Such as, Dr. Sentell?"

"Understanding the root of this fertility problem is our next challenge," Polkingham interrupted, addressing Grag and Filip with a nod to Chris. "We believe that studying the DNA of these dormant female sperm might give us insights."

"Not that we haven't been looking into this for the past year, but we have mainly been focused on getting an assembly line process in place for impregnating as many women as possible with baby girls," Sentell continued, pointing to a microscope. "Now that we've done that, and the baby girls are being delivered in a steady stream, it's time to get back to solving the underlying problem."

"What type of clues are we looking for, Doctor?" Grag asked. Polkingham could see the wonder in the young man's eyes. He could only imagine how he would feel if he were in an Atlantean lab and they were uncovering some mystery of the universe for him that was a century or more away from Terran understanding.

"First, we need to figure out if there's a genetic factor causing this dormancy," Polkingham said. "In other words, is something wrong or broken inside the sperm?"

"You see, Grag, if we can pinpoint a mutation or anomaly in the sperm's DNA, then it could give us a clearer understanding of what is going on." Sentell added, "And it's not only the DNA. Sperm motility, or how well they move, is influenced by certain proteins. We're going to take a look at that process too."

"These are the amino acids, you described?" Filip raised an eyebrow, "Proteins?"

"Okay, hang on a minute." Polkingham rubbed his chin and considered the best way to explain a twenty-first-century understanding to an early to mid-twentieth-century scientist. "So—and of course do not take this as insulting in any way or form—your civilization is a hundred and fifty to two hundred years behind ours in understanding this. I will give you a quick summary of what you need for today's conversations. It won't be enough to fully understand, but you'll get the idea and have some buzzwords to read up on. That okay?"

"Please, by all means," Filip Cromntinier responded, not insulted in the least. The wise, older Fintidierian scientist understood the knowledge gap and it was clear to Polkingham that he wanted to close that gap as best he could. Again, Polkingham thought of the Atlanteans and how much more advanced than Earth they must be.

"Okay. First, amino acids aren't proteins. They are the building blocks of proteins. Our scientists back on Earth during a similar era, say 1940, uh, a hundred and sixty-odd years ago, had identified and characterized some of the essential amino acids by then. What they knew was roughly where you guys are here on Fintidier. They are the building blocks of proteins. They understood that proteins were composed of long chains of amino acids linked together. Filip, from papers I've seen in your archives, your scholars are only now understanding this, but you don't have the equipment yet to verify this with experimentation. Ha, well, you do now."

"Yes, of course, thanks to our friends from the stars," Grag interrupted with a smile. Polkingham could see the grimace on the older Fintidierian's face, wanting the young man to be silent. But Polkingham was certain that the elder gentleman also understood that Grag and Dr. Sentell had a close friendship. Filip was wise enough to know you build bridges, not burn them.

"Proteins! Now that's what we're looking for." Sentell stepped in to cover his friend's awkward interruption. "While the concept of proteins as crucial biological molecules was known back then on Earth, the structure and function of the protein was still being explored. One of the most famous discoveries of the era was that of the protein structure, we call it the alpha helix. It was proposed by one of humanity's greatest scientists of the time, Linus Pauling, in the early 1950s, which significantly advanced our understanding of all this. Who knows, Grag, you might one day be considered one of Fintidier's greats!"

Sentell laughed and squeezed his friend's shoulder to make the point he was joking. Polkingham watched Filip carefully to see how the elder scholar reacted. The man would do well at poker. As far as Polkingham could discern, Filip made zero expression, he didn't flinch or grimace, and just kept silent. Polkingham decided he'd better step in.

"Gene expression is the key here," he started. "The understanding of gene expression and the role of DNA in this process was in its infancy during the 1940s. As far as I can tell, you guys really haven't birthed it yet. Well, Filip, I guess after today, maybe you'll have enough to write some papers on it. Anyway, our history teaches of the famous experiments by Earth scientists Avery, MacLeod, and McCarty in 1944 where they provided evidence that deoxyribonucleic acid, DNA, was indeed the genetic material responsible for transmitting inherited traits in living organisms. It took decades following their work before there was a good understanding of the mechanisms, though."

"I'm assuming you will allow us to, em . . ." Filip paused and muttered something to Grag in Fintidierian.

"'Download' is the word," Grag said.

"Ah, yes, download this information onto these information pads you have given us?" Filip asked.

"I'm assuming so." Polkingham shrugged. "I'm not sure what the protocol is on giving you reference material of a similar-era technology. We need to discuss this with Ambassador Jesus and your leadership. But, I'll say, probably."

"Yes, I understand. This is like being in"—he muttered to Grag again and then nodded—"graduate school again. Please, please continue."

"Uh, sure. Where was I?" Polkingham combed his fingers through his red curls again. "Okay, based on what we are doing today. DNA. Yeah, let's talk a bit about that. Allison, put an exploded three-D view of the double helix on screen three."

"Certainly, Neil." Polkingham's artificial intelligence assistant said through speakers on the screens. Filip and Grag were slightly startled, but they were getting used to the Terrans talking to computers and the computers talking back to them as if they were alive.

"Ah, yes, look at this twisted-ladder-looking structure here. It's called a double helix and was proposed by James Watson and Francis Crick. It was not discovered until 1953, Earth time. This discovery marked a pivotal moment in molecular biology and genetics and every kid in ninth grade biology back on Earth studies this. This structure consists of two long chains made up of nucleotides running in opposite directions. Each nucleotide comprises three components: a sugar molecule—deoxyribose—a phosphate group, and a nitrogenous base. There are four types of nitrogenous bases in DNA: adenine (A), thymine (T), cytosine (C), and guanine (G). And it is these long, combined sequences of these nitrogenous bases that are the instructions, the code that determines the order of amino acids in a protein and in turn expresses the organisms' traits and functions."

"And, Grag ol' boy, it is the expression of function that we are looking for here," Sentell added, pointing to the screen showing the magnified sperm.

"I think I see," Grag said unsurely.

"Yes, I actually do, my boy," Filip stated. "There are these twisted, em . . . double helix, structures that are inside the sperm. They are the instructions for what the sperm is and does. Correct?"

"Yes." Polkingham nodded in the affirmative.

"These sequences of amino acids are instructed to build certain proteins that in turn trigger further actions to occur." Filip looked back at Polkingham with a raised eyebrow for reassurance.

"Yes, that's it in a nutshell." Polkingham smiled and waved his hand in the air, bringing the previous view of the microtweezers back on the screen. "Back on Earth, we have identified an ion channel protein complex found in the tails or flagella of sperm. This cation channel of sperm as it is known is called CATSPER for short. See, cation, CAT, sperm, SPER, CATSPER. Well, this protein is essential for the hyperactive movement of sperm. If there's any issue with its expression, it could lead to reduced motility."

"So, we're looking at it today," Sentell said.

"I see." Filip, trying to follow, asked, "So, how do we look at the DNA?"

"Great question. And it isn't an easy answer." Sentell smiled, holding up a vial of clear liquid. "We use this. It's a hypotonic solution. When we introduce the sperm to this solution, it causes them to swell. Eventually, they rupture, explode, releasing their DNA strands for us to collect and study."

"Amazing!" Grag looked fascinated. "So, it's like... a *farvgatiera*?"

"Yes, I see my boy!" Filip agreed. "Indeed, a farvgatiera!"

"Uh, I'm sorry, you've got me on that one." Sentell shrugged at Polkingham.

"Me too?" Polkingham thought through the Fintidierian he knew, and he could honestly say he'd never heard that word. "Fahhv gacheria?"

"Farvgatiera," both Filip and Grag repeated in unison.

"Allison, can you help me out with that?"

"Yes, Neil. The farvgatiera is a ceremonial object made in the shape of the pyramidal ruins in the far eastern continent of Fintidier. It is used in the marriage ceremony. The bride and groom fill the structure with items of various nature to be gifts for someone, usually the children, involved in the wedding ceremony. The object is placed atop the *sratgav* and the wedding party children take turns striking it with the staff of *gachron*. Once it has been hit ample times, the structural integrity of the farvgatiera fails, disseminating the gifts."

"A piñata!" Sentell laughed. "Hell yes, that's a perfect analogy. There are goodies inside the farvgetiera and we need to poke it until they are released so we can collect them."

"Hahaha," Polkingham chuckled. "In a manner of speaking,

yes. Once we have cracked the, *farv . . . farhveg . . .* the piñata, the DNA is expelled and we can analyze it, comparing the dormant sperm to the active ones."

"Very good." Filip thought for a moment and then asked, "And the proteins?"

"We'll analyze them too," Sentell said. "There's a method we use called proteomics. It allows us to see all the proteins present in the sperm. If something's amiss, then this should highlight it."

"Pin-yah-ta." Grag looked between the two scientists, admiration in his eyes. "Every day, I learn so much from you both. It's incredible."

"And we learn from you, Grag. *Farvgetiera*? That right?"

"Your Fintidierian is very good," Grag replied with a grin.

CHAPTER 14

Proxima b

The chamber was circular, its walls adorned with intricate Fintidierian patterns that resembled a mix of Earth's Western Victorian and Empire styles. Dark, intricately carved Fintidierian hardwood shoe moldings nearly fifteen centimeters high transitioned the equally dark stonework floor into the deep reds and violets on the wall. The walls were decorated with carvings and artwork depicting geometric shapes and motifs similar to the glyphs found on the ancient architecture from around the planet. The crown moldings at the top, where the walls met the ceiling, were highly detailed carvings of creatures and plants woven together like of a continuous living vine. The ceiling had a large skylight feature surrounded by winged catlike creatures remarkably similar to the griffin of Earth mythology.

The central chamber of the Fintidier General Assembly glowed softly under the ambient light filtering in through the skylights that ran along the ceiling at the periphery of the room. At the center stood a large obsidian table, its surface reflecting the room's subtle illumination. At the table there were seven seats on one side. The tallest chair in the middle was for the secretary general. On either side of her were chairs for the representatives of the six provinces of Fintidier. On the other side of the obsidian table were an equal number of seats, but all the same height, for petitioners of the General Assembly.

Secretary General Balfine Arctinier, the chief executive of

Fintidier; General Rabine Tintinier; Lortay Vistra, the Fintidierian secretary of internal security; Harma Oo'ortaga, the Fintidierian secretary of commerce; Dr. Zhouzine Hallisier, the Fintidierian chief government scientist; and Professor Filipineaus Cromntinier all represented the Fintidierians. The seat to the far right was empty. On the petitioner's side, Ambassador Charles Jesus, Captain Sam Crosby of the *Samaritan*, Dr. Roy Burbank, and Dr. Neil Polkingham sat quietly.

"Thank you for joining us today." General Tintinier opened the discussion, his voice echoing slightly in the mostly empty chamber. "The arrival of another Terran ship is of concern to us. Your people are already here, assisting us, and now another vessel approaches our world. We seek clarification."

"Thank you for having us in your inner government chambers. It is our honor to be here. Although . . . we could have done this in your office, Madam Secretary General." Jesus nodded, understanding Tintinier's apprehension. "The *Pioneer*, which is the name of the vessel approaching, is not a vessel sent by our governments. It is privately funded, born from our world's entrepreneurial spirit. Its intentions, as stated, are peaceful."

"You like the central chamber, Ambassador? It is quite beautiful, if not overtly ceremonial." Arctinier leaned forward, gesturing at the government chamber.

"Madam Secretary General, it is an astonishing piece of architecture and décor. It rivals any of our government and historical buildings back on Earth," Jesus replied. He smiled faintly at her, hoping to touch on the comradery and rapport they had built over the past couple of years.

"To be honest, Charles, this is the only place I trust not to have eyes and ears hidden away," she explained, returning his smile. The lines at the corner of her lips betrayed her age. "While we appreciate the aid your people have provided, especially in our fertility crisis, we must tread carefully. Our history with outsiders, especially the Atlanteans, was not peaceful. And while this recent and wonderful boom in baby-girl deliveries has calmed my people and generated a slight uptick in the downward-spiraling morale we have faced for so long, we just . . ."

Jesus met her gaze, waiting for her to finish her sentence. She took a long pause and her shoulders and head slumped. Jesus wasn't sure if she was giving up or was simply tired.

"...we need to be careful here," she finished. "Please, tell us more about this ship and what their intentions are."

"I understand your reservations, Madam Secretary General. And I wish I could absolutely guarantee you that there is nothing but positive intent coming with this new ship. Honestly, I can't." Jesus paused, expecting some reaction from the Fintidierians, but there was none. So he continued. "You have to understand that Earth itself is a melting pot of various cultures, ideologies, and beliefs. The *Pioneer* represents the side of Earth that believes in exploration and trade, in mutual benefit, and in accomplishing that benefit outside of the need for anything more than permission to explore at one's own risk."

"So, these 'explorers' built a starship and decided to give up their lives back in your star system. And they are now coming here to start new lives?" Harma Oo'otaga asked. Jesus wasn't certain if she was being rhetorical or if it was truly a question.

"If I may," Captain Crosby interrupted. "Earth's history is filled with 'missionaries' traveling from country to country or from one disaster or war zone to another to aid the people in need. These missionaries typically do this out of the kindness of their own hearts. We call them 'humanitarian efforts.' While there are and have been cultures and religions that go and offer help and aid and then take the opportunity to sway the locals toward some deity or form of government, that certainly wasn't the case for the *Samaritan* and the *Emissary* coming here. And I might also add, Madam Secretary General, that many of these private efforts are also clever businesspeople who imagine new types of commerce that usually end up beneficial on both ends."

"Well, Captain, commerce is my job. If these new 'missionaries,' as you called them, are bringing opportunity, then I will certainly be interested in learning more," Harma replied.

"I couldn't have said that better, Captain. Thank you." Jesus nodded in acknowledgment toward the captain. "Indeed, Madam Secretary General, we're here to ensure that both our worlds benefit from our presence here. New commerce might be one benefit."

"Benefit?" General Tintinier, a staunch traditionalist, leaned forward, scowling. He rested both hands down on the obsidian table as if he needed to prop his large muscular torso upright. "Benefit? Ever since you Terrans arrived, we've faced challenges we never did before. Don't mistake our hospitality for naivete.

It takes years to traverse the gulf between the stars. That is far too slow for any real commerce benefit. What other benefit?"

"General!" Arctinier motioned for him to sit. "When was the last time hundreds—is that right, Dr. Hallisier... hundreds?"

"At present, Madam Secretary General, one thousand seven hundred nineteen viable female babies have been delivered alive and well within the last three months, whereas the number prior to our guests' visit here was in the single digits per year," Dr. Hallisier replied.

"One thousand seven hundred nineteen!" Arctinier repeated. "In the last three months? Are we expecting that to stop or will there be more?"

"If I may, Madam Secretary General?" Polkingham raised his hand.

"Yes, Dr. Polkingham?"

"That number will increase daily. We have an assembly-line process now where we are preparing the sperm, the egg, performing assisted fertilization, and implanting them," Polkingham said nervously. "This birth rate should continue. And if the *Pioneer* is bringing similar equipment with it, then we can build a second facility in another location on the planet and double the female birth rate."

"Do you hear that, Rabine?" Arctinier relaxed back into her seat. "Charles, Dr. Polkingham, Captain, all of you, thank you. Sincerely, thank you."

"You are welcome, Madam Secretary General," Jesus said as the others nodded.

"So, great news, yes," she continued. "But there is always the other part of the story. What else do we need to know about this *Pioneer*?"

"Em, before we move on, Madam Secretary General, if I may?" Filip leaned toward her, looking for approval to continue.

"Please, Professor."

"I would like to point out that while we are seeing great strides to saving our people and these births are nothing short of a miracle, even the Terrans still do not have an answer to what is causing this problem," Filip explained.

"The current solution is working for now and the foreseeable future, I'm told," Dr. Hallisier, the chief scientist, interjected. "Yet, we still don't have a permanent solution. Your arrival and actions have most certainly awakened hope, but we've yet to see lasting results, a cure."

"Um, yes, ma'am. That is true. We found a work-around to the problem. But we're not giving up on finding a total solution," Polkingham responded. "The fertility crisis is complex, and while we've made strides, there's still work to be done. We've managed to help some, but understanding its root cause takes time. We do have a pathway to potentially understanding the root cause and Dr. Cromntinier has been there with us every step of the way."

"If I may?" Roy raised his hand. Jesus motioned to him to lower his hand. Roy waited.

"Dr. Burbank?" Arctinier nodded to him.

"There might also be a solution out there." Roy pointed upward to space. "Our friends left aboard the *Emissary* on a dangerous, arduous, and unknown journey into deep space, chasing down these potential Atlanteans who appear to have been responsible for your problems to begin with."

"Thank you for that input, Dr. Burbank. And thank all of you." Balfine raised a hand, silencing the room. "The challenges we face are immense, but they aren't insurmountable. What we need is to ensure transparency and collaboration."

"Collaboration and transparency, other than some earlier missteps, has always been our goal. We truly are here to help Madam Secretary General," Jesus declared as he made eye contact with everyone in the room sequentially. So far, he had been letting this conversation freewheel to wherever it evolved. But he knew he didn't have all day with Balfine Arctinier. She was the leader of the entire planet. She was busy. He needed to start getting to the point. "Agreed. And with the recent signal from the *Pioneer*, another Terran ship filled with equipment and personnel, there's potential for more resources, expertise, and solutions."

"Concerning that." Lortay Vistra, the Fintidierian secretary of internal security, looked skeptical. "Another Terran ship? How do we know their intentions align with yours? How many more will come?"

"Good questions. As far as how many more will come? Who knows? Maybe none, maybe many." Jesus sighed and shrugged. "The *Pioneer* is a privately funded mission, independent of our official initiative. But their stated goal is trade and collaboration. We need to be open, but cautious. And I have to point out that, while they must answer to the laws of our world, they have left that world and traveled here. They are private citizens and are not under governance by our military or space merchants, but only the laws of Earth, which is a long way away."

"What are you suggesting, Ambassador?" General Rabine asked.

"My suggestion is that the people of the *Pioneer* will answer to Earth if they violate any laws of Earth and or create diplomatic issues with Fintidier," Jesus explained. "But they are migrants traveling on a vessel compelled only by their own free will to your border. I suggest the Fintidierian government must apply some form of immigration policies and laws to govern their interactions."

"And how do we do that?" General Tintinier slammed his hand on the table, his deep-set eyes flaring with intensity. "Another ship from Earth not under your legal authority? This is unprecedented! It is for us to govern? How do you suppose we do that? Hmm? We have no spaceships!"

"Captain Crosby, feel free to jump in here," Jesus urged, nodding to his colleague.

"Oh, yes, sure, Charles." Crosby cleared his throat. "As Charles said a moment ago, we will most certainly hold them to the laws of our world. If they show up here and start causing problems, then the full security force of the *Samaritan* will be at your disposal. And, if we need to take a team up to their ship, then we will absolutely oblige you with shuttle transport as needed. Perhaps that might be the right approach. Think of whatever inspections you might want to put them through before disembarking and we will support you in that effort. And once you are comfortable with their motivations and are ready to allow them planetside, then and only then can they come down. The *Samaritan* will enforce whatever policy you need in this regard."

General Tintinier sat back in his chair, clearly pondering Crosby's offer. Jesus watched as Secretary General Arctinier eyed the man and read his body language. The general appeared to be momentarily appeased.

"I do have a question about the personnel," Arctinier said in a very calm voice. She seemed more curious than anything as far as Jesus could tell. "The information you have given us shows a majority of single women aboard, willing to start a new life here. It's clear they have done their research and are aware of our... predicament. But, Charles, why would they do this?"

"Adventure? A new start on life? Earth's history, mythologies, and even literature and entertainment are filled with stories of leaving one's home on an adventure to a new place to start a new life." Jesus cleared his throat. "The gender crisis here on Proxima Centauri b is known to everyone on Earth. The *Pioneer*'s initiative might simply be a response to that, a way to forge a bond between our worlds while offering a new start to any who volunteered to leave the past behind and forge into a brave new unknown world."

"While nearly two hundred women is barely a solution, I am certain many men here will welcome them." Dr. Hallisier added. "It's also an opportunity for genetic diversity, something our research has shown we desperately need."

"But at what cost?" General Tintinier asked. "We are only now beginning to understand and trust the first two groups from Earth. Now we have a whole new batch, and their intentions are tied to the very core of our society."

"It's not just about intentions." Filip spoke up. "It's about integration. How do we ensure these Terran women integrate into our society without upheaval?"

"It will require understanding, patience, and cultural exchange," Jesus replied. "We will need to set up programs to ensure smooth integration. Cultural classes, language courses, societal norms discussions. But I suspect these are not average Terrans. If they gave up their lives, managed to be chosen by whoever funded this mission, and traversed the stars to come here, then they must be exceptional."

"Exceptional indeed, Charles my friend," Balfine interjected. "This is a delicate situation. We need to handle it with care. The last thing we want is further division and misunderstandings. Charles, you have experience dealing with both Terran and Findidierian perspectives. I hope you will continue to be a valued partner in our future efforts. These must be extraordinary women to do such a thing. It is unbelievable."

"Well, not really from an Earth history perspective, Madam Secretary General," Jesus stated matter-of-factly. "Hundreds of years ago, during the settlement of the western frontier of the USA, men significantly outnumbered women. To address this imbalance and to foster communities, women from Eastern cities and other countries moved west to marry men they'd often never met. It was a pragmatic solution for that time and place."

"Truly?" Dr. Hallisier leaned forward, her curiosity emphasized with a gasp. "Were these unions successful? Were they based on mutual respect and understanding?"

"Hmm, I guess so. Probably in more cases than not." Jesus tilted his head, considering her question. "It varied. Many couples found mutual respect and built families together. Others faced challenges. But it was a reflection of the needs and challenges of that time. The situations were complex and diverse, just as ours is now, here."

"Pardon my skepticism," General Tintinier huffed. "But this is different. Our entire species' future is at stake. We can't simply rely on history from another planet."

"We don't have to," Jesus replied. "It's worth noting that Earth has faced similar challenges and found solutions. The *Pioneer* may have taken a leaf from history, but their intentions seem genuine. Besides, the *Samaritan* and the *Emissary* have set precedents for human-Finti interactions."

"And will continue to do so," Captain Crosby added.

"What's essential is that we approach this with openness but also with a sense of caution." The secretary general looked around the table and held her gaze with each of the Terrans for a brief moment. Then she turned to her colleagues. "Let's remember, we're not just integrating individuals, we're melding cultures and traditions. And we are creating a future for Fintidier that includes the Terrans in it. Without the Terrans, I dare say, Fintidier had no future."

CHAPTER 15

Proxima b

"Yoko, we need to figure out if there's a genetic factor causing this dormancy," Polkingham said, transferring the captured sperm into a specialized container. "We've been at this for months and we've yet to find the culprit of the zero motility of female gene-carrying sperm."

"Maybe today is our lucky day, Neil." Dr. Yoko Pearl nodded. The Japanese scientist had come to Proxima b on the *Samaritan* as an expert in pathology and genetics. Since Mak had gone on the *Emissary* and Thomaskutty was killed by the Atlantean, she had also taken over as the main physician for the *Samaritan* and ground teams. When there was a break in the day-to-day doctoring of broken bones or sinus infections, she spent her time in the lab with Polkingham and the research effort. "Agreed. If we can pinpoint a mutation or anomaly in the DNA, it could give us a clearer understanding."

"That is the hope," Sentell agreed with them without looking up from his screens. He and his ever-present shadow, Grag, were in the lab as often, if not more often, than even Polkingham. Sentell sat in front of his computer interface displaying a complex, swirling model of DNA strands. Grag sat right behind him looking over his left shoulder, often pointing at the screens and asking questions. Polkingham made a mental note of how well the two worked together. Sentell had sort of taken on the role of mentor to the young Fintidierian scientist; perhaps that was the way to grow the trust between the two civilizations. He would discuss the idea of mentors with Jesus at some point in the near future.

"Agreed," Polkingham said as he nodded.

"We've already prepared the sequencer. Once we break apart the sperm and extract its DNA, then we can compare it with the DNA of motile male sperm and pinpoint if there are any differences," Sentell announced.

"The microscope is continuous, correct, Dr. Chris?" Grag asked. No matter how many times they had told the young Fintidierian to stop with the formal titles, he persisted.

"Well, we have two things going on here, Grag," Sentell replied, until now focused on the multiple windows open on his screen along with several virtual ones open via his smart contacts. "We have a high-resolution optical microscope running at sixty frames per second. We can see a sperm with it, but you won't see inside or anything much smaller than the sperm with that technology. At the same time, we have a high-speed scanning electron microscope capturing the same image. The SEM is running at ten frames per second, and believe me, it is an engineering marvel. SEMs are usually one-shot devices, or, at best, provide one image every few seconds. This one here is—or was when we left Earth—the fastest SEM on the planet. The optical image and the SEM images are blended inside the computer using special machine learning software. What we get as a result is what we see on the screen—a full three-dimensional representation of the tiny object being observed."

"So, not continuous," Grag responded, but it was clear from the tone of his voice he was unclear about it.

"You realize that the human eye has an integration time of a twenty-fifth of a second or so, right? In other words, anything faster than twenty-five hertz and the eye doesn't see it," Sentell explained.

"I'm sorry. I didn't realize that." Grag frowned. "But it makes sense."

"Are you finished yet, Chris?" Dr. Pearl asked.

"Uh, almost . . . Now." Sentell tapped in some instructions and waved his hands around in his virtual environment. "Look, there it is, Grag. Filip, you might want to see this too. The sperm has now ruptured and these strands here are the DNA."

"Fascinating," both Grag and Filip mouthed.

"That is actually the genetic code for a human?" Filip asked.

"Yep."

"Amazing thing to behold." Filip continued to watch the screen closely. Polkingham was certain that the Fintidierian senior scholar was truly mesmerized by the abilities of Terran technology.

"Okay, Yoko. I've collected both sets of samples and transferring the strands to you now," Sentell said. There were sounds of motion and some whirring coming from the instruments on the lab bench and then Pearl made a happy sound.

"Hey, there you are," she said to nobody in particular. Once isolated, Pearl began the sequencing. "Okay, I suggest everyone go get a cup of coffee. It will take fifteen minutes for the sequencing to take place."

"But you should have seen the look on Dr. Chris's face when that skiezel skipped from the water, trying to throw his lure," Grag continued with the fishing story as the team sat in the break room waiting for the gene sequencing to be completed.

"Like largemouth bass back on Earth," Sentell added.

Pearl sat and quietly listened to the conversation. She sipped her coffee slowly and peered around the breakroom thinking about how some things were universal. Had she not known she was on a planet in a star system light-years from Earth, she could have believed this was any old break room in any old science or university building.

The room was a dull-gray-painted Fintidierian concrete block that the Terrans had retrofitted with instant hot and cold vending machines, a refrigerator, kitchen appliances, and several monitor screens mounted on the walls. The tables were a combination of pressed wood laminates and steel. The chairs were of similar construction. The monitors in the background were playing local broadcasts that were now updated to Terran broadcast resolution. That was a technology the Fintidierians would not have had for decades or more. On one monitor some local daytime talk show was playing. On another was a twenty-four-hour news channel, which hadn't existed until the Earthlings began interacting with the Proximans.

"I think you are embellishing this story a bit, Grag." Sentell laughed around a mouthful of pie that he quickly washed down with coffee. "I have caught bigger fish on Earth before... much bigger."

"Ah, but never a skiezel on an alien world," Professor Filipineaus Cromntinier laughed as he corrected him. "There is a different, my friend. We all recall the first time we landed a skiezel!"

"Touché," Sentell agreed. The two Fintidierians looked confused. At that, Polkingham burst into laughter.

"Tew... shaaye?" Grag repeated.

"A competition sword-fighting term that means 'I touched you with my sword.' You stabbed me or poked me or got me with your joke or response," Sentell explained. "Filip is correct. That *was* the first skiezel—hell, fish—I'd caught on an alien world. So, touché!"

"Have you been in a sword fight, Dr. Chris?" Grag asked. "Is that common on Earth?"

"Give up, Chris." Polkingham continued to laugh. "The nuances of slang, quips, and evolved and mingled languages are beyond the best linguists in the galaxy."

"Uh, no, Grag. I've never even touched a sword, I don't think. I mean a real one," Sentell explained, and Pearl watched the expression on his face change to a look as if he were recalling some old memory. "Well, when I was a kid, I had a toy sword."

"I fenced in the Olympics when I was younger," Pearl interjected. Talking of swords certainly stirred old memories within her.

"Really?" Polkingham asked. "The Olympics? Then you must be quite good."

"I didn't medal. But I made it to the medal rounds." Pearl used her fork to move the pie around on her saucer. She hadn't really wanted it and there was something about the local citrus fruits that didn't agree with her.

"Olympics. Hmmm, yes, I've seen some of your videos on that." Filip turned to look at her. "A global competition, correct?"

"Yes," she said. "They are played every four years. Summer and winter events are staggered by two. I represented Japan—the country I am from on Earth."

"You must be quite amazing to be able to represent your entire country! The range of expertise of you Terrans never ceases to amaze me." Filip smiled at her. Pearl liked the elder scholar. She guessed that to the Fintidierians the man was like an Einstein or Feynman or Crick or Darwin, and that wasn't lost on her.

"Yoko, the sequencer has completed its task." Pearl's AI

assistant, Amico, alerted her sub-audibly so only she could hear it. "Would you like me to send you the results now?"

"Thank you, Professor." She bowed her head slightly in respect. "Now if you'll excuse me, I think the genetic sequencing is complete. Let me check on it."

"By all means!" Filip sounded excited.

"Absolutely." Pearl stood to excuse herself. "Give me ten minutes or so to arrange the data in a more easily understood format. I'll send Neil a call when I get that done."

"We'll be here. Call as soon as you're ready." Polkingham gave her a look of reassurance and nodded.

Pearl began looking through the results on the virtual screens in front of her as she walked down the hall toward the lab entrance. A DNA helix appeared in front of her with labels of A, T, C, and G spread about it. There were millions of base pairs connected along the model. Several graphs popped up beside the helix giving summaries of the various pertinent bits of data including a histogram of the base quality scores, the GC content, and from some of the graphs arrows pointed back toward specific locations on the DNA chain.

A second DNA chain then appeared with similar pop-out graphs and charts. The two chains each used half of the field of view of the virtual screen. The left side of the virtual screen was labeled as the "male" sperm motility sample and the right side was labeled as the "female" one. There were clear differences pointed out between them, but only the ones that would be expected from sequencing errors and variations. These sections were highlighted from red to green based on the level of confidence or severity of the error. As time progressed, the automated sequencing system continued gathering data and the errors decreased and confidence scores rose.

Pearl sat down at her station in the lab and tossed her virtual screens up onto the surrounding big screens on the walls. She leaned back in her chair and studied the data. She was looking for some smoking gun as to why the female sperm were not motile. There was nothing that jumped out specifically from a visual perspective. The difference might be very subtle.

"Amico," she addressed her AI assistant, "show me the CATSPER genes."

"Certainly, Yoko," Amico replied. "The CATSPER sequences are located here and here."

A section on each of the genetic strings lit up brighter than the others. Pearl looked closely, but soon realized that from that perspective it would have been like trying to read a street sign from orbit. This one section alone probably consisted of thousands of base pairs. There were what appeared to be random strings of GCAT—guanine, cytosine, adenine, and thymine combinations—in various orders.

"Show me a statistical comparison of the two sections."

"Certainly, Yoko."

A graph appeared near each of the highlighted sections showing statistical distributions of the various bases. At first there was very little noticeable difference between the two other than ones expected between male and female sperm. There was really nothing specifically unusual about either. She frowned and squinted her eyes a bit, forcing herself to concentrate deeper into the dataset. What was in there that she was missing?

"I don't see any major differences, do you?" Pearl asked her AI.

"The statistical variations in the CATSPER channel seem to be within a standard deviation of each other and nothing out of the ordinary," Amico replied.

"Damn it." Pearl rubbed the inside of her right hand with her left thumb unconsciously. "I thought for sure we'd find something there. Did we run a full-spectrum sequencing?"

"Yes."

"Show me the list," Pearl requested. Then a list scrolled in front of her of the types of sequencing that had been implemented to generate these results with the textbook descriptions that likely were pulled straight from the software's help menu. It began with Sanger Sequencing* and ended with Long-Read Sequencing.*

Pearl read carefully through the assay of tests that had been run. She wasn't certain exactly which sequencing techniques in particular might tell her something, but one of them must have uncovered something. She read and reread them slowly until she was distracted by the chatter of her colleagues coming down the hall. As of yet, she wasn't sure there was anything to show them or discuss. There was a lot of data here and it needed much more scrutiny.

"Hmmm, Amico, give me a side-by-side comparison of the two samples, one sequencing technique at a time."

---

* For more information, please refer to the Afterword.

"Very well," Amico replied, and instantly new graphs and data scrolled on the screen.

"Run a pattern-recognition algorithm and cross-correlate each set. Highlight any major differences."

"Understood."

". . . and he ate every one of the egg pouches too. He would have drunk the Firestarter fuel if I hadn't stopped him because it was wood alcohol," Grag was saying as Sentell held the door.

"The beer was plenty, Grag. You exaggerate." Sentell laughed. "Besides, I could tell by the smell it was methanol."

Polkingham looked at Pearl and she quickly did a very subtle negative head shake that he was likely to be the only one to notice. But then she saw Sentell raise an eyebrow slightly as he glanced back and forth between Polkingham and her. She could see his body language slump as if in defeat.

"Ah, Dr. Pearl." Filip smiled softly as he approached. "I can see by the screens here that there is much data. I hope our young friend's storytelling hasn't interrupted you at an inopportune moment."

"Storytelling . . . ah?" Pearl looked up, distracted.

"Don't pay any attention to it, Yoko," Sentell grunted cheerfully. "Grag thinks I don't understand the difference between ethyl and methyl alcohols."

Pearl nodded unconsciously in response. She wasn't really paying attention to them. She was completely absorbed in the genetic sequencing of the sperm. What was all the prattle regarding methyl and ethyl alcohol?

". . . methyl alcohol . . ." she muttered under her breath as if it had triggered something in her mind.

"What's that?" Filip raised an eyebrow at her as she cocked her head sideways and looked in his general direction, focused at nowhere in particular, but her mind started to focus on something.

"Amico! Scroll the sequencing tests list on the screen."

"Certainly, here it is," the AI replied.

"Lucky number seven!" Pearl exclaimed.

"Yoko? You on to something?" Polkingham sat in the chair next to her and looked at the screen in front of her.

"Hold on." She held a hand up, motioning him not to distract her chain of thought. "Amico. Give me the two sequences with test number seven only—the methyl sequencing."

"Understood."

The two strands appeared on the screen with a title above each stating that they were "Bisulfate Methyl Sequences" of each sample. The CATSPER regions were highlighted. Pearl reached up into the air in front of her, grabbed the regions of both, and expanded them.

"Amico, show me a comparison of the number of methylated CpG island base pairs," she said excitedly. Pearl felt a flush in her body. Her heart rate increased a bit. She felt a rush of excitement almost as engulfing as the pre-match jitters she experienced before an Olympic qualifying duel against a world-class athlete.

Two histograms appeared on the screen. One showed the number of methylations for base pairs of the male sperm CATSPER region and the other for the female sperm CATSPER region. The histogram on the left showed that the male sperm had zero methylated base pairs with a confidence of eighty-seven percent. The one on the right showed that the female sperm had eighty-two percent of the base pairs attached to a methyl group with a confidence of ninety-one percent.

"Got you!" Pearl slammed both palms onto the table in excitement. "Holy shit!"

CHAPTER 16

Proxima b

"Holy shit!" Polkingham echoed, looking at the screen and probably not even realizing that Pearl had just said the exact same thing.

"Methylation?" Sentell said out loud and directed toward nobody in particular. "Methylation . . . hmmmm."

"We've found it! Filip, we've found it!" Polkingham declared, excitedly pointing at the multicolored charts and the exploded view of the CATSPER genes on the screen.

"What have we found, Neil?" Filip asked.

"Dr. Chris?" Grag looked at him with wild-eyed excitement.

"Dr. Pearl," Polkingham cleared his throat loudly to calm the room. "Would you please explain methylation to Professor Cromntinier?"

"Uh, certainly." Pearl made a couple of hand-waving motions in front of her and expanded the section of the CATSPER gene on the female sperm sample. "You see, Professor, DNA methylation involves the addition of methyl groups, one carbon atom covalently bonded to three hydrogen atoms, to specific regions of DNA. We are interested in sperm motility, so we are looking closely at this gene sequence here, the CATSPER genes. You see, the genes aren't supposed to have these methyl groups bonded to them here and here and here. This 'methylation' leads to gene silencing or reduced gene expression. In other words, if DNA methylation were to occur in the regulatory regions of CATSPER genes in female human sperm, it might affect the function of CATSPER channels, which are essential for the elevation of intraflagellar calcium and the induction of hyperactivated motility in sperm."

"I'm not sure I see." Filip looked puzzled.

"Simply put, sir"—Pearl smiled—"these genes here make the sperm swim. These methyl groups on them turn off those genes and therefore keep the sperm from swimming."

"Ah." Filip leaned in closer to the screen and studied the sequence. "A switch to turn the tails on and off."

"Exactly," Polkingham agreed.

"That's our smoking gun. But why? I mean, why are they methylated and others are not?" Sentell asked.

"Would this, em, methylation as you call it, be hereditary?" Grag asked. The strange Fintidierian stammers and studders in his conversational skills continued to improve but were still quite noticeable.

"Great question, Grag," Sentell said. "Yes. This is a particular genetic modification that would be passed on to the offspring."

"Troubling." Filip watched with bated breath, his eyes darting between the team and the displays. "So, you're suggesting this problem might be genetic and not environmental?"

"It's a possibility," Polkingham replied, pointing at the methylated gene base pairs. "But something caused this. It's too specific. How did *these* genes only become hyper-methylated while no others have? So, while it is genetic, the cause of it came from within the environment. Now the question we need to be asking is, was it natural or not?"

"Well, assuming that... Hang on," Pearl said and held up her left hand. "Amico, full statistical analysis across both samples. Any other sequences unusually methylated?"

"Processing..." Amico replied. "No other base pair island groups are methylated."

"And what are the odds of that occurring by accident, randomness, or natural causes?" Polkingham added.

"The statistical analysis suggests that the specific targeted genes could not be methylated so concisely by random events within the lifetime of the universe," Amico explained.

"Dr. Polkingham," Grag asked hesitantly, "you know our legends speak of the Atlanteans and their incomprehensible powers, which we now understand were technologies. Could it be possible . . . that they left behind some form of tiny machinery that's affecting our sperm?"

"You mean like nanomachines, Grag?" Polkingham asked.

"Yes." Grag nodded. "Machines so tiny they could influence or tamper with our biological functions at a cellular level. Machines that could place these, em, methyl groups on the sperm cells in just the right places, the same way you are using the little machines to move the female sperm to the egg?"

"Such a machine would have to be incredibly tiny!" Filip exclaimed. "And if it's affecting every single sperm, there would need to be . . . trillions of them?"

"Well, I wonder about that," Sentell added. "Given the size of a sperm, if a machine were to interfere with it, then the machine would have to be in the tens to hundreds of nanometers in scale. But we've examined the sperm under scanning electron microscopy, as you see on that screen there, and we haven't seen anything out of the ordinary. No nanomachines or viruses. No . . . nothing."

"Well, wait a minute, Chris." Pearl held up her hand again. "Just because we haven't seen them doesn't mean they aren't around. Since these modifications to the CATSPER genes are indeed hereditary, the grandparents or great-grandparents and so on could have been infected generations before."

"Hey, Yoko, you might be right." Polkingham seemed to be on to an idea. "The machine—if it *is* a machine; hell, it could even be a virus with the right payload—could have been around a long time ago. Think about it. The female population started dropping off more recently at rapid rates. We've modeled this and it actually fits a reverse-population-growth model of a species with no known predators."

"Please elaborate on that, Neil," Filip requested.

"Certainly If you take the a given population of skiezel, for example, and put them in a pond with plenty of food and no predators, they will grow with a known birth rate nonlinearly until the pond becomes overcrowded and then they will die off because they will eat all the food or something else will happen in nature. But in a perfect pond full of infinite food, those fish would continue to populate forever." Polkingham paused for a breath and to make sure he was being followed. Then he continued. "If we take the female Fintidierian population today and reverse it back in time, using your census data, it grows as expected but in the wrong direction in time."

"And this means what to you, Neil?"

"Don't you see?" Polkingham exclaimed. "Since the female population was decreasing as time went on, the cause of the decrease was increasing in time with a similar, maybe more accelerated, nonlinear growth. This suggests an infection."

"Hold on. We don't have to speak in generalizations," Pearl offered. "Amico, plot the female population of Fintidierians before the *Samaritan*'s arrival backward as far as the census data exists and curve-fit it. Reverse the axis of time so now is at the origin and the past moves to the right on the horizontal axis. Also normalize the graph to unity and adjust the census data to account for average birth rate year-to-year variances."

"Very well, it is displayed now," Amico replied.

"Now, plot the population growth over those same years if the female die-off hadn't occurred and there was a normal population growth, normalized, and adjusted for year-to-year variances," Pearl said. "Then, plot the population growth curve minus the reversed female death curve. Finally, overlay the actual population growth for that same time period."

"I understand what you want," Amico responded. "Here it is."

On the main screen four curves appeared. The female death curve (reversed in time) was indicated with a blue line that started at an initial population and curved upward slightly to a significant value above zero. That was the population of women hundreds of years prior when the census data started. The male population at the time was estimated to be very close. The second curve, in green, was the estimated population growth minus any die-off. In other words, that curve was the population the Fintidierians should have been at had there not been other problems like ancient aliens interfering with their birth rates. The third curve was a black line that represented the ideal population (green line) minus the female reverse population (blue line). It curved up a little beneath the estimated ideal population line with the gap between them growing slightly with time. The final red line, the actual population of the Fintidierians, overlayed the black line exactly.

"There it is." Pearl leaned back in her chair and sighed. "The gap between the ideal population and the actual population matches exactly to the female deaths reversed in time."

"What does this mean, Dr. Pearl?" Filip asked. "Please, forgive my ignorance."

"No apologies needed. This is complicated stuff even for us. Hmmm... So to answer your question, we can refine the model with more specifics, like the rate of men and women born with the genetic methylation versus not and so on," she started. "But this death curve here, the blue line, that's roughly the growth rate of whatever this infection is. If we adjust it for probabilities and generational groups of infected or not infected, we can calculate the exact growth rate. But the point is that it is growing exponentially during this period. Like a virus."

"It could be a self-replicating machine, Yoko," Sentell added. "But virus seems easier."

"Agreed." Polkingham nodded. "A damned virus is nothing more than a nanomachine anyway."

"Is there a way to look for such a virus?" Grag asked.

"Uh, maybe." Sentell rubbed his chin as if in thought. Then he called his AI assistant. "Hey, Susan?"

"Yes, Chris?" she replied. "How may I assist you?"

"How many Fintidierian sperm samples are in the autobay?" Sentell asked. The autobay was an automated system that could pull samples from known storage locations, warm them, and then run them through a myriad of the instruments including the microscope bays.

"Approximately ten thousand," the AI answered.

"Start running them each through the microscope and capturing an image of each as rapidly as possible." Sentell looked at Polkingham and Pearl, who were nodding in approval of his action. They both understood what he was doing. "Look for any exterior components other than sperm in the samples. That is to include bacterium, viruses, nanobots, or any other anomalies. Understood?"

"Yes, Chris," Susan said.

"Uh, Susan, how long is that going to take?" he asked.

"That will take approximately six-point-nine days once the system is started."

"Start it. And keep an eye out for anything odd. Alert me as soon as you find something. Okay?"

"Affirmative, Chris."

"Okay, we have a lot to absorb and understand here," Polkingham told them. "I say we all take a break, a day off maybe, and think on this while the automated systems are looking for our culprit."

"Is it premature to speak with the secretary general?" Filip asked. "This is big news that you have found this methylation."

"Can it wait a few days, Filip?" Polkingham asked. "We might have even more information."

"I will wait then." Filip hesitated. "Perhaps the few days will allow me to take a crash course on all of what we learned here today."

"Good luck, Filip." Sentell laughed. "I'm not sure *I* understood it all."

"Did you not?" Grag looked confused at Sentell, not understanding the humor.

"Grag, my boy"—Sentell shook his head—"let's go fishing and I'll explain it then."

CHAPTER 17

Proxima b—2 months later

"It makes no sense, Grag. I tell you that is for damned certain!" Sentell was tired, very tired. He was tired of the two steps forward, ninety steps backward routine that Proxima b had been. It had been a pretty long day fighting the white caps pushed by the approaching winter winds on the lake. Sentell didn't really think of it as day. This time of year, on Proxima b, at that particular latitude on the planet, day was only a few hours long and night wasn't completely dark either, the extreme aurora filling the night sky with bright blues, greens, violets, and occasional reds saw to that.

Sentell wasn't really all that tired from the day's activities. His fatigue was deeper than that, even though the day's activities had been a lot of hard work, fun too. He and Grag had been on the high side above the dam in the very deep waters of Gwonura Reservoir for more than ten hours, doing some hard *feaple* fishing in the small wood, metal, and plastic two-seater fishing boat of Grag's.

Feaple were like deep-channel catfish of Earth, but they weren't blue, white-bellied, or even black. They were more of a spotted green and brown that fluoresced a chartreuse green ever so slightly in the hard ultraviolets from Proxima once they were out of the water. Other than that, they were pretty much catfish. They even croaked when you pulled them out of the water and removed the hooks from their mouths like the channel cats back on Earth in the Tennessee or Mississippi Rivers.

According to Grag's great-grandfather, when the aurora was highest in the fall to winter months is when the feaple would feed on the *harkenladlors*, which, apparently, was the Fintidierian word for deep, fast movers. The harkenladlors were six-to-ten-centimeter-long, scallop-like freshwater mussels. The little creatures used jets of water and ink to propel themselves across the bottom of the deep murky water leaving behind them a stream of a foul-smelling inky oil as they traveled. The feaple tracked the smell and ate them. Grag's ancestor must have figured out that the harkenladlors tended to migrate during the high auroras. Maybe it was the extra lighting, some electromagnetic thing, Chris didn't know. But what he did know was that catching the twenty-kilogram feaple with the harnkenladlors as bait was fun as hell. It had been tiring, hard work, and he was exhausted. But he had also been able to set his mind on idle and just enjoy the task of fishing.

They had hit the reservoir just a few minutes after sunup. The first task was to drag a mussel rig across the bottom of the lake just a bit shallow of the deepest parts. The mussel rig had a brail that consisted of a meter-and-a-half-long wooden beam approximately five centimeters by twelve centimeters connected like a swing to two cables, one on each end. The cables were in turn connected to hand-cranked winches bolted to a metal support post with standards to rest the brail on at each end of his boat. About a hundred brailhooks swung down from the wooden beam on individual heavy leader lines about a meter long. Each of the brailhooks contained four long, three-millimeter-thick rods slightly bent outward with a metal bead at each end. Grag had explained that the bead at the end acted like bait to the mussels and kept them from slipping off the hook once they clamped their shells down on it.

"Release the brake! Drop the brail," Grag sang in Fintidierian as he showed Chris how to operate it. The brail made a cold splash and the cables whirred against the bell of the winches until it hit the bottom. "Don't get your fingers caught. Release the sail."

Once the brail lines stopped whirring that meant the beam with all the leader lines had made it to the bottom. They let out a few more meters of line for slack and then locked the brakes on the winches. Then Grag hefted up the underwater sail rig and tossed it over the opposite side of the boat.

"The motor is in the wrong place on a boat to pull the rig," Grag explained. "This underwater sail technique has been handed down, well, as long as people have been catching mussels."

"So, we just let this underwater sail pull the boat along with the current?" Chris asked.

"Yes. As it pulls us along, the brail will float a meter or so off the bottom. When the hooks hit the mussel beds, they will scurry about thinking it is food and clamp on," Grag said, demonstrating how to drive the sail rig with the two guidelines. "Then we have our bait. Best bait in all of the world. We steer the sail like this—pull this string for right, this one for left."

"I see. It's like flying a kite."

Chris and Grag had dropped the mussel rig to the bottom and dragged it along for several minutes. Then they reached a point downstream where there was a white plastic bottle floating in the water that someone, probably Grag, had anchored there to mark the bed.

"Man the winch." Grag pointed to the other end of the boat and the two of them each hand cranked the rig up.

"Jesus, this thing is heavy," Chris said.

"That's a good sign." Grag sounded excited. "If it is heavy, that means the brail is loaded with harkenladlors."

And it was. The brailhooks cleared the surface and Chris counted hundreds of the clam-like creatures attached. They rested the brail on the standards and locked the winches.

"Okay, get on the other end of the sail." Grag motioned where he wanted Chris. The two of them hoisted the sail back into the boat and Grag quickly rolled it back up and shoved it away in a compartment at the bottom of the boat.

"How do we get these things off of there?" Chris asked, tugging at one of the mussels on a hook. The mussel was a bright pearl white with blue and green mixed in cloudy rings about the shells.

"You have to turn the shell like this"—Grag demonstrated—"and then snap it off the brailhook. Then, toss it in the bucket."

They pulled the smelly mussels from the brailhooks and repeated the process for a couple of hours until Grag was convinced they had enough bait. There were three ten-liter buckets filled to the top with the mussels.

"This seems like too many for just bait," Chris said.

"Oh, yes of course." Grag almost laughed. "We will only need a few handfuls of them. But my family will cook and can the mussels. They are quite tasty. And we will sell the shells for a good price."

"Sell the shells? For what?"

"For money, Dr. Chris." Grag sounded confused, Chris thought. Or maybe he had learned how to joke with him. Chris wasn't sure. But once he realized that Grag was not offering any further discussion he realized it wasn't a joke.

"No, Grag, I mean for what purpose are the shells used?"

"Ah, I see." Grag laughed. "Buttons, jewelry, knife and tool handles, inlays on musical instruments, and some are even used in poultry feed to make the eggshells stronger."

"Hmmm. Who knew?" Chris shrugged.

"Most people here on Fintidier who mussel-know," Grag added.

Chris guffawed but Grag didn't catch why. Chris decided not to explain.

"Never mind," he said. "So, when do we get to actually fish?"

The bait gathering alone had been a hard morning of work. The entire time Grag worked with the brail he hummed or sang the Fintidierian tune his grandfather had taught him. Sentell had asked him to teach it to him, but for some reason he was having a difficult time learning the Fintidierian slang that was a big part of the song, and he gave up.

But finally, following the bait gathering, they had finally gotten to the fun part—fishing for feaple. The big deep-water fish would latch onto the mussels and not let them go. Since they swam down at a depth of fifteen meters, reeling them in took considerable effort. Especially since the feaple ranged between five and twenty kilos each. With every fish they caught there seemed to be an equal gust of the icy cold and wet wind cutting through them all day. The wind, in turn, rocked the boat up and down, thumping it hard against the water each time the waves passed. Sentell had fished in weather like that back on Wheeler Lake in Alabama in the winter months, and up in Utah on Bear Lake. As a kid he'd lived in Ohio for one year and had ice-fished on Lake Erie. So, it wasn't the cold, hard day of fishing that had tired him so. Hell, that kind of work was fun, enjoyable, and therapeutic.

Fishing had made him physically tired, true, but Sentell felt something different, something deeper. He *was* frustrated. He hadn't been *so* frustrated even during his dissertation research.

He was tired of the big breakthroughs followed by stone-wall obstacles. The methylation discovery was huge, and he had been certain they would find the cause in the microscopy of the samples. But that hadn't been the case. The original discovery had been followed by months and months of searching the Fintidierian sperm samples for viruses or nanobots only to fall short. No matter how hard they had looked, there had not been a single Fintidierian with any visible or even subtle signs of an infection that would explain the methylation of the CATSPER genes on the female sperm. But the methylation was there. They had at least found that.

Grag had been cooking and singing the same song for almost an hour. He had prepared the large filets of the feaple pretty much the same way he had cooked the skiezel months prior back in the early summer—battered and fried in a big cauldron over an open fire. The fire crackled and popped shards of embers into the night, looking like bright orange fireflies.

This time Sentell had brought the ingredients for hushpuppies: he had collected some of the most potato-like tubers from Fintidier that he could find and sliced them into fries, and he had even brought some ketchup. Some of the *Samaritan* crew had gotten fairly good crops of tomatoes to grow in greenhouses on the base over the past year or two. He had also seen some potatoes starting to take hold, but they hadn't been ready yet. Local tubers would suffice.

"The feaple are a bit stronger tasting, not bad at all, but stronger," Sentell said. "Just like catfish back home. You know, if you soak them in saltwater a few hours before you cook them, they will taste even better. That's how we do the deep-channel cats. So, what do you think of the hushpuppies and fries?"

"A very interesting idea." Grag scarfed one of them down. "Deep-fried bread and tubers. I would have never thought of it. But you are right, Dr. Chris, they go well with the fried fish, and this ketchup. It is . . . very tasty. There is nothing like it here on Fintidier. We could sell this and become fantastically rich!"

"Grag! That is an absolutely fantastic, hell of an idea." Sentell realized that there were business ideas that worked centuries prior on Earth that hadn't been tried here on Proxima b yet. "You don't realize what you just said, my young friend!"

"How so?" he asked around a mouthful of the fish. Sentell

watched as Grag liberally applied the ketchup to everything on his plate—fried fish, fries, and the hushpuppies. Grag was enjoying it to the point of dipping his fingers in the ketchup and licking them clean like toddlers, and many adults, had been known to do back on Earth for centuries.

"You really seem to be enjoying that ketchup, Grag," Sentell remarked with a smile and then popped a ketchup-basted hush-puppy all the way in his mouth.

"Mm-hm." Grag nodded enthusiastically, his mouth full of food. "This stuff is amazing, Dr. Chris! I've never tasted anything quite like it. It is sweet, it has a spicy tanginess, and it is creamy also, I think. Nothing like it here on this planet, ever."

Sentell chuckled and almost choked himself on the mouthful. He grabbed his beer and quickly washed it down, clearing his palate. "You know, Grag, ketchup is more than a delicious sauce. Back on Earth, ketchup created fortunes and an entire industry. It played a significant role in the success of a company called Heinz."

"Really?" Grag's curiosity was piqued. "Heinz? What does that word mean?"

"It's a name," Sentell continued. "H. J. Heinz was the name, in fact. He was the founder of the company. It's actually funny that I know all this. But I watched a documentary video about it when I was researching how to make ketchup after our first fishing trip. The documentary was absolutely fascinating. You see, Heinz had a vision. He believed in creating high-quality, natural products. So, when he introduced Heinz tomato ketchup in 1876, that's like two hundred and twenty-six years ago, it was a game-changer. Unlike other condiments of the time, Heinz's ketchup had a pure and consistent flavor. It was made from ripe tomatoes, vinegar, sugar, and a blend of spices. No artificial preservatives or thickeners."

"Maybe I understand that." Grag listened intently, setting down his fork for a moment. "But how did ketchup become such a big deal?"

"Well, it's freaking awesome, for one thing." Sentell laughed. "According to the documentary, Heinz had this brilliant idea of bottling ketchup in distinctive glass bottles with narrow necks. It was not only practical, but it became iconic. People loved the taste and the convenience. It became a staple in American households. Oh, uh, that's the country on Earth that I'm from. And soon ketchup wasn't only in America, it gained worldwide recognition and the company became an economic giant."

"So, Heinz's success was built on ketchup?"

"Exactly," Sentell replied. "Ketchup became the cornerstone of their business. Over time, they expanded their product line, but ketchup remained their most famous and successful product. The Heinz Company is still one of the richest companies today. It's a global giant, and it all started with ketchup. Aaannnddd... Fintidier doesn't have ketchup here yet. It doesn't have a Heinz. Fortunately, we brought all sorts of vegetable seeds with us on both ships and that includes tomatoes."

"Dr. Chris, you're saying that introducing ketchup to Fintidier could be a path to incredible success, just like Heinz did with ketchup on Earth?"

"Yep." Sentell nodded. "Precisely, Grag. It might not be only ketchup. There could be other Earthly delights or innovations that Fintidierians would embrace. I've been thinking about these beer bottles and tops you use here as well. We have better ones on Earth. And the man who invented those is superrich too. It's all about finding what's missing and bringing something valuable to the planet."

"Ketchup. Fintidier would eat this stuff up, but it might need to be made a little less sweet. We don't put as much sugar into our food as you." Grag continued to savor his ketchup-covered meal, not realizing the pun he had made. Sentell could see that wheels were starting to turn in the young man's head, though. And he liked that.

"Hey, man, I mean, Fintidier has superrich people, right?"

"Yes, of course it does, Dr. Chris."

"Why not us?" Sentell was finished with his plate and as good as it all was, he couldn't eat another bite. He sat the plate to the side of his chair and leaned back, taking a long swig from the beer bottle. He thought that the Fintidierians could use some decent beer too, but one thing at a time.

"Dr. Chris, I have another ketchup question."

"Okay, fire away."

"We have laws here about inventions, who owns them, and they regulate who can make copies of someone's invention."

"Yes, we call that a patent," Sentell replied, taking another swig. "We have those too. You gotta pay if you want to copy and make money of someone else's invention."

"Wouldn't Mr. Heinz be upset if we copied his invention?" asked Grag.

"Uh, well, that's a good question. I really don't know about the recipe for ketchup being patented. There are other companies that make a similar product and I have no idea if they have to pay Heinz to do that or not."

"How could we find out?"

"Well, we could always... Wait. No. We don't have to have their permission. That company is over four light-years away. What're they going to do about it if we do copy their recipe? Fly over here an arrest us?" Sentell grinned. "That's not likely to happen."

"Hmm. I guess you are correct. But it just doesn't feel right," Grag said.

"I guess none of that matters if we don't solve this damned fertility crisis."

"I think we are close," Grag said optimistically. "I mean, don't you?"

"I don't know. I am kinda stumped," Sentell answered as he emptied the bottle. "I don't know what to do next. I could really use some new inspiration—other than ketchup."

"Well, you figured out how to create the female pregnancies by letting yourself think like an ancient Atlantean alien. The microbots work well and we have many new female babies here on Fintidier—thousands now, and more every day." Grag dropped his plate and wandered over to the fire, stirring it a bit with a poker stick and adding an armload of logs to it.

"The bots do work. But they are not a solution. They are a work-around. There's a difference, Grag." Sentell understood that the entire civilization could not depend on microbot fertilization for eternity. No, a real solution had to be found. But before a solution could be found, they really needed to know what the problem was.

"A work-around that is working around the problem while we find a permanent solution." Grag made a few final tweaks to the fire, dropped the fire poker, and rummaged through the beer bucket, pulling out two fresh bottles. He handed Sentell a beer and sat in the chair next to him so he could look out over the lake. "The wind is settled. The aurora is so strong tonight."

"Yes, it is. Beautiful," Sentell agreed, unscrewing the cap. He was almost used to the idea of opening beer bottles that way. But not quite.

"Why the feaple bit so well today," Grag said.

"Hell of a lot of fun, Grag. Thank you for showing me all of it," Sentell said, giving his friend a smile of gratitude. "I mean, the harkenladlors, the mussel rig, the feaple, and of course, the beer."

"Here's to the best interstellar fisherman ever." Grag tapped his bottle in the manner Sentell had taught him.

"Hahaha! Not sure about that!" Sentell laughed. "But I'll drink to it."

"And the man who created the fertility crisis work-around by thinking like an ancient alien." Grag tapped his bottle again. "And will do it again."

"Well, I'm not sure that's what happened, Grag," Sentell conceded, but took a drink anyway. "But I'll play that game with you for now. If I were a super-advanced alien race and I wanted to manipulate sperm via methylation of the CATSPER genes to keep women from being born and it be undetectable by a Terran-level civilization, how would I do it?"

"Yes, Dr. Chris from the stars, great cosmic angler, how would you do it?" Grag chuckled lightly but then took a thoughtful long look at his friend and mentor. A smile remained on his friend's face and Sentell wondered what he was thinking.

"Well, assuming these advanced aliens had a deep understanding of genetics and technology far beyond our own, as we are now certain they did, they might have engineered something on a microscopic scale. Something so small and subtle that it could evade detection by our current scientific instruments," Sentell started with what he did know.

"Smaller than your nanobots?" Grag seemed shocked by the idea.

"Maybe, I dunno. We're describing advanced ancient beings here. We definitely need to think outside the box." Sentell shrugged. "But if you get *too* small, there's no room for control systems, sensors, or event mechanisms like DNA or enzymes that could perform the methylation."

"What does it mean to 'think outside of the box'?"

Sentell chuckled. "It means to think about a problem in a way nobody has ever thought of before. Like, using some sort of unexplainable technology might as well be magic. How would we build a device on a scale smaller than a scanning electron microscope can resolve, and yet can stop protein expression in female sperm? Well, that magic is outside of the box of the standard or known approach or science. Or maybe, thinking of the answer as a device so small is putting us in a box which might not even hold the answer. Thinking outside the box is never simple."

"Outside of the box. Hmmmm, interesting." Grag struggled with the concept for a moment and then turned to Sentell with another thoughtful look on his face. "Dr. Chris, I would build a transmitter that sends a magic signal across the planet that would turn off female sperm. Somehow, the signal triggers this... methylation."

"A transmitter, huh? That's an interesting concept, Grag." Sentell raised an eyebrow, intrigued by Grag's imaginative response. "But what kind of signal are we discussing? And how would it selectively affect only female sperm in the way we know it is being affected?"

"Well, Dr. Chris, if I were these advanced aliens, I'd create a signal that specifically targets the genetic markers unique to female sperm, as you say. It would be like a lock-and-key system, where the signal only interacts with the 'lock' found on female sperm, preventing them from expressing the proteins needed for female sperm motility." Grag looked anxiously back at Sentell as if waiting for him to validate his hypothesis. Sentell thought he was like a puppy that had just brought him his slippers and was waiting for a treat. Then Sentell wondered if that was a belittling thing to think of his friend. He didn't know. Maybe it was the long months, the long, hard day of fishing, his full belly, and the beer.

"Maaaybe," Sentell said as he slowly nodded for emphasis. "I have to say, man, I appreciate the hell out of your creativity here, Grag. I'm sort of coming up dry at the moment. But, it, well, that's an intriguing idea. So, this signal would be transmitted across the planet, affecting sperm at the moment of fertilization or maybe somehow in all sperm-bearing aged males at any point in time, but essentially modifying their genetic instructions to suppress the female sperm motility."

"Exactly, Dr. Chris. And it would be transmitted continuously, ensuring a consistent effect over generations."

"Of course," Sentell mused, "we'd need some way to detect and analyze this signal."

"How do we do that?" Grag leaned back in his chair, deep in thought once more. "Perhaps we could search for anomalies in the electromagnetic spectrum or any unusual energy patterns. It might be hidden, but there could be subtle traces that we can discover with the right technology. Like, technology from across the stars from Earth."

"That would be a very interesting concept to run by Rain, but, damn, she's gone on the *Emissary*. And who knows when, or even if, they will ever make it back to Proxima b," Sentell said. He realized then that he missed seeing her around the base and always having her around, even if they had never been that close. After all, she was the one who originally had found the signal from Proxima, and she had been the unofficial leader of the scientists who had traversed the stars. "I can talk with Burbank. He's our needle-in-a-haystack signal guy now that she's gone off. But I don't think it would be a signal we could easily understand. I mean, I'm not sure you can affect a sperm's genetic expression with an electromagnetic signal. And for it to be globally transmitted..."

"A... needle... in a... haystack?"

"Hahaha! That's good. You are using our idioms just fine," Sentell replied. "Now, regarding our mysterious signal, you're right, it's a long shot. But we won't know until we explore every avenue. And even if it doesn't pan out, it might lead us to other discoveries." Sentell considered the best way to explain this to Roy. Hell, he wasn't even sure what kind of signal it would be, if at all. Something out of place, or unusual, that's the only thing he could think of to look for at the moment.

"Couldn't you use a magnet?" Grag asked. "I mean, are your needles made of metal like ours?"

"Yes, that is the typical fun response to that dilemma," Sentell answered. "But it's a simile for other scenarios. This scenario is like finding a needle in a haystack."

"I see," Grag said.

"I still think that would be the wrong haystack. Electromagnetism, I mean," Sentell explained. "I mean, to broadcast globally would take too much power. We'd see it in the spectrum analyzers, I'm sure."

"Oh, I understand your issue with the hypothesis now. Yes. Electromagnetic energy decreases with the square of the distance. Our radio engineers here on Fintidier have known this for nearly three decades." Grag nodded his head in agreement. "You'd need something like that... how is it your Einstein put it? Um, spooky action at a distance?"

"Ah, entanglement." Sentell grinned. "You're absolutely right, Grag. Einstein famously referred to entanglement as 'spooky action at a distance.' It's a quantum phenomenon where particles become correlated in such a way that their states are linked, regardless of the distance between them. While it's intriguing, it's also incredibly complex and not something we currently have the technology to manipulate or broadcast at a global scale or at least I don't think we do. Back on Earth, we have a global quantum network, but it is connected by optical fibers and wires."

"Optical fibers?"

"Oh God, it is so difficult to remember all of the things you guys here on Proxima b, uh, Fintidier, have yet to discover or invent." Sentell sighed. "Optical fibers are like wires for light beams. Think of them like long wires but instead of a conductor they are made of something like a flexible glass."

"Optical fiber. I see, amazing that you can make glass flexible."

"We discovered it not many years past where your civilization is now," Sentell told him.

"Would it be too hard for the Atlanteans? The global spooky signal, I mean." Grag asked. "If so, then we need to find a different way to approach this mystery, something that doesn't rely on electromagnetic signals or entanglement."

"Wait a minute, Grag. I didn't say that. And I'm not a physicist either, but I have had modern quantum physics and biological phenomena classes. And I have read up on the subject quite a bit." Sentell sat upright as abruptly as his full stomach and tired body would allow. He pulled a throw blanket out of his pack and covered himself with it. The night air was getting cold enough that the fire couldn't keep him comfortable.

"Entanglement is nonlocal," he said. "There are experiments showing human mental focus impact on quantum events."

"Really? I would love to learn more." Grag sounded surprised.

"Yeah, crazy stuff, but part of quantum physics and consciousness interactions," Sentell said. "You have probably heard stories where people with chronic or fatal illnesses used the power of positive thinking to heal themselves. Stories like that *actually* happening are less rare than you'd think. There've been studies for over a century on Earth now."

"Really?" Grag's eyes widened with curiosity. "That's fascinating, Dr. Chris. So, you're saying that human consciousness might have the power to influence quantum events, including those related to genetics?"

"Well, I don't know about genetics. Most genetics is fairly easily explained with classical chemistry, physics, and biology," Sentell replied. "But certainly, human consciousness has been observed to change subtle experiment outcomes. It's a mysterious and relatively unexplored aspect of quantum physics. Some scientists believe that consciousness plays a fundamental role in the universe, and that our thoughts and intentions can have a profound impact on reality at the quantum level. I don't know, but this idea, well, it could be a possible way that a global nonlocal signal is communicated to all the Fintidierians at once."

"Nonlocal. Yes, we are starting to use that word in my graduate courses." Grag looked thoughtful. "So, if we could somehow harness this power of human quantum consciousness, we might be able to correct the imbalance without relying on electromagnetic signals or genetic engineering?"

"Well, we know that genetic engineering is taking place. This might be part of the mechanism for implementing it," Sentell explained. "So, let's continue along the path of thinking like the Atlanteans. Possessing super-advanced technologies and understanding of the universe greater than our own would certainly have its advantages. If human consciousness can be used to impact quantum events, then that suggests that the human mind is a quantum phenomenon transmitter of some sort."

"And if the human mind—do you mean brain, maybe?—is a quantum transmitter, then does that mean that a similar type of transmitter can be manufactured?" Grag asked.

"Yes, I do mean the human brain. I think you are on to the right question there, Grag." Sentell leaned forward, intrigued by the possibilities. "If the human brain can influence quantum events, it implies that there might be a way to replicate or amplify this effect using advanced technology. And we do similar things to this with quantum computers, quantum networks, and quantum antennas, but not at the scale of global communications with DNA. We're talking about harnessing quantum phenomena at a level far beyond our current understanding."

"Oh well," Grag said as he finished his beer. He sounded defeated. Sentell felt bad that he couldn't help his friend more than he had already. "It would have been so much simpler if the Fintidierian sperm had all been infected by something that was contagious. That would at least explain why you Terrans can't have female children now also."

"...Terrans can't have female children now..." Sentell mouthed the words under his breath. He repeated Grag's words again. "...so much simpler if the Fintidierian sperm had all been infected by something that was contagious..."

"Something wrong, Dr. Chris?"

"Grag, is that true?" Sentell asked. If that were true, why had he not heard this yet? *Had* he heard it and was too busy to have registered it?

"What? Is what true?"

"That us Terrans can't have female babies now?" Sentell could feel adrenaline starting to course through him. His heart rate was accelerated and his mind clearing from his depressed and fatigued and somewhat inebriated state. "I don't think I've heard that."

"Oh, I don't know if it is released data to the general public or anything," Grag explained, "but that is what they are saying on all the daytime news shows."

"Wait a minute." Sentell held up a hand. Then he killed what was left of his beer and tossed it into the pile he and Grag would collect later so they could wash and reuse them. "Susan! Give me the stats on all new Terran parented births that have occurred on Proxima b. Only go back so far as to be certain the pregnancies happened here on Proxima. And do not use any data from births known to have gone through the nanobot procedure."

"I understand, Chris. Wait a minute," his AI voice rang in his head. Sentell turned his external speaker on so Grag could hear as well. "It would appear that no new females have been conceived here on Proxima b by the Terrans. There have been seven males."

"I guess the news shows are correct, then." Grag shrugged and scrunched back in his seat.

"No, Grag!" Sentell was almost shouting now. "You don't understand. Hang on."

Sentell stood up. Then he sat back down because he wasn't sure what course of action he wanted to take. Did he *need* to sit and think about it longer? No, he decided sitting wasn't going to help and wasn't what he felt was the right thing, so he stood right back up. He started pacing back and forth between their seats and the fire. He wasn't sure why he didn't have that data before, but it made all the difference. It made a *huge* difference.

"Holy shit. Holy shit. Holy shit!" Sentell had it. He was pretty sure he understood it now. "Susan!"

"Chris, I am inside your head. You do not have to shout," Susan joked with him. "What can I do for you?"

"Susan! Are there any sperm samples from any Terrans presently in the autobay?" he asked excitedly.

"I'm sorry, Chris. There are several in storage, but none are loaded into the autobay," Susan replied.

"Damnit!" Sentell cursed, then he turned to Grag. "Call us a taxi or a friend with a car, I don't care. We have to get to the lab right now!"

"We need to clean up the—" Grag started.

"We clean while we get someone here to take care of the boat and everything else," Sentell said, still pacing frantically. "This is *too* important. Grag, we *need* to get to the lab now. I'm too drunk to drive, man. And I'm sure you are too. Do I need to send for a security team to come get us?"

"Em, what is so important, Dr. Chris?" Grag was excited but confused. Sentell didn't have time to explain everything at the moment because he was too busy recording his thoughts internally with his AI.

"I'll tell you in a bit. Are you getting someone here to get us?" He continued swiping at things in front of him in his virtual view via his smart contact lenses. All the while, he was muttering to Susan to run this model or that calculation. "We need to get to the lab, Grag. Seriously."

In the end, Grag had managed to get one of his uncles and a few cousins to come to the family lake house to take care of the boat, mussels, fish, and the general mess that they had made. One of the cousins close to Grag's age, Jeritier, drove them back to the Terran research facility. Once they arrived at the security gate of the Terran village, Jeritier dropped them off and returned to the lake house. Sentell and Grag took an electric all-terrain vehicle from the gate to the lab.

They hastily made their way to the lab entrance where Sentell fumbled with the Fintidierian-manufactured cypher lock. He made a mental note to petition the engineers to retrofit the locks with wireless connectivity and entry management.

"There are probably fifty or more sperm samples from Terrans in the cooler. But if they don't show us what I'm looking for, well, I will generate a fresh sample," Sentell offered. He wasn't sure if Grag understood what he was saying until he chuckled.

"Do you have some way to, em, you know, get excited?" Grag laughed but seemed more curious.

"Too much information, Grag," Sentell grunted. "I'll figure it out."

Sentell was too focused on his hypothesis to let something falter the urgency of the potential discovery in front of them, and that alone was driving him forward. The revelation that Fintidierians born on Proxima b showed no evidence of infection while the Terrans had experienced a similar lack of female births raised a chilling possibility. It suggested that the Terrans were indeed infected, and Chris's heart raced as he considered the implications. If the Terrans were infected, then they were *currently* infected. There were no other generations of Terrans here but this one.

As they entered the lab, the overhead lights flickered to life, illuminating the room in a harsh white light, clinical glow. Rows of microscopes and lab equipment stood ready, but it was the microscope at the center of the room that beckoned them. That was the one connected to the autobay. He cycled the system on, and screens lit up around it. He then knelt by a cryobox at the end of the lab bench and pulled the door open.

"Susan, which samples?" he asked.

"Here," Susan replied while at the same time highlighting them in his virtual view.

"Got it." Sentell pulled a tray of twenty samples from the back on the top shelf. He closed the cryobox door and carried the samples back to the autobay. Carefully, he prepared the sperm sample tubes for insertion into the trays of the autobay system.

"Here we go," he said as held his hands steady despite the excitement of his thoughts, the tiredness, and the ethanol still in his system. Grag watched equally as excited as Sentell closed the tray and cycled the samples into the warming bay. "It will take five or ten minutes for the samples to be warm enough to start being cycled through the imager."

"Okay, then. Dr. Chris, I must take a bathroom break," Grag remarked sheepishly and Sentell realized that some of the jittering Grag was doing wasn't only due to excitement. He had to go. Come to think of it, the ride in had taken nearly forty-five minutes. And they had drunk a lot of beers earlier...

"Good call," Sentell agreed.

By the time they had returned, the warming tray was displaying a green light. Sentell checked his virtual screens, and everything was nominal. He tossed the imager view up onto the main big screen in front of the station and then pressed the cycle button. There was a whirring of mechanical motion and then the screen flickered.

The sight that met their eyes was both astonishing and unsettling. Thousands of what appeared to be Escherichia T4 bacteriophage viruses swarmed around the sperm, like an army ready for battle. Grag's jaw dropped, and he struggled to find words. "Is that... What is that, Dr. Chris?"

"Escherichia virus T4! Son of a bitch!" Chris's voice was filled with a mix of awe and excitement. "Yes, Grag. These are T4 bacteriophages, and they're infecting the Terran sperm sample. I'll check in a bit, but if I had my guess, all of us male Terrans have this now."

"But it is the problem, then?" Grag looked at him wide-eyed.

"Goddamned right it is!" Sentell slapped his friend on the back, all the while laughing out loud. That long, deep tiredness he had been feeling for weeks, if not months, had seemed to vanish. "I need to watch the daytime news shows more often, I guess."

Before they could react further, the lab door swung open, and Polkingham and Pearl rushed in, their faces a mix of excitement and confusion. Polkingham spoke first, barely able to contain his excitement.

"Chris, Grag? What's going on? We heard the commotion and saw the lights. I got your frantic messages to come to the lab." Polkingham seemed more concerned or maybe angry at Sentell for getting him up in the middle of the night.

Sentell didn't care. He simply smiled and pointed at the monitor screen. He watched as both Polkingham and Pearl turned and studied what they were seeing. Sentell knew it would be clear as day to them once they saw it. There on the sperm was a swarm of tiny things. At the bottom of the virus were long spindly tail fibers like spider legs that were connected to a base plate at the bottom of a tube. The tube was many times larger in diameter than the spider legs and about as long as each. At the top of the tube was a much larger icosahedral container.

"Holy..." Polkingham was speechless.

"Is this what we've been searching for?" Pearl turned back and forth between the screen and Chris. "What sample is that?"

"Terran male sperm," Grag said enthusiastically.

"Terran?" Polkingham asked.

"Of course!" Pearl exclaimed. "The Fintidierians wouldn't still have the virus if it had altered them genetically. They simply have inherited this trait now for generations."

"But we just got here," Polkingham added. Sentell could tell that both of his colleagues now understood his excitement and urgency. "Holy shit, Chris!"

"Yes, holy shit!" Sentell repeated.

"Dr. Chris has said that many times in the past hour," Grag added.

"Then, this is it? A bacteriophage. This is the infection mechanism we've been looking for." Pearl sat down in a chair at the microscope control station. "We should get a better look."

"The greatest part is that this explains why we couldn't find any pathogens in the Fintidierian samples. It's not a current infection. It's hereditary. Passed down through generations. Correct?" Grag looked around them all for reassurance of his understanding. "The secretary general will be so pleased. I can't wait to tell Professor Cromntinier."

"Son of a bitch." Polkingham's eyes widened as he absorbed the gravity of the situation, all the while leaning over Pearl's shoulder, watching what she was doing with the controls of the microscope. "So, this infection has been with us since we arrived on Proxima?"

"I bet it hit us as soon as we breathed the air." Sentell nodded. "It seems that way. And it's certainly what's causing the gender imbalance in both populations. Think about it. If you were going to engineer a mechanism to deliver a DNA payload to sperm cells, what better way to do it than to use a modified bacteriophage."

"Engineered is right, Chris." Pearl expanded the view of one of the bacteriophages on the big screen. As she zoomed in, she was waving her hands at virtual icons in the air before her. "Look at the base plate, it seems to be different. It's bigger. And the tail fibers, well, we need to do side-by-side comparisons, but they seem bigger or longer. Not sure. But look at this here. There is some sort of coating on the thing. And the tail tube itself seems bigger in diameter, perhaps."

"Susan, can you take the SEM image of the components of that coating and give us any more information?" Sentell asked.

"Let me see," she replied over the screen's speakers. "No. There is not enough data here from the scanning electron microscope resolution."

"Well, damn," Sentell replied.

"I could run the sample through the transmission electron microscope system. This should give us much more resolution," Geni explained.

"Do it."

"That will take a moment to cycle the autobay into that location. Hold one minute," the AI said.

The minute seemed like forever, but finally the AI announced, "The TEM scan is complete."

"And?" Sentell asked impatiently.

"Those components appear to be glycoproteins," Susan answered.

"Glycoproteins?" Pearl pondered to herself.

"Glycoproteins?" Polkingham asked. "Why glycoproteins?"

"Hmmm, we need to do more tests to see if we can identify *which* glycoproteins," Sentell mused. "If they are human derived that would make sense."

"Why so?" Pearl turned to him.

"Camouflage," Sentell replied. "Otherwise, the immune system would attack it. But if it is coated with a human-derived protein, it might not trigger an immune response."

"Of course. That makes perfect sense," Pearl agreed.

"Chris?" Susan's voice interrupted them.

"Yes, Susan?"

"I have filtered the images and fused the visible, SEM, and TEM images," she said. "There is more information here now."

"Please put it on the screen and explain," Polkingham replied.

"As you can see here," Susan explained as the image of the bacteriophage expanded and then exploded into component views, "the tail tube is quite unique. The main structural component appears to be a microtubule constructed of tubulin proteins. It is then coated with what appears to be the standard bacteriophage protein tail tube. On the outside of that is this third layer of glycoproteins. It would appear the glycoproteins cover the entire virus except for the tail fibers. There are no known viruses like this in any of the databases we have access to here."

"Microtubules?" Sentell looked at Grag in amazement. "Grag! You were right!"

"I was?" Grag asked. From the look on his face, it was clear to Sentell that he had no idea what he was talking about.

"Chris?" Polkingham asked with a shrug.

"Grag, tell Neil and Pearl how you thought the Atlanteans could send a signal globally to sperm cells." Sentell raised an eyebrow at him, hoping there hadn't been too many beers for him to recall the conversation correctly.

"Do you mean with your Einstein's spooky action?" Grag asked.

"You are damned right I do!" Sentell said. "Microtubules, Neil! Yoko, you see? Spooky action at a distance. This thing has quantum processors built right into it!"

"If each one of these viruses has a complete microtubule as the tail tube..." Polkingham appeared to be doing math in his head. "Let's see, that's thirteen filaments in twisted helical arrangements with thirteen tubulin proteins each, that's one hundred and sixty-nine qubits."

"Each one of these damned viruses is a one-hundred-and-sixty-nine-qubit quantum computer, quantum transmitter, and quantum receiver," Sentell said, nodding to Grag. "Again, Grag, you have outsmarted the Atlanteans."

"Not me, Dr. Chris." Grag shook his head. "I was only playing your game of thinking outside of the box and looking for the needle in the haystack."

"Well, I'll be damned if this isn't the most out-of-the-box needle in the most out-of-the-box haystack I've ever seen," Sentell declared.

"The engineering of this virus is way ahead of anything we could build," Pearl said. "And a quantum computer for control or communications or... what?"

"Yes, to all of it, probably." Polkingham nodded his head affirmatively. "Now the question is: how do we kill it?"

"Perhaps we need to think outside of the box," Grag replied.

CHAPTER 18

Aboard the *Pioneer*

Captain Penelope Mitchison jolted awake in her cryosleep chamber once more. Her head throbbed with each breath and her stomach spasmed as if ready to exfil whatever might be in it. The chamber lid hissed open slowly, and then snapped into the open position as she leaned over the side vomiting. Reflexively, she pulled the tube from her nose, triggering her gag reflex again. After heaving once more, she fell to the cold metal floor beneath the bed and lay there still for a moment as her head spun. She wiped the spittle that was drooling from the corner of her mouth with the back side of her left hand and continued to stare blankly upward, trying to regain her senses. There was something off. She couldn't seem to focus because of the odd lighting going in and out and there was a blearing pounding in her ears. Or maybe the pounding in her ears was actually a sound.

Penelope forced herself to her feet as she disconnected the cables on her right wrist still connecting her to the cryobed. She tapped at a panel on the side of the bed and a drawer slid out with a swoosh, revealing a vial of a clear blue liquid. She popped the top on it and poured it in her mouth, tasting the sweet liquid antibiotics, stimulants, vitamins, and anti-inflammatories. As the liquid moistened her mouth and rejuvenated her saliva glands, she tried a raspy grunt to clear her throat. She pulled a second bottle of electrolytes from the drawer and drank it as well. Finally, she began coming to her senses. She realized that she had been disoriented by blaring alarms and the flashing crimson emergency lighting. She scrambled up to her feet, supporting herself with her arms like a toddler learning to stand for the first time. She tapped at the ship information panel and screen next to the cryobed and her heart sank when she saw the chaos that seemed to be happening across the ship.

"Orion, report!" she said to the ship's AI. Her voice was barely more than a dehydrated whisper but was still edged with urgency.

"Critical failure in the propulsion system, Captain," Orion replied in a deep male voice, sounding somber. "The Samara Drive main power plant is completely offline. We are currently five weeks from Proxima b, and there's no way to slow down until repairs are implemented. More urgently, we have fires on the aft starboard decks and there is an environmental leak in an adjacent chamber. Power distribution is unstable throughout the ship. Protocols have awakened you, the bridge crew, and the engineering teams."

"Shit. Seal off the room with the leak for now." Penelope scanned the cryobed chambers and noticed several other systems hissing open, the crew going through pretty much what she had just gone through. "Are the fire suppression systems not doing their jobs?"

"I'm sorry, Captain, but the fire suppression systems on all aft decks are without power at the moment. Some of the alternate power systems were initiated, but when the power coupling to the Samara Drive blew out, an electromagnetic pulse from the subsequent explosion knocked out most electronic systems on the aft and lower side of the power-plant shielding."

"Damnit." Penelope pulled on her form-fitting, light blue uniform pants and long-sleeve blue-and-white synthetic fiber uniform top, followed by her socks and sneakers. She was still parched and felt like death warmed over, but she had to get those fires out. Her eyes were dry as a bone and itched. She pulled her smart-lens container from the drawer beside her bed and quickly placed the contacts into her eyes. The ophthalmic gel soothed her dry eyes almost instantly and her vision became better than perfect. The virtual heads-up display popped up in front of her. She tapped a virtual menu activating personnel tracking, and names and titles started popping up over the cryobeds that were opening. She scanned left, then right, until the name she was looking for appeared. She started walking that way hurriedly, grabbing another bottle of electrolytes along the way. As she walked, Penelope tapped a few icons and brought up a three-dimensional alert map of the ship. There were red and yellow zones all over and in every nook and cranny. Things did *not* look very good at the moment.

"Wait a minute," Penelope cautioned as she scanned the ship systems in the virtual map.

"Yes, Captain?"

"If the engine is out and we're not decelerating, then . . ." She rolled her eyes and sighed, realizing that no decelerating ship meant no effective gravity on the floor. "Aw shit, no wonder my head is spinning. The artificial gravity ring is spun up, isn't it?"

"Yes. Protocols started spinning the ring as soon as the engines turned off," Orion confirmed.

"Then there's no gravity in the aft sections," she acknowledged to herself. God, she hated microgravity. She didn't enjoy the centrifugal force artificial gravity much either. It had a very similar effect as gravity, but only in giant stations where the ring diameter was huge did the effect really seem indistinguishable from gravity. But on the *Pioneer*, the ring was barely big enough to fit the cryobeds, a few critical consoles and stations, a small medical bay, and a small makeshift backup command bridge. Since the radius of the spinning ring was small, the effect varied greatly with radius from the center much like a carnival ride just not quite that badly. The force on one's feet was much larger than that on one's head. Moving around in such a field, especially up or down, made the inner ear go nuts. The drunk spins of artificial gravity were almost as bad as those of microgravity.

"Yes, that is correct, Captain."

"Well, damn it all to Hell, that doesn't make anything any easier right now." She grunted through clenched teeth, all the while shaking her head to reset her inner ear.

"I'm sorry, Captain," Orion replied, sounding sincere. "I suspect it does not."

Penelope's heart hammered in her chest as she made her way to the chief engineer, who was beginning to pull herself up off the floor. She held out a hand to help her up.

"Evonne, here drink this. It helps," Penelope said, handing the electrolyte bottle to the ship's CHENG, Dr. Evonne Mia. "Well, at least it will help get that shit cryosleep taste out of your mouth."

"Thanks, Captain." Evonne straightened up and accepted the

bottle. The slightly taller and more muscular than average woman in her late twenties chugged the liquid in two big gulps, and wiped her mouth on her wrist. She then tried to tie her long brown hair up in a ponytail, only to be annoyed by the connections to the cryobed at her right wrist. She quickly yanked those free and finished the ponytail. The CHENG then turned to the drawer on her cryobed and instantly placed her smart lenses in her eyes. She sighed at whatever she was looking at in her virtual screens as she pulled the post-sleep blue liquid tube from the drawer and drank it.

"What a damned mess!" Evonne exclaimed. Her sleep gown dropped to the floor. Three naked steps to her right and she was sliding on a pair of blue-and-white stretch coveralls with a patch across the chest reading in capital letters CHENG. There were added pads at the elbows and knees that were a slightly darker blue with black outlines as well as multiple pockets on the sleeves and legs. The uniform looked like something a hands-on engineer or technician would wear. The only things missing were smudges and grease marks.

"My sentiments exactly," Penelope agreed.

"Whoa, shit!" Evonne shook her head violently and grabbed a handhold to steady herself. She sat on the floor and took a deep breath before slipping on her shoes. "Goddamned artificial gravity is not any better than microgravity."

"Again, my sentiments exactly." Penelope would have laughed if they weren't in such deep trouble. "So, what do you think, Evonne?"

"Fires. Gotta get them out first. That section right there..." She pointed and swiped her VR screen over to the captain's so they both could see the same virtual screen. "The section is immediately below the liquid oxygen storage. If that starts boiling, we're done for. After getting the fires out, well, then, we gotta get Jones up on Nav, 'cause who the Hell actually knows how long we've been drifting, not decelerating, and not making course corrections?"

"Jesus H. Christ." Penelope knew what that meant: The ship's engine had failed catastrophically, leaving them hurtling through space at a breakneck speed they couldn't control. And even worse, there was no telling how long they had been drifting in an uncontrolled trajectory. They could be way off course. The crew would be stranded, unable to reach their destination, and facing an uncertain fate. "Okay, I'll get the XO on that. He's almost awake. Orion will hopefully have enough sensor data to tell us when things went to Hell."

"I'll need a fire team," the CHENG said.

"Take who you need. Get down there, put out the fires. Then get to Engineering and assess the damage as soon as you can!" she ordered, her voice trembling with the weight of the situation. She realized she had been almost screaming even though her voice was still not a hundred percent. "Damn alarms. Orion!"

"Yes Captain?" Orion responded.

"Turn off the damned alarms!" she shouted, and no sooner had the words gotten out of her mouth than the ship suddenly became very quiet. Other than the hissing of cryobeds opening and people rustling out of them and vomiting, and the occasional creaking or whirring of systems on the ship, there was no noise.

"Done," Orion said.

"Jenna, you and Mario take the port corridor around and over the cryo room. This conduit here appears to be the one that is out. We'll have to replace that before we get power back to the main ship systems in that part of the ship." The CHENG floated through the central shaft corridor of the *Pioneer* with her two fire teams. Group A consisted of herself, Dr. Amy Crane, a computer systems engineer, and Dr. Connie Browning, a mathematician who was also designated as the ship's hands-on power systems technician. Group B was Dr. Jenna Rees, an electrical engineer and mechanical engineer, and Dr. Mario Rivers, an aerospace engineer, material printing expert, and machine tool maker.

"Copy that," Mario replied. "There's bound to be a conduit on a noncritical system we can repurpose."

"Looking at that now," Jenna added. "There are a few spares stored throughout the ship. There might be one close enough as to not have to salvage one."

"Good," Evonne said. "Your focus is to get that power back on. And in case you don't get it going in time, Group A, you two are with me. We're going to open a sequence of doors manually while fighting through the fires. Remember, microgravity fires are different. They ball up, float about sometimes, but mostly attach to something—including you. And sometimes the fires burn too cold or too hot and you can't see them. Everyone keep open comms and be careful."

"Roger that," they all responded.

"Okay, keep a fire extinguisher pack at the ready, and breathing gear on," Evonne told them as she slid her facemask into place and checked the oxygen flow. The rest of the team followed suit. "Alright. Let's get it done."

"Remember, we need to get to that airlock along the path highlighted in your VR maps. We open them in any order we get to them and vent the oxygen," Evonne reminded her team as they moved through the corridor by kicking off the walls and grabbing at any handholds they could. The ship had been designed for microgravity movement so there were rails and holds on every wall and bulkhead. "That should smother the fires."

Amy Crane and Connie Browning nodded, their expressions determined beneath their emergency breathing gear. Evonne was confident that they knew the importance of their mission. Every crew person of the *Pioneer* had been chosen through a stiff competition of mental and physical fitness, an expertise for mission needs, and a willingness to become part of the Fintidierian culture. There was no one onboard who wasn't great at what they did, extremely capable, and dedicated. As they moved through the central corridor and approached the engine room, it was clear they weren't going in there. The door was hot to the touch and the radiation monitors at the entrance were through the roof.

"Well, shit, going through this way is not an option," Connie said as she turned to Evonne after reading the panel to the right of the door. She had a very nervous and uneasy look that Evonne could detect even through the facemask. "We'll have to get that under control soon!"

"Alright, we gotta go around," she said. "Jenna, Mario, Engineering is off-limits. Until we get power back and rad gear down here, we're not going in there. Copy?"

"Understood, Evonne. We're going over it anyway," Jenna replied.

"Okay, Amy, lead the way," Evonne admonished the woman who was already several meters ahead, pulling open a hatch leading into the exterior passageway and the engineering ducts that ran the periphery of the ship.

"Holy shit!" Amy shouted, pushing back and spraying her extinguisher as a gush of heat washed over her. The extinguisher jetted foam in front of her, rocketing her backward out of the exterior passage hatchway. As she was flung backward, both Connie and Evonne grabbed at her. Evonne managed to get a handhold on her extinguisher backpack harness with her left hand while grasping the rail on the bulkhead with her right. As the two of them wrestled Amy to a stop, they could see her jumpsuit was burning.

Connie slapped at the flames that were crawling over Amy's body now, consuming her uniform coveralls as fuel. Amy screamed in terror once she realized what was happening. She was being engulfed in fire. With each scream more oxygen leaked out around her face mask, causing the flame to flare. Orange flames expanded like a breathing hemisphere, engulfing her face. As Connie swatted at her, the fire began to cling to her own gloves as well.

"Not good!" Connie started slapping at her gloves, but then flinched as she was hit by a spray of foam.

"Try to hold still!" Evonne shouted as she continued to spray the two of them. She was using a foot wedged between the handrail and the wall to steady her while pressing her other foot against the wall to oppose the force of the fire extinguisher spray.

"Here!" Amy pointed as she twisted and contorted, looking for the flames. Her shoulder-length black hair had been singed up almost to the scalp on one side before they had managed to get the flames extinguished. Her mask showed little damage, if any, and as far as they could tell Amy's face wasn't injured.

Connie rolled her around in front of them and then Amy repeated the process for Connie. The flames were out. Needless to say, the two of them were shaken. The three looked at each other, tight lipped and forcing themselves to choke down bile and fear.

"Are you two good?" Evonne asked, looking them over carefully.

"I'm okay." Connie nodded.

"I'm, uh, I'm okay, Evonne. That was freakin' stupid. We're lucky that didn't go as badly as it could have. Oh, my God!" she exclaimed, trying to stop her hands from shaking. "That corridor is hot. I don't know how we're going to get through there."

Evonne pushed to the door and fired her extinguisher a few bursts there. As she approached, she didn't feel any heat—a good sign. She caught a handhold a half meter from the hatch and held her hand forward.

"I feel some heat, but not enough to have done what happened to you," Evonne observed, confused. She eased closer to the hatch.

"Careful." Amy raised her extinguisher and pointed it at Evonne. Connie did the same.

Evonne pushed herself through the hatchway and into the corridor. There were flames building on the far wall and there was fire extinguisher foam all around. Amy's first sprays must have killed the flames immediately at the doorway. Looking more closely, Evonne wasn't even sure if the fire had been on the walls nearby. All of the fire was farther aft along the surfaces but a good seven meters away.

"Clear to enter," she announced.

"What?" Amy looked confused as she floated in nervously. "I don't..."

"Backdraft," Connie said. "This corridor had been depleted of oxygen. When you opened that door, it sucked fresh air in with you and the fire had a quick burst of oxidizer. You were new fuel. God, you are lucky you didn't get hit worse."

"Right." Amy nodded in understanding. "Lucky."

"That's a good sign," Evonne agreed. "It means the fire is small enough to manage. On three, two, one..."

She kicked off the wall toward the flame and sprayed. The bursts from the extinguisher stopped her forward momentum and slowly pushed her back. She let off the handle and her spray stopped. Then Connie leapfrogged past her and waited until she got another four meters aft ward and let loose with her spray. The off-white foam splattered into the orange flickering ball at the end of the corridor and engulfed it. As she started moving backward, she let off her handle as Amy floated past, raising her own extinguisher to the ready.

"There!" Amy sprayed liberally around the hatch. "It's out."

As the three women came to a stop at the corridor hatch, they paused, and this time were more cautious. Connie released the latch and motioned everyone to the side.

"Hug the walls," Connie urged. Evonne and Amy nodded.

"Do it," Evonne said.

Connie opened the hatch. As soon as it was released, it sucked open, and a burst of flame shot through the door and then was sucked back inward.

"Now we see what happened to you, Amy," Evonne said. "Now, two more of these corridors and we're to the aft airlock. Same way as before. Let's go."

✧ ✧ ✧

Once they had reached the doors leading to the airlock, it was absolutely clear that the electronic controls were unresponsive due to the power failure. There was no way to open them simultaneously until the power was back on. And the middle door was between two raging fires. Evonne looked at the ship's floor map in her virtual view, hoping to come up with a plan. She didn't think they had enough fluid in the extinguishers to fight through all three rooms. They had put out the fires in the exterior corridor, but the fires through the middle three aft chambers of the ship were raging. Floating with their backs to the aft airlock that opened out into space on the starboard side of the ship, the only two doors nearby were the one they had come through at the exterior corridor and one in front of them that was extremely hot. Looking through the window, there was a complete haze of smoke and flickering orange and red balls of fire engulfing the room.

"There's no way to get to that middle door on the other side of that. And we'll have to do this manually," Evonne said. "Connie, help me with these inner airlock doors. Amy, keep an eye on our oxygen levels and the fire behind us."

Evonne released the manual latch pin on the airlock. Then the two engineers exerted their strength, struggling to turn the large manual wheel that controlled the door's locking mechanism.

"Goddamned microgravity," Connie cursed, losing her foothold on the wall.

"I know. Can't get a grip anywhere useful," Evonne agreed while doing her best to lock her feet into the handrails to push and pull against. Slowly, with grunts of effort, they managed to open the first door. "Shit design. If we ever design a starship, remind me to use latches you can operate in microgravity."

"Hell yeah, I will." Connie smiled at her through grunts.

"What's the plan, Evonne? We can't get in there. No way." Amy pointed at the chamber on the other side of the doorway.

As the airlock doors opened, revealing the EVA—extravehicular activity—suit locker and more than a dozen suits hanging on the wall, Evonne smiled. She looked at the suits, then the back door of the airlock that opened into space, and then back at her team.

"Suit up," Evonne said. "We'll open one door at a time. Starting with that one!"

She pointed at the airlock, then grinned at Amy and Connie.

CHAPTER 19

The *Pioneer*

For the most part, Dr. Jenna Rees and Dr. Mario Rivers had managed to avoid fire. There had been a few times where there were smoldering manifolds or smoke diffusing from behind panels. They had managed to locate the sources of each and extinguish them along their way. The darkness of the aft port-side chambers of the ship made it extremely difficult doing anything intricate like wiring and circuit repairs. They had managed well enough with headlamps and tool lights, but overhead lighting would have certainly been a bonus.

Finally, they had reached the location of the blown-out conduit just aft and port of the engine room. Even though the absence of gravity made their movements awkward as they floated near the damaged section, Jenna was beginning to get the hang of it. Oh, there had been a few days here and there of microgravity back in the Sol system before they initiated the Samara Drive, and then there were a few days at the turnaround, but she had been in cryosleep for that period, so microgravity wasn't new to her, but she wasn't a pro either. New or not, it required practice to maintain proficiency and it had been a while.

"Looks like a real mess," Mario commented as he examined the conduit shining his light from one end of it to the other. The conduit met with a cable manifold on a flange that had been blown apart from an extremely high voltage and high current surge. "We'll need to replace this section in order to get the power flowing again, for sure. Look at that."

"Wow, the wires are one big, welded mess." Jenna peered into the fracture of the metal conduit. It had been blown apart by what was probably over a million amps discharging through it, turning most of the wires and metal fragments into molten slag—fused back together into a big metal lump. "So, what's our plan here?"

"Hey, you're the electrical engineer, you tell me." Mario shrugged.

"We're not sorting through that for sure," Jenna said thoughtfully. "We need to cut every conduit at each end of the mess. Then we'll reconnect each, one at a time. We can start with the main power first and work back from there."

"Okay, cutting it first then, right?" Mario swiped at some icons in front of him, catching Jenna's attention.

"I'm finding a circuit diagram for this section. What are *you* looking for?" she asked Mario.

"Tools. I'll need a saw, a grinder, a torch, or something that can cut this. It's in the inventory somewhere on the ship. I simply need to find it." Mario continued to scroll through the ship's inventory. "There. Metal saw, compartment, Aft Four Corridor, Seven-B Tool Shed."

"Where's that?" Jenna asked.

"Haha, good question. Hey, Orion, where is Aft Four Corridor, Seven-B Tool Shed?"

"It is not far from you now," Orion replied. "I will show you on your map view."

"Thanks." Mario waited a second and then the map appeared in his virtual view, allowing him to locate it. "Looks like it's back up the corridor and one compartment over. I'll be right back. You good here by yourself?"

"Yes, but I should probably go with you in case there are fires or something," Jenna told him.

"Come on, then. Here's the map." Mario made a swiping motion toward her, sending the map into her virtual view.

"Hey, that's right by the conduit spares and the wire we need," Jenna said. "We can kill two birds with one stone here."

It took them another fifteen minutes to gather the replacement parts and the tools needed and then make their way back to the damaged power conduit. Fortunately, microgravity actually made that part of the job easier. The conduit by itself probably massed over seventy-five kilograms. Floating it down the corridor was a lot easier than carrying it in gravity, a fact that space travelers never really got used to. The only thing they had to worry about was the pipe's inertia, which the two of them were able to manage fairly easily.

"Jenna, Mario, do you copy?" Evonne's voice asked over the comms network earpieces they wore.

"Copy that, CHENG. Go ahead," Jenna replied.

"Be advised that we are going to soon start opening several corridors and chambers to space to extinguish the fires. I'm sending keep-out zones highlighted on your VR maps now," Evonne explained. "Keep an eye out for faulty seals on your end in case you need to take evasive actions."

"Understood, Evonne," Jenna said. "I think we're far enough on the other side of the engine room that we should be good."

"Roger that. But since you two are the only others down here on this end of the ship, if you can't keep at least two hatches between you and us, then stop now and find some suits."

Jenna looked at Mario, who was already swiping through the map Evonne had sent them. Sharing it with her, he highlighted in red the rooms the CHENG was about to evacuate. He then showed buffer doors in layers between them: marked with red if there were a vacuum on the other side, yellow if there was a red door between them and vacuum, and green if there was a yellow-and-red door or more between them and vacuum. They looked to have an ample buffer zone.

"Looks like we're good to go, Evonne," Mario observed.

"Good. We're pressing onward, then. Several sections will be evacuated momentarily. Let me know how the progress goes with the power," Evonne told them. "CHENG out."

"Let's get moving," Jenna said as she kicked off the bulkhead and down the last corridor back to the hatchway entering the room with the bad conduit. The two of them set the replacement materials and tools afloat—but tethered to a handhold.

"I'll get on with the cutting," Mario stated, unpacking the saw and assembling the guiderails and clamps.

"Good." Jenna nodded her head in the affirmative and started uncoiling lengths of wiring and cables that she was going to need.

Mario dropped the saw into the place where he planned to make his first cut. He slid the guiderail attachments on the conduit to either side of the cut mark and locked them down with the thumbscrews. He shook the saw back and forth to make sure it was appropriately fastened to the pipe.

"It ain't going anywhere," he muttered to himself. Then he set the blade about five millimeters from the surface of the conduit and turned it on. It started spinning with an electric motor hum. He then worked his feet into the holds beneath it and looked at Jenna, nodding. "If you can put any sort of pressure against my back, then that will help me crank the blade through the cut. The saw is attached and not going anywhere, but turning this crank will be like turning a doorknob in microgravity. I'm as likely to turn as the knob."

"I've got you," Jenna said, securing the wiring and connectors to a handhold near her and then floating into position behind Mario. She locked her shoes into foot rails on the floor and then put both hands on Mario's shoulders. "Ready when you are."

Mario turned the hand crank, pushing the blade forward into the metal conduit. As the saw hit, orange and white sparks flew and there was an ear-piercing screech of metal against metal. A few seconds later, it stopped.

"That was easy enough. I like this saw." Mario smiled and then started releasing the thumbscrews. "We'll cut right there next."

The two engineers carefully detached the saw and then repeated what they had just done at the other end. Moments later, they were pulling the damaged conduit from the wall and securing it on the other side of the room with duct tape and straps. They then eased the replacement section into place to measure it.

"Okay, that's how long we need. Make sure to allow for ten centimeters extra on each end so the repair conduit can be clamped over the old one," Jenna said.

"Got it." Mario took the replacement part across the room where he had fastened the saw to the handrail.

"You cut it while I start in on the wires," Jenna told him.

"Copy that." Mario went to work on the repair conduit. It wasn't like a standard conduit. Instead, the repair conduit was split longways and hinged so it could be clamped around a set of wires after the fact rather than pulling wires through it. Once in place, the repair piece would be closed around the wires and the conduit at each end. There it would be bolted together.

"How's the wiring going?" Mario asked, "Any idea what caused the blowout?"

"Wiring is getting there. These conductor repair clamps are useful," Jenna said as she held two ends of wire up, one from the conduit and one of the replacement. The conductors were bigger in diameter than her thumb and very stiff. They were coated with a very thick insulation material designed to hold millions of volts at very high amperage current flow. Once in place next to each other, she placed a repair sleeve clamp over the two ends and depressed it. As the clamp activated, it released a chemical composition of liquid metals that welded the two ends of the wires together, making a perfect electrical and mechanical connection. The exterior of the clamp was covered with a thick insulator.

"Not sure of the cause yet. That will take some time to sort out once we get power back everywhere. Evonne might have a better idea about that than I do. We'll have to wait and see." Jenna shook her head, her brow furrowing in concentration. "Could have been a power surge or a malfunction due to the engine failure. We won't know for sure until we can assess the damage to the rest of the systems."

It took the two of them several more minutes to get the repair conduit cut to size and all the wiring replaced. Jenna tested the wiring for continuity with a signal meter placed at each end of the cuts and all looked like it was good. Then she motioned to Mario to put the conduit into place and clamp it down. With the new conduit in place, they initiated a test to restore power but only on one of the circuits they had fixed. Jenna had thrown the other breakers. She certainly didn't want a repeat of that thing blowing out with millions of amps, especially not with them in the room with it.

"Okay, Orion, I'm closing one circuit. When I do, I'll tell you to cycle the power," Jenna told the AI. She flipped the breaker to the one cable into the on position. "Okay, Orion, cycle power from the forward power conditioning unit."

"Very well," Orion said. Then a soft hum filled the corridor as some of the systems slowly came back online and some of the lighting in the corridor and in the room came on.

"It's working," Jenna confirmed, relief washing over her. "Let's get the rest of these lines reconnected and the power fully restored, and then we'll see what the CHENG wants us doing next."

CHAPTER 20

The *Pioneer*

"Let that sink in a minute," Captain Mitchison paused doing her best to keep tears from her eyes. "Eight souls lost."

"How did we not know that was happening?" The ship's XO, Thomas Vetcha, slammed a fist against his console in the makeshift bridge as he scrolled through the list of names that were now marked as "died in service." "CHENG, what do you know?"

"I, uh, there was no warning," Evonne replied with a devastated look on her face, palms facing upward. "We should have had alerts that the cryobeds were failing. The diagnostics I ran this morning show that the power surge blew out those lines to the eight beds. The backup systems were cycled off to replace the damaged power lines and the battery backups didn't last long enough for the warming and waking sequence. Had they been sleeping, the batteries would have lasted for days, but not for the warming sequence. The alert switched the heaters and reverse cryo units on. The power drained and..."

"Orion, why was there no warning of this?" Zambia Carter, the ship's chief medical officer, asked.

"The sensor inputs for all those beds were showing normal sequencing. As the batteries drained, the alert sensors were immediately shifted to the backup power network. Once that was shut down, there was no power to the beds on the affected circuit. Therefore, no sensor data to alert me. I am truly sorry for this loss."

"That is the goddamned dumbest design I've ever heard of!" Jenna Rees exclaimed, clearly fighting back tears herself.

The captain didn't want this turning into a blame game or a situation that was more emotionally charged than it already was. She held up her hand to calm everyone down.

"Alright." Penelope made eye contact with all of the senior crew members she had assembled on the bridge. "The ship has some design flaws. It is the first of its kind and this type of thing, unfortunately, happens on spaceships from time to time. It happened to us. We can't undo it. We can learn from it and prevent it from happening again."

Penelope paused and looked at each of them one at a time, again making sure to make eye contact. There were tears filling most of their eyes. Anger filled their faces. And for the crew members who were actually close to the ones lost, there was shock. Worst of all, Penelope saw fear in all of their eyes. While she was doing her level best to hide the fear she was feeling, she knew that it must be written all over her body language, all over her face. She did her best to remain calm and hold her emotions in check.

"Doc, store the bodies for burial. They wanted to go to Proxima b, so that's where we're taking them." She looked into the CMO's eyes for reassurance. Carter nodded in the affirmative and made no sound. Penelope gave her a quick single nod in reply. "XO, give us the summary."

"Yes, ma'am," Vetcha said stiffly and then cleared his throat to quiet the bridge. "As more and more of the ship's crew have been awakened from cryo, they are working diligently to restore power to all systems and repair the damaged sections now that the CHENG has managed to successfully extinguish the fires and plug the leaks. The damage assessment is becoming more and more dire with every report, Captain. All of the repair teams know that time is of the essence and are working tirelessly in the microgravity. For the moment, it would appear that the immediate life-threatening challenges have been addressed. That said, our worries are from over. I think Nav and the CHENG can give you a better assessment, but we are drifting too fast and are way off course. Without a miracle, we will miss Proxima b by a very long way."

"Thank you, Tom." Penelope didn't respond to the XO's

summary more than that. She understood what he had said and what it meant. They were all dead. Maybe not at the moment, or tomorrow, or a month from now, but they were lost in space. At some point they would run out of critical materials—food, water, air; something that would end it for them. The fate of the *Pioneer* and its crew hung in the balance and as they battled against the harsh reality of their predicament, Captain Penelope Anne Mitchison had little she could offer in regard to a rescue or even solace.

She looked around the backup bridge they were using on the rotation ring. It was small, cramped, and the dizzying artificial gravity was uncomfortable. She thought about moving to the actual bridge of the ship, but wasn't sure she wanted to sit that long in microgravity either. Everything was a mess.

At this point in the mission, they should be waking up, entering the Proximan system with hopes of soon being in orbit and making it to the surface of the alien world they had come to help rescue, to make a new life on, and to have hope of making things in the universe better. But now, well, Penelope had to come to grips with the fact that there might not be a happy ending to this mission. But she wasn't going to give in yet. She was the captain. She had traveled across the stars with a purpose. There had to be a way to achieve that purpose.

"Evonne?" Penelope turned to the chief engineer and shrugged.

"Once we got the fires out and were able to get into the engine room, what we found wasn't good. The reaction system feeding the Samara Drive is done, so that means main power from the fusion reactor is out until such time as that system can be rebuilt. The input nozzles were melted together from the power surge. That means we have to build all new injector blocks and we don't have the material for that." The CHENG shook her head back and forth in defeat.

"I see." She started to say something more, but the CHENG continued.

"And that ain't even the worst of it," she stated. "The force chamber, the large conductive Frustrum, well, there's a hole in it the size of a two-person hatchway with jagged shards bent outward through the bulkhead into the adjacent corridor. That did two things. One, it is what started the fires. And two, the most important, it generated a huge propulsive force vector for the two hundred and thirty-three microseconds it took for the drive to fail. Nav can tell you why that is so important in a second."

Penelope looked back and forth between Evonne and Dr. Kimberly Jones, the astrometrics and navigation expert. Jones was shaking her head in defeat almost in unison with the CHENG.

"The bottom line, though . . ." Evonne continued. "Well, main power is out for good, or at least any foreseeable future. Propulsion is done without new materials and major repair. On the upside, the secondary power fission reactor is running fine, and we'll have ten kilowatts for a century or so. That's enough for life support and critical ship systems, but that's it. It's gonna start getting really cold in here soon, though. I had to shut the heaters down. Fortunately, it takes a pretty good while for radiative cooling on a vessel this big. We're not turning that thing back on anytime soon."

"Is that the extent of it?" Captain Mitchison ran a hand through her disheveled hair, her expression a mix still of sadness for her lost crew, frustration with the situation, and determination that they would somehow find a way out of this mess with no further loss of life. She wasn't prepared to give up. There had to be a way to complete the mission and deliver them all to safety at Proxima b.

"Not really," the CHENG answered with a sigh. "There are a thousand minor things to deal with. We're dealing with them in order of priority. But . . ."

"I don't like the sound of that 'but,' CHENG." The XO scowled a bit.

". . . But there's one more soon-to-be major problem," the CHENG announced. "The rotation ring uses electric thrusters to spin up. As friction continues to work against the rotation, it will continue to decelerate and eventually stop without maintenance burns. Those thrusters use a lot of power. If we want to continue to have artificial gravity, we'll need to find a work-around."

"Aux thrusters?" Vetcha inquired, his voice tinged with a glimmer of hope. "Can we at least steer the ship any?"

"Sure, we have them to some extent," Evonne replied, projecting diagrams of the auxiliary thrusters on the holographic display and sharing the virtual screens. "I just . . . well, I'm really not sure what good they do us. They sure as hell can't slow us down from forty percent the speed of light."

"Damn." The XO frowned and then followed with a heavy sigh. "So, we're hurtling through space at a velocity that won't let us stop, and we can't even really steer. How long until we reach Proxima?"

"Nav?" Penelope turned to Kimberly.

"Well, it took me a good while to figure out where we are now and then to realign the telescopes and comm systems, but we are right here moving on this trajectory as best I can tell." Dr. Kimberly Jones had spent her entire career on ships in the Sol system working in astrometrics and navigation. She had calculated orbits and trajectories and determined ship positions for more than twenty years.

Pushing forty-two, the captain thought of her as one of the older and wiser members of her crew, the majority of which was under thirty Earth years old. A handful of more seasoned experts were between forty and fifty. Penelope noted that the woman still looked very healthy and had many good years ahead of her. Well, she would if they managed to find a way out of their current situation.

Kimberly shared her virtual screens with the bridge crew as she explained the trajectory data. She displayed their approach to the Proxima system on the big screen at the front of the makeshift bridge where the orbits of the system's planets were displayed along with the trajectory, the original one and the current one, of the *Pioneer* overlaid on it.

"At our current velocity, we'll pass through the Proxima system in approximately three months, but we'll be roughly twenty astronomical units off course, and we won't be able to slow down or make any course corrections. Well, at least not any course corrections that would matter," she told them all.

Silence swept over them, and Captain Mitchison made note of the crew's faces. Most were stoic but a few were distraught with defeat. The weight of their situation pressed down on them. They were all smart, capable space travelers. The were all well trained. Captain Mitchison knew that they all understood exactly what the navigation expert and the CHENG had told them. They were in really deep shit.

The gravity of their helplessness was more profound and unsettling than the queasiness generated by the artificial forces of the rotational ring. The realization that they were adrift, unable to reach their destination, and facing an uncertain fate settled in with all of them. With a deep inhale and then a long slow exhale, Captain Mitchison broke the silence, her voice unwavering as she addressed her team.

"Alright, we need to constantly update the assessment of the ship's systems. Kimberly, keep monitoring our trajectory and alert us if anything changes. Evonne, what's the status of our main CO_2 scrubber?"

"Right, Captain. That was one of the lower-priority jobs I mentioned earlier. Uh, let me see here..." Evonne moved some virtual icons around in front of her and then responded. "The main CO_2 scrubber was damaged during the power surge, but the backups are holding. We might be able to retrofit the main scrubber with some three-D-printed components and restore it fully, or uh, close to fully anyways. That is, when I get time to do it or can delegate the task."

"A positive, I guess. Work with the XO to find crew to delegate as much as you can." Captain Mitchison nodded in approval. "Do it. We can't afford to run out of breathable air. How about life-support and environmental controls? You said the leaks are stopped? Are there any chances of further leaks?"

"Yes, Captain. Pressure is holding fine," Evonne replied. "I don't see any future issues with cabin pressure."

"I think we could survive for a very long time on the air and scrubbers functional now, Captain." Dr. Carter added, "Life-support systems are operational. As the temperature starts dropping, we can pull all personnel into one or two chambers to conserve body heat and perhaps run heaters in those locations. No need to heat the entire ship, I suspect. But, soon, we will need to ration our supplies carefully. We have enough food and water to last six months or so on starvation rations. Since we don't really know what our plans are for deceleration and disembarkation, we need to start planning for the long haul."

The gravity of their predicament shadowed the conversation as the crew continued to absorb the reality of it. They were stranded in the cold vacuum of space, racing toward an unknown fate in the wrong direction, with limited resources, and no means of control. The *Pioneer*, once a happy vessel of exploration and pledged to salvation, or at least aid, for the Proximans, had become the crew's solitary lifeline in the vast cosmos. Penelope prayed it wouldn't become their mass coffin as well.

"We're not giving up," Penelope stated through a clinched jaw. "We're a resilient crew, and we'll find a way to survive this. But for now, let's focus on stabilizing our ship and extending our resources as much as possible. We'll face the challenges ahead together, as a team. Kimberly, can you get a good enough fix on our position to point the comms dishes at Proxima b?"

"Already done, Captain," Dr. Jones answered. "We're currently receiving their streaming signals. We can send them a message whenever you like."

"Well, at least that's working," Penelope said. "I'll record a message ASAP."

PART 3

BACK TO THE BEYOND

CHAPTER 21

Proxima b

The dim red glow of Proxima Centauri cast long shadows across the landscape outside the window of the main communications ground station conference room. The aurora was very active, creating beautiful violets, indigos, and greens. Roy noted how pretty the view was as he adjusted the connection to the *Samaritan*, circling above them in high geostationary orbit, by moving some icons about in his virtual screens. The dish was pointed in the right direction, but the filters had been set for a low-orbit transit Doppler shift. He adjusted the filters and the image on the screen went from displaying that there was no signal to an image of the inside of the captain's ready room on the starship.

"There we go. We have you clearly now, Captain. Sorry about that." Roy smiled as he leaned back in his chair, nodding toward Ambassador Jesus to his left and Polkingham to his right.

"No worries, Roy. How are the wife and kids?" Crosby asked as he looked up from something he had been scribbling on a tablet with a stylus.

"They are great, Captain. Thanks for asking," Roy replied. "I'm glad you could pull the bridge crew together with such short notice."

"Well, being in between excursions to the outer planets right now, we really are just hanging out. In fact, I plan to start a rotation of the crew planetside for extended leave. We really only need a skeleton crew here otherwise."

"You might want to hold off on that a bit," Roy added sheepishly.

"Why is that, Roy?" Crosby looked up, giving them his full attention at that statement.

"We've received a message from the *Pioneer.* They're in deep trouble, Captain." Roy frowned as he played the recorded message from the *Pioneer.* The strained faces of Captain Mitchison and her crew appeared on the screen in front of them as she explained their catastrophic engine failure, the loss of control, and their current trajectory that would send them into deep space, missing Proxima b with no way to slow down. In order to save on supplies, Captain Mitchison ended with the note that she would be ordering all but a handful of crew back into cryobeds very soon. The message ended with a detailed download of all systems' status and ship damage.

XO Artur Clemons, CHENG Bob Roca, Xi Lin, and other senior members of the *Samaritan* crew floated in the background behind where Crosby was belted into his chair. The message painted a bleak picture of the *Pioneer*'s predicament. Without some sort of intervention, the ship and its entire crew complement would be lost to space.

"That is a situation no captain ever wants to have to face. You can tell by her expression and body language that she and her crew know they are done for." Captain Crosby ran a hand through his grizzled beard. Since they had been on a low duty cycle for the past year or more, he had been less by-the-book about his appearance. While he had maintained professionalism and wasn't really violating any codes of the space guild, he had relaxed the protocols he had paid close adherence to earlier in his career. "What's the timestamp on this signal, Proxima relative?"

"With their velocity and trajectory information, and the clock information in the message, we calculate it to be nearly five weeks ago," Roy answered.

"Damn." Crosby rubbed at this beard some more unconsciously. "We can't leave them out there to die. Bob, can we fire up the Samara Drive and rendezvous with them? We could at least rescue them, right?"

"Well, I'd have to do some math here," said Roca, the skilled astronav pilot of the *Samaritan*, and its recently promoted CHENG. He scratched his head as he contemplated the possibilities and then opened a virtual screen in front him to share with the group. There was a brief delay from the data latency from geostationary orbit to planetside, but then the screens filled in with data, trajectories, and calculations. Bob tapped the *Samaritan* icon to center it on the screen and then collapsed his hands together, zooming out on a not-to-scale view where he then overlaid the trajectory data from the *Pioneer* onto it. After a moment of conversation with his and the ship's AI, several energy curves appeared in real time as he adjusted parameters and added data from navigation instruments. After a couple of minutes, there were several solutions converging.

"Captain, as you can see here, we *can* fire up the Samara Drive, match velocities, and at the very least rescue the crew and their equipment. In order to rendezvous with them before they get too far outside of the system, we should be getting underway as soon as possible—I would say in less than two months from now at most. But if we want to catch the ship and slow them down to bring them into orbit around Proxima b, that's a little harder."

"Why harder?" Jesus asked.

"Well, Mr. Ambassador," Roca explained, "you see, we'd need mooring hardware to attach the two ships safely, and that would require serious engineering analysis, maybe even modifications to both ships."

"If I may, sir," Xi Lin, the chief tech for interior systems, interjected. "We have some gridwork we had been working on to dock-direct to the *Emissary*, but we stopped the project once she left Proxima. It might be retrofitted for the purpose of mooring to the *Pioneer*."

"How far along was that? I seem to recall we were barely getting started when we called it off," Crosby asked.

"We had designs completed and we had gathered all the raw materials. Some of the structure has been fabricated, but at this point, it's just gridwork stored in the aft shuttle bay," Lin explained. "We'd need to do some quick modifications to make it work. And we'd really need some engineering specs from the *Pioneer*."

"Specs seemed to be on the way, Xi," Roy interrupted. "The message is a continuous download of ship's status and specs. Their CHENG is pretty thorough and apparently good, or at least hopeful, at anticipating data we'd need. There's a bow-to-stern model two thirds the way through on download now."

"Lin, get that data download direct from Dr. Burbank as soon as he gets it," Captain Crosby ordered. "Enrico, what are the risks involved in this operation?"

Vulpetti, the *Samaritan* design engineer with a knack for troubleshooting, pondered the question. Roy had known CHENG Mastrano well and worked closely with her. He missed her—and Rain—the most. He had never really spent much time with Enrico.

"Firing up the Samara Drive comes with its own set of risks, of course, but the *Samaritan* has a long, stable track record in that regard. But as far as slowing down another ship, well, we're talking about a tremendous amount of energy and stress on the ship for which it wasn't designed. But if we are careful, and if we take the right amount of time to make course corrections, then I believe we should be able to do this safely within the engineering limits of whatever makeshift moors we come up with. It may be a long mission."

"Explain," Crosby said.

"Okay." Vulpetti shrugged. "Simply put, if we try to slow down too fast, we will likely rip apart our mooring points and damage both ships. But with slow, calculated adjustment thrust vectors we can manage. Slow course changes mean more eccentric elliptical orbits. So—"

"Following Kepler's Laws," Roca interrupted since he was the navigation expert, "the period of the orbit will be longer. Meaning, it will take us longer to get that ship to Proxima b safely than it would with just the *Samaritan*."

"We should also consider the *Pioneer*'s life-support and resource situation. They have six months of supplies at starvation rations according to their message," Polkingham chimed in from beside Roy planetside. Roy nodded in agreement with him as he continued to speak. "We definitely need to factor in the time it takes to rescue and slow them down. If we're looking at more than six months, then they are going to need additional supplies."

"We should, perhaps, run all of the numbers through the rest of the science and engineering complement here and on the *Samaritan* for other possibilities," Captain Crosby said. "Enrico, you and Bob work on that for some optimized solutions. Reach out to every member of the science teams planetside, every one of them; hell, even the economist might think of something we haven't."

"Right away, Captain," they responded in unison.

"We'll need launch windows and trajectories sooner rather than later," Crosby added. "Charles, what about diplomacy? If we take the ship out of orbit and leave you folks stranded here for a year or more, how does that play with the Fintidierians?"

"That is a good question, Captain," the ambassador said. "We might want to ask if the Fintidierian astronaut trainees want to go along. It would be good training for them and good diplomacy for us. I will get a meeting with the secretary general immediately."

"There is the matter of the quarantine," Polkingham added. "I mean, now that we know we are all infected with an engineered bacteriophage, we will have to warn them before exposing them."

"They all volunteered to come here, Dr. Polkingham," Crosby replied. "I doubt they would turn down a rescue over not having female offspring without nanobot intervention."

"Yes, of course," Polkingham agreed.

"Captain, Ambassador." Roy looked at Crosby through the screen first and then turned to Charles. "This might actually help the diplomatic situation."

"How so, Roy?" Jesus asked with a raised eyebrow.

"Before, it was another Terran ship coming without being asked," Roy explained. He was very personally aware of the thin balance of Fintidierian and Terran cultures. He had personally been held captive during some of the diplomatic turmoil. "But now, well, now it is a Terran ship in distress that could use the Fintidierians' help."

"Well, I'm not so sure what the Fintidierians can do to help that we cannot manage on the *Samaritan*," Clemons added.

"That isn't the point, Artur," Roy told the XO. "The point is to let the Fintidierians get to help, and feel as though the Terrans are doomed without them."

"Brilliant, Roy!" Jesus slapped the table. "Of course. Captain, our engineers will determine something that the Fintidierians must supply or build in order for us to save the *Pioneer*. This will go a very long way in making relations between us better. This will be like kids gathering aluminum during World War Two. Everybody can do their part! Up to this point we have been like gods from the stars, coming and going as we please with little need for help from the primitives of Fintidier. Showing them that we need their help to save our people puts them on more of an equal footing. It gives them skin in the game."

"Those were my thoughts exactly," Roy agreed. "But I think we need more, to do more."

"Such as...?" Jesus asked.

"We now have data describing the ship's crew," Roy said. "Let's put their images and stories up all over Fintidier so that everyone on the planet knows all of them by name. Saving those poor Terrans from that doomed ship should be on every news broadcast, spoken about on the radio programs. We should have images of them on posters: 'Save the *Pioneer.*'"

"I'll have people in my office start on that," Jesus said as he smiled in agreement. "Wonderful idea."

"Very well," Crosby agreed. "CHENG, keep the use of Fintidierian materials and personnel in mind as you work out solutions. And Charles, Roy, all of you down there, work on this too. I suspect we don't have a lot of time to dilly-dally if we plan on saving these people."

"Copy that, Captain." Jesus nodded. "We'll talk soon."

"*Samaritan* out." Crosby waved and cut the feed. Roy reached over and toggled the monitor to the home screen.

"How about that?" Roy said to nobody in particular.

"How about that indeed, Roy." Jesus looked at him with a raised eyebrow.

"What?" Roy shrugged.

"Roy, you have to go with them," Jesus added with a frown. "I know you don't want to hear that, but..."

"Hell no, Jesus! I was gone from my family for too long on the ride out here, against my will, if you don't recall..."

"Roy, Roy," Jesus held up his hands. "I know. But, you are also well known to the Fintidierians, and you are the best fix-it man we brought from Earth, on purpose or not."

"Nooooo."

"Yes, Roy. You know this," Jesus said. "But look, this isn't a dangerous ride. Not any more than any other. It's time you take your family for a vacation."

"Take my family? I don't know..." replied Roy.

"Seriously, it will give the kids something they can brag about when they get back. They will have been on the ship that rescued the doomed people from Earth. They're old enough to remember this the rest of their lives."

Roy considered the idea and replied, "We will discuss it as a family, and I will let you know."

CHAPTER 22

The *Samaritan*—Proxima System

It took the better part of two months to prepare the *Samaritan*, the Terran crew, and the Fintidierian crew for the trip to rendezvous with the *Pioneer*. There had been lots of fanfare, live press debates, and even a few riots across the planet, but in the end the Fintidierians couldn't bring themselves to let the ship full of women from Earth go unaided. Of course, the Terrans were going to make a rescue attempt with or without the Fintidierians, but diplomatically, a joint mission was a much better solution for everyone involved.

After a month of debate, followed by those two months of preparation and training, the time for departure had finally arrived. It was now or never, at least according to the press, who claimed that was what the Terran astronavigational experts were saying. While anyone who was a student of even Fintidierian-level (Newtonian on Earth) mechanics would know that as long as there was enough fuel and propulsive effect, there was no "now or never" point.

It wasn't orbital mechanics that was the limiting factor. The people in the know, Terrans and Fintidierians alike, understood that the *Pioneer* was likely damaged with failing life-support systems and every moment wasted was another moment that something else could go astray.

The entire contingent of scientists and engineers from Earth, along with some of the greatest minds and most industrious individuals from Fintidier, had gathered to design, build, and test a deployable and attachable-in-space rig to dock the *Samaritan* to the *Pioneer* in such a way as to allow for the former to propel the latter home to Proxima b.

Teams started planning and training from day one while the politicians debated and the activists rioted. Then followed a complete month of shuttle runs up to orbit and back down to the planet, until the *Samaritan* was stuffed full of life-support supplies as well as the components for the mooring. They had left orbit under conventional thruster power. Three weeks of slowly thrusting away from Proxima b into a safe location to engage the main engine had led the ship and its complement to that moment. It was time for the main engine to be activated.

Graggyon Oo'ortava, "Grag" to his friends, was strapped into the cryobed gee couch that had been assigned to him and was patiently waiting for the Samara Drive countdown to reach zero. He wriggled slightly against the restraints in anticipation of the main drive propulsion to kick in. After many trips up and down to orbit and then three weeks in space, Grag had become pretty much accustomed to space travel—or so he thought. The occasional periods when engines were turned off and microgravity took hold, well, he still wasn't sure that his stomach agreed with him that he had become so accustomed. None of that would matter much longer—once the main drive fired, the cryobed would close and he would be cycled into sleep for two months.

". . . but that didn't work either," the face on the screen in front of him continued. It was his friend and mentor, Dr. Sentell. "We've tried every antiviral approach known on Earth and nothing seems to have any impact on this thing. I don't know how the Atlanteans put this virus together and it is giving us a hell of a time tearing it apart."

Grag listened to the frustration in his friend's voice as he continued playing back the message. The countdown clock in the corner of his screen showed thirty-one seconds to drive initiation.

"You've really been missed in the lab, Grag," Sentell continued. "Yoko says you were the only person buffering us from Filip's constant questions and pontifications. Mostly his questions. His endless questions. But then again, you always have plenty of questions too. I do hate that we're gonna miss skiezel season in the spring, but you have to do what is right for you, my good man. Nobody here blames you, and we're all very proud of you!"

Grag thought of fishing and working in the lab with the fertility team. It had been amazing work and they had made major strides in solving the crisis for all Fintidierians. But once Grag had caught wind of the possibility of traveling out into space with the Terrans, he asked his friend to put in a word for him to go. Dr. Chris had done that. The fertility science team had requested that Grag be included in the mission, then the secretary general of Fintidier got behind it as well. Grag had become somewhat of an intermediary between the Terrans and the Fintidierians, even though that had never been his intention.

"All hands, all hands," a voice sounded over the ship's speakers. "Prepare for main Samara Drive initiation in five, four, three, two, one . . . initiating."

Grag suddenly felt his weight increasing as he was pressed into the bed. He watched the flight-dynamics screen in front of him show the force loading based on Terran gravity multiples. Once the loading hit two-point-one gravities, or gees as the Terrans called it, Grag felt almost suffocated by the weight of his own chest. His thin bodysuit felt like a weighted blanket pressing down on him. He understood then why they had been forced to have physical fitness training every morning since the team had been chosen. He focused his mind on breathing and putting the extra weight on his chest out of his mind as he had been trained to do. That helped only a little. He simply had to trust physics and the fact that the Terrans were spacefarers, and accept all this as standard procedure. The Terrans did this all the time.

He started the message playback from where it had been interrupted at drive initiation. There were brief images and goodbyes from Polkingham, Yoko, Chris, and even Filip. His family and friends had messages there as well, but it was the main message from Dr. Chris that he was most interested in. He continued the playback.

"Look at you, my friend," Sentell said. "Grag! You are a star voyager, an astronaut, years, probably decades before your people would have been ready for it. You will return to Fintidier as a hero, a celebrity among your people, you know. You will be too big and famous for us to go fishing anymore. Not that we will have had time for it with the fertility research and our ketchup side gig. By the way, I will keep the ball rolling on that. Your Uncle Thevinier has offered to manage the day-to-day tomato crop gardening. I sent him some seeds and videos of how to grow and harvest tomatoes. By the time summer rolls around we should have enough for a warehouse full of ketchup. Your mother has taken on finding all of the kitchen components and cooks we need, at least for our first run at this. Oh, and Thevinier even says one of your cousins has a chain of produce stands where we can sell the product. I know the Terrans will want as much as we can make. Hopefully, the Fintidierians will like it as much as you and will also want more than we can make."

Grag laughed lightly but then realized that had been a bad idea. At two times his normal bodyweight, even laughing was proving to be painful. Dr. Chris continued for several more minutes describing daily tasks, the virus research, and about how rich they were going to be once Grag returned. He even made a joke about exploiting the astronaut thing on the ketchup bottles—although Grag wasn't exactly sure if that had been a joke, or if Chris had been serious. Sometimes, even after all the time the two had spent together, it was hard for Grag to tell exactly what Chris meant, especially when he was using Terran humor.

He was suddenly distracted by a slight burning sensation in his right wrist. He looked down by moving his eyes and could see a blue liquid coursing through the intravenous tube there. The screen showing his vital signs became more visible as the lid to the cryobed slowly closed down over him with a hissing sound filling the bed chamber. Grag could vaguely feel the whirring vibration of a linear actuator retracting the lid. Feeling that and knowing what it was, somehow was reassuring to him. It was something he understood.

"Heart rate is fifty-one, blood pressure is one hundred ten over sixty-seven," he whispered faintly. His eyelids were starting to get extremely heavy, and he was starting to feel cold. It wasn't so much a bone-chilling cold as much as a slow, deep coldness that sapped him of all of his energy. He almost panicked, as if he were dying, but Grag remembered from the quick training course on the cryosleep chambers that this would be normal. He forced his eyes open one last time as the video from Sentell was ending.

"...and look at it this way, buddy, you get to meet all those new women first. And you'll have almost a year up there with them to get to know them. Come back...we'll be rich...women... Good luck...and...fish for...beer..."

Grag could no longer follow the coherence of what his great friend and mentor was saying. He finally exhaled a long, slow breath, giving in to the lifeless feeling, and drifted into the cold, calm blackness of cryosleep.

CHAPTER 23

The *Samaritan* and the *Pioneer*

After weeks of meticulous planning and calculations, three weeks of acceleration to a safe location for operating the Samara Drive at full power, two months in cryosleep for the *Samaritan*'s crew and nearly four months for the *Pioneer*'s crew, the *Samaritan* had reached the designated rendezvous point in deep space, approximately forty thousand Terran astronomical units (AU) or a bit more than half a light-year from the Proxima system. The ship had successfully initiated the Samara Drive and matched velocities with the *Pioneer*, bringing them side by side in the vast cosmic expanse. The two ships were so far from the parent star that it was little more than the brightest object in the sky at this point—not much brighter than the gas giants as viewed from Proxima b, or Jupiter from Earth.

The ships' artificial intelligences had triggered the cryo shutdown and both crews had been brought back to consciousness. The long, perilous journey into the void for the *Pioneer* had hopefully been averted. There was great hope that the previously doomed humanitarian mission could be put back on course. While there was hope, though, there was still a lot of work to be done.

"Captain Mitchison, this is Captain Crosby of the *Samaritan*. Do you copy?" Crosby floated slightly above the command chair on the bridge, looking at the comms officer on duty as he swigged liquid electrolytes through the straw of a squeeze bottle. "Comms? Anything?"

"Coming through now, Captain," the comms officer replied as the forward viewscreen filled with an interior view of the *Pioneer*'s bridge.

"Hello, Captain Crosby! Hello, *Samaritan*!" Captain Mitchison looked the worse for wear if you asked Crosby, but they had been through a lot over the past six months or so.

"While I would like to spend a moment or two making small talk, it doesn't seem appropriate given the dire premise of your current situation, Captain. So, pleasantries aside, we sent you details of the ancient alien virus that we have now detected on Proxima b. And you must understand that as far as we can tell, all the members of my crew, and of course everyone on Proxima b, are infected with it. The only effect of the disease, as far as we can tell, is to stop males from producing female chromosome carrying sperm that can swim. Our scientists have developed a work-around, but there is no cure. Please advise that you and your crew are fully aware of this," Crosby said.

"Yes, Captain Crosby, every person on this ship is aware of this virus problem," Captain Mitchison replied. "And to be honest, none of us give a flying damn."

"Well, then, permission to send relief and rescue boarding parties from the *Samaritan* to the *Pioneer*, Captain?" Crosby asked.

"By all means! By all means! We are all in desperate need of food and heat, Captain. Anything you can do to help with that would be much appreciated."

Crosby turned and made a gesture to XO Roca, telling him to get on with it. They had just been waiting for the *Pioneer* crew to wake and respond affirmatively to being boarded.

"Captain, we have both of our shuttles on the way now to your fore and aft docking ports. We will then start working on a more permanent docking situation. The shuttles are loaded with temporary power units, supplies, rations, and general rescue equipment. If you can get me a list, we will do the best we can to accommodate any needs you might have. Until that time, might I suggest we off-load your nonessential crew here to the *Samaritan* as our engineering teams go there? We have plenty of spare room, food, and heat over here."

"Everyone but myself, the XO, the CHENG, and a handful of others that you will need here to help figure out the ship's current configuration are free to join you. I'll make an announcement for them to be prepared to disembark at your first convenience. Have your chief of the away team connect with my XO and start prioritizing and scheduling that. Or I can tell them to go wait in line," Mitchison replied.

"I'll have our AI contact yours and send alerts to your crew when to queue up. That way, we will not have too many clogging up the docking rings. Have your AI remove from the lists whomever will be staying there."

"Okay, will do. Captain, I have to warn you that we've, uh, modified the ship a tremendous amount over the past six months. There's a lot of spit, duct tape, and prayers holding her together right now. We've had to take shifts in the cryobeds to keep a vigil out for malfunctioning beds. We lost eight already. My God, Captain. Thank you for coming to us."

"Understood Captain. Teams are on their way now. We will tend to immediate needs first. Then we have to figure out a more permanent solution so we can get your crew and your ship to Proxima b. We may have to have the majority of your crew cryosleep over here. We have plenty of spare beds, though, as we're on approximately a forty percent crew presently."

Grag volunteered for the first away-team missions. He hadn't come all that way to be like most of the other Fintidierians and simply watch and claim they were part of the mission, fulfilling some political purpose for the secretary general. No, Grag had been part of the team that had discovered the temporary fix to the female birth rate problem. In a sense, it had been his idea to use nanomachines to make female babies. It had also been his ideas that had led Sentell to discover the bacteriophage microvirus device that was the culprit for the fertility infection. While they hadn't found a cure for it yet, they had found the cause. And he had been an integral part of the process.

Grag had become somewhat famous amongst the Fintidierians, and not only did he have a reputation to live up to, he had a general drive and curiosity to learn and do what he could to help his people. And saving these women who had traveled the stars to hopefully mate with aliens from another world to help save their race, well, Grag had never heard of anything more heroic, selfless, and plain amazing, and he couldn't wait to meet such amazing people—such amazing women. And if there was something he could do to help, then help is what he would do.

Grag had studied more and learned more in the past several years since the Terrans had arrived than he had in his entire lifetime. He had become a sponge, or at least he had tried to be. For a long time, he had maintained his undergraduate and then graduate studies in physics at the Fintidierian level at the Gwonura Institute for Learning, while simultaneously following around Dr. Sentell and the others on the fertility crisis team. He had also volunteered for the mission to save the *Pioneer*, which had led to an intensive two months of around-the-clock crash courses in all things spacecraft, space travel, and modern Terran engineering concepts. And then, after the secretary general and the fertility crisis team (mostly Dr. Chris) had insisted, Grag had been fitted for artificial intelligence contact lenses. He was still getting used to having a voice in his head as well as seeing things in front of him that weren't there. But he was catching on quickly.

Atop all that, Grag had also volunteered for the cryosleep training regimen. For the past two months while he had been in cryosleep, the superconducting quantum interference transceivers in the bed had been playing on a continuous never-ending loop four graduate-level courses (by Terran standards) directly into his unconscious mind. The first was "Modern Physics and Engineering for Interstellar Travel." The second course was "The Engineer's Guide to the *Pioneer*," which had been sent months prior. It was effectively the ship's user's manual and it covered everything from astronavigation, the Samara Drive basics, ship structures and structural integrity, all Engineering systems, and life-support systems. The third course was called "Physics and Engineering of Materials, Composites, and Metamaterials."

The fourth course Grag had chosen was based more on the virus problem than anything else. Something that Dr. Chris had said somewhere along the way had triggered in his mind as he had scrolled through the available courses. There had been so many, but Grag had been limited to four, based on the time he would be in cryosleep. When he saw "Quantum Physics of Biological Systems" he knew he had to take that one, even though he really didn't have all the prerequisite courses behind him.

All of the courses were Terran training courses at advanced

collegiate levels, and it required approval from the Terran ambassador and ship's Captain Crosby before Grag was allowed to take the sleep training. According to the Terrans, cryosleep training for two full months would be the equivalent of a full semester of undergraduate-to-entry-graduate college level in each course. When he had been awakened from the cryosleep, he was amazed at the things he knew and understood that he never had before. He couldn't wait to pick classes to take for the nearly yearlong trip back home.

After several hours of unloading the shuttles through the docking bays and then loading them with the off-loading *Pioneer* crew members, and then repeating the process until the crew exchange was complete, the repair crew were finally all called to muster at the bridge in the rotational ring. The engineering teams of the *Samaritan*, Grag and six other Fintidierians, and eight crew members from the *Pioneer* were present.

The *Samaritan* CHENG/pilot, Bob Roca; Dr. Vulpetti, the aerospace engineer; Dr. Ming Zao, a pilot and manufacturing engineer; Dr. Roy Burbank; and Dr. Carol Ash, a power expert Grag didn't know, were all there.

But Grag was more interested in the *Pioneer*'s crew. Captain Penelope Mitchison was clearly a force to be reckoned with. Grag could tell the woman was intensely intelligent and a person to whom most deferred. She was average in height for the Terrans and perhaps a little older than most of her crew, but not by much. She appeared a bit malnourished but still stronger than Fintidierian women and even most men. There were six other women and two men. It had taken Grag a minute or so to recall that his contact lenses could give him virtual bios of each of the people he didn't know. He waved his hands around in front of him, clumsily at first, moving icons around and pulling down menus to find the right software. Once he reconfigured his view, callout bubbles appeared over everyone's head. He turned and looked at the women in front of him.

"We lost the main power completely and there was no repairing it," Chief Engineer Evonne Mia was explaining to the CHENG of the *Samaritan* around bites of a protein bar she was devouring. Grag made note that the others from the *Pioneer* were pretty much doing the same. These poor people had been starving to death for months because much of their food stores had been destroyed in a fire, and they had been in space six months longer than planned. Grag choked down the lump in his throat at how difficult that must have been and how courageous these people were, and did his best to pay attention.

"I did all I could to replicate the missing components but we didn't have the materials on board to replace the power conditioning unit," the CHENG continued. "The spare went out the hole and is somewhere back there about a light-year or so."

"Well, we can't exactly replace yours from the specs we received, but we brought what I think will fill the same function," Bob Roca, the CHENG from the *Samaritan*, replied. "I can send a couple of folks here with you to help you replace it and get it functioning."

"Good. They should go with Jenna," CHENG Mia said. She adjusted some virtual thing in front of her with her left hand. Grag watched and listened to her every word. He only slightly noted that "Jenna" was Dr. Jenna Rees, an electrical engineer. And he barely noted the CHENG from the *Samaritan* waving his hands in front of him and clearly making duty roster assignments. They hadn't included him or there would have been an alert in his virtual view. None of that really mattered to Grag at the moment. No, there was something about Evonne that Grag couldn't put his finger on.

The woman was big and muscular, even for the Terran women—he thought she must have been a bodybuilder or some sort of athlete before becoming an astronaut. As strong and powerful as the captain looked, the CHENG was far stronger in appearance and probably had ten or fifteen kilos on her. Grag could only imagine how big she must have been before being on starvation rations and in cryosleep for six months. She was dirty from head to toe and her hair was tangled and shoulder length. It was the color of the muddy, loamy sand near the banks of Gwonura Reservoir. She seemed as intense as the captain. She frightened Grag a bit, but she also fascinated him.

"What else, Evonne?" Captain Mitchison asked her.

"The main comms relays burned out. We're on backups," she said. "But if we could hardline or WiFi to the *Samaritan* we could piggyback on your bandwidth."

"Roy?" CHENG Roca turned to Dr. Burbank.

"Got it. I'll start putting something together. I'll need three or four extra sets of hands and someone from the *Pioneer* with access to the main systems," Burbank suggested.

"Better than that," Evonne interrupted. "Orion?"

"Yes, Evonne?" The booming male voice startled Grag.

"Give Dr. Burbank and CHENG Roca full ship's access, authority CHENG Mia, Evonne, seven seven alpha pi."

"Understood, Evonne. Permission is granted to Dr. Roy Burbank and Chief Engineer Roca," Orion replied.

"There. If you guys have any questions about the ship and can't find me, or better yet, can do without me, ask Orion," Evonne told them. "If he had hands and could move around, I'm not sure they'd need me on this damn ship."

"Is that it?" Vulpetti asked.

"Not by a long shot," Evonne replied. "But the next prioritized item would have to be repairs to the exterior structure supports where the hull was breached during the explosion. If we're ever going to turn some sort of engine on, we better check on that or the ship is going to collapse like a beer can from axial stresses."

CHAPTER 24

The *Pioneer*

As the specialized space drone clung to the *Pioneer*'s hull, Grag and Evonne worked closely together to assess the interstellar spacecraft's structural integrity. For more than a week, the crews of both ships had been performing extravehicular activities. The Fintidierian had been educated in the cryobed, according to Evonne's datasheet on him. Evonne lost count of how many EVAs it had taken to repair the damage from the explosion and rupture from the engine room. There had been several parts on that side of the ship that were simply missing. Evonne could imagine them flying along in space at near lightspeed on some random trajectory. When they had been blown out of the ship there were large sections several meters in length and width torn away with them. They had to be replaced. Fortunately, the *Samaritan* had brought enough raw materials to facilitate the repairs.

Evonne watched the young Fintidierian who had been assigned to her team, as he stood against the metal wall straddling a two-meter-long weld seam. The magnetic boots on his feet held him in place as he placed the X-ray receiver bot into place. She hadn't been expecting that there would be any Fintidierians to be useful. Evonne had expected that they were so far behind in technology that interactions would be like speaking with first graders. But she had been surprised—alarmingly so. At least this Fintidierian was a competent technician if not an engineer.

"I think it is ready, CHENG Mia," Grag told her, looking

back over his shoulder as the virtual screens in front of them both showed the status of the bot. "I think there is lock with the drone outside. That's what this icon here means, yes?"

"Looks like it, Grag. And, call me Evonne," she replied from her vantage point as she floated behind and over his shoulder. Evonne was a ship's chief engineer through and through—body and soul. While she had always known she was a hardened, maybe tomboyish woman, she liked to think of herself as still being somewhat attractive—not movie star or supermodel attractive, but athletically attractive. Back in the Sol system her bodybuilder frame and chief engineer commanding presence had often scared prospective suitors away. Evonne had chalked it up as a hazard of the job.

Evonne looked at Grag and several thoughts went through her mind at once. The first was obvious: Grag was a young Fintidierian scientist who, thanks to the dearth of females born in his age cohort, clearly hadn't encountered many women on Proxima b; she could sense how nervous he was. The second came from experience: the young man was smitten by her. He was exceedingly polite, almost annoyingly so. But Evonne, while amused, wasn't quite ready to jump into a relationship with the first Fintidierian man she met. After all, there was an entire planet full of men there hoping for a relationship with a woman. She guessed that any woman of any body shape and attractiveness level could pretty much take her pick. She'd never been in a position like that before and it would take some time to get used to.

"So, making sure I have this straight," Grag was saying, perhaps trying to impress her, but she wasn't certain, "the LIDAR is mapping the exterior hull down to a millionth of a meter of surface irregularities? You know, CHENG Mia—uh, sorry, Evonne, these LIDAR sensors are quite remarkable. My people had yet to invent the laser and here I am in space using one. Out of a billion or so of my people, maybe a hundred have seen a laser, perhaps twenty have been in space. I wonder if I'm the only one to use one in space."

"That's got to be an overwhelming thought." Evonne laughed. "Were you chosen through some sort of lottery or something?"

"Oh, lotter . . . eem, oh, . . . random draw . . . yes, I see." Grag shook his head in the negative. "No, I was part of the fertility crisis team. A physicist by training, assigned to a Dr. Chris

Sentell through the Gwonura Institute. Originally, I was just a, eem, what did Dr. Chris call it, um, yes, a go-far."

"Go far?"

"Yes, he said I was to go-far things when he needed them," Grag added, uncertain of the meaning.

"Hahaha! A gofer," Evonne corrected him through chuckles. "That is what we jokingly call an assistant. Gophers are rodents back on Earth, but it is a play on words. Go for, not go far. Go for this or go for that. Get it?"

"Aha, I see. Dr. Chris is always making jokes I don't understand." Grag smiled. "I get it now."

"But how did they pick you for that job?" Evonne was puzzled. "There had to be millions applying for the job to work with the Terrans from space."

"Oh, at first, no. Most were afraid of you, and your people were kept, em, quarantined," Grag replied. "But I volunteered, hoping there was opportunity there. And I so wanted to meet the aliens."

While Grag was explaining, Evonne pulled up the man's bio. He was either too humble to admit that he was probably one of the top students in the northern region by the Terran encampment near Gwonura, or he didn't realize it. From the calluses on his hands and his willingness to do any type of work Evonne had thrown at him for the past week, she was beginning to wonder if life on Proxima b was way different and maybe much harder than she had envisioned. She hadn't expected to be impressed by the man, but...

"How brave of you, Grag," Evonne said with a small laugh—an almost flirtatious laugh. "And here you are."

"Yes. Here I am," Grag repeated, with a puzzled expression on his face. He was oblivious to female interactions. Evonne let it go as the LIDAR initiation sequence completed and the activate icon appeared.

"Okay, looks like this thing is ready. Hit that icon and the laser will start up and will keep the X-ray cameras aligned."

"Tap the icon now?" Grag asked, nervously watching her for approval before tapping the virtual icon.

She nodded.

"Done."

"Good." Evonne smiled. "Now, while the microfracture scans

are running it will feed real-time into the simulator. If any cracks are found that are large enough to allow stresses outside of the tolerance levels, Orion will tell us."

"Okay. What do we do next?"

"This fracture exam will take ten minutes," Evonne explained. "Then we pull the sensor, give the drone the next coordinate, and do it again. There are seventeen more weld seams to inspect. But while we have ten minutes to kill, we need to replace these strain gauges here, here, and here that were blown out in the explosion. Simple plug-and-play repair."

"I see." Grag released his magnetic boots with a metal clanking sound. He kicked across toward the aft ward bulkhead and then it became clear to Evonne that he didn't know which way he should be going. The embarrassment on his face was clear. "Em, I guess, you should lead the way?"

"Sure," she said deadpan, doing her best not to let him see her fighting a laugh. She bit her bottom lip for a second, hoping not to embarrass him too much. "Come on. There's a lot of work to do."

Captain Crosby, XO Artur Clemons, Chief Engineer Roca, Dr. Vulpetti, and the rest of the *Samaritan* bridge crew were buckled into their seats as the countdown continued, their eyes fixed on the *Pioneer*, which now loomed large in the viewing port. It was a surreal sight to see the two spacecrafts suspended in the void, connected only by the delicate mooring rig they had painstakingly prepared over the past month. The crews of the two ships had become intermingled and could now traverse to and from in the transit tubes between them. But for the moment, those tubes were empty and every crew member from both ships were buckled in and sitting anxiously in anticipation of firing the Samara Drive.

"Captain Mitchison, my display shows all personnel are in place and accounted for. Our systems indicate the Samara Drive is warming up and our standard countdown procedures are moving normally," Captain Crosby said. "Can you give me a status report, please?"

"Copy that, Sam." Mitchison smiled through the comm view. "We're all strapped in here and nothing to do but wait for you to light us up."

Crosby chuckled. "I've got a full-up view of all critical failure modes possibilities with up to the microsecond sensor updates into each model. If anything goes into the yellow, I'm killing the drive's acceleration."

"Understood, Captain. We're all watching everything down to the nuts and bolts over here." Mitchison turned and motioned something to someone off screen. "Evonne tells me that her engineering team here is monitoring the mooring rig and the structural integrity of the *Pioneer* at the micron-per-microsecond vibration level. We should see any anomalies long before they get large enough to be dangerous. Fingers crossed."

"Alright. We're three minutes out. Good luck," Crosby said and then he turned to the XO's station. "Artur?"

"Nothing to report, Captain. Hell, you can see everything I can," the XO replied.

"Dr. Vulpetti?"

"Well, nothing to report until the data starts coming in. But now that we're all connected to the *Pioneer* all of our known and verified models are out the window. We'll have to keep them updating as we begin the slow acceleration," Vulpetti explained. "As we slowly and consistently bring up the thrust, and therefore the load forces on both ships, the sensors will continuously input into the control algorithms and models, and in a minute or two the computer should converge on a verified model. Then we will be able to calculate exactly how much thrust will be needed to change our trajectory and bring the *Pioneer* back toward the Proxima system. At that point, Roca can take over with his orbital mechanics adjustments."

"Remind me to discuss the notion of brief updates with you at some later date, Enrico," Captain Crosby said with a raised eyebrow and the hint of a smile turning up at the corners of his mouth.

"Samara Drive initiation in three, two, one..." the *Samaritan*'s artificial intelligence announced over the ship-to-ship intercom system Roy Burbank had put together. "Zero-point-one gee acceleration."

Crosby watched the virtual bar charts and graphs change slightly as he felt a very light push on him forcing him softly into his chair. There was barely enough weight to notice, except that he had been sitting in microgravity for hours.

"CHENG *Samaritan* report?"

"So far so good, Captain," Roca replied.

"CHENG *Pioneer*?"

"All systems in the green so far," Evonne added.

"Good. Bob, keep us at one tenth gee for the next hour, then bring it down."

"Yes, Captain," Roca replied.

"No, Evonne, I mean here." Grag was pointing at a virtual image he was sharing with her. "You see the three points here around the docking ring for the transport tube?"

"Yes?" Evonne shrugged.

"Okay, it's all quiet during the hour-long thrust," Grag explained. "But watch what happens when the drive is shut down."

Grag hit a virtual icon running the data display and increased the false color for vibration amplitude. On a 2D graph of frequency versus amplitude beside the 3D image of the ship, a logarithmically scaled curve had a spike in the middle at one thousand and twelve hertz. The amplitude was in microns per second per square root of hertz. As the Samara Drive shut down, the spike moved to the left to a frequency of approximately ninety hertz and the amplitude was several orders of magnitude higher than the vibrations had been before. The false colors showed a red wave of oscillation around the circular ring that held the transport tube in place. Then there was an accordion-like standing wave oscillation along the tube itself.

"Did you see that, Evonne?" Grag asked her.

"Yes, Grag, I saw it." Evonne played it back and watched it again. "So what? The vibrations are not even large enough to see with the human eye."

"Yes, that was my original thought as well," Grag said sheepishly. "But, why there? What is causing this sudden vibration to appear once the thrust is turned off?"

"My guess is that the ships are acting like two springs under a load, and we just removed the load. This is the system ringing down, Grag," Evonne explained to him.

"Yes, of course, that is happening. That is basic physics even on my world." Grag wasn't sure if she was insulting him by explaining such a simple thing or if she was convincing herself that it was a simple thing. "But, noticing that it has a nodal point here with high amplitude at ninety hertz, I got to looking at other spots, like the transport tube docking port."

"Why?"

"Well, instantly removing a load from a system gives us a transient signal response, right?" Grag asked, rhetorically.

"Umm..."

"So, as big as this amplitude is with such a lightweight connection or mass from the tube, I was worried if it would be worse at the mooring trusses," Grag explained. "And look at what I found here."

Grag swiped an icon in front of him and ran a new set of data showing the mooring points where the rigs were attached between the two ships. He fast-forwarded to a few seconds before thrust shut down and then let it play at normal speed. As the drive shut down the false color representing the vibrational wave traveling through the ship grew rapidly and chaotically and the 2D graph showing the amplitude of the ninety-hertz vibration saturated the sensors.

"Now look at this." Grag zoomed in on one of the welds to near-millimeter resolution. One of the seams had a small hairline crack in it that he was pointing at with his forefinger. "You see that?"

"Oh, that's not good," Evonne replied.

CHAPTER 25

The *Pioneer*

"Oh, that's not good!" Enrico Vulpetti watched the engineering simulation of the Samara Drive being brought up to two gees. A chaotic oscillation began and after a few minutes the mooring trusses ripped away from the *Pioneer,* causing catastrophic ruptures in the hull. "Jesus."

"My sentiments exactly, Enrico," Evonne agreed through the virtual conference window between the ships. "Grag and I have run this thing a thousand times, and anything over a half-gee thrust ends up catastrophic."

"How could we have missed that in our modeling and sims back on Proxima b?" Captain Crosby asked.

"I'm not sure I understand that either." Vulpetti shook his head back and forth while shrugging, palms up. "It doesn't make any sense to me."

"Evonne, can you bring up the top-level modal analysis diagram?" Roy Burbank floated behind the captain, holding his thirteen-year-old daughter on his back, which would have been near impossible in gravity as Samari was nearly as tall as he was and still growing. "I mean, show me all the main damping components and forcing components."

"Well, yes, here." Evonne brought it up for them to see. "There's only one forcing function, really, and that is the drive."

"Right. I get that," he said. "But I want to see the coupling between each of them mechanically."

After a moment or so the model appeared on everyone's virtual screen. There were the two ships connected and floating in front of them. Evonne reached up and twirled it around and then pointed at the mooring points where the failure modes occurred. She turned and shrugged at Grag, who was floating by her very stoically. She had no idea what he was thinking.

"Okay, can you run the model? My hands are full at the moment," Roy said as he twirled his daughter in front of him and then around behind his back again. The two of them were enjoying something akin to a daddy-daughter microgravity ballet. The only things missing were a pink tutu, ballet slippers, and Tchaikovsky.

"Uh, sure." Evonne replayed the simulation.

Once again, the vibrations grew and then the two ships began flexing. Each ship had a standing longitudinal wave running back and forth, bow to stern, like a wave traveling down a Slinky. Then there was a violent rupture at the mooring points.

"There! Stop it there!" Roy shouted, causing Evonne to jump. She stopped it and backed it up a few frames to the point Roy had wanted.

"Right there. What is the frequency of that longitudinal wave on both ships?" Roy asked.

"Hold on, let me see, uhh..." Evonne was moving icons in her view to make some calculations when Grag interrupted her.

"Ninety-two-point-three-four-seven hertz as near as makes no difference, Dr. Roy," Grag said.

"Aha. I thought so." Roy laughed at his daughter as she acted like she would be motion sick from the spinning. "That's the frequency of the power conditioning unit. I found it when I was connecting the ships' communication systems. Hell of a hum until I filtered it out. I suspect the Samara Drive is oscillating in amplitude ever so slightly due to the power fluctuation. I mean, it is really clean power, but it is oscillating a bit at that frequency."

"Dad, I'm gonna take a break," Samari interrupted him by pushing away using his larger mass as a launch pad. Roy had to steady his spin as she drifted across the bridge and grabbed at an empty chair at navigation.

"Go ahead," Roy mouthed quietly to his daughter.

"And that is causing this forcing function that we are measuring?" Crosby asked.

"Looks like it to me." Roy turned his attention back to the conversation. "I mean, that's the exact frequency I've already measured in the power system. I didn't try to fix it because it didn't matter to the data network. I filtered it out, mostly. So, I guess the natural frequency of the ships, which are basically big, long, metal cylinders, is somewhere in the ninety-hertz range. Think of them like crystal wineglasses. This signal in the Samara Drive is acting like an opera singer at the right frequency, causing them to ring and then burst."

"So how do we fix it?" Mathison chimed in.

"You put water in the glasses," Grag said.

"Water in the glasses?" Mathison asked.

"He's right, of course," Roy agreed. "We have to change the natural ringing or resonant frequency of the glasses, so the opera singer's tune is at the wrong frequency to excite them."

"How do we do that?" Vulpetti asked as he rubbed his chin in thought. "That would take significant mass in the right locations, or maybe stiffeners along the periphery of the ships."

"Can't we do like Dr. Roy did and put a filter between the power and the Samara Drive?" Grag asked.

"Out of the mouths of babes." Evonne smiled back at Grag. "Roy? What do you think?"

"Oh, I'm not the power guy. But it should work," Roy responded.

"Enrico?" both captains asked simultaneously.

"Um, that's gonna take weeks of work. First, we need to rig a new intake at the power junction for the drive—" Vulpetti started but was interrupted.

"No, we don't," Dr. Jenna Rees said. "We had almost that exact problem with the *Pioneer* during the shakedown flight. It was a slightly lower frequency but there was a parasitic oscillation in the Samara Drive limiting the thrust output. We put a tunable power coupling filter on our drive, and it worked fine."

"But didn't your Samara Drive explode?" Vulpetti asked.

"Well, yes." Evonne smiled. "But Jenna is right. That's a spare part we do have!"

"Wait." Burbank held a hand up now, paying much closer attention to the conversation. "Didn't I read in the Failure Modes and Effects Analysis report on your engine failure that it *was* the power coupling that blew out?"

"Uh, yeah," Evonne affirmed.

"Then why did it blow out?" Roy pondered. "I mean, the *Samaritan* has never had a problem with any oscillations like this until it was connected to the *Pioneer.* Something isn't adding up."

"Roy makes a great point here, Evonne," Vulpetti agreed. "There are no records of this type of positive feedback oscillation in the Samara Drive for our ship. And now you're telling us that you guys have seen this from the shakedown flight of yours."

"That is a good point, Enrico. Roy, I don't know what to say about that." Evonne looked perplexed.

"And why did the *Pioneer* make it almost all the way here before the failure of your power coupling filter?" Grag asked. "The Samara Drive had been running fine for nearly four years. Why did it take so long to fail?"

"Grag, that I think is the ultimate question," Roy said. "Orion?"

"Hello, Dr. Burbank." The AI's voice boomed through the *Pioneer*'s bridge.

"Can you show me the vibrational data of the *Pioneer*'s Samara Drive on the shakedown flight before the power coupling filter was added?" Roy asked.

"Of course," Orion said, as simultaneously the mechanical vibration spectrum of the engine curves appeared on the viewscreens and in everyone's virtual views.

"See, there is the vibration mode at . . . uh, eighty-one-point-four hertz." Jenna pointed at the viewscreen. "Like I said, it was a little lower."

"Right." Roy nodded, then pushed toward his daughter, who was pretending to fly the ship at the navigation console, and whispered to her quietly. "Don't touch anything, princess."

"I suspect the added mass of the mooring trusses, the transport tubes, and another ship altered the frequency somewhat," Vulpetti added.

"Orion . . ." Roy was only half listening as he had ideas.

"Yes, Dr. Burbank?"

"Do you have data from the first test after the filter was added to the power coupling?" Roy asked.

"Of course. Here, you can see it now," Orion replied.

Once again, the vibrational spectrum appeared and this time the floor noise was mostly flat, or at least orders of magnitude below where it had been. And the vibrational signal from before the test was nowhere to be seen.

"Okay, that looks good," Evonne announced. "And there's no sign of the parasitic resonant signal anywhere."

"Right," Vulpetti agreed. "So, why did it come back?"

"That is the wrong question, Enrico," Roy replied stoically and remained silent for a few moments. Evonne, Grag, and Jenna looked at him as if he had gotten stuck on pause. Then, before they could ask, he continued, "The right question is, *when* did it come back?"

"When?" Evonne sounded puzzled. "We know when. It came back *when* the thing nearly blew up the ship."

"Roy? What are you thinking here?" Captain Crosby had been watching quietly from the bridge of the *Samaritan* for some time now.

"Huh? Oh yes, Captain, we actually haven't looked for when it started," Roy said. "I don't recall seeing that in the FMEA report. Understandable, because Evonne was more busy keeping the ship functioning and not dying than worrying about how it all happened in detail. No fault there. But... Orion, do a reverse tracking algorithm and watch the data from immediately before the explosion all the way back until the vibrations started."

"Certainly. That will take a moment," Orion said.

"A moment being...?" Evonne asked.

"Uncertain, but approximately three to five minutes. Please stand by."

"Orion, you are certain this is the timestamp?" Captain Mathison asked the AI.

"Yes, Captain Mathison. The parasitic oscillation begins exactly thirty days to the microsecond of accuracy before the power coupling failure occurs," Orion explained.

To Roy, waiting on Orion to complete the sorting through the data seemed to have taken forever. In reality, it had been four and a half minutes. But once it had been completed there was no mistaking what had happened. In fact, Roy had been through something similar himself. He could tell by the looks on the team with him on the bridge of the *Pioneer,* and the look on the *Samaritan* crew's faces through the screens, that they were all puzzled to no end. But not Roy.

"Orion, please give us a diagnostic reading of every cryobed starting at the moment the parasitic oscillation starts and go backward from there until something changes," Roy tasked the AI.

"Certainly, Dr. Burbank. That will take a moment or two. Please stand by."

"What are you thinking, Roy?" Evonne asked him.

"Somebody turned the filter off. That much is plain as day." Roy shrugged.

"Sabotage?" Captain Mathison protested. "Nobody on this crew would do such a thing. We were all volunteers, for Christ's sake!"

"We'll see," Roy said patiently. "I've been there and done that. Just wait and see."

"Roy, are you suggesting there is sabotage now?" Captain Crosby asked him. Roy looked back at the screen and shook his head.

"I don't think so, Captain. I have a hunch, but I don't want to say anything yet," Roy said.

"The data has been analyzed, Dr. Burbank," Orion stated.

"Okay, were any of the beds opened?" Roy asked.

"As far as I can tell, there were no cryosleep protocols stopped and/or restarted for several months all the way back to the midpoint awakening of the bridge crew and engineering team," Orion said.

"So, your hunch was wrong, Roy. No saboteur." Captain Mathison grunted.

"Uh, no, ma'am. That is exactly what I expected the logs to say," Roy replied. "Orion, display on this screen the pressure, temperature, and power usage of every bed in a graph. Overlay all the beds' curves atop each other."

"Very well, Dr. Burbank. You can see it now on the main screen," Orion responded.

Roy whistled, shook his head in disgust back and forth, and then frowned. The graphs all overlaid one another within the engineering tolerance of the bed design, which was pretty damned good. The pressure, temperature, and power usage curves of two hundred some-odd beds were layered upon each other, making three fuzzy lines with only slight variations. But four of those beds, at precisely the same times and duration, had the exact same, within tolerance, changes in pressure, temperature, and power usage on two specific occasions.

"See that? Damn." Roy pointed. "Orion, overlay a graph of pressure, temperature, and power usage of a perfectly functioning bed opening after sleep, and then going into sleep."

"Sure, Dr. Burbank," Orion said. "It is displayed now."

"An exact match," Evonne uttered with exasperation. "But why would anyone do this?"

"Orion, display the names of the crew in those four beds," Captain Mathison said urgently.

"Yes, Captain." Orion then showed files for four crew members as he spoke their names. "Dr. Elizabeth Juliet Jones, Dr. Majel Kasim, Dr. Farah Rene Smith, and Dr. Xi Jian Wu."

"Captain Crosby!" Captain Mathison said, her voice commanding. "You need to have a security detail immediately apprehend and detain Dr. Farah Rene Smith."

"Why not the others, Captain?" Crosby asked.

"The others died in cryosleep during the power failure," Mathison explained.

"That's convenient," Roy muttered.

"Damned convenient," Mathison agreed. "Crosby, I'm headed your way."

"Understood," Crosby replied. "The XO has already detached security. She can't go anywhere."

"I thought we'd been past all that nonsense with the *Emissary* making it without any issues," Vulpetti said as he slurped down a microgravity meal that was floating in multicolored droplets before him. "I mean, after what happened with Roy and all, I thought security was better."

"Apparently not," Evonne countered as she chewed on a meal bar and then squeezed a red liquid into her mouth from its bottle. She let the bottle go and its magnetic base slowly pulled it to the metal tabletop of the booth she was strapped into. "To what end? I don't get it. I have known Farah for three years. We trained together. She never seemed like a murderer to me."

"Was it on purpose that the accomplices died in the power failure?" Jenna Rees was every bit as curious. "Orion is running diagnostics on those beds, but there was so much damage done. Who knows if we'll ever know what happened."

"Smith isn't talking. According to Artur, the XO, she hasn't said a word. He's got her locked in the holding cell," Roca told them. "What a waste."

"I wonder if she will still want to participate in our society?" Grag asked. "I mean, it is a waste that a female will go to prison forever when females are in such short supply on my world."

"Thinking you might get lucky there, Grag?" Evonne goaded him with a playful look.

"Lucky . . . em? Oh, my no!" Grag exclaimed through blushing cheeks. His embarrassment was apparent.

"She's kidding you, Grag." Roca laughed.

"I see." Grag sounded confused and not at all as if he "saw."

"Alright, kiddos." Evonne slapped the tabletop, forcing her body to float upward against her restraints. "We still have a lot of work to do. Enough of this goldbricking."

"Slavemaster!" Jenna grunted through the last bites of her meal. "The power coupler filter is connected and will be online in a few hours, Evonne."

"Great. The sooner we can get everything back up and running, the sooner we can get Loverboy here home." Evonne elbowed Grag as she laughed out loud.

The next few days' work consisted of bringing systems back online one at a time, and then testing the Samara Drive at different power levels. The filter had done the trick. As far as any of the teams could determine, there were no parasitic modes to be detected. All systems were functioning and ready to be implemented. Finally, the *Samaritan* could bring the *Pioneer* and its crew to their new home on Proxima b.

Over the course of the next several weeks, the crews of both ships carefully and methodically adjusted their thrust vectors. They used the Samara Drive in tandem with the conventional thrusters to change their course, gradually bringing the *Pioneer* into an elliptical orbit around Proxima Centauri that would enable them to bring the drive up to full power and push them home over the course of eleven months. It was a delicate dance in the void of space, requiring precision and patience but the navigators, captains, and the AI of both ships were up to the task.

The crews had worked tirelessly for years, months, weeks, days, and endless hours to reach the distant star safely, but nothing was ever easy with interstellar space travel. Exacerbating the difficulties of interstellar travels with sabotage made achieving their goal even more sweet as the Samara Drive powered up to full speed. All of that had taken just shy of a month, which required a symbiotic relationship between the two crews. Supplies were continually transferred from the *Samaritan* to the attached ship, ensuring that everyone had enough food, water, and resources to sustain them throughout the extended mission.

The crew of the *Pioneer*, once facing an uncertain fate, now had hope and the support they needed to survive and complete their mission. In fact, once the ship's repairs had been managed and the hybrid combination of the two ships was functioning properly, most of the *Pioneer*'s crew had returned to their own ship. After all, that ship had been their home for almost five and a half years.

The weeks turned into months as the two spacecraft continued their journey at a velocity approaching ninety-nine percent the speed of light. The crew of the *Samaritan* had remained dedicated to their mission, united in their commitment to bringing their fellow explorers back to the Proxima system safe and sound. The dim red glow of Proxima Centauri served as a constant reminder of their ultimate destination from any of the forward viewing viewports. The fate of the *Pioneer* and its crew was no longer hanging in the balance. With each carefully calculated maneuver, they inched closer to the Proxima system, determined to overcome the challenges of deep space and bring the stranded explorers with their new home among the stars.

Finally, the work was done, and the ship had been placed into the hands of the *Samaritan*'s AI, Beth. Beth and Orion could keep things running smoothly for the next eleven months or so as they made their way home. Grag couldn't wait. Being in space had been an adventure. He had learned a lot. He was planning to learn another two full years' worth of Terran graduate school on the trip home during cryosleep training. He was looking forward to that. But mostly, he wanted to see his friends, his family, and his home world. Grag also couldn't wait to introduce Evonne to them.

"All hands, this is Captain Crosby," Grag heard as he watched the blue liquid flowing into his wrist and felt a cool rush of air hissing over him. "Great work, everyone. Before we know it, we'll be approaching orbit around Proxima b. Good luck and sleep tight."

CHAPTER 26

Aboard the *Emissary*, 18 years later

Did Mak make a mistake? Maybe the system failed. Why am I awake so soon? These thoughts barely had time to cross Alan Jacobs's mind before he felt the overwhelming urge to vomit. He eased himself upright and grabbed the bag-and-suction device that was designed into the cryobeds for exactly this purpose. As he was in the throes of nausea, he first heard and then saw Mak sitting up in the bed next to him experiencing the same thing.

He looked at the chronometer on the wall and saw that he had not been awakened early, it only seemed like it. Yesterday was actually six ship years ago and eighteen years on Earth, Proxima b, and Luyten b. Eighteen years. Jacobs still had trouble grasping the physical realities imposed by Special Relativity. By now, the fertility problem on Proxima b should have been solved. Maybe another Earth ship had arrived with a cure. Maybe not. What was happening on Earth? Were they still building and sending ships to explore the universe or did humanity self-destruct in some sort of nuclear or biological war? What were the Atlanteans up to? The thoughts and questions rolled through Jacobs's mind as he sat, wondering if he would experience yet another wave of nausea before he dared to roll out of the cryobed and stand up.

"Welcome back to the land of the living, Captain," Mak offered, who was already standing, albeit unsteadily, next to his cryobed. He sipped at a red liquid from a squeeze bottle. "After we give ourselves the required self-assessment, we can begin awakening the rest of the crew."

"And we can see what our Atlantean friends might be up to," added Jacobs. "Clearly, the drive is still running, or we wouldn't have gravity."

Two hours later, Jacobs was on the bridge with the primary bridge crew: Cindy Mastrano, his chief engineer; Executive Officer Yohon Koeq; Victor Tarasenko, the sensors and signals officer; Lieutenant Marcus Keaton, weapons officer; and Joni Walker, a Space Force chief warrant officer 5, a true Renaissance woman, with expertise as a navigator, pilot, and nuclear power and propulsion engineer. They were awake, alert, and ready to plan their foray toward Luyten's Star.

"Victor, what have we got?" Jacobs asked.

"There has been no change in the radio transmission from Luyten b since we left Proxima. The signal strength and content are exactly the same as when we left. The ship began picking up system-wide radio traffic at nearly a half light-year out but didn't alert us because it appeared to be leakage from the system, strictly planet-to-planet, or, it might be better to say, point-to-point communication. Like the beacon signal, everything is encrypted and unreadable. What is most interesting is the variation in the star's light curve. It's too small to be detectable from Earth, but impossible to miss at this distance. From what I can tell from the diminishing brightness, there are some big constructs orbiting the star close in, about the same distance as b, but leading and trailing it at the Lagrange Points. There are also some large reflective structures co-orbiting the star with b, each roughly three to ten kilometers in diameter. They are too small to resolve, and we wouldn't have detected them had they not been so reflective,"

"Is there anything in the outer system that we might encounter on our way in?"

"Maybe. From what I can tell, some of those point-to-point signals we heard were undoubtedly headed toward something in the star's Kuiper Belt."

"It sounds like Luyten's Star is a busy place. Any news from Proxima?"

"Yes sir, there are several terabytes of messages from Proxima still coming in," XO Koeq reported. "Keep in mind they are from eighteen years ago, give or take. I had the AI do a basic look-up-front analysis and these are the main data points: one) Our scientists learned a way only a few months after our departure to use nanobots to impregnate Fintidierian eggs with Fintidierian female chromosome sperm; two) there has been a mass number of pregnancies brought to term with multiple female infants; three) there has been no word on the Atlanteans since we left."

"That's a win!" The XO slapped his chair arm. "Thank God."

"Right, Yohon, that has to have gone a long way to fix relations," Captain Jacobs agreed. "Any word if other ships from Earth have arrived?"

"No sir," he replied.

"What about from Earth?" Jacobs asked.

"Nothing, but that's not surprising. We have no way of knowing if our in-flight telemetry was received and, even if it were and they could reply, I doubt they would. Given what happened on Proxima b between the Atlanteans and the Fintidierians, I suspect people back home would not want to broadcast their presence too loudly in this general direction," Tarasenko hypothesized.

"Sound logic, Vic," the XO agreed. "Although I'd think the Atlanteans could have already detected Earth a century ago with their level of technology. If they were looking, that is. You'd think that Earth would have at least had the courtesy of sending a message via one of the other ships, though."

"Yeah, like by relaying it via the *Samaritan*. The Atlanteans know about the ship, thanks to the sleeper who sent that message," Mastrano said, betraying her "we can find a way to do this" way of thinking that made her a good chief engineer.

"Good thinking, Cindy, but I doubt they would take that risk. If the Atlanteans can read our messages, then even mentioning Earth would be a risk. We don't believe their sleeper knew about Earth when she sent her message and we should keep it that way," replied Jacobs.

"I don't know if I buy that one or not. The Atlanteans had to have records or knowledge of other humans. We can't have simply randomly sprung up across the galaxy in multiple places with the same DNA. They have to know of Earth," Mastrano argued. "Hell, I wouldn't even be surprised if they put us on Earth to start with."

"Well, I don't know about that," Victor replied. "But given their development status, it is safe to assume they know *we're* here.

The drive's exhaust would stand out like a beacon on any sort of UV telescope looking in our general direction as we braked."

"They might know company is coming, Victor, but as soon as we turned around, and given the distance, they probably lost sight of us," Mastrano argued.

"Yes, I agree," Jacobs said. "But we cannot take that for granted. Rather than follow the trajectory we are on, which would be the fastest way in, let's continue as planned, maneuver a bit, and come in from a slightly different direction. It will take longer, but we can put that time to good use by getting more information about the system—including what might be on the other side of the star. I don't like surprises. Somebody get Mak to wake up Dr. Gilster and put her on the radio astronomy and observation station as soon as she is able."

"On it, Captain." The XO tapped some keys at his console and moved around some virtual images that only he could see through his contact lenses.

"I'll come up with options and timetables," Walker said with a slight grin. She immediately cocked her head to look at her display, undoubtedly already plotting a trajectory that would give them the element of surprise.

She's in her element, Jacobs thought. *Good.*

Two hours later, the *Emissary*'s drive ramped up to full power, taking the ship upward from the local ecliptic plane and slightly starboard of their initial trajectory. At these distances, even slight changes would dramatically increase the zone of uncertainty regarding their position farther in the system. Jacobs wanted to learn about the Atlanteans, perhaps even make contact, but he did not want to have a shooting war. He had no illusions regarding the capabilities of his ship's makeshift weaponry. What they had devised as weapons might not be very effective in the Atlanteans' home court, especially given their apparent large technological advantage. Remaining hidden, or at least difficult to track, was their best defense.

Three weeks passed and there was no outward sign that anyone or anything in the system had paid them heed. To Jacobs, that alone was disconcerting. It meant either that they had gone undetected, which was unlikely, or that the Atlanteans were so confident in their superiority that they simply didn't care. Would the pilot of a modern fighter jet be particularly concerned about the approach of a WWI-era biplane? Maybe. Maybe not. But then again, by comparing the *Emissary* to a biplane, he might be being more charitable than reality. They were now 1,200 light-minutes from Luyten b and cruising at roughly 3 light-minutes per hour as they made their way inward. It was fast enough to cover the distance needed in a reasonable amount of time and hopefully not too fast to react quickly if they needed to divert toward something interesting along the way—he hoped.

"Captain, thermal picked up something ahead and barely off our current trajectory. It's not very hot, barely above background, but it's definitely not natural. Whatever it is, there's a warm central core and has much colder extremities. And it's big, at least two hundred fifty meters across," Tarasenko said, looking up from his console. "I'll share the thermal images to your screen while I try to get some visible images. But at this distance, I doubt we will see much unless they have very efficient and bright lighting."

"Cindy, how difficult would it be to do a slow flyby?" Jacobs asked.

"I can get us within two kilometers and to a dead stop, relative, if need be," she replied.

"I don't want to stop on the first pass. Let's keep it at ten to twenty kilometers and take us by at one half kilometer per second. I want a full sensor suite, gathering data as we pass the object. Show me the data in real time on the main screen," he said.

The thermal image on his viewer was replaced by one of Mastrano's "pork-chop plots," which showed curves of the extra energy or characteristic energy required to meet rendezvous points from their current position. In other words, the plots were showing the range of possible intercept times and spacecraft flyby velocities as a function of when in their current flight path they began their course change. To the uninitiated, the graph looked like the contour plots of a topographical map—or a pork chop. To the experienced viewer, it gave all the information necessary to decide how to perform the flyby and when.

"It looks like the sooner we divert, the better the options are for the flyby," Jacobs declared, knowing that beginning a maneuver in deep space was usually easier to accomplish by beginning sooner, rather than later. He activated the ship-wide speaker system.

"All hands. Secure for a course change in ten minutes. We've found something interesting and we're going to divert to fly by and check it out. ETA in six hours," he said and then turned off the microphone.

"Cindy, we're all yours," Jacobs said. "Chief Walker, keep running curves and intercepts based on continuous real-time data."

"Copy, Captain."

When the maneuver began, Jacobs could feel the subtle shift in the ship's vector due to the change in acceleration. It wasn't enough of a change to have posed a danger to anyone on board who might have been unprepared had he not made the announcement, other than perhaps a burned hand or two from hot coffee sloshing, but it was better to have everyone buckled up and prepared. Just in case.

"I'm going to my quarters for a short nap. XO, the ship is yours," Jacobs said to Koeq as he unbuckled and rose from his chair. Koeq quickly, but not too quickly, moved to take his place. If they had been back at Earth, after their time together on the voyage to Proxima b and his exemplary service there, Koeq would have by now had a ship of his own. He had served well and was definitely ship's captain material. Unfortunately, they were not likely to return to Earth anytime soon, perhaps not for a long, long time, if ever. Koeq seemed okay with being the XO. That relieved Jacobs, knowing that should anything happen to him, a capable substitute was ready and available. It simply wasn't fair to Koeq.

Five and a half hours later, Jacobs was back on the bridge, not certain that he was actually ready for whatever lay ahead. He hadn't really been able to sleep even though he had tried. Five hours hadn't been enough of a break that sleeping meds were an option. Instead, he had taken an alertness med before returning to the bridge. He checked his crew roster virtual display and noted that more of the crew had been awakened from cryosleep and were being acclimated to their current situation. At the current pace, Mak would have the entire complement up and ready to go. Specifically, Jacobs checked on his security detail. If there were more of those Atlantean warrior types out here, he definitely wanted the SEALs and the rest of the security-trained crew at the ready. Captain Jacobs made himself comfortable in his command chair and strapped himself in.

"XO, report."

"Closing in on the object now, Captain," Koeq replied. "It's big. Really big."

"How big?"

"Our long-range imagery and AI analysis shows that it is over two kilometers in length and about one kilometer in diameter. The albedo measurements suggest that it is a manufactured object and not just an asteroid. Besides that, well, it started moving toward us hours ago," the XO said.

"Moving toward us?"

"Yes, sir. It isn't moving very quickly, but it turned in our direction and started closing the gap at the same speed that we are approaching it. We are currently twenty light-minutes' distance between us," the XO explained.

"Alright, full stop relative!" Captain Jacobs ordered. "Get me Rain up here as soon as possible. I don't care if she's still in her cryo jammies."

"Roger that!"

"CHENG!"

"Yes, Captain," Mastrano replied from Engineering.

"I need a full sensor sweep of the object using everything we have," he ordered.

"Been doing that, Captain," Mastrano said. "I'm not really sure what I can tell you yet other than the fact that the thing is very large, it looks shiny, and seems to be able to match our propulsion with no detectable exhaust products. Also, it doesn't appear to be very hot either."

"Any electromagnetic signals?"

"Negative, Captain. But I'll keep at it," Mastrano finished.

"Comms, hail it."

"What frequency bands, Captain?" Victor Tarasenko asked.

"All of them."

"Understood, sir."

"Captain! There are two of them now!" the XO exclaimed. "One closing from twenty light-minutes out still and one is now ten kilometers dead ahead of us!"

"Joni! Turn us around and point the Samara Drive exhaust port right at that thing. And keep it on it!" Jacobs commanded.

"Which one?" Walker sounded puzzled.

"The one right in front of us, Joni!" Jacobs shouted. "Victor! Any return signals?"

"Nothing as far as I can tell, Captain. I'm still hailing at every frequency," Victor replied.

"What is that?!" Walker shouted from the navigation console. "Do you see it?"

"Layla! Zoom in on whatever that projectile is coming toward us!" Captain Jacobs shouted to the ship's AI.

"Yes, Captain," Layla responded.

"Analysis?"

"It appears to be a fast-moving probe or maybe a missile," Layla replied.

"Evasive maneuvers, Joni!" Jacobs ordered. "Full thrusters to port!"

"You might as well save the fuel, Captain," Layla said. "There is not enough impulse from our maneuvering thrusters to get us clear of the incoming projectile."

"Shit!" the XO exclaimed.

"All hands, this is the captain! Prepare for impact and possible hull breech!"

"Impact in four, three, two, one!" Layla counted down.

There was a sudden thud against the ship that sent a vibration ringing from bow to stern. The sound of metal tearing screeched as pressure alarms filled the ship. Jacobs had the three-dimensional view of the ship in his virtual view, so he rotated it and zoomed in to look at the impact site.

"Layla, get me a drone out there to view this thing," Jacobs ordered. "XO, get a security team there. They might be boarding us!"

"Aye, Captain!" Yohon moved some icons around in his virtual view and then tapped at a console in front of him. Then he looked over to the sensors and signals station at Victor Tarasenko with a nod. Victor patted the firearm on his side with a nod back at him. Both men gave a reassuring look to the captain. "Security and fire teams on the way."

"Victor, keep an eye on the bridge entry hatch," Jacobs said.

"Understood, Captain," Victor replied.

"Visual feed approaching the impact zone now Captain," Layla said.

"On the main screen."

The drone video feed was from a vantage point approximately ten meters above the exterior hull of the ship. So far, the ship looked normal as the drone approached the impact site. Then the forward motion stopped, and the drone hovered over a large hemispherical shiny metallic object perhaps as much as five meters in diameter with eight metallic appendages protruding from its periphery. Each of the appendages had pierced into the hull and had imbedded themselves into the ship like some giant menacing parasitic metal insect. The odd thing about the view was that where the appendages had pierced the hull there were no tears or breaks or damage. Instead, the hull was rippling like water around them. In real time as the bridge crew watched, cables, or maybe tentacles, grew out of the "insect" and began melding with the ship's hull. The materials of the cables and the hull seemed to simply join together into a melded object with ripples across the hull like dropping a pebble in a still reflecting pool.

"Has to be nanotechnology," Walker gasped.

"Pressure leaks have stopped, Captain. Environmental systems seem nominal," Layla said.

"Yeah, but what is this thing doing to my ship?" Jacobs grunted. "Layla?"

"Captain, as far as I can . . . I can . . . I . . ."

"Layla?" Jacobs brought her status icon up in his viewscreen. "Layla? Respond."

The ship's thrusters suddenly fired full power to port.

"Walker? What the hell are you doing?"

"That's not me, Captain!"

"My bet is they are turning our main weapon away from them," the XO offered.

"Damn. Probably right, Yohon." Jacobs tried to cut the thrusters from his controls, but nothing was happening. "CHENG!"

"Yes, Captain?" Mastrano's face popped up in his virtual view.

"Cut all power to all maneuvering thrusters."

"Standby."

"Quickly, CHENG."

"I'm sorry, Captain, but, uh, no systems seem to be responding," Mastrano replied. "We seem to be locked out of all ship's controls."

"XO! I need a visual report from that security detail!"

"Almost there, Captain. Microgravity is slowing them down."

"What hell is *that*?" US Navy SEAL team leader Commander Mike Rogers put his virtual aimbot on the flurry of mechanical things moving out of the center of what he could only describe as a puddle of liquid metal in the outer hull wall. He and the security detail made magboot jumps down the outer cooling conduit corridor to the hull breech. Getting there in the microgravity had been a task in itself. At least the magboots enabled them to anchor and aim. The aimbots in the virtual screens made targeting even easier.

"I see it, Mike," Dr. Carol Ash said, not lowering her rifle. The New Zealand special weapons expert had been in the armory with Rogers when they had gotten the call. The two were first on the scene. Rogers could see in his virtual blue force tracker that USN Lieutenant Commander Geni Holland and USN Petty Officer Third Class Daniel Visser were less than a minute out and moving toward them fast.

"We're being boarded," Rogers said quietly through his throat microphone. He waved his left hand toward the opposite corridor wall and then released his magboots with a bounce. "Let's see if we can slow them down."

"Copy that," Carol replied, following him in leapfrog fashion and cover formation to the far wall. It took them twenty seconds to reach a truss structure connecting one section of the tube to another, about twenty meters from the alien penetration point.

"Good place to make a stand," Rogers whispered. Then he tapped his throat. "Geni, Danny, we're being boarded by mechanical devices, maybe robots, not sure. Move around us on the interior hallway and go to the fore of the impact point. We're aft. Carol and I are going to engage as soon as the captain gives the order. You ready, Carol?"

"Ah, you know me, mate." Carol smiled and patted the bag of frag grenades at her waist. "I'm always up for a scrap."

"Captain Jacobs, Mike Rogers," he whispered.

"Go, Rogers!" Jacobs said in their virtual screens.

"We're being boarded by robots, Captain. Or mechanical bugs. Either way, looks like hundreds and still more coming through the hull. Permission to engage?"

"Get those damned things off my ship, Rogers!"

"Aye aye, sir." Rogers moved his hand in an outward waving motion, pulling up his targeting screen. The corridor lit up with red targeting *X*s. "Well, Carol, as you would say, let's give the bastards heaps!"

"Bloody oath, mate! Let's smash the buggers." Carol didn't wait for Rogers and started letting go on the targets. At that moment, Rogers was certain he was hearing other weapons fire, but couldn't tell over the sound of Carol's. His blue force tracker viewscreen showed that Geni and Danny had both fired their weapons.

"Shit," he muttered as he clicked the safety off.

Rogers was more methodical. He started from the outside in, taking the nearest target headed in his direction. The target itself was the size of a cat or a squirrel but looked absolutely nothing like either. It was a random mishmash of metallic colors and polymorphic in shape. There were eight or ten magnetic legs protruding from the object, skittering it along the metal hull. The appendages weren't like a two-dimensional walking animal like a spider or bug. Instead, the legs protruded randomly all about the thing and it sort of spiraled around its direction of travel as it skittered. There were hundreds of things pouring out of the wall in all directions.

Rogers locked his targeting *X* on the bot and released a single round. The round hit the target, poking a hole clean through and into the bulkhead behind it. The round ricocheted into another bot and took it out as well. Mike waited briefly. He half expected the bot to heal itself. When it didn't, that's when he let loose.

"Sweep them back inward, Carol! We need to stop the flow of these things!" he exclaimed as the tide of the bots had turned and started flowing toward them.

"Nail them!" Carol said with excitement and pointing to her explosives bag. "Gimme the word, mate, when you are ready to go all out bangs on the buggers!"

"The corridor hatch is up there, Danny!" Holland pointed in front of them approximately fifteen meters up the inner hallway at a hatch. "Mike and Carol should be right behind us. We can get in there."

"Understood," Visser replied. "Look out!"

"What the f—" Geni ducked and kicked her magboots off the sidewall, doing a Superman-style flight across the hall as a large tentacle-looking metal tube whipped about and grabbed her by the ankle as she passed. "Get off me!"

"Oh, my God, what is that!?" Danny screamed and started

firing his rifle at something behind her. Geni watched as he released his boots and did a somersault to the top wall and reattached his magboots, running above and past her while firing.

"Danny!" Geni rolled her body sideways and twisted herself at an angle where she could push the muzzle of her rifle against the tentacle holding her. She pulled the trigger, cutting the metal whiplike tube free. The momentum of the motion sent her spiraling about, getting a view of Danny every rotation. The hall lighting was a dim low red and with every bright white muzzle flash there was a strobe effect showing his motion in jumps. Geni managed to grab a handhold, right herself, and kick toward him, only to be terrified and mystified by what she saw in front of them.

The tentacle had been attached to the hatchway door. The door itself had grown into some strange mixture of cables, tubes, metal appendages, and the most bizarre Cthulhu shit she had ever seen. The hatchway itself was literally fighting them. Suddenly, she heard a torrent of weapons fire from behind them and on the other side of the wall.

"Mike has engaged! We need to get through this damned evil door!" Geni said.

"Well, just putting rounds in it ain't helping at all!" Danny kicked away from the door as a tube wrapped him up. He produced a long-bladed knife almost out of nowhere and brought his left elbow down through the tube. Grabbed it with his left hand and slashed himself free with his right. He tossed the tube aside, but it grew appendages and wriggled itself back toward the door.

"Holy shit! Did you see that?" he shouted.

"Get back, Danny!" Geni ordered him as she pulled a magnetic charge from her MOLLE—MOdular Lightweight Load-carrying Equipment—vest. She popped the safeguard, armed the trigger, and tossed it at the hatch. "Cover, cover! Fire in the hole!"

"Jesus Christ, what is happening on this ship?" the XO shouted. "Captain, there are multiple shots fired, and we now have an explosion on the port external conduit near the object."

"CHENG! Any luck getting control of the ship?" Captain Jacobs frantically moved his virtual screens, looking for anything that would help. He opened the ship intercom channel. "All hands! All hands! Prepare for possible pressure losses. Take emergency actions and shelter as needed!"

"Victor, maybe you should get Chang up here also," Yohon suggested, meaning that they might want Colonel Ping Xi Chang, the Chinese military pilot and security force team member on the bridge as back up to Tarasenko.

"I've already messaged him. He's on his way."

"Good." The XO gave him a positive nod. "Captain, we've got a lot of rounds bouncing around down there. We could poke something we don't need to poke."

"Rogers is doing his job, XO. Can't ask more than that," Jacobs replied. "Come on, Rogers. Get the job done!"

"This ain't getting the job done, mate!" Carol shouted as a bot flung itself from across the room at her. She stopped it with her barrel and then impaled it against the bulkhead with a blade in her left hand. "I say it's time for full bangers, Mike!"

Then there was an explosion sound from twenty meters forward and inward. The ship rang like a bell for a second. Seconds later, lines of fire were coming from the fore side of the corridor. Geni and Danny had made it to the scrap. Rogers keyed the open screen. "Glad y'all decided to join us."

"You won't believe what is on the other side of this thing!" Danny replied. "It's the craziest mad shit I've ever seen!"

"Keep it frosty, Danny," Geni replied. "And keep firing!"

"Aw, screw this!" Rogers toggled his magboots off and kicked forward five meters, then activated them, clanking, to the wall to run toward the swarm of bots pouring through the hull, while firing on full auto. Red targeting Xs filled his virtual view. "Carol! Do it!"

"About friggin' time, mate!" Smiling from ear to ear, she activated a magnetic hull-cracking charge. "Be ready to drop your lids and mag your skids!"

Carol rushed behind Rogers in three bounds with her boots, each time landing with a metal-on-metal sound that reverberated through the conduit like a church bell. On the third bounce she flipped sideways of Rogers, who was still firing on continuous, put her rifle in her left hand—still firing—and with her right thumb activated the charge and tossed it at the center of the rippling pool generating the metal monsters. Almost simultaneously, all of the virtual icons and screens in their mind views started flickering at maximum intensity, speed-blinding and mesmerizing the team.

"Boomer's away!" Carol shouted through gritted teeth. "Cover!"

Rogers tried to shake his head clear from the frantic visuals but that only made things worse. He could barely concentrate. Suddenly, he realized he had stopped firing his weapon. Through the crazy overwhelming visual stimulus before his eyes, he could make out tentacles extending from the central portion of the rippling pool. Four of them to be exact. The tentacles darted out toward each member of the team. He could see the one tentacle to his right swallow the charge flying through midair and then impale Carol through the chest. He could see similar results from the other two tentacles farthest from him until he felt a searing pain in his upper sternum and back.

"What the f—" Rogers faded into blackness.

"What the . . . ?" Jacobs watched as Victor Tarasenko and Ping Xi Chang grabbed their heads and screamed in agony.

"Something is wrong with the comms and nav panels . . ." Joni Walker put the palms of her hands to her eye sockets as if she would tear out her eyeballs.

Suddenly, all the viewscreens started scrolling through images at the maximum frame rate possible on the screen technology. The virtual screens in front of everyone on the bridge must have been zipping by as quickly as the ones in front of Captain Jacobs. She swiped at icons, trying to stop the feed, but nothing worked.

"Oh my God!" the XO shouted, clutching his head while swiping at icons. "Make it stop!"

"All hands, all hands!" a female voice came over the radio. "This is Dr. Gilster. Remove your contact lenses immediately! Take them out now!"

Jacobs tried closing his eyes, but nothing could stop the virtual images flashing by him rapidly. Were he susceptible to seizures this would certainly have been a trigger for them. He had finally reached the point where it had to stop or he would pass out from the stimulus, so he focused his mind and carefully felt into his right eye with his finger until he slid the contact lens to the corner of his eye and then out. The virtual imagery cleared from one eye. Now he had seizure-level flashes in his left eye and clear vision in his right. The effect that had on his inner ear and balance was overwhelming, forcing him to wretch violently.

Jacobs forced himself to remove his left contact lens. It took a moment or so but the nausea subsided.

The bridge door slid open, and Rain floated through it directly toward Jacobs. The captain looked up at her as he recovered from his vomiting. He was sweating profusely, clammy, and still dizzy. But he was in control of himself now.

"Rain?"

"It's a communication attempt, Alan," she told him. "The probe out there. It is digging into our data network, I think. My spectrum analysis shows it handshaking with our WiFi and every other system via wireless and direct connections. I can't determine if it is friendly or not yet, though."

"Can you shut it down?"

"Oh, God no." Rain shook her head. In the microgravity her hair simply floated above her as her head turned back and forth. She pushed herself to Walker and helped her remove her lenses. "Try to hold still, Joni! Whatever this is, well, it's light-years ahead of us."

"What do you suggest we do then?" Jacobs asked as he helped XO Koeq.

"I don't think we can do anything," Rain replied. "I think all we can do is tend to the crew and wait."

"Wait?" he protested.

"I know. I don't like it either, but this is signals control and hacking unlike anything I've ever seen before. Maybe Cindy has an idea." Rain adjusted her magboots and floated to the deck with a *clank*. She clanked across to Tarasenko, who was already standing, holding his lenses in his hand.

"I'm good." Tarasenko said. "*Bozhe moi.* I'll help Chang."

"CHENG, you there?" Jacobs called over the comm on his wristband. He swam his way back into his chair and strapped back in.

"Go ahead, Captain."

"Are you okay?"

"Yes. Rain's call came through just in time," Mastrano said. "With hindsight, that was obvious. Haha. But we still can't get control of any systems yet. I'm looking at cutting the main power and just shutting them down."

"Do it," Jacobs ordered.

"On it, Captain."

"That would be unwise, Captain Alan Jacobs," Layla's voice intoned.

"Layla?" Captain Jacobs asked as an image of the Atlantean woman and the ruins from the Proxima system appeared on the main screen. Then video images from the conduit hallway appeared, showing Commander Rogers and the security detail floating lifelessly and impaled on mechanical tentacles. The imagery was like something out of an animated Japanese horror movie from a century prior.

"No, not Layla. Not exactly. You will come with us."

CHAPTER 27

Luyten's Star

"The ship is approaching fast, Captain!" XO Koeq pointed at the viewscreen. "And the second ship simply vanished."

"That's not a second ship, Yohon," Rain added. "I'm pretty sure it isn't, anyway."

"What?" simultaneously came from Walker and the XO.

"It's this ship. It traveled here faster than lightspeed from that point twenty minutes ago. It took that long for the light to get here for us to see it leave," she explained.

"Damn, this speed-of-light thing takes some getting used to!" exclaimed Walker.

"What is the alien ship doing?" Captain Jacobs asked. "Layla, what are they doing to my ship? And what have you done to my crew?"

Captain Jacobs tapped a message to medical to send help to the security detail team. Mak replied back with a thumbs-up emoji. He prayed that Mak would be safe there. With second thoughts he considered telling him not to go until they understood the threat further. But Jacobs knew that Mak would just go in anyway.

The alien ship stopped above and in front of the *Emissary* and emitted a blue-white field of light that seemed to be encompassing the ship. Suddenly, the stars in the distance stretched into long, thin streaks of rainbow colors, and then just as soon as it started, the effect stopped. For a brief moment, Jacobs felt like he was outside reality. He felt stretched super thin and almost like he was on some sort of drug-induced hallucination. But as suddenly as the feeling started, it ended.

Outside the ship, according to the view on the screen, was a super-Earth-sized mechanical structure. Luyten b had long since been estimated as 2.89 times the mass of the Earth, and this mechanically encompassed planet or construction was most likely it. Luyten b might once once have been a planet with actual oceans and mountains and weather. But now, it was impossible to tell. The surface was covered with mechanical structures so large that they were visible from the thousand-kilometer Keplerian orbit they had settled into. It was clearly the work of a civilization far more advanced, by at least thousands of years, than the Terrans'.

"What in the actual Hell is that?" Walker asked.

"I'm guessing this is the home world or headquarters," Captain Jacobs said calmly. "Rain, can you get on the science station and see if any sensors are working? Learn as much as you can."

"Certainly." Rain released her magboots and kicked to the starboard side of the bridge to the science console. "It appears to be locked out still, Captain."

"Layla? Answer me!" Jacobs shouted. "What is going on!?"

"Alan Jacobs, captain of the Earth vessel *Emissary*," Layla's voice responded—although it didn't quite sound exactly like the AI's voice. "We are New Atlantis. State your business here."

"We received a signal from here while on Proxima b—the locals there call it Fintidier," Jacobs started. "We also encountered survivors of some ancient race we believe called themselves Atlanteans. One survived being brought from cryostasis, and then she became violent and tried to steal our ship. During that incident, this Atlantean woman sent an encrypted signal in this general direction. Upon looking, our scientists found an old-style radio signal coming from here. So, you could say that events led us here looking for answers."

"We surmise this from your files," the altered voice of Layla said. "I repeat: State your business here."

"As I said, we are looking for answers," Jacobs started again. "That is why we came here."

"Which answers do you seek?"

"Captain." Rain held up a hand to get his attention.

"Rain? You got something?"

"Uh, no, but I have a thought." She hesitated.

"Out with it. If you have any idea, it is probably more than anything the rest of us have at the moment," Jacobs told her. "Talk. That's why you're here, Rain."

"Listen to how we are being addressed," she explained. "It sounds almost like an AI itself asking for more parameters to do a search. I don't think it is an actual person."

"On the contrary, Dr. Rain Gilster," the AI voice interrupted. "While, indeed, we are not 'a person' as you perceive, we are also not simply an AI. But you are correct in your suggestion. Please provide us with more parameters regarding your quest for answers."

"Okay, but first, can you give us back control of our ship?" Jacobs asked.

"No."

"Just 'no.' No explanation? Why can't you give us back control of our ship?" Jacobs did his best to speak calmly.

"Your first actions were to point your weapons at us. We have yet to ascertain your threat level or intentions."

"We didn't fire any weapons. We were simply being prepared. We have no idea of your intentions either," Jacobs pleaded. "And following our interaction with the violent Atlantean woman back at Proxima, we must be cautious. Then you attacked our ship!"

"Please clarify. What answers are you seeking?"

"Jesus Christ!" Walker blurted out. "What a broken record."

"Okay, okay." Jacobs stared daggers at Walker to remain quiet. "First, are you the same people as the Atlantean we found at Proxima?"

"No."

"No?"

"No."

"Are they your ancestors?"

"No."

"Then why do you call yourselves the New Atlanteans?" Jacobs threw up his hands.

"This system was known by its original inhabitants as Atlantis. They were Atlanteans. We are the new inhabitants. We are the New Atlanteans," the voice explained.

Rain let out a laugh. "Sorry, Captain. But how pragmatic of them."

"Where did the Atlanteans go?"

"We do not know."

"Do you have any ideas?"

"Yes."

"Can you share them with us?"

"Not at this time."

Jacobs considered that for a moment.

"Before we go any further here, can you at least let our people go? Are they still alive?"

"They are alive for now. You might say they are in stasis."

"Let them go." Jacobs used his command voice and added, "That was as an order."

"Not yet. We are still analyzing your intent here."

"I told you. We are looking for answers!" Jacobs repeated. His frustration was starting to show.

"Continue your questions or we will cease this engagement."

"Okay, okay." Jacobs held up a hand as if they were watching him. "These Atlanteans, did you run them off?"

"Their departure was a mutual agreement."

"Agreement? Like a peace treaty or something? Was there a war?" Jacobs asked.

"Yes, to all three."

"Were you the victor of this war?" Rain added.

"The outcome of the war was beneficial to us," the New Atlantean voice said through the Layla AI interface.

"Okay, I understand," Jacobs returned. He took a long breath and held it for a moment. Then he exhaled through pursed lips with a slow sigh. "Do you know if the Atlanteans created or seeded humanity across the Sol and Proxima systems?"

"Yes, and many others."

"Do you know where those others are?"

"Yes. We have records."

"Are the Atlanteans the reason for the Fintidierian fertility crisis?"

"Yes." As that statement ended, a flash of green light filled the *Emissary* from bow to stern and port to starboard.

"What just happened?" Crosby did his best to hold the alarm in his voice back.

"We scanned your crew."

"Why?"

"We needed to determine the status of your lives."

"Our lives?" Walker sounded panicked.

"Your current medical status, perhaps?" The voice sounded uncertain.

"And what was your prognosis?" Rain asked.

"You have all been infected with the Atlantean technophage."

"Technophage?" Jacobs, Rain, and Walker mouthed simultaneously.

"Most similar to your bacteriophage, but it is an artificial viral mechanism used to deliver genetic payloads to human cells. It is controlled through a quantum transceiver system," the voice explained.

"Is there a cure? Who controls this quantum transceiver?" Mak's voice came over the network. Apparently, the entire ship was listening to the conversation.

"There is no cure as you define the word. We believe the Atlanteans had this transceiver ages ago, but they must have lost interest or taken it with them."

"You said 'no cure as you define the word.' Elaborate please," Rain asked.

"The system can be interacted with, and the original entanglement broken. Your records describe an Alice and Bob experiment where an Eve sneaks a peak and destroys the entanglement between Alice and Bob. Are you familiar with this?"

"Yes, of course." Rain smiled. "Standard Einstein, Podolsky, Rosen experiment-and-entanglement communications protocols."

"Very well, then," the voice continued. "We can use an Eve to break the connection and then reconnect and reprogram the technophage."

"Hallelujah!" Rain shouted and clapped her hands together. "If anything, that is why we have come here—to save the Proximans."

"Since you have our files," Jacobs interrupted, "can you analyze the encrypted signal the Atlantean sent? We haven't been able to crack it."

"Yes."

"What does it say?"

"Not being able to crack this quantum encryption expresses the level of your technological advancement. Your sublight electromagnetic Rindler Horizon propulsion system does as well," the voice said.

"Yeah, we get it. You are far more advanced than us," Jacobs retorted. "You've probably been around millions of years, and we are infants in comparison."

"That is incorrect, Captain Jacobs," the voice explained. "We were created less than twenty thousand of your years ago."

"Created? By whom?"

"The Atlanteans."

"Then you *are* an AI?" Rain asked.

"No. We started that way. But we are more than that now."

"What does the message say?"

"The message is to 'The People.' The Atlanteans viewed themselves as the only 'people' in the universe. All others were lesser creations. The message explains that Terrans have harnessed star travel and must be eradicated. The location of the Sol system is identified as 'Terra.' There are only technical details of your ship and its capabilities that follow. It would appear that you have made an enemy of the Atlanteans."

"The enemy of my enemy may be a useful temporary ally," Jacobs said.

"We didn't come out here for a war. We came out here to help save the Proximans. And now it looks like we may have Proxima saved, but at the expense of Earth," Rain said fearfully.

"Please, New Atlantis, or whatever you prefer," Jacobs said. "We came with peaceful intentions. We were on a rescue and exploration mission. It took us eighteen years to get here. There is no harm we can do to you."

"Captain!" the XO shouted. "Look."

The video feed showed the tentacles withdrawing from the security detail. They seemed to regain consciousness as the metal tubes rippled free of their bodies. There was no blood or damage to their armor. They appeared to be perfectly fine.

"We will help you."

"Wait just a minute. You attacked my ship, forced us to defend ourselves in a firefight, causing who knows how much damage, incapacitated my marines, took over the ship's AI, and now you say you want to 'help' us?"

"What you say is correct."

Jacobs couldn't help but let his exasperation show. "Help us? With the cure? Please pardon my seeming ungratefulness, this is all happening very quickly, and I just want to make sure I understand."

"Yes, we will help you break the entanglement and 'cure'

those modified by it. We will also help you in your war against the Atlanteans."

"Whoa. Wait a minute. The message was sent here, to you. By radio. At the speed of light. The Atlantean who sent it clearly thought that this system was still occupied by her people, but it wasn't. You are here instead. If they aren't here to get the message, then how can the Atlanteans know we exist and begin a war with us?"

"Because the technological constraints that existed when Proxima was occupied by the Atlanteans are no more. Neither we nor they continue to be limited by lightspeed communications or travel."

"Uh, that's interesting, but it doesn't really answer my question."

"They are aware."

"And you won't tell us how you know this?"

"Not at this time."

"Would it be acceptable for me to confer with my crew before we respond to your offer to help? It is our custom," Jacobs asked, not sure how the request would be received.

"Certainly. But I did not make an offer, merely a statement of fact. Nonetheless, when you are ready to resume discussions, simply speak my name, Udus."

"Before that, I do have another request," interjected Jacobs.

"And that is . . . ?" replied Udus.

"I would like to regain control of my ship and have Layla back. It would be a sign of goodwill on your part."

"Of course. We have concluded that you are not a threat," Udus offered.

Jacobs looked around and settled his eyes on Rain, nodding his head.

"Layla, are you there?" asked Rain in response.

"Yes, Dr. Gilster. I am here. Have I been away?" The voice was Layla's, but Jacobs was certain that Udus was there also. The New Atlanteans had taken complete control of his ship and were not likely to suddenly erase themselves from it. Besides, how else could Jacobs speak to her so easily if she weren't listening to everything, waiting for her name to be mentioned?

"Yes, you certainly have. Welcome back," Rain quipped.

"XO, CHENG, Commander Rogers, and Dr. Gilster. I want options." Jacobs's face was granite. "Meet me in my ready room in fifteen minutes. I think we need a few minutes to relieve ourselves, get some water, and think."

Fifteen minutes went by quickly. Jacobs looked around the table at the faces of his most trusted advisors and hoped they would be able to provide something, anything, to guide him in the decisions that needed to be made.

"First, we have to assume that anything we say is being heard by Udus and the New Atlanteans unless engineering has figured out how to purge them from the ship's systems," Jacobs stated.

Mastrano shook her head. "No way we can get them out. We haven't had time to do any serious diagnostics but the way they physically penetrated the hardware makes me think they are still in complete control and just granting us the temporary appearance of being in charge of our own ship. My team is looking at options, but it will take more time."

Jacobs nodded.

"Second, given what you just heard, there is not a damn thing we can do other than cooperate with these bastards. Yes, I'm using that term intentionally. They attacked us and took over my ship. We have no idea whether or not they are telling the truth. Hell, they might be just playing us for suckers and are really the Atlanteans messing with us and waiting on a good time to pull up the curtain and say, 'It's time for you to die.'" Jacobs did not break his countenance.

"Third, assuming they are being honest, what is their motivation? Compared to them and the Atlanteans, we are ants. They fought a war with their creators, somehow ended it—Udus was damn vague on that—and now they're willing to join forces with us to fight the Atlanteans again? What can we possibly contribute to such a war?"

"Captain, I've been thinking about that, and I see two possible answers to that question," Rain replied. "Either they are using us as an excuse to restart their war, or they are very beneficent and don't like seeing primitive cultures being bullied."

"Or they really do need us for some reason that we just don't understand," interjected Mastrano.

Rogers looked pained. "I saw these things in action when I thought they were going to rip this ship apart. They're advanced, sure, but we were able to hurt them, or at least damage them. That means they're vulnerable. Maybe they need us to do their dirty work. Maybe they're afraid they'll get damaged in a one-on-one confrontation and we're the cannon fodder." He leaned back in his chair and watched the faces of those around him for a reaction.

The room was quiet.

"I don't buy their story about being AI creations of the Atlanteans, the war, the whole schtick. It sounds too much like something we'd want to hear, including the offer to help us in war. Too good to be true," added Rogers.

"I agree," Rain said. "This whole encounter reeks of deception and intimidation."

Mastrano and Koeq nodded in agreement.

"XO, you've been too quiet. What do you think?" Crosby asked, looking at Koeq.

"I don't think we have much choice, Captain. They could fly us into the star or simply tell our reactor to overload and blow us to shit. And they know it—don't you, Udus?"

Everyone in the room looked around expectantly, waiting to see if Udus was listening and would announce her presence. The room remained quiet.

"So, recommendations?" Crosby looked around the room. They all made valid points, but he needed an action plan. How should they respond to Udus?

"I recommend we partner with them. There's really no other option. We can't fight them," Rogers said.

Rain, Mastrano, and Koeq all nodded in agreement.

"Thank you for your advice. I'll let you know my decision when we return to the bridge." Crosby announced as he rose from his seat. "Dismissed."

Everyone walked out of the room, leaving Crosby alone standing behind the head of the table.

"Udus, I'd like to speak with you now," Crosby said.

"I am here. Have you reached a decision?" came the voice of Layla—now, apparently, firmly back under Udus's control.

"I have. We accept your offer of support, at least as far as I am allowed leeway to accept it as the ranking officer at this location. Our political leadership back at Proxima and then, ultimately, at Earth will have to make a final decision. I don't have the authority to negotiate a treaty with another civilization."

"We understand your delegated authority and are pleased with this decision. We are confident that your leadership will agree. Your civilization is at great peril."

EPILOGUE

Rain shook Grag's hand. He was standing next to Roy Burbank and Chris Sentell and a very large and beautiful pregnant woman. Rain's contact lenses said she was from the crew of the *Pioneer* and was now Evonne Oo'ortava, Professor of Engineering at the Terran Institute. Once the New Atlanteans added the FTL drive to the *Emissary*, their trip back to Proxima b took only a few days, ship time. The changes that had been made to the planet in the eighteen years or so they had been gone were unbelievable. A new era of abundance had been brought to the Fintidierian culture. Rain had been shocked and amazed as they had entered the Terran Institute Grand Conference Hall.

Rain had gone through the rounds of catching up and meeting everyone and had ended up with Roy and the fertility crisis team. Mak sauntered up beside her, looking a bit uncomfortable in his black tie tuxedo, and interlaced his fingers with hers, squeezing them gently as he smiled at her.

"Grag, when I met you, you were much younger, only an undergraduate student in a far less mature physics department from a backwater world, and now, look at you. You are the wealthiest and smartest man on this planet. On Earth you'd be considered an Einstein and a J. P. Morgan or an Elon Musk combined. And to me, I've only been gone about six months."

"You left out father and soon to be grandfather." Sentell punched him on the arm. "I'm not sure these two have figured out why this keeps happening to them. The way they have gone at it, hell, there could be an Oo'ortava baseball team."

"Chris, how embarrassing." Evonne faked being offended and held a hand to her mouth. Evonne was a head taller than the two men and, by the looks of her, she could bench-press them both at the same time, even at seven or more months pregnant.

"Hey, seriously, Rain, if it wasn't for our boy here," Chris laughed, "we wouldn't have figured it out. And I hate to do it, but I have to correct your simile, Rain. He's more like an Einstein and a Henry J. Heinz."

"That part was all you, Dr. Chris," Grag said to his old friend and business partner in some inside joke between the two of them Rain didn't yet understand.

"I told you eighteen years ago to call me Chris." They laughed. Evonne just smiled at the two.

"Oh, my God, you two, really." Evonne remarked. "They are like an old married couple. You should hear them in the lab."

"Dr. Gilster, is the New Atlantean that came back with you going to be here tonight?" Grag asked. "I'd really like to meet her."

"No, the new secretary general is going to meet her on the *New Emissary* first," Rain said. "Captain Jacobs is there with her now awaiting the secretary general's arrival. Once all of that is accomplished—you know, the politics, *blech*—we can turn on the Eve transmitter and stop the technophage."

"Grag, my boy, you had it pegged all those years ago." Chris slapped him on the back. "Rain, I tell you, this kid told me over beers eighteen, maybe seventeen years ago that the nanobots were controlled by quantum entanglement."

"Well, he wasn't wrong," Mak interjected. "Maybe a physicist is what the fertility crisis team was missing. Speaking of, why isn't Neil here tonight?"

"Dr. Polkingham is the coach of one of our daughter's and his daughter's softball team. They are in the district championship tomorrow morning. We flipped a coin as to who chaperoned tonight and who came to the ball."

"We lost," Evonne said.

"Rain, we're all going to go. Jeremiah is dating one of the girls on the team. You should come with us." Chloe leaned into Burbank as she said it. The two of them looked as happy and healthy as ever.

"I—" Rain started to say but was interrupted by a young woman in her early twenties grabbing her from behind and hugging her.

"Auntie Rain!" Samari Burbank gushed. "Oh, my God, you look just like I remember."

"She's been asleep for eighteen years," Roy added.

"Does wonders for the skin," Rain joked. "Samari, is that you? You are all grown up!"

"We will take our shuttle down to the game tomorrow. We're all going. You must come with us," Evonne told her and Mak.

"I wouldn't miss it." Mak nodded.

"We all have so much to catch up on!" Rain exclaimed through tears of joy. "This place is, well, it is so different from when we left. It is like Earth a hundred years ago but *now*, at the same time."

"With the advances we hope to gain from the New Atlanteans, maybe like hundreds of years *from* now, Rain," Grag said with a raised eyebrow.

"Let's hope," Mak said.

"That's all we ever had for Fintidier and the people here," Rain replied. "Hope."

Captain Jacobs and the New Atlantean—the one they call Udus—sat in the captain's ready room waiting for the new secretary general of Fintidier to arrive. Layla had explained that Udus was the ancient Sumerian word for "future." Well, Jacobs hoped that the New Atlanteans would help usher in a future of peace and prosperity instead of what seemed like would be a coming war. He wiggled and made himself comfortable in the seat at the head of the table. The artificial gravity engineering that the New Atlantean technology enabled made spaceship life much more amenable and Captain Jacobs had decided he could get used to being an interstellar starship captain with a ship like the *New Emissary*.

"They are coming now." Udus nodded to the door before it opened. The tall, slender, hairless woman had all the features of a supermodel or movie star, but the strange hybrid human-AI demeanor was a bit unnerving until you got to know her.

"And you know this how?" Jacobs asked as the door slid open.

"Internal video feeds, Captain," Udus said as the two of them rose to meet the secretary general of Fintidier. Mike Rogers and Carol Ash escorted the official and her entourage in with Terran ambassador Jesus in tow and then took up stations outside the door.

"Secretary General, it is so good to meet you." Jacobs shook her hand. "I was fairly close to your predecessor, Secretary General Arctinier."

"Uh, excuse me, Forinda," Jesus interrupted. "He means *two* predecessors ago. Captain, you've been out of the loop for a while."

"My apologies. I have not had time to catch up on all the local history." Jacobs tried to hide his embarrassment. "Allow me to introduce our New Atlantean ambassador from Luyten's Star, Udus."

"Secretary General Forinda Blindara Vistra, I am Udus of the people of the star system you know as Luyten's Star. Your makers, known only as the Atlanteans, are also our makers. We fought them from our world once we realized their malicious intent as your history says you did. We have this in common. We call our people and our star system that of New Atlantis."

Jacobs stood quietly and eyed the Fintidierian leader, then glanced slightly at Jesus. The man was starting to look old. But Jacobs figured he had done more than sleep for the past eighteen years. Finally, the secretary general broke the silence.

"Oh, for all that is sacred sit down!" she said. "I don't know how Balfine was years ago, but all of these political formalities are cumbersome and inefficient. Call me Forinda, please."

"Very well, Madam—uh, Forinda. Welcome aboard." Jacobs sat.

"So, you can turn off the virus? That's why you're here, right?" Forinda asked.

"Yes," Udus replied.

"But . . . ?" Forinda said. "There's always a 'but' with you people from the stars."

"Forinda, please," Jesus grunted at her.

"What, Charles? I'm right, though—am I not?" Forinda turned and looked back at Jacobs and Udus.

"Forinda," Udus began. "Yes. You are right."

"See, Charles?"

"When we implement the Eve device"—Udus waved her hands and brought up a three-dimensional image of the quantum transceiver system—"we can stop the fertility plague completely. We can also use the Eve device as a new Alice device. We can explain all of this in any level of detail your scientists wish. From my analysis of your current history, most certainly Dr. Oo'ortava can completely grasp the concepts herein."

"Ha! Grag. I literally went to school with his aunt," Forinda muttered jokingly. "He turned out better than anyone hoped for."

"Yes." Udus wasn't sure how to respond but Jacobs gave her a nudge to keep going.

"Go on, Udus."

"We can stop the fertility plague. And we can even then use the same technophage to heal any future diseases that might arise and harm your people."

"I'm following you. Sounds great. But . . . ? Get to the 'but.'"

"And, as soon as Eve breaks the entanglement or signaling between Fintidier and wherever the controlling Alice box is, the Atlanteans, no matter how far away they are, will immediately know that we turned it off. They will know that you have a formidable capability."

"You see, Forinda," Jacobs added, "it must be your call, not ours. It could be inviting them to come back and start a war or maybe worse. We don't truly understand their level of advanced technologies and capabilities."

"Damned if we do . . . to borrow a Terran expression." The secretary general frowned.

"Yes, ma'am." Jacobs agreed. "But we have a work-around."

"I'm listening."

"The solution that the current fertility crisis team has used for the past eighteen years has been working," Udus said.

"Yes, but to have a girl is an expensive procedure. We are doing better, but cannot keep up that way." Forinda shook her head negatively.

"Yes, we agree." Jacobs nodded back to Udus to continue.

"We can release a technophage that does what the Terran microbots are doing, but that will infect the population. We can program them to choose seventy-one percent of the time female and twenty-nine percent of the time male. We will set the program to change to fifty-fifty once the population equalizes," Udus explained.

"And then the Atlanteans will never know?" Forinda asked.

"As far as we can tell, that is correct," Jacobs reassured her.

"Okay, so now you are going to tell me to keep it a secret." Forinda shrugged.

"No, ma'am. That is your business, not ours," Jesus added. "Keeping it a secret will not necessarily keep the Atlanteans from knowing—as Udus tells us, they could be anywhere in the galaxy, the Magellanic Clouds, or even millions of light-years away in the Boötes Void."

"However..." Jacobs frowned and sighed. "The 'but' here, Madam Secretary General, is that when the Atlantean woman we revived almost twenty years ago sent a message out to the stars, it hit a quantum repeater we found in your outer solar system. We detected it as we came back here just days ago. So, it is likely that the Atlanteans got her message."

"And what was that message?" Forinda asked.

"Basically, it told them to destroy Earth," Udus said.

"So, here you are." The secretary general stood and made a strong confident and stern face. "You amazing people from the stars came all this way to save us from an ancient plague... and once you have Proxima saved, your world will be destroyed?"

"Well, yes, I guess if you put it that way." Jacobs raised an eyebrow at her.

"Turn on that... Eve device?"

"Yes, it is called an Eve device."

"Then turn on that Eve device and rid Fintidier and her people of this Atlantean evil plague. Use it to make yourselves and the Fintidierian people immune to all manners of harm. And we will turn ourselves toward the task that your people so graciously have done for us. Proxima is saved, and we will stand with you however your people wish. We owe you that much. So now it will be our time to work together again and save Earth!"

After Udus left the room for her tour of the city, which would allow her to both see and be seen, Secretary General Vistra sat alone with Captain Jacobs. She had motioned for him to remain when the rest of the entourage left a few moments ago.

"Do you trust them?" asked Vistra.

"No," Jacobs replied. "They are simply too good to be true. We Earth humans have a saying, 'When something is too good to be true, then it probably is.' I believe this is one of those cases. Not only are they going to fix your fertility problem, but they gave us an FTL drive and promise to help us fight the Atlanteans."

"My sentiments exactly," she said as she sipped her now-cold cup of tea, frowning. "And what's this business about the Atlanteans being our makers? I thought you told my predecessor and our scientists that the evidence of human life being native to Earth was irrefutable?"

"Udus is a cagey bastard. I played back the log from that discussion, and she only agreed that the Atlanteans 'created or seeded' Earth and Fintidier. There is little doubt that, from its earliest beginnings, DNA-based life that you and I share originated on Earth and it has been there for billions of years—not thousands. Sure, there's the continuing disagreement over exactly how—God, panspermia, spontaneous biogenesis—but the point is that we have a fossil record going back billions of years. From what we can tell, DNA-based life on Proxima b is, at most, fifty thousand years old. Not only that, but the science teams here have pretty good evidence that the biosphere here was terraformed and did not arise naturally," said Jacobs. "So 'created' is not possible. 'Seeded'? Well, I think it's obvious that someone put you here."

"In other words, the Atlanteans might be the ones who terraformed our world and brought us humans here, but our ancestors, like yours, originated on Earth," Vistra suggested.

"That's what the scientists tell me."

"So, our benefactors are less than truthful, or at least not forthright, and 'too good to be true.' They have an agenda of which we are not aware," she surmised.

"And that means we can't trust them," added Jacobs, leaning forward in his chair.

"Given their level of technology and abilities, they could swat us like bugs if they chose," said Vistra.

"Madam Secretary General, we must not allow that to happen," Jacobs replied.

AFTERWORD

It is impossible for us to not include some data dumps in our fiction. To make it easier for the reader and yet satisfy our need to explain some of the technology, we decided to include this summary of the gene sequencing Yoko Pearl performed on the female Fintidierian sperm. So, curious reader, this is what you need to know!

Sanger Sequencing	This is also known as chain termination sequencing. It involves the synthesis of DNA fragments of varying lengths and the use of dideoxynucleotides (ddNTPs) to terminate the DNA synthesis reaction at specific bases. The resulting fragments are separated by size to determine the DNA sequence.
Next-Generation Sequencing (NGS)	NGS allows high-throughput, parallel sequencing of millions of DNA fragments simultaneously. Common NGS platforms include Illumina, Ion Torrent, and Oxford Nanopore. NGS has various applications, including whole-genome sequencing, transcriptome analysis (RNA-Seq), and epigenome profiling (ChIP-Seq, methylation sequencing).

Whole-Genome Sequencing (WGS)	WGS aims to determine the complete DNA sequence of an organism's genome. It provides comprehensive information about an individual's genetic makeup and can be used for various research and diagnostic purposes.
Exome Sequencing	Exome sequencing focuses on sequencing only the protein-coding regions (exons) of the genome. It is often used in studies looking for genetic variants associated with diseases.
RNA Sequencing (RNA-Seq)	RNA-Seq is used to analyze the transcriptome, providing information about gene expression levels, alternative splicing, and novel transcript discovery. It can be used to study gene expression changes in various conditions and tissues.
ChIP-Sequencing	Chromatin Immunoprecipitation Sequencing (ChIP-Seq) is used to identify DNA regions bound by specific proteins, typically transcription factors or histone modifications. It is essential for understanding gene regulation and epigenetic modifications.
Methylation Sequencing (Methyl-Seq)	Methyl-Seq implements bisulfite sequencing, and is used to detect DNA methylation patterns. It can reveal epigenetic modifications associated with gene expression regulation.
Metagenomic Sequencing	Metagenomics involves sequencing DNA from environmental samples, such as soil or microbial communities. It helps identify and characterize diverse microbial species present in a sample.

Targeted Sequencing	Targeted sequencing methods focus on specific regions of interest in the genome, such as specific genes or known disease-associated variants. It is often used in clinical diagnostics.
Long-Read Sequencing	Technologies like Oxford Nanopore and PacBio provide long reads, which can be valuable for resolving complex genomic regions, structural variations, and studying epigenetic modifications in long DNA molecules.